SHAWN LAMB

TRADER OF
ELDAR

Allon Books

TRADER OF ELDAR
by Shawn Lamb

Published by Allon Books
209 Hickory Way Court
Antioch, Tennessee 37013
www.allonbooks.com

Cover illustration by Robert Lamb

International Standard Book Number: 978-0-9964381-5-5

Other Books by Shawn Lamb

Young Adult Fantasy Fiction

SON OF ELDAR

ALLON – BOOK 1 – STRUGGLE FOR ALLON
ALLON – BOOK 2 – INSURRECTION
ALLON – BOOK 3 – HEIR APPARENT
ALLON – BOOK 4 – A QUESTION OF SOVEREIGNTY
ALLON – BOOK 5 – GAUNTLET
ALLON – BOOK 6 – DILEMMA
ALLON – BOOK 7 – DANGEROUS DECEPTION
ALLON – BOOK 8 – DIVIDED
ALLON – BOOK 9 – IN PLAIN SIGHT

GUARDIANS OF ALLON – BOOK ONE – THE GREAT BATTLE
GUARDIANS OF ALLON – BOOK TWO – REPRIEVE
GUARDIANS OF ALLON – BOOK THREE – OVERTHROW

PARENT STUDY GUIDE FOR ALLON ~ BOOKS 1-9
THE ACTIVITY BOOK OF ALLON

For Young Readers – ages 8-10
Allon – The King's Children series

NECIE AND THE APPLES
TRISTINE'S DORGIRITH ADVENTURE
NIGEL'S BROKEN PROMISE

Historical Fiction

GLENCOE
THE HUGUENOT SWORD

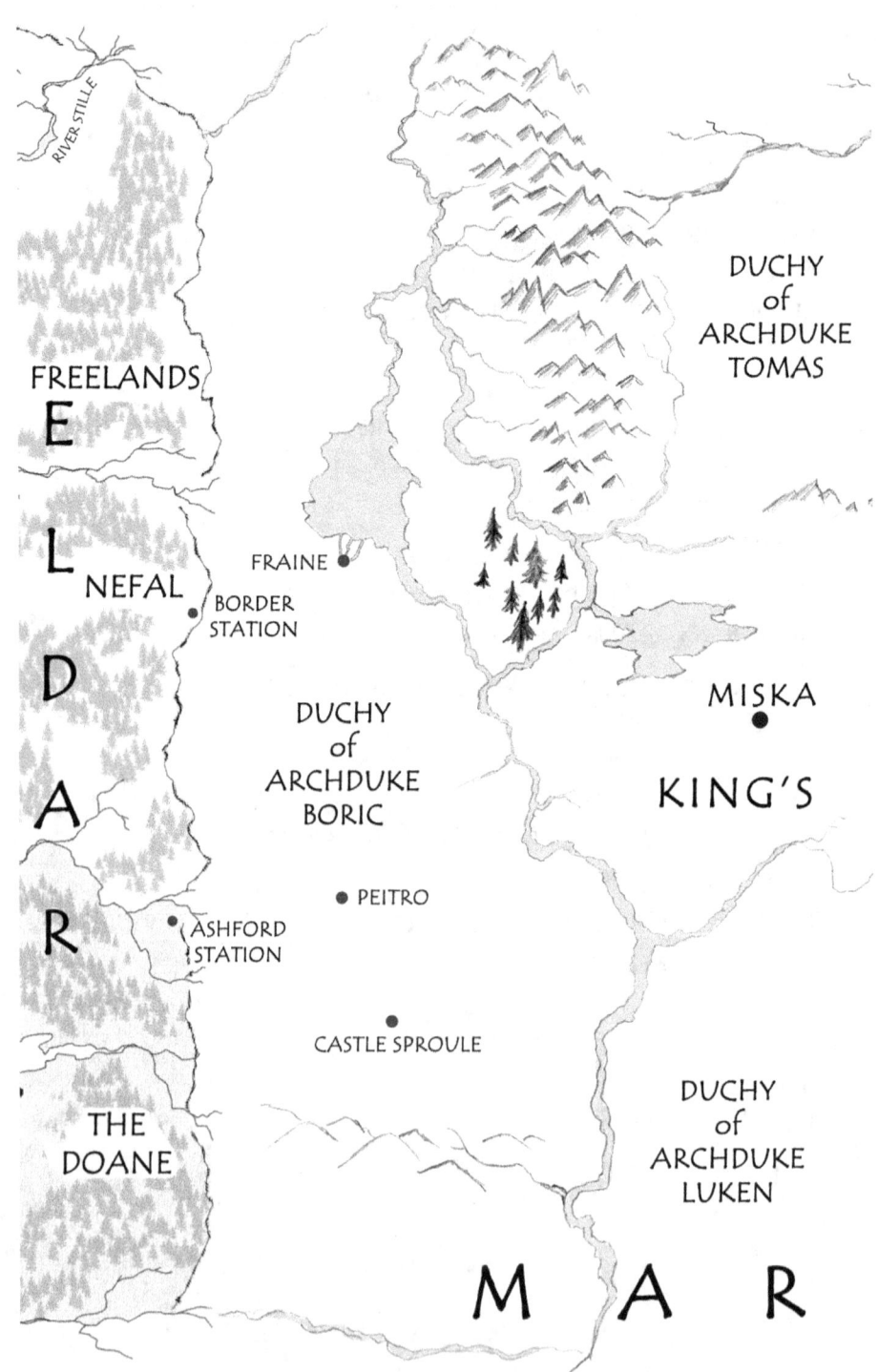

ANDROS SEA

KRANSTON

DEVIL'S GORGE

BLACK MOUNTAINS

BUSHLIK
FOREST

DOMOVAY
SETTLEMENT

LAND

DUCHY
of
ARCHDUKE
PANKO

K I T A

CHARACTERS

ELDAR

PEOPLE
King Axel
Sir Gunnar
Nollen of Far Point
Arctander, High Priest
Ida, Nollen's sister
Jarred, Ida's husband
Lord Ronan, First Minister
Baron Irwin
Lord Cormac
Lord Leon
General Mather
Captain Castor
Jonas, Innkeeper at Gilroy
Sharla, Jonas' wife
Sheriff Ezer of Gilroy

ANIMALS
Othniel, Great White Lion
Artair, Eagle King
Alfgar, Lord of the Unicorns
Bardolf, Leader of White Wolves
Callie, she-wolf
Ajax – son of Artair
Alydar – former unicorn

MARKITA
King Montre
Archduke Boric
Archduke Panko
Archduke Tomas
Archduke Luken
Lord Carl
Baron Albric
General Tilbic
Captain Horst

KRANSTON
Milos, priest
Kean
Jann
Arnie
Lexi
Alicia
Lorraine

Chapter 1

A CRISP, LATE FALL BREEZE STIRRED THE WATERS AS THE FERRY to Gilroy reached its destination. Mid-morning sunlight sparkled off the gently flowing waters and dewy bank. Once the ramp was clear to disembark, Nollen led his pony off the ferry. He mounted to ride the last mile to Gilroy. Since the defeat of Elector Javan three years ago, much had changed in Eldar. Commerce became easier. Nollen no longer needed to take secret routes, and freely traveled the country.

Now age twenty-three, his youthful features matured into a comely young man with brown hair and blues eyes. Still, habits formed over a lifetime of alertness kept him aware of his surroundings. He gave the watch a friendly smile as he passed through the town's southern gate. He barely steered Gilen through the busy streets since the pony knew the way to the inn. In a corral adjacent to the main building, he dismounted.

A seventeen-year-old lad came from the barn. "Nollen, welcome."

"Bart." Nollen gave the lad a quick embrace. He motioned around the corral. "I see a few more horses. Business picking up?"

"A bit."

Nollen softly smiled at the tacit response. He removed the saddlebag. "Don't feed him too much. We still have a ways to travel today."

Gilen snorted and stomped his front leg in mild protest.

"I'll give you an apple," Bart partial whispered to Gilen.

Inside, the small breakfast crowd began to leave. Nollen placed the saddlebag on the bar to watch another teenager and older woman tend the remaining guests. He widely smiled when she noticed him.

"Nollen!" She greeted him with a warm embrace.

"Sharla." He kissed her cheek.

"Abe, tell cook to fix a special plate."

Being twins, Abe bore a strong resemblance to Bart. "Aye, Mama. Welcome, Nollen."

Sharla escorted Nollen to the booth nearest a roaring fire. He removed his cloak to place over the saddlebag on the bench.

"How is everything at Far Point? Is Ida well? How are the children?" Sharla asked in rapid questioning.

Abe arrived with a tankard. "Mulled cider. Breakfast should be ready shortly."

Nollen drank before answering Sharla. "Ida is well. Of course, Jarred is excited to become a father again. He thinks Dinah looks like Ida."

"Corey? How is he doing?"

Nollen drank again. "A rambunctious two-year-old. He is curious about his baby sister but doesn't understands what being a big brother means."

Cook arrived with breakfast. She happily smiled at Nollen. "Eggs and potatoes cooked just the way you like them."

"Thank you, Meara." He glanced around the room. "Where is Jonas?"

Sharla's heavily sighed, which prompted Abe to place a supportive hand on his mother's shoulder. "Back in his room," she lamented.

"Why? He's been doing so well the past year," said Nollen, confused.

Sharla didn't directly answer the question. "Abe and Bart have been wonderful in helping me run the inn. Abe has his father's old exuberance." Her voice trailed off.

Nollen reached across the table to take her hand. "I'll talk to him."

She flashed a plaintive smile. Hearing a patron call, she left.

Abe occupied the seat she vacated. His voice low yet harsh. "Galt returned, and stirred up others against Papa."

Nollen paused in eating. "I thought he moved his family east?"

"Aye, but business brought him back. He can't forgive Papa for what happened to Destry. That's what drove Papa back to his room." Abe fought to contain his anger when a patron passed in departure. "Have a blessed day," he made the usual parting comment.

Nollen's features turned hard. "Destry's own treachery is to blame."

"We told Papa so, but Galt launched such a vicious verbal attack that even Alderman Flynn joined in the condemnation."

When Sharla returned, Nollen changed his expression to encouragement. He patted his saddlebag. "I have something that will greatly interest Jonas and help him recoup."

"I hope so." She then spoke to Abe. "Time to clean up and prepare for luncheon." They left Nollen alone to eat.

Once finished, Nollen placed the saddlebag over his shoulder, and grabbed his cloak. He winked at Sharla, as he made his way to the main staircase. Aside from the family quarters, the inn had six guest rooms. He knew which door. He waited for an answer to his knock. Nothing.

At the second rap on the door, he said, "Jonas, it's Nollen." To his identification, he heard the scaping of a chair, footsteps, and finally the door opened. Immediately, he noticed discouragement had taken its toll on Jonas' appearance. He tried not to let personal dismay show in his smile. "Hail, cousin."

Jonas grinned, but a dull sadness remained in his eyes. "Come in."

Nollen noticed a small brazier barely warmed the room, but he was more interested in Jonas. The voice in greeting sounded weak and weary. He mustered a smile of encouragement. "I see more horses in the corral, and patrons enjoying Meara and Sharla's cooking. That's good."

"Aye, business is picking up. Slow, but better."

"Because it is *you* they come to see. Your reputation for hospitality is known throughout The Doane." Though he spoke with enthusiasm, Nollen kept a keen eye on Jonas for reaction.

A brief smile, like of old, appeared, and even reached Jonas' eyes. It faded when he said, "Those days are gone." He returned to a table upon which sat a pitcher, cup, and book.

Nollen sat opposite. "All the days under Javan are gone. A new age of Eldar has enlivened those in The Doane, and other provinces."

For a moment, Jonas regarded Nollen. The expression weary, but a small grin appeared. "It is good to see you so cheerful."

"It grieves me to see you so dejected. The cousin I always admired for his jovial nature, even in the dark times." Nollen seized Jonas' arms. "You must let the past go. Please! We need you to do that."

Jonas closed his eye with a heavy sigh of lament. "I've been trying."

"Galt," Nollen spat the name with indignation.

Jonas' eyes snapped open, guarded, and quizzical.

"Abe told me," Nollen answered the unspoken question. "He's as bad as Destry – for whom you are *not* responsible."

"I have come to accept that, at least in part," droned Jonas.

"If that is true, why let Galt send you retreating to your room?" Nollen spread his arms.

"You don't understand!"

"What? Guilt?" Jonas' sharp glare prompted Nollen to say resolutely, "Oh, I do understand." He thumped his chest over his heart. "I carried it inside for years. Guilt for not protecting them." His eyes grew misty. "Watching them dragged away as traitors to be executed."

Jonas grew sympathetic. "You were a boy, and no match for Javan's soldiers."

"That fact didn't lessen the guilt. Instead, it drove me to prove myself. To be as good as my father in our clandestine ventures." Nollen grew reflective in recollection. "Not until meeting Axel did I begin to understand what guilt had done to me. He challenged me, and once I let go of it … well," he smiled, "you know what happened at Sener on the day of battle, and since that victory."

Jonas smiled, this time, his eyes reflected genuine affection. "You became the Royal Officer of Commodities."

Nollen chuckled. "Aye. With Ida and Jarred taking over daily operations of Far Point, I freely travel in my new endeavor. But," he stressed, and returned to the main point. "If I had not let go of the guilt and moved forward, I wouldn't be where I am today." He looked earnestly at Jonas. "We need you. True, Sharla and the boys are capable of running the inn, but *you* are the heart of it. Jonas of Gilroy, proprietor of renown. Let the world see that again. Ignore Galt, Flynn, and others."

"It's not so easy."

"I didn't say it was. In fact, I know it's difficult, but you must start somewhere. Now is a good time since I, the Royal Officer of Commodities, rely upon your knowledge of quality goods."

Jonas laughed. "You don't need my help in that."

"I do," said Nollen emphatically. "I'll prove it." He pulled a box from the saddlebag. "What do you think of these?" He lifted the lid to show the contents.

Jonas' eyes grew wide with astonishment. "Are those—?"

"Palleteen diamonds. At least, I believe they are. I want your *expert* opinion since I remember Uncle Oberon had one."

"A fragment from an ancient priestly vestment." Jonas lifted two precious cut stones out of the box for examination. "These are more refined."

"Do you still have it for comparison?"

"No, it's long gone. Given as Tribute." Jonas grew curious. "Where did you get them?"

"A group of foreigners passed through on the way to Gorland. I happened to be in Edison where they paused for supplies."

Jonas glanced up from admiring the gems. "Foreigners?"

"I haven't seen their like before, nor had Rafe, the innkeeper."

"I know Rafe. He's part of the Guild."

Nollen motioned to the diamonds. "They claimed these are Palleteen diamonds and wanted to use six of them to trade for what they needed."

Jonas hurried to a dresser where he scrambled to find a magnifying glass. He returned to closely examine the diamonds. "You must have traded a fortune for these."

"Actually, I didn't trade anything." At Jonas' skepticism, Nollen explained. "Since Rafe wasn't familiar with them, he asked my advice. I might not know about diamonds, *but* I do know trading," he said with emphasis. "I noticed a difference in the box originally shown, and the one placed on the counter after Rafe agreed."

Jonas cocked a wry smile of understanding. "Bait and switch."

"Aye. So, I asked to see the diamonds in the original box. Of course, he insisted it was the original, so I played coy while Rafe wanted to call off the exchange. Along comes another foreigner, who whispered to the first in their language, and the original box was handed to Rafe." Nollen sly grinned. "I got these as a reward. I want to present them to Axel."

Jonas heartily laughed. "And you said you need my help."

"I said I noticed the different *boxes*. Despite having only a fragment, you should know real from fake."

Jonas again picked up the magnifying glass to look at the gem. "Hand me your dagger." He held out a hand, though still focused on the gem. Once he had the dagger, he placed the point against the gem.

Nollen seized Jonas' arm. "What are you doing?"

"Glass will scratch, a Palleteen diamond won't. A nick will not diminish the value of a real one. The fragment father had, paid a whole year of Tribute for The Doane." Jonas turned the diamond over to the bottom part. He used the tip of the dagger to scrap along the gem. He placed the dagger down and lifted the magnifying glass to view the area. He turned the gem over several times.

"Well?" asked Nollen with impatience.

Jonas widely smiled. "This is a real Palleteen diamond. The rarest of them all." He placed the gem back in the box.

Nollen smiled with triumph. "Now, I can tell Axel these are authentic."

"You're off to Sener again?"

"Aye." Nollen donned his cloak and hefted the saddlebag over his shoulder. "I just stopped for breakfast." He held out his hand to clasp Jonas' arm. "Your help is always appreciated, cousin."

Jonas took hold of Nollen's arm. "I will see you on your way."

At the bottom of the stairs, Nollen caught Sharla's surprised look at seeing Jonas. He carefully patted the saddlebag slung over his shoulder.

Sharla happily smiled, and told Nollen, "You'll find a bag of provisions on the bar. I included a loaf of Meara's apple bread."

"Woman, see to lunch preparations," Jonas said in his normal well-meaning gruff manner. He steered Nollen from the inn to the corral.

Chapter 2

Nollen casually rode north up the Freeroad on the east bank of the mighty River Leven. Despite bordering Ha'tar territory, the Freeroad was now alive with traffic. In the past, traveling the main highway required stealth and alertness. The same proved true for the west bank highway that ran alongside Leven in Nefal territory. Dragons, bandits, and harpys ignored the law regarding safe passage on the Freeroads.

Since the defeat of Javan and Dolus, the Eagles drove the harpys from Eldar while all adult dragons were killed during the conflict. King Axel ordered the remaining Ha'tar to turn over all dragon eggs to the royal hatchery to control the population. One Ha'tar breeder would be assigned to aid the caretaker to help train the hatchlings to defend Eldar. Becoming protectors of the Kingdom was the only way for the Ha'tar to remain in the country. Two dozen agreed to the condition. The majority returned to their ancestral home far beyond the Black Mountains.

Nollen glanced across the river. The Nefal numbers became decimated by battle. All that remained were women, children, and a few older men. The last chieftain signed a pact of non-aggression, so Axel dealt mercifully with them. Previously, he avoided the province. Now, he frequently visited Nefal in his new role. He used his skills to encourage farming in exchange for vegetables and fruits to serve at the King's table.

Indeed, Eldar changed for the better. There were times he wondered if he would live to see it restored, especially when aiding Axel and Gunnar in fleeing Javan and Dolus.

Around the bend, the magnificence of Sener came into view. The royal castle and fortified city gleamed with a splendor dimmed during the two-hundred-year reign of Electors. Marble gleamed in the daylight. Sunlight sparkled off the colored windows while gold ornamentation of the buildings dazzled the eyes. Each year, he spent the winter months in Sener. For two months, he visited family at Far Point, with the rest of year spent traveling Eldar on royal business of commodities.

Nollen reached the gatehouse on south side of Lake Helivan. The settlement of Wyckton had grown into a village named after the inn's owner. With so much traffic coming and going from Sener, he steered Gilen on and off the bridge that connected the royal city to Wyckton. From the wide main square, he guided Gilen up the winding levels to the apex. In the main castle courtyard, an older groom scurred to meet him.

"Welcome back, sir."

"Ben. Feed him and rub him down well. Traveling in the cold is not good for the old boy."

Gilen snorted, his breathing a bit heavy.

"He'll be well taken care of," Ben said.

Saddlebags in hand, Nollen headed to a door nearest the eastern wall. He walked through a small foyer and up two flights of stairs. Down the hall, he entered a spacious apartment. A flurry of activity went on, as men set about cataloguing commodities, taking inventory, or other tasks related to the daily supplying of the castle.

An older man in his forties dressed in fine clothes, looked up when the door opened. "Ah, Nollen."

"Sir Hastins." Nollen set the saddlebag on a desk. From the bag, he withdrew two ledgers. "These are the accountings of my summer route."

Hastins took them. "We've already received some of shipments."

"Good. See they match the agreement."

Hastins cocked a wry grin. "Nefal or Ha'tar?"

"Ha'tar. Oh, and Gair of the Highlands. He stills tries to pass off diseased sheep or inferior wool."

Hastins gave the ledgers to a clerk. He drew Nollen aside. With a sober expression, he asked, "Have you seen Arctander yet?"

"No. Why?" Nollen asked, immediately concerned.

"Let's just say, it's good you're back."

"That bad?" A hint of fear slipped into Nollen's voice.

Hastins tried to offer a sympathetic smile, only short-lived.

Nollen grabbed his saddlebag and headed to the chapel. Workers, and lay clergy, cleaned and repaired the interior. During the Electors' reign, the chapel fell into disrepair, doing only minor renovations when absolutely needed.

Nollen made his way through the sanctuary to the rectory behind the altar. Arctander, sat near the front window. Beside him, stood Lord Leon, a fifty-year old man from The Doane.

"Nollen," Leon greeted him. "Your grandson is here," he told Arctander.

Stiffly, Arctander rose from his seat. "My dear boy."

Nollen quickly put down his saddlebag to escorted Arctander to the hearth. "It would be warmer for you by the fire. Where is your robe? The room should be warmer. Mendel!" he shouted. "Mendel!"

"You fuss over me like I'm an old woman," Arctander complained. He embraced Nollen. "It is always good to see you, my child."

A young cleric quickly arrived. He carried a fur-lined robe. "Sir?"

Nollen snatched the robe. "It is too cold for him to be without it."

"I've been telling The Reverend that all morning," Mendel said.

"What about the fire?" Nollen wrapped the fur robe around Arctander.

"I sent for more wood," replied Mendel.

"Where are his gloves?" demanded Leon. "He should be wearing them at all times. The cold badly affects his joints."

"Gloves are in the pocket." Mandel indicated the robe.

Leon pulled out the gloves. They were knitted fingerless gloves with a short string and buttons on the glove and end of the string.

"Those look new," observed Nollen.

"Aye. He lost the others." Leon buttoned the gloves to the sleeve of Arctander's robe then helped put the gloves on Arctander's hand. "I had these specially made so he wouldn't lose them again." He turned to Mendel. "Why were these in the pocket?"

"Greta cleaned the robe."

Leon rolled his eyes. "Leave us," he dismissed Mendel.

The young cleric sent a hapless glance to Nollen before he left.

Leon noticed the exchange. "Incompetence," he chided to Nollen.

"Mendel? He's always been dedicated."

Leon shrugged. "Lately, he's been derelict."

"Strange," Nollen muttered in consideration.

"He ignores my instructions concerning Arctander's care."

"Your instructions?"

"We are friends," Leon proudly insisted. "It is only right I help him in your absence. After all he has done to help me. Greta isn't much better than Mendel."

"You can tell Ida it won't work," Arctander argued.

"What?" Nollen asked with confusion.

Leon leaned closer to speak quietly. "He confuses Greta for Ida."

"Now where are my glasses," Arctander complained.

Nollen hid a painful express when his grandfather looked curiously at him. "You're wearing them."

Arctander felt his face. "Oh, so I am."

An older woman entered with a tray. "Time for supper, Reverend," she announced. "Master Nollen, welcome back," she happily greeted.

"Greta." He flashed a plaintive smile. With painful sympathy, Nollen watched Leon escort Arctander to a table for supper. He heard the wall clock strike the hour. "I must see the King to give my report. I'll be back afterwards."

"The Reverend usually takes a nap after he eats," said Greta.

Nollen kissed Arctander on the head. The old man simply grunted an acknowledgement. He retrieved his saddlebag then waved for Greta to accompany him into the hall. "Has he been taking his medicine?"

"Only when forced."

With distress, Nollen glanced back at the open door.

"Sir." Greta touched his arm to get his attention. "Even when he does, the effect is minimal. His mind grows more confused. Daily he mistakes me for your sister, and believes he is either at Far Point or in the forest. The King—"

"What about the King?" Nollen pressed.

"It may be best coming from him."

Nollen blinked back a sudden wave of fearful tears. "I need to see the King anyway." He readjusted the saddlebags to head for the royal study. He knew Axel was there since guards stood at the door. "The Royal Commissary to see His Majesty."

Nollen listened, as the inside guard announced him. He heard Axel give permission to enter. He tried to keep the dismay from being seen.

Axel sat behind a large wonderfully crafted desk. In three years, he had not changed. Strong handsome features, tall and sturdy frame, with black hair, trimmed beard, and clear hazel eyes.

"Sire." Nollen stopped before the desk to bow.

"Welcome back, my friend." Axel warmly smiled and rose in greeting.

Nollen let down the saddlebag to receive the embrace.

Axel's smile faded. "Something troubles you."

Try as he might, he couldn't fool Axel. "I just came from the rectory to visit Grandfather."

Axel's gaze shifted from Nollen to the guard. "Close the door behind you." Once the guard let, he guided Nollen to the hearth. "Sit." He indicated a chair. He sat opposite. Sympathetic, he said, "Arctander has changed much in the few short months of your absence."

Nollen fought to find his voice. "Aye." His gaze grew pleading. "Is there nothing that can be done? Alfgar? Surely the lord of the unicorns can help. Othniel? The Great White lion brought you back from the dead."

"What happened with me, was by the Almighty's design, to fulfill prophecy, and save Eldar. Though Arctander is a loyal and faithful servant, it is the way of all creatures due to age. Thus, beyond unicorn power or Othniel's intervention."

Nollen bit his lip to contain a sob at the news. "How much longer?"

"Only the Almighty knows. But he wants for nothing."

"Who will ... I mean when he ..."

"Verner. You know he's been Arctander's dedicated assistant these past three years. In fact, he has already assumed many duties of the High Priest. What Arctander does throughout the day is minimal routine to keep him occupied." Axel compassionately regarded Nollen. "It is good you have returned for the winter. Spend all the time you can with him. Send for Ida and Jarred."

Nollen soberly shook his head. "She gave birth to a baby girl two weeks ago. She won't risk traveling in the cold with a newborn."

Axel happily smiled. "Another child. How wonderful."

"Bittersweet. She already laments being unable to visit Grandfather this summer."

Axel drew Nollen to his feet. "Refresh yourself with food and drink then visit him this evening. Tomorrow will be soon enough to hear your report."

Nollen gathered his saddlebag and left. The word *bittersweet* repeated in his mind. He roused himself enough to direct his steps to his grandfather's bedchamber. Mendel had difficulty with a combative Arctander. Nollen dropped the saddlebag on the dresser to intervene.

"Here, let me. Stop fighting," he calmly said to Arctander.

"Oh, it's you." Arctander partially smiled. He sat on the edge of the bed. He turned on Mendel. "Now, I have someone who will do as I ask."

Mendel fought vexation. "I will return in the morning, Reverend."

"Bah!" Arctander roughly waved at Mendel.

"You shouldn't be so harsh with him. He's just trying to help."

Arctander tugged on Nollen to sit beside him. His voice a harsh whisper. "They think I don't know. But are wrong. I fight a battle daily … in here." He motioned to his head. "Something they can't understand."

"We want to."

Arctander dolefully sighed. "No, you don't. It's more disturbing than dealing with any physical malady."

"Grandfather—"

Arctander seized Nollen's face between his hands. In a voice of desperation, he urged, "You must be strong! They need you to be strong. I need you to be strong."

The imploring made Nollen momentary speechless.

"Do you hear me, my dear grandson?"

Nollen swallowed back his discomposure to reply. "Aye."

Suddenly drained of all energy, Arctander's hands fell away. "I'm tired. So very tired."

Nollen aided Arctander under the covers. When he pulled up the blankets, Arctander grabbed his hands.

"The Almighty has allowed me to see Prophecy fulfilled. To see my grandchildren blessed. Do not forget that. Remain faithful, and call upon Gott, and He will answer."

"I will remember. Now, please, rest." Nollen kissed Arctander's forehead.

He watched the rising and failing of the blankets. Assured his grandfather truly slept and nothing more, he blew out the lamp on the nightstand. He sat in a cushioned chair between the hearth and bed. He wrapped the cloak about him to get comfortable. This time, he didn't fight back the tears. *You must be strong,* he heard Arctander again. *Bittersweet* followed those words. He already lost so much in his young life that he believed all would be well when Axel became king. Of course, he knew it naïve to believe Arctander would live much longer, especially considering his advanced age.

A small smile appeared, as he thought about Ida, Jarred, Corey, and Dinah. His sister finally married the man she loved and had children. Far

Point prospered like never before, while he gained the friendship and trust of the King. Indeed, the Almighty blessed him, and his family. In truth, all Eldar now lived in a state of peace not seen in hundreds of years. Images filled his mind until he fell asleep.

Chapter 3

RONAN, LORD OF GANEL, WALKED IN HURRIED STEPS BESIDE AXEL. His long black hair tied back, his blue eyes worried. Ronan held a lantern, as they hastened from the King's bedchamber down darkened halls of early morning.

"I tried to calm him, but he repeats your name with urgency," Ronan said.

"He told you nothing more?" asked Axel

"No, though he kept mumbling *sirin.* Whatever that means."

When they arrived in the guest room, Cormac, another Ganel with long brown hair, fought to restrain the man thrashing upon a bed.

Ronan rushed to help. "What happened?"

"I don't know. He became combative and began screaming."

Axel pushed Ronan and Cormac aside. He took the man by the shoulders and pinned him to the bed. "Sylvan, be still! I am here," he forcefully declared.

Sylvan's eyes snapped open. His wild gaze glanced around. He breathed heavy, and his body drenched in sweat. His eyes finally came to rest on, "Ax...el?"

"Aye."

Sylvan smacked his lips and panted.

"Water!" Axel snapped at the Ganels.

Cormac rushed to comply. Axel supported Sylvan's head to help him drink. He gently laid Sylvan back on the pillows. He gave Cormac the cup before he sat on the bed.

"Better?" he asked.

Sylvan nodded and brought his breathing under control.

"Ronan said you called for me. Why? What happened to you?"

The wild look returned, which caused Sylvan's eyes to wander.

Axel again seized Sylvan. "Look at me!"

Sylvan battled to comply. "Sire?"

"Focus on me. Nothing else," commanded Axel. "Now, what happened?"

"Horrible! Sirin!" He grew agitated.

"I said focus on me," Axel repeated his command.

Sylvan again did so.

"Did you reach Kranston?"

Sylvan frantically shook his head. "No. Black Mountains. Sirin!"

"What is sirin?"

The wild look began to overtake Sylvan, but Axel wouldn't allow it. "By the Almighty, begone whatever ails him and restore his wits!"

Sylvan took in a sudden gasp of air. When he exhaled, his whole body relaxed.

Cormac and Ronan watched with anxious fascination. Ronan flinched with dread when Sylvan mentioned the Black Mountains.

Keen to Ronan's reaction, Cormac whispered, "Do you think—?"

Ronan made a curt wave for silence.

Unaware of the exchange, Axel asked Sylvan, "Can you answer me now?"

"Aye," he replied in a weak yet resolute voice.

"You and Gunnar never reached Kranston?"

"No, at least not before …" he forced himself to continue, "before meeting—," he couldn't say the word.

"The one you kept mentioning?" Axel discreetly asked.

Sylvan nodded. It took great strength of will not to revert to the wild state. "Gunnar told me to return. Too dangerous. I didn't want to ... but that one ... I couldn't continue."

"Did Gunnar go on alone?"

Sylvan nodded then shook his head.

"Well, which is it? Aye or no?"

"Aye, until captured."

Axel flinched at the news. "Who captured Gunnar?"

Sylvan's struggle became visibly more difficult. "Don't know ... I saw when leaving ... Fear! Fled!" With hysteria, he cried out then fainted.

When Axel tried to rouse Sylvan, Ronan stopped him. "No, Sire." The Ganel lord motioned Axel from the bed. "I need to consult the Ancient books, to find a clue to this *sirin*. However, I do know, there is great evil in the Black Mountains."

"I know! Gunnar and I crossed the mountains on our journey to Eldar," Axel sternly rebuffed.

"No doubt the Almighty kept you safe." Ronan's glance brief went to Sylvan. "I heard tales of many, who were not so fortunate."

Axel took a breath to calm down. "Aye, we found a route less traveled through the lower elevation. I'm sure Gunnar will take that path. He would not knowingly place anyone at risk."

"Sir Gunnar's loyalty and bravery are not in question. Yet something terrible happened to Lord Sylvan. He is struggling to maintain his sanity."

"The same incident may be responsible for Sir Gunnar's capture," Cormac suggested.

For a long, silent moment, Axel stared at Sylvan. Without looking at Ronan, he issued instructions. "Consult the Ancient books. I have deep prayer and meditation to consider this dangerous turn of events."

Axel didn't take a candle or lamp to his bedchamber. A small adjacent room served as his private chapel. Many times, since becoming King, he spent hours in prayer and meditation for wisdom. None felt more urgent than now.

Panic gripped him when Sylvan spoke of Gunnar's capture. Naturally, a return trip involved more risk, yet necessary to fulfill a promise. Gunnar never hesitated. Then again, Gunnar didn't back away from any challenge. Axel's prayer went so deep and fervent that he did not realize someone stood beside him until a voice spoke.

"Son of Eldar."

Axel knelt with his head touching the altar platform. He pushed himself back onto his knees. "Othniel?" He balked in wonder at sight of the Great White Lion of Eldar. The door to the room remained shut.

Othniel bowed his head to touch Axel's forehead in greeting.

"What are you doing here?"

"Where else would I be when the King is in need?"

Axel came off his knees to sit on the floor. "It is not I who needs help."

Othniel also sat. "You fear for Sir Gunnar."

"The Almighty said it was time to fetch them, so he went. I should have accompanied him," Axel chided.

"Your place is here. Gunnar knows that. So did Lord Sylvan. Do not minimize them with such a selfish statement."

"I don't mean that. Ronan's right, the Almighty protected us when we traveled the Black Mountains. My presence might have spared Sylvan such torment, and Gunnar … from an unknown fate."

"Concern for those in your charge is admirable. However, as King, all of Eldar needs you more than individuals."

Distressed, Axel rebuffed, "How can you speak so about Gunnar?"

"I speak from reality, you from the heart. Those don't always agree." When Axel went to protest, Othniel placed a paw on his shoulder. "That does not mean you are prevented from taking action."

"Sire!" Ronan anxiously called a moment before he burst into the chamber. He paused in astonishment. "Othniel."

"Your appearance does have a profound effect upon humans," Axel wryly commented to the lion. He stood to speak to Ronan. "I take it you found something in the Ancient books to be so agitated."

"Aye. *Sirin* is an old monster long thought vanquished."

"Sirin?" repeated Othniel with concern.

"Sylvan's condition is due to an encounter with it," Ronan explained.

The Great Lion growled. "It is not simply a monster, rather an evil spirit banished for rising up against the First Ones when the world was young!" Othniel turned to Axel and spoke with dread. "If it has reached the Black Mountain, the intent is to return to Eldar for revenge."

"How do we stop it?"

Othniel's mane shook with a negative indication. "I don't know."

"Eldar just came out darkness. It can't happen again," Ronan said with desperation.

Axel gripped Ronan's shoulder. "We shall do everything to prevent it."

"Finding Sir Gunnar, and completing the task, is vital to that end," a new voice spoke. A large white alpha wolf joined the group.

"Bardolf. Welcome," Axel greeted.

"Alfgar and Artair await us in stables. We have matters to discuss," Bardolf announced.

Axel stiffened with anticipation at the mention of the Unicorn lord and eagle king. They followed Bardolf to where Alfgar and Artair waited.

"Greetings, noble First Ones." Axel saluted.

"Son of Eldar." Alfgar lowered his noble head to where his horn nearly touched the ground.

Artair spread his wings and bowed his head in acknowledgement. He tilted his head quizzically at Ronan.

At the eagle king's regard, Axel spoke. "Ronan became my First Minister and Counselor last year. I trust him implicitly, as should the First Ones."

"I do not doubt his loyalty or discretion. I sense uneasiness," said Artair.

"Indeed, I am uneasy with the discovery of what I read in the Ancient books about Sirin. The thought of Eldar threatened should concern all," said Ronan.

"Sirin is why we are here," said Alfgar. "However, what is said cannot go past these walls."

"Upon my word, it won't," insisted Ronan.

"Will you take the blood oath?"

"Alfgar—" began Axel in refute, only stopped by Ronan.

The Ganel Lord spoke resolutely to Alfgar. "I will take the oath."

"Hold out your left hand."

When Ronan did so, the Unicorn Lord used the tip of his horn to prick Ronan's palm. The Ganel flinched but did not withdraw his hand.

"Now, swear."

Ronan held up his pricked left hand with a trickle of blood visible on the palm. "By my life's blood, I swear to keep all secrets entrusted to me."

Axel took hold of Ronan's hand. "You should not have had to take it twice."

"He took the oath?" Artair asked Axel.

"The day he became my First Minister and Counselor. That is what I tried to say earlier."

Alfgar made a low whinny and bowed his head. "I should have known, and not questioned you. Forgive me, my lord," he said to Ronan.

"There is nothing to forgive. Loyalties are often tested under great threat."

"To the matter at hand," said Bardolf.

Othniel made a low roar then announced, "We are free to speak. None shall hear us."

Chapter 4

OLLEN FOUGHT DROWSINESS, AS THE GUARD ESCORTED HIM TO the King's study. He reckoned about three hours of sleep while watching over his grandfather. Arctander didn't move when the royal guard informed him of the King's summons. At the study door, he tried to straighten his wrinkled clothes from spending the night in the chair. The attempt was short-lived when ushered inside. Ronan and Othniel were with Axel.

Nollen pushed aside momentary surprise at sight of Othniel to address Axel. "You sent for me, Sire?"

"I take it you didn't rest well."

Nollen colored with mild embarrassment. "I stayed up with him last night."

Axel kindly grinned. "Understandable." He motioned to a table with food and drink. "Take a moment to eat before we discuss why I summoned you."

Nollen removed his cloak to place it, and his saddlebag, on a windowsill. He proceeded to enjoy some food.

Othniel approached and sniffed the saddlebag. "What have you in the bag?"

Nollen swallow the food. "Precious gems for the King."

"Show us."

He rose from the table to comply. "A rare find. Palleteen diamonds." He opened the box.

"Palleteens? In Eldar?" Othniel growled.

The anger of the Great White Lion startled Nollen. "I don't know. I've never seen a Palleteen."

Axel seized the box. "Where did you get them?"

"A group of foreigners stopped in Edison—"

"Where is Edison?" demanded Axel.

"A southern border town with Bertrand. Is something wrong?"

"You got these from them? In trade?" Axel continued the interrogation.

"Not me. Rafe, the innkeeper. They wanted supplies in exchange and claimed those are Palleteen diamonds. I simply kept them honest during the negotiations when they tried to switch fake for real. Rafe gave me two for helping."

"You're certain these are real?"

"Aye. They passed the dagger test."

"What?"

"Glass will scratch, Palleteen diamonds won't. What is the problem?"

"They may have been scouts," Ronan told Axel.

"Aye." Axel slammed the lid shut.

"Scouts for what?" asked Nollen, frustrated.

Axel crossed to the hearth where a fire warmed the room. He tossed the box into the flame.

Nollen gasped in astonishment and hurried over. Axel stopped him from doing anything to retrieve the box. Othniel breathed upon the flame, which caused the fire to glow with white hot heat. The intensity made them back away.

"Why did you do that?" asked Nollen, utterly confused.

"Intense fire is the only way to destroy them," replied Othniel.

"But *why?*"

"He obviously doesn't know," Ronan said to Axel and Othniel.

"Before we explain, describe the foreigners," said Axel.

"Physically they were swarthy with dark hair, beard, and eyes. Never seen their type of clothing before. A bit more colorful than ours." Nollen indicated his waist. "Used a cloth sash rather than a belt to close the inner vest and shirt. Lots of embroidery on the long outer coat. The hat was round and flat on top."

"Were the swords curved?"

Nollen shrugged. "I didn't see any weapons other than elaborately carved dagger hilts. The one who talked to Rafe and me, had an unfamiliar accent." Then with thought, he added, "They spoke to each other in a language I've not heard before. And I know Markitan and Bertrandian."

"Sounds like Palleteens," Ronan said to Axel.

"*Now,* tell me why you destroyed the diamonds, and are concerned about the Palleteens?" Nollen firmly said.

"Have you even seen a Palleteen diamond before?" asked Axel.

"Only a fragment Uncle Oberon had. He claimed it came from a priestly vestment once worn by one of our ancestors."

Othniel took up the explanation. "Rare diamonds were gifts to Eldar's first king by Emperor Beldon of the Palleteens. Eventually, the diamonds were used as ornamentation on royal and priestly garments."

"Aye, and so valuable Jonas used the fragment to pay a year's tribute for The Doane when gold became scarce. I believe them a kingly gift." Nollen motioned to the hearth where the fire returned to normal.

"Valuable, and deadly," stressed Othniel. "Within a year of the gift, strange things began to happen. Things even the First Ones were hard pressed to explain."

"Such as?" Nollen listened with rapt attention.

"Unknown plights upon crops, mysterious human illnesses, and creatures behaving unnaturally."

Ronan spoke. "My ancestor was the High Priest then. During study at the Mathena University, he stumbled upon the truth. The diamonds contain evil properties that mesmerize the wearers. He hurried to King Nandor with the information. Alas, the King had ridden to battle when word came of a Palleteen invasion from the east through Nefal."

"Back then it was called Greenlands, due to the lush forest," said Othniel. "By the time the Palleteens reached Leven's river plain, many innocent Eldarians died. The First Ones rallied to fight against the enemy."

"When my ancestor reached the King, he urged Nandor to destroy the diamonds with fire in hopes of stopping the evil. Just like Axel did," said Ronan.

"Destroying them, turned the tide of battle. It ended in utter defeat for the Palleteens. Sadly, also costly for Eldar in lives," said Othniel.

Axel retrieved a very old book from a shelf, opened it, and placed it on the desk. "Through the High Priest, the Almighty cursed the Palleteens for their treachery. And placed a supernatural blight on the barrier between Palleteen and Eldar to ensure such invasion would not happen again." He beckoned Nollen to the desk. The page was a map. With his index finger, he pointed to location.

Nollen looked up from the map to Axel. "The Black Mountains."

"Aye," Axel grimly confirmed.

The young man still appeared confused. "To reach Eldar the Palleteens would have to pass through Markita."

"They did so last time," Othniel stoutly said.

Nollen's gaze shifted between the Great White Lion and the map. "With our treaty, it is doubtful King Montre would allow that."

"There is more," said Axel in a tone suggesting a complication. "The only way to Kranston is through the Black Mountains by way of Markita. It is how we came to Eldar. And where Gunnar went two months ago."

"Gunnar? Why?" asked Nollen, surprised.

"To fulfill a promise. Sylvan went with him, only returned in a horrible state. Driven the point of madness by an encounter with Sirin."

Hearing Axel's lament, Nollen asked, "What is Sirin?"

"A creature of darkness. Many such creatures are said to inhabit the Black Mountains," Ronan explained.

"What happened to Gunnar?" Nollen asked, wary of the answer.

"Captured. That's what Sylvan said," replied Ronan.

"By whom?"

Ronan shook his head. "Sylvan didn't say. Or more rightly, couldn't say. His mind almost gone."

"Like Grandfather," murmured Nollen with despair.

"No!" insisted Axel. "Arctander suffers from old age. Sylvan's condition is the result of evil. Two different things. Do not connect them." He sent a nod to Ronan and Othniel. The Ganel lord and Great Lion withdrew.

Nollen didn't speak until Axel stared at him in a way he took to mean trouble. "You have something to tell me you either don't want them to hear, or they already know, and I'm about to be told."

"You have grown into an astute young man. Keen in ways beyond your years. Yet it is your *other* expertise that is needed, as pathfinder and trader extraordinaire to avoid trouble with Montre."

Nollen returned the direct gaze. "You want me to find Gunnar."

"I *need* you to find him, so he can finish his mission."

"Why keep it from Montre?"

"For reasons I cannot tell you at present." Axel took hold of Nollen's shoulders to look at him directly. "You are the only one I trust for this task. It is extremely dangerous, so I will understand if you refuse."

"How can I refuse? Gunnar is missing. I nearly brought evil to Sener with those diamonds. And Palleteens again threaten us."

Axel's expression softened to a kind smile. "An innocent gift for me." The smile faded. "Will you go?"

"Aye."

Grateful, Axel embraced Nollen. "Now, rest. I mean really rest. Meet me an hour after supper in the corral behind the stables."

Chapter 5

DESPITE UPSET AT HIS GRANDFATHER'S CONDITION, GUNNAR'S reported capture, and the impending journey, Nollen managed to get six uninterrupted hours of sleep. The remainder of the day, he tended to his duty as royal commissary then personal preparation for departure.

Fully dressed for travel, he slung a saddlebag over his shoulder. In one hand he carried a small loaded sack, while in the other, he held his crossbow. With the early sunset of late autumn, most had gone indoors for the evening. Soldiers made rounds while a few servants scurried between buildings.

At the corral, Nollen found Axel along with Othniel, a white wolf, and an eagle. Yet one thing struck him as odd—a beautiful black horse with a star on its forehead fully saddled. A small crossbow sheath was attached to the front of the saddle by leather straps. A quiver of arrows hung from the saddle horn. Two more leather straps held a bedroll in place behind the saddle. He put down the sack.

"Why is Alydar saddled? Is someone else going?" he asked.

"No. For this journey, Alydar is your mount." Axel patted the horse's neck.

"I haven't traveled anywhere without Gilen in over a decade."

"A most noble pony, indeed. However, Alydar is an unusual horse."

"I'm a unicorn. Or rather was," lamented Alydar.

Briefly surprised by the speech, Nollen asked, "Why haven't you spoken before now? I've seen you in the stables the past two years."

Othniel explained, "Alydar lost his horn in the battle to restore the Son of Eldar. That day, he became a mortal horse, in years of life and loss of magic."

"Like Teva?" asked Nollen in reference to the Queen of the Unicorns.

"Teva was my sister," said Alydar. "I still have my strength, speed, and centuries of knowledge."

"While speech has been restored for this task," added Othniel.

"Being among the original herd, Alydar knows the secret pass through the Black Mountains to Kranston." Axel again patted Alydar's neck. "In fact, he accompanied my ancestors when they fled."

"Then why do you need my pathfinding skills?" asked Nollen.

"For the rest of the journey, and any deviation that might occur. The secret pass requires knowledge you do not possess, nor can I adequately impart the location." Axel pointed to the sack. "I assume those are items for trade."

Nollen cocked a grin. "No, food and supplies. Trade items are in here."

He picked up the sack to finish preparation. He placed the arch of the saddlebag under the bedroll to hold it in place. He put the crossbow in the sheath then slung the quiver across his back. He made certain everything was secure.

"I hope I didn't tighten the girth too much," he said to Alydar.

"I would let you know, if you did."

"Alydar is not your only companion for this venture," began Axel. "Callie is the youngest of the Halvor White Wolves. Ajax is Artair's son."

"Hello," Nollen greeted each.

Axel proceeded to give instructions. "Even in Eldar travel mostly at night. Callie will be your ears and eyes in the darkness. Ajax will keep the day watch."

"Why in Eldar?"

"If Palleteens have infiltrated The Doane, there is no telling how much further they have travelled. Leave by the back gate and cross over to the Freelands via the north bridge. Only, don't enter Stellan. Travel the eastern border until you come to Ashton Station then cross into Markita."

"I haven't forgotten my secret paths so soon," Nollen wryly said.

Axel ignored the statement to continue. "Once in Markita, avoid as many settlements, cities, and towns as possible. Trade only for what you need. The journey to the Black Mountains, could take as long as three weeks." He took Nollen's face in his hands. "The Almighty bless you and guide you, my dear young friend." He kissed Nollen's forehead.

Nollen flashed a timid smile. He reached inside his pocket and withdrew a sealed letter. "If anything should happen to me … see this is delivered to Ida."

Axel accepted it. "I will. Now, off with you." He and Othniel accompanied them to the rear gate. He ordered the guards to remain silent about the departure.

Once away from Sener, Ajax landed on the bedroll behind Nollen.

"Eagles don't fly at night?" asked Nollen.

"Why fly when I can ride?" Ajax countered.

"*Humpf.* He rests while we walk," complained Callie.

"I need to rest sometime if I'm to keep watch from above during the day while *you* sleep, she-wolf," Ajax retorted.

"Callie. My name is *Callie*, not *she-wolf*."

"If we're to travel at night, silence is best," Nollen stressed.

"So says the human who doesn't want to talk to animals," chided Callie.

"I didn't say that. During darker times, night travel was always done in silence. To avoid detection by jackals and bandits."

"The King said Palleteens may be in Eldar," Alydar reminded Callie.

"And," began Nollen with emphasis to Callie, "while talking animals are common in Eldar, it might not be so in Markita."

"You can't argue with that logic … *she-wolf*," Ajax purposely said.

Callie lowly growled at Ajax.

"Silence," Nollen snapped in frustration. "I think Gilen may have been better for this," he muttered the last sentence to himself, or so he thought.

Alydar did a short whinny-laugh. "I know what Gilen would tell if he could."

"Excuse me?" began Nollen, offended. "Gilen is very special to me. I treat him like a member of my family."

"He returns your affection. However, you didn't always listen to him when he tried to steer from trouble - to protect you."

Nollen scowled. "There were times I didn't have a choice of how to react."

"Silence!" Callie took up position in front of them.

Alydar abruptly stopped, and raised his head, with ears straight up to listen.

Nollen leaned down to whisper to Alydar, "What is it?"

An owl swooped down in front of him. Startled, Nollen sat back in the saddle, which made him pull on the reins. Alydar tossed his head in protest. Ajax hopped off to avoid Nollen's backward movement.

"It was an owl!" Ajax chided Callie.

"I know. I just wanted to quiet the human."

"Next time, do it in a less dramatic way," complained Alydar. "I'm still getting used to the bit."

"We will all be quiet," Nollen chided. He waved Callie to take the point. He waited until Ajax settled back on the bedroll to follow.

The grey light of pre-dawn peeked over the eastern horizon. They reached the north bridge, which crossed the narrowest part of the Stille into the Freelands. Nollen yawned and rubbed his eyes.

"Do you wish to stop and rest here or over the bridge?" asked Alydar.

"There is an old shed in a forest grove a mile from the bridge. I've used it multiple times in the past." Nollen fought another yawn in reply.

"Very well, only we should hurry before you fall asleep." Alydar began a lope that for any normal horse, would equal a gallop.

Taken back by the speed, Nollen woke enough to hold on. At the spot to turn off the road, he jerked Alydar's head. "This way."

"Easy on the bit!" Alydar complained, as he changed direction.

By the time they arrived at the shed, Nollen felt sleepy again. He slid off the saddle. "I thought my clandestine night rides were over." The shed door creaked when opened. "There is enough room for everyone." He went to take the reins, but Alydar proceeded inside on his own.

Callie sniffed the shed floor. "Others have been here, not just you."

"It served as a common hideout for the Brethren." Nollen removed all his gear and saddle from Alydar.

"No, recently," insisted Callie.

Nollen paused in removal of the bridle to ask, "How recent?"

"The scent is strong. A day, maybe two."

"Replace the saddle for quick escape," said Alydar.

"No. Let Ajax explore the area first," replied Nollen.

Ajax hopped out of the shed before he took flight.

Alydar shook his head when Nollen completely removed the bridle. "I hope you can hold on tight enough if we need to leave in a hurry."

Nollen sat on a roughhewn stool near a small fireless hearth. He tried to stifle a yawn and blinked his eyes to concentrate on the bridle.

"What are you doing? You need to rest," said Callie

"Taking off the bit to reposition the reins." He looked at Alydar. "It will more comfortable when I'm done."

"Gilen is right. You are a merciful and kind human." Alydar nudged Nollen.

"At least, he said something good about me."

"He said many good things. Especially sorrow when the King fetched me instead of him." Alydar lowered his head to meet Nollen's gaze. "In truth, he is not fit for such a journey. Age is catching up with him."

"I know," droned Nollen with lament. "In the spring, I plan to turn him out in the pastures around Far Point." He stretched and yawned.

"Sleep." Alydar nudged Nollen so hard that he fell off the stool.

Nollen fetched his bedroll. Callie laid beside him while Alydar laid down in front of the closed door.

Chapter 6

FOLLOWING THE INSTRUCTION OF NIGHT TRAVEL, IT TOOK FIVE days to reach Ashton Station on the border of Eldar and Markita. At the break of dawn, Nollen stopped inside the tree line. Activity at the inn showed signs of beginning for the day. Smoke rose from the chimney, accompanied by the smell of cooking.

"I need to stop at the inn," said Nollen.

"The King told us to avoid settlements," refuted Ajax.

"I only packed enough supplies for a week. Now that I know how long to expect, I'd rather resupply in Eldar than risk any trouble in Markita."

"Can't argue with that logic ... *eagle whelp*," Callie said.

Annoyed, Ajax spread his wings and cried at Callie.

"Quiet!" Nollen scolded. "When I am done at the inn, we cross the border."

"In broad daylight?" asked Alydar.

"I haven't decided yet. With traffic, we can enter unnoticed. At night, we could draw patrols, if we're not careful," replied Nollen, though considerate in tone. "Still, someone may recognize me."

"You have visited Markita before?" asked Callie.

"As Royal Commissary, Axel sent me, Gunnar, and two others to negotiate a trade treaty with King Montre. Of course, we dealt with Archduke Boric first since his duchy is the border territory. We stayed a month before he finally decided to take us to Montre. Since then, I've been to Markita on three different occasions."

"Getting supplies is risky enough," said Alydar sternly.

Nollen didn't immediately reply. He stood in the stirrups to survey the surrounding area. "There are remains of a ruined outpost on that ridge. We can stop there when I'm done. Ajax, keep watch from above. Callie, wait here. Sight of a wolf might scare them." He made a slight kick for Alydar to continue.

They arrived just as the innkeeper opened the shutters and front door. "Hail to the house, Friend Danika," Nollen greeted.

It took a moment to recognize him. "Why, Nollen of Far Point, it's been ages. Welcome."

Nollen dismounted and tied the reins to a post. He retrieved his supply sack and saddlebag. "How goes it, Danika? Is Oscar recovered?"

Her face fell. "Alas, no. He passed four months back."

"Oh, I'm sorry."

"Thank you. It was for the best. His pain is ended, and he rests with the Almighty." She waved him inside. "Come. Breakfast is ready."

Nollen took a big whiff. "Smells wonderful. Tell me, do you still make raisin cakes?"

Danika laughed. "Of course." She then called, "Ron! Three raisin cakes, eggs, and bacon for Nollen." After receiving an acknowledgement, she escorted him to a table. "Morning cider or light ale?"

"Cider. Thank you." He sat at a table with his back to the wall in such a way as to view the door. Another old habit honed over years of clandestine travel. Of course, this was a secret mission, his first in years. His wandering gaze of surveillance changed to a smile when Danika returned with a tankard.

"I see you're packed for travel. Coming or going?"

He swallowed a drink before making a vague reply. "Business is robust since becoming Royal Commissary."

Ron arrived with the food. Danika impatiently waved him away and took a seat opposite Nollen. Her voice lowered to a near whisper. "You know the value of trade goods."

Her statement and peculiar behavior made him cautious. "Aye," he tentatively answered.

She reached into the pocket of her apron, yet kept her fist closed when she withdrew it. "I took these in trade three weeks ago. I can hardly believe my good fortune, yet uncertain what to do with them. Though perhaps the Almighty is blessing me after the passing of my husband." Her eyes grew misty. "It's been difficult. Only Ron and Kaye remain."

Concerned, he asked, "Business has not been good?"

She solemnly shook her head. "It is slow to return since … There is a new inn closer to the border."

Nollen tapped her close fist. "What is it want to show me?"

She slowly opened her fingers and spoke with a breathy voice of anticipation. "Palleteen diamonds."

Nollen tried to keep the harsh reaction from being visible.

"That's what they said," she insisted at his silence.

"Who?"

"Foreigners. They traded these for supplies."

"Bertrandians or Markitans?"

"Neither. I had not seen their kind before, but with things so difficult …" She picked up a diamond to hand him. "Can you tell me their worth?"

Nollen turned it over several times. From his experience with Rafe and Jonas, he feared the outcome. He readied his dagger.

Panicked, Danika seized his hand before the blade touched the diamond. "What are you doing?"

"A test to authenticate it. Glass will scratch, a diamond won't." To his great dismay, a scratch appeared. This time, he couldn't keep his expression neutral.

"Well?" she asked, a hint of hopelessness in her tone.

"I fear you have been badly cheated."

Danika covered her mouth to contain a sob of lament.

Nollen held her hand in support. "Do not weep." He reached into his purse for five silver coins. "Fifty talents. I will take the imitations off your hands."

Danika's expression changed to shock. "I can't accept this much for glass."

Nollen held her hands between his. "To aid you in a time of need. And to spare you further grief. As a friend, and Brethren."

Momentarily speechless, she pocketed the coins. "I'll fetch your supplies." She took the sack but left the fakes on the table.

Nollen scowled in regard of the imitations. He snatched them up and place them in a pouch on his belt. He finished eating when Danika returned with a filled sack.

"A dozen raisin cakes are on the top. Give my regards to Ida."

Nollen paused in taking the sack. "I … I will. Blessings to this house." He picked up his saddlebag and left.

He secured everything to the saddle before he mounted. At an eagle's cry, he glanced skyward to see Ajax. He didn't look toward the forest. He assumed Callie waited. He turned Alydar east toward the Markita border.

Once around a bend, Nollen paused to observe the other inn located within eyesight of the border crossing. The building appeared newer, with a few unfinished sections where workers applied their craft. He noticed more patrons than at Danika's inn. Whoever built this place knew what they were doing. He vacillated between learning the owner's identity or proceeding. His indecision didn't last long when Alydar made an angry snort and stomped his right front hoof. Nollen took the cue. He picked up the reins and headed into the forest. He didn't backtrack to where he left Callie. Instead, he steered Alydar up the hilly terrain.

Forty minutes later, they reached the ridge ruins. The roof was long gone, yet enough of the walls remained to hide them from view. Brush and trees once cleared, threatened to overtake the ruins. With a log blocking the narrow opening, Nollen dismounted to lead Alydar inside.

"You know many hidden places," Alydar commented.

"Comes from living most of my life secretly traveling Eldar in service of the Brethren. We used this particular outpost to stay close to the border before traveling through Nefal to the Freelands."

At a lower part in the wall, Nollen waved his hand at the horizon. "Markita stretches as far as the eye can see. At least twice the size of Eldar with four duchies laid down like a compass around a central city where the king lives." He huffed an ironic laughed. "They barely agree to anything with each other. It's a wonder we managed a trade treaty."

"I remember Markita from the beginning," Alydar said.

Nollen lightly chuckled with slight embarrassment. "Sorry."

Ajax landed on a crumbled wall a moment before Callie arrived.

"What made you deviate from the plan?" she asked.

"Curiosity." Nollen removed his bedroll from behind the saddle.

Despite his terse response, she scolded him. "Curiosity could get you hurt or killed."

Anger prevented Nollen from replying. He spread out the bedroll in preparation for sleep.

Irritated by his avoidance, Callie stopped him from laying down. "We're supposed to protect you. We can't do that if you follow human *curiosity!*"

"A good friend lost her husband, is being deprived of business by a greedy rival. *Worst of all,* cheated by Palleteens with fake diamonds! My *human curiosity* came from a desire to help, not satisfy some arbitrary choice."

Callie lowered her head in submission at the rebuff. "We're only concerned for your welfare."

Nollen sighed with regret. "I'm sorry, Callie. Emotions get the best of me when someone I know is in trouble."

She responded by licking his hand. He patted her head.

"Were Palleteens at the inn just now?" asked Alydar.

"No, Danika said they traded the diamonds for supplies three weeks ago." He removed them from the pouch. "Glass cut to resemble diamonds." His brows knitted in deep consideration. "Her encounter happened before mine in Edison. They tried to cheat Rafe by switching real for fake, only I was keen to their attempt thus thwarted them." He glanced up at Alydar. "Sounds like they entered by way of Ashton Station before proceeding further into The Doane."

"Othniel told us about destroying the real diamonds. Perhaps, your success deprived them opportunity of fooling anyone again by taking possession of the real ones."

"I can only hope." Nollen put the fakes back into the pouch. "I made it right. I gave her money for the fakes."

"Compassion does you credit," Alydar said.

Nollen nodded since he yawned.

"Rest. I'll keep watch." Ajax took off.

Nollen laid with an arm under his head. "Don't let me sleep past suppertime." Callie laid down near him.

Chapter 7

ARTAIR FLEW HIGH ABOVE THE RIVER LEVEN COMING UP FROM the south. He reached Lake Helivan as twilight grew nigh. Below, the day's commerce between Wyckton and Sener was coming to an end. The watch shouted for the guards to begin clearing the bridge for gate closure. None of that deterred Artair, as he descended toward the castle at the apex of Sener.

Even at night, the glow of lamp and torchlight sparkled on the magnificence of Sener Castle. Artair directed his flight path to the balcony of the King's study. The carved wooden and glass balcony doors were shut. Firelight and the softer glow of lamps showed a presence within the room. Artair landed and used his beak to rap on the glass. Ronan opened one of the doors to admit him. Artair hopped inside then made a short flight to land on a table near the hearth. He spread his wings to absorb warmth from the fire. Othniel rose from his place by the hearth when Artair arrived.

Axel worked at his desk. He paused to ask Artair, "Have they left Eldar?"

"Aye. They crossed the border just north of Ashton Station."

Axel tossed aside the quill pen. "I still regret not telling Nollen everything."

"It is for the best," assured Artair.

"Really?" chided Axel. He rose to pace, his steps long and agitated.

"Artair is right, Sire," began Ronan. "What Nollen doesn't know he can't tell."

Axel paused before the fire to stare at the flame. "He will take it as a lack of trust."

"For his survival," insisted Othniel.

"From our point of view," said Axel, soberly.

Ronan moved to stand beside Axel. "You saw what it did to Sylvan. Innocence, and ignorance will protect Nollen."

"Let us pray he doesn't encounter Sirin—or any of the other creatures."

"The Almighty had you summon Nollen for this task," said Othniel.

"I believed the same about Gunnar," Axel droned heavily.

"Do you doubt the Almighty, Son of Eldar?" Othniel harshly questioned.

For a long moment, Axel stared resolutely at the Great White Lion. "No, but it doesn't mean I can't be concerned when I knowingly place people in harm's way. Two with knowledge, another without. One returned only to lose his mind. The others—" He couldn't finish for personal discomfort.

"We understand your feelings toward Gunnar and Nollen," Ronan spoke with sympathy.

"There is something I have not yet told you," began Artair.

"What is that?" Axel asked tersely.

"I spoke with Ajax while Master Nollen slept – before they crossed the border. Palleteens cheated the widow of Ashton Inn by switching real diamonds with glass. Nollen took them and gave her a generous compensation."

"That's the second report," Ronan said emphatically to Axel.

Artair continued. "Ashton is on the eastern border. Nollen's encounter happened on the southern border. According to the reported times, it is believed the Ashton switch happened prior to Edison."

Axel's eyes narrow with wrath. "The Doane is compromised. Summon General Mather!"

Ronan quickly informed the guards to fetch Mather.

"Are Bardolf and Alfgar still in Sener?" Axel asked Othniel.

"Aye. They remain, awaiting word from Artair."

"You fetch them," Axel instructed Ronan.

A heavy silence hung in the room, as they waited for those summoned to arrive. Axel didn't move from his place in front of the hearth. With fixed gaze, he stared intensely at the flames. This would be the greatest threat since assuming the throne. Dealing with the Ha'tar and Nefal after the defeat of Javan and Dolus perhaps served as a test to prepare him for this challenge.

Even when the door opened and closed several times, he didn't move from his transfixed position. His concentration went so deep, that not until Othniel nudged his arm did he rouse himself.

Ronan, General Mather, Alfgar, and Bardolf stood at the ready. For a moment, Axel regarded Mather. The loyal Freelander gallantly fought to overcome evil. Since that day, he remained at Sener in service of the royal new army. In three years, his dedication, faithfulness to the Almighty, and military intellect helped him rise through the ranks.

"General, are you aware of the history between Eldar and Palleteen?"

"Aye, Sire. They are our sworn enemies since the beginning."

"The presence of Palleteen spies in The Doane has been confirmed."

Mather slapped his sword. "Say the word, Sire, and I will root them out!"

"The word is given, General, only do not upset the populace. The army is to be placed on full alert with orders to capture any Palleteen. Also, investigate any report of diamonds, fake or otherwise. Have them confiscated, locked in a secure box, and brought to Sener by loyal and faithful men. Do not trust them to just any soldier. Be generous to compensate those wronged by a dishonest trade."

"Aye, Sire." Mather again slapped his sword and began to leave.

"General!" Axel's sharp tone caused Mather to pause for further instructions. "I cannot stress enough the danger of those diamonds, nor the importance of them being brought here under lock and key."

"A severe sentence for any derelict soldier may be necessary," Ronan strongly suggested to Axel.

"Prison, Lord Minister?" Mather asked.

"Death."

Stunned, Mather looked to Axel for confirmation.

"It is *that* serious."

"Aye, Sire." Mather bowed and departed.

When the door closed, Axel directed his attention to Bardolf. "Take a pack of Halvor Wolves to The Doane. The Palleteens may try to elude the soldiers. We need to confine them to one province."

"The eagles will watch from above," said Artair.

"That was my next order." With new consideration, Axel asked Ronan, "What news of the juvenile dragons? Have they been successfully trained to defend Eldar?"

Ronan hesitated to answer. "To a point. However, I don't believe they are trustworthy yet."

Axel cocked a brow of curiosity. "How do you trust a dragon?"

"I mean the Ha'tar trainer."

"Myn has given you trouble?"

"He's more cooperative than in the past. However, he feels he hasn't received all the support necessary for proper training."

His interest piqued; Axel folded his arms. "In what way?"

"The armory quartermaster, Lord Leon."

"Didn't you place Irwin in charge of the armory?"

Ronan flushed with some embarrassment. "Aye. It is a personal matter that Irwin has been trying to rectify without bringing it to your attention."

"A little late for that now! Send for Irwin and Leon."

While Ronan dispatched soldiers to fetch the men, Alfgar spoke to Axel. "The Unicorns can form a defensive barrier between The Doane and other provinces."

"How?"

"Nicor. The water spirit of a unicorn. I can summon a herd to patrol the waterways separating The Doane from Ha'tar and Nefal."

"Will they be able to discern a Palleteen from an Eldarian?"

"Most assuredly."

"Sire. Lord Leon and Baron Irwin," Ronan announced.

Irwin appeared every inch a Ganel with handsome features and long blond hair. Lord Leon stood shorter than the Ganels, a bit rougher looking than the elegant beings. The Ganels almost defied the appearance of aging, while Leon's sagging jowls and reddened eyes showed years past his age of fifty.

Axel dismissed Bardolf, Artair, and Alfgar. Othniel remained. The king directed his attention to Leon. "I hear there is difficulty with the Ha'tar trainer and juvenile dragons."

"That's putting it mildly, Sire," huffed Leon.

"Do you find Myn's request for supplies unreasonable, my lord?"

"Well, they aren't exactly the usual requested supplies. In fact, I'm not exactly certain what half of them are."

Irwin spoke. "What is required is found mostly in their territory."

"So? Why not find ways to accommodate him?" Axel asked.

Leon fought to contain his disdain, while Irwin scowled at the shorter man. Axel noticed the reactions. "Gentlemen, I have neither the time nor patience for petty squabbles. Now, why are the Ha'tar requests not being properly addressed?"

"If you don't tell him, I will," Irwin scolded Leon.

"It's not that easy!" Leon snapped.

"What?" demanded Axel.

Leon balked with unwillingness to answer, so Irwin replied.

"Lord Leon bears a grudge against the Ha'tar. A grudge I have been diligently trying to resolve."

"Grudges have no place in this court!" Axel rebuked Leon, then to Irwin, "If you have been unsuccessful in coming to a resolution, it should have been brought to my attention before now."

"Sire, I only learned about this grudge two days ago when Master Myn came to me with proof. I have since confronted Lord Leon, and tried to mediate a truce, if not a compromise between them."

His patience gone; Axel waved his hands. "There is no time for this! Lord Leon, tell me now, and tell me true, can or cannot you deal rightly with the Ha'tar?"

"Sire, let me explain—"

"Aye or no!"

Leon took a deep breath and squared his shoulders. "No. Even under orders, I cannot in all good conscience deal with those who killed members of my family when they raided The Doane."

Some of Axel's anger faded at the confession. "My sympathies for your loss. However, understand my position. Despite old wounds and injustices, I must find common ground to bring peace and harmony to Eldar."

"Then let it be done without me."

"My thoughts exactly. You are immediately relieved of duty. Gather your things and return to The Doane." Axel grabbed Leon's arm when he turned to depart. "I bear you no ill will. I hope you can do the same towards me, even if you can't for the Ha'tar."

Leon clapped a hand to his chest in a salute and bowed. He left.

"My apologies, Sire. I tried to deal with it," said Irwin with contrition.

Axel took a moment to regain his composure. "See Myn is accommodated. We may soon need the juveniles."

"Sire?" asked Irwin, a bit taken back.

"Ronan." Axel indicated Irwin and waved for the Ganels to leave. He returned to his position before the fire to once again stare at the flames. Quietly, under his breath, he prayed. "Lord, protect Nollen. Help him find Gunnar, so we can fulfill the task at hand, and perhaps determine the source of this threat."

Chapter 8

OR THREE NIGHTS, THEY TRAVELED THROUGH THE MARKITAN forest. Being late autumn, the nights grew colder in the hills. When they paused before sunrise to rest, Nollen kept a fire just hot enough to heat food and warm up from the night's ride. Each morning, Callie lay beside him to provide more warmth and protection. Ajax kept a sharp eagle-eye out for any threat that could disturb or discover Nollen. Alydar went between sleep and standing guard. As a unicorn, he rarely required recuperative sleep. Fortunately, normal horses only need three hours to recover from any activity.

By the fourth dawn, Nollen drew Alydar to rein at the edge of a clearing. Callie strolled alongside with Ajax perched on the bedroll. A half-mile down the road, the rising sun outlined the shape of a town. Flickering lights and rising smoke gave more definition against the growing morning colors.

"This is the first town we've seen since arriving. The only way to get information about Gunnar is by talking to people," said Nollen.

"I thought you were a capable tracker?" asked Alydar.

"Pathfinder," Nollen corrected. "There's a difference between finding one's way and tracking someone. However, I haven't detected anything to suggest someone passed the same way we did."

"I can pick up a scent if you have something from Sir Gunnar," said Callie.

"It's been over two months. I don't think even a wolf's keen sense of smell can find a track that old."

"No, but once I know the scent, I will be able to determine *if* he has been some place or is nearby."

"Unfortunately, I don't have anything to help with that."

"Do you speak Markitan?" asked Alydar.

"Aye. Part of my trading is knowing languages, specifically the border countries." Nollen observed the countryside surrounding the town. "Callie, skirt the forest north of town, and avoid contact. Ajax, make sure all is clear between here and town."

Ajax lifted off from the back of the saddle. Once out from under the trees, he flew upwards. He reached the sleepy town in a matter of moments. He made several circles overhead before he landed on the highest roof for a few moments of observation. People woke to start the day. Satisfied, he flew back to the forest where he landed on a branch above Nollen's head.

"I saw nothing of concern," he reported.

"Good. Take the day watch." Nollen snapped the reins for Alydar to move.

In a casual walk, they approached the town. When Nollen received some wary attention, he simply smiled. To one man he asked, "Where is the inn?"

The man curiously eyed Nollen. "Your accent is strange."

"A traveler passing through."

Another man appeared. "He sounds Eldarian," he tersely commented to the first man.

"You have a keen ear, friend," said Nollen with a friendly smile. "The inn?"

"Two streets down and turn left."

"Thank you, friend." Nollen touched his forehead in the Markitan gesture.

Once at the inn, he dismounted and tied the reins to a post. He arched his back in a stretch from the night's ride. He removed his crossbow to place over his shoulder then went inside. Two large hearths for cooking, warmed the inn. In a brief glance, he spied the proprietor, an older man with a bald head.

"Innkeeper," he said with a nod and smile.

Stone-faced, he motioned Nollen to a table. "What do you want?"

"Food and drink, please, friend." Nollen sat with his back to the wall.

The innkeeper's brows furrowed. "You have money? Markitan, not any foreign stuff."

Nollen reached into his pouch. One of the glass fakes appeared among the Markitan coins. He quickly brushed it back into the pouch before he showed the coins. "Will this do?"

"It will." He left to fetch food and drink.

Nollen noticed the man who identified him as "Eldarian" arrived. He averted his eyes to avoid the man's attention again. Didn't work. The man approached the table.

"Eldarians aren't a common sight in these parts." He spoke in the same unfriendly tone as earlier.

Nollen shrugged. "Like I said, I'm just a traveler passing through."

"To where?"

"Personal business. Nothing to be concerned about."

With a menacing snarl, he leaned on the table to bring his face closer to Nollen. "I said *where?*"

Nollen refused to be intimidated. "And I answered: *personal business.*"

He seized Nollen by the doublet. "We don't need your kind here!"

"Dimitri!" The innkeeper rushed over.

Dimitri roughly released Nollen. "We don't need more trouble."

"I'm not here to cause trouble," Nollen refuted.

"Tell that to your *friends!*"

"What friends? I came here alone," Nollen replied, though curious about the reference.

"Dimitri, that was months ago," the innkeeper sternly said.

"Ya, and I'm still rebuilding!"

Nollen stood. "Friend, I don't know what you're talking about. However, if an Eldarian has done you harm, I sincerely apologize."

"Apologies don't pay for supplies to rebuild a home."

"Fair enough." Nollen reached into his pouch for some Markitan coins. "Will this compensate?"

The man's sneer softened at sight of the money. "Maybe."

"Not as much as a diamond," the innkeeper told the man.

"Diamond?" Dimitri echoed with interest.

Nollen held up his hands in refute. "It is not what you think. The coins are better."

Dimitri stepped threateningly close to Nollen. "I will decide."

By now, other men had entered the inn, and Nollen found himself outnumbered. With slow reluctance, he opened the pouch and carefully withdrew a single glass diamond.

Dimitri snatched it. With eyes of delight, he examined it. "Have you more?"

"No, just the one."

"Let's see."

When Dimitri reached to grab his pouch, Nollen drew his dagger. "That's enough! I have endured your wrongful accusations, and now you would rob me. Take it as compensation for your suffering and let me leave in peace."

This time the innkeeper physically stepped between Dimitri and Nollen. "He's right. I will tolerant no violence."

Dimitri's eyes narrowed on Nollen. A haughty smile appeared when he regarded the diamond and coins. He tossed a last glare at Nollen before he left.

"The rest of you, out!" the innkeeper ordered. "The Eldarian has made amends."

Nollen held his dagger ready, as he cautiously watched the men leave. "What was that about?" he demanded of the innkeeper.

"You heard Dimitri. Two Eldarians made trouble a few months ago."

"They destroyed his home?" Nollen asked with confused concern.

"No, Chika did."

Baffled, Nollen shook his head. "Chika?"

"The goddess from the Black Mountains. Now, enough talk. I'll fetch your provision to go. It's not safe for you to stay here any longer."

Nollen wouldn't be put off. He sheathed the dagger and followed the innkeeper. "This Chika destroyed Dimitri's home because of the Eldarians? Is that what happened?"

"Ya! Now, no more questions. You'll take the food and leave."

Knowing he couldn't push any further, Nollen left without accepting anything from the innkeeper. Commerce of wagon, people, and horses began to crowd the town. Nollen ignored them to jerk loose the reins and vaulted into the saddle. When he turned Alydar to leave, he noticed Dimitri across the street with two other men. A bit harder than intended, Nollen kicked Alydar for more speed in departure.

Dimitri's gaze followed Nollen until a female voice spoke to him from behind him.

"Are you going to let him cheat you?"

Dimitri snarled in anger at sight of a ugly old woman. "Sveta, you old hag! I confronted him like you said only to be thrown out!"

"Ya, all your bewitching ways are useless," added a companion.

She ignored the complaints to fix dark eyes on Dimitri. Her voice throaty and commanding. "I said, are you going to let him cheat you?"

"We have no mounts."

"Oh?" She motioned to three ponies across the street now tied to a post. The backs of the owners disappeared into the building. "You must hurry to enact revenge on the Eldarian."

Nollen didn't slow Alydar until they reached a bend in the road a mile from town. He saw no signs of pursuit. "I think we lost them."

"Who?"

"Men who aren't friendly toward Eldarians. They blame two countrymen for an incident involving a creature from the Black

Mountains called Chika. It apparently destroyed a man's home because of them."

"Sir Gunnar and Lord Sylvan?"

"I don't know. And I'm not going back to find out." Despite the unsettling events, Nollen fought a yawn.

"We need to find a place for you to rest."

Nollen and Alydar just entered the forest when someone jumped down from out of the trees. Both men tumbled to the ground, where Nollen's head snapped back and hit the ground hard. Dazed, he had difficulty fighting off the assailant.

Alydar reared and loudly whinnied in protest. Another man snatched the reins to control Alydar. The mighty stallion wouldn't settle down. A second man tossed a rope around Alydar's head. The stallion grunted in anger but forced to comply. From above came an eagle's call, which prompted a responding whinny from Alydar.

Dimitri straddled Nollen and roughly tore open the pouch. "Let's see how many more diamonds you have!"

Nollen managed to knock Dimitri aside. He tried to roll over and get to his knees, but experienced dizziness. When grabbed, Nollen ignored pain and wooziness to fight back. He landed a punch to Dimitri's face. His struggle didn't last long when mounted soldiers arrived.

"Break it up! Dimitri! Back off!" Impatient, he waved at the other soldier. "Arrest them all!"

Once on his feet, Nollen swallowed back sickness to say, "They ambushed me, and tried to rob me."

"Captain Laban, *this* Eldarian cheated me!" Dimitri spat.

"No! And leave off my horse!" Nollen tried to shake free of the soldiers to reach Alydar.

Laban confronted Nollen. "Eldarians have caused a lot of trouble here lately. Why should I believe *you* over an Markitan?"

"I don't know about any trouble. I'm here on business."

"What business could an Eldarian have in Markita? And one well-armed and supplied?" Laban challenged.

"Do you speak Eldarian?"

"Aye," came the gruff reply.

Nollen rose to his full height, and shoulders squared in defiance. "I will only answer to Lord Carl or Archduke Boric," he spoke in Eldarian.

Offended by the bold rebuke, Laban struck Nollen across the face. The force split Nollen's lower lip and increased the earlier dizziness.

Alydar angrily snorted and stomped at the assault.

"Easy, Alydar," Nollen soothed. He blinked several times to recover.

"I will ask you again, what is your business in Markita?" Laban demanded in Eldarian.

Unwilling to reply, Nollen glared from under shrouded brows of pain. When Laban grabbed him by the hair, he declared in Eldarian; "I am the Royal Emissary of His Majesty King Axel! I will only answer to Lord Carl or Archduke Boric."

Thunderstruck, Laban released him. "You claim diplomatic rights?"

"I do!"

"Release his horse. Sergeant, take Dimitri and the others back to town," he ordered in Markita.

"He cheated me!" Dimitri harshly insisted.

"I'll deal with you later! Return home."

Nollen removed the rope from Alydar's head and kindly stroked the unicorn's neck. "I hope they didn't hurt you."

Alydar made a soft grunt and placed his head against Nollen's chest.

"I'll be all right," Nollen quietly replied to the gesture.

With a more contrite and respectful attitude, Laban spoke in Eldarian. "The Archduke's castle in Sproule is two days ride. Do you need something for your injuries, sir?"

"Rest and food would be nice."

"Won't be good to take you back to Peitro. There is a waystation two hours from here, can you make that?"

"Aye." Nollen took a drink form his water flask before he and Laban proceeded. He glanced skyward at hearing an eagle. He resisted the impulse to give any attention to the forest. With all the commotion, he wouldn't be surprised if Callie lurked nearby.

Once at the waystation, Laban gave orders about Nollen's care, and stabling Alydar.

"We can get a fresh start in morning, sir," Laban said.

Nollen simply nodded, as he ate the stew provided. His head spun, but uncertain if due or injury or fatigue. Whatever the cause, he needed sleep.

Chapter 9

TWO NIGHTS OF COMFORTABLE SLEEP IN BEDS, HEARTY MEALS, bathing, and shaving helped Nollen to recover from the assault. Being daily in the company of Captain Laban or people at the inns, he never had the opportunity to speak confidentially with Alydar. He talked in general terms when grooming Alydar at night or during preparation for morning departure. The unicorn/horse replied in either soft whinnies, grunts, or tossed his head in agreement. Nor could Nollen interact with Ajax and Callie. However, an occasional eagle's cry told him of Ajax's presence. He could only assume about Callie since the she-wolf never appeared.

Archduke Boric's castle stood situated on a ridgeline overlooking the heavily fortified town of Sproule. Plain in comparison to Sener, the sand-colored stone walls rose thirty feet in height by fifteen feet thick. Square turrets dominated the four corners of the castle. The interior buildings and courtyards occupied roughly two acres, less than half that of Sener. A hive of activity greeted them.

Laban spoke to a groom in both Markitan then Eldarian for Nollen's benefit. "Take good care of this one," he motioned to Alydar. "He belongs to a diplomat. A guest of Markita." He nodded to Nollen.

"Ya, Captain." The groom partially bowed to Nollen. "He … be goodly," he said in broken Eldarian.

Nollen replied with *thank you* in Markitan. He gave Alydar a friendly pat before he followed Laban to the main building.

They no sooner left, than Dimitri accosted the groom. "Give me the horse," he demanded.

"What?" said the stunned groom.

"The horse! Give it to me."

Alydar tossed his head with a loud grunt and stomped his front hooves in an act of protest.

The groom stopped Dimitri from snatching the bridle. "This horse belongs to a guest of the Archduke."

Disgruntled, Dimitri crossed the courtyard to join his companions.

"What now?" asked one.

"We wait. When he leaves, we follow," replied Dimitri.

"Then what?"

"You will use this," said a female.

They grew leery at seeing Sveta emerge from the shadow of the wall.

Dimitri tried to mask his uneasiness. "How did you get here, hag?"

An eerie glow appeared in her narrowed eyes. "The ways of a Baga are not to be questioned." She held three small packets. "Each take one."

Dimitri swallowed back fright to accept one. "What is that?"

"Bushlik venom. Carefully tear off a corner and wipe it on the arrowhead before you shoot. And hope you don't come in contact with the venom while applying it."

The men balked, wary of the packets.

"Make sure to finish the Eldarian this time. I won't give you a third chance." That said, Sveta faded back into the shadows and disappeared.

Inside, Nollen and Laban discovered more activity. Servants scurried about. Some nobles walked the corridors en route to the Great Hall.

"Halt," commanded a guard. "State your name and purpose."

"I am Captain Laban from Peitro. I'm escorting this Eldarian ambassador to the Archduke. He is here on a diplomatic mission."

The guard skeptically eyed Nollen. "Papers?" he said in bad Eldarian.

"Lord Carl and Archduke Boric can vouch for my identity."

Laban interceded when the guard appear unconvinced. "He is who he says."

Though reluctant of the explanation, he said, "No weapons allowed."

Both yielded their weapons, which for Nollen included a crossbow, quiver, and dagger. Laban handed over his sword and dagger.

Laban led Nollen through the crowd in an effort to be near the raised platform. A guard stopped their progress twenty feet shy of the destination.

A heavy-set bear of a man with full salt-and-pepper beard, Archduke Boric sat wrapped in an embroidered fur-lined coat. He patiently listened to petitions. After which, he would respond with an appropriate finding. Realizing the event, Laban quietly explained to Nollen.

"Annual day of judgement."

"Are there no local magistrates to judicate issues?"

"Ya. The more difficult ones are delayed for this day, when Boric will hear them. If he can't render a verdict, King Montre has the final say."

For an hour, they listened and observed. Nollen grew antsy. He risked a great deal when he revealed his true identity to Laban. Now at Sproule, he began to second guess his impromptu action. Private would be better than public. He looked for a way to discretely withdraw.

"If there are no further petitions, this court is dismissed," said a nobleman dressed in elaborate robes.

"Now!" Laban gave the distracted Nollen a hard nudge. So hard, in fact, that Nollen stumbled forward into the aisle leading to the platform.

The action caught the nobleman's attention. "You have a petition?"

Nollen gathered his courage, as he recognized the noblemen. "I do, Lord Carl."

Some in the crowd grew suspicious when Nollen spoke in Eldarian.

"Come forth." Carl beckoned with this hand. His brows knitted. "You look familiar. Your name?"

"Nollen of Far Point, my lord. Royal Commissary of King Axel."

Everyone recognized the name *King Axel.* This brought disgruntled murmurs from the crowd.

"Silence!" Carl shouted in Markitan. He then confronted Nollen in Eldarian. "You make a bold appearance in this court, Nollen of Far Point."

"By grave necessity, my lord. Otherwise, I would not risk anger of the Markitan people or the displeasure of the most gracious Archduke Boric."

"Carl!" Boric made a faint nod.

With a bow of acknowledgment, Carl escorted Nollen to the platform.

"My lord Archduke." Nollen deeply bowed.

"This visit … about Sir Gunnar?" asked Boric, who obviously struggled with Eldarian.

Nollen covered his initial surprise at the question. He cast a sideways glance at the crowd. Discretion came in reply. "It would be a violation of my lord King Axel's wishes if I spoke in the presence of too many ears."

Boric's agreeable expression turned harsh. "Year long time, much happen since."

"Much, which we are unaware of, I assure Your Grace."

"To chamber!" Boric hastily rose.

Carl waved for Nollen to accompany him.

As soon as the door closed, Boric accosted Nollen. "You want me believe Axel know not of wrong visit?"

At Nollen's confusion, Carl clarified. "Unauthorized. Sir Gunnar did not present himself to the Archduke—before the trouble started."

With understanding, Nollen addressed Boric. "Upon my word of honor, my lord King Axel is ignorant of any trouble. All we know is Sir Gunnar is missing, and his companion, the king's cousin, returned half out of his mind."

"How did that happen?" asked Carl.

"A reported encounter with a creature called Sirin."

"What *Sirin?*" asked Boric.

"A creature from the Black Mountains."

Boric grew hot with intense anger. "Gunnar and companion bring wrath of Chika on us. Destroy."

Momentarily dumbfounded, Nollen asked, "Who or what is Chika?"

"The supreme goddess from the Black Mountains," said Carl. "She invaded Markita centuries ago, and some still worship her."

For a moment, Nollen considered the explanation then inquired, "Could Chika and Sirin be one and the same?"

Carl shrugged. "There are many creatures in the Black Mountains that people worship or fear. Some live in caves and mines."

"Mines? With diamonds?" asked Nollen, his interest piqued.

"Ya! Curs – ed," Boric impatiently snapped.

"People of the Black Mountains," Nollen murmured in further consideration. "Palleteens?"

Boric looked quizzically at Carl, then asked several questions in Markitan. The archduke spoke so rapidly that Nollen only caught the words Chika, Sirin, and Palleteens.

Carl addressed Nollen. "These people you call *Palleteens*, do they claim their diamonds and gems have magical powers?"

"Aye."

Agitated, Boric spoke Markitan to Carl in quick, short phrases. Carl tried to calm the archduke, with little success.

Nollen boldly interjected. "My lords, if the Palleteens are the same people of the Black Mountain then Eldar might be to blame for your trouble. Yet, not in the matter you think, I assure you!"

"Explain!" Boric demanded.

"Palleteens are the sworn enemies of Eldar. They seek to enact revenge. Sadly, Markita lies between Eldar and the Black Mountains."

"Gunnar say same."

Another surprise, to which Nollen asked, "You spoke with him?"

"After Chika attacked. You not listen?"

"Forgive me, Your Grace. I'm trying to discern what happened, why, and the present location of Sir Gunnar."

Boric threw up his arms. "He left. And glad!"

"May I ask how long ago?"

Boric appeared to count on his finger. He asked something of Carl.

"A month," Carl clarified for Nollen. "Sir Gunnar should have returned to Eldar by now."

Nollen soberly shook his head. "He has not. King Axel sent me to learn his whereabouts, especially after the tragedy of his royal cousin."

"Stop Eldarian at border!" Boric declared.

"Your Grace, our treaty—"

"Worthless." Boric picked up a piece of paper to wave in Nollen's face. "Markitans die because of Eldar."

Nollen clenched his fists against inward trembling at the archduke's rightful anger. "My humblest apologies, Your Grace."

Boric loudly spouted Markitan and stormed out of the antechamber.

"Leave Markita," Carl said in warning.

"To do so without Sir Gunnar would go against my King's wishes."

"You defy one royal to please another?"

Nollen remained steadfast. "If I must."

Carl regarded Nollen. Despite visible discomfort, he acted bravely in the face of royal displeasure. In a hushed voice, Carl spoke. "Your mettle is of the same quality as Sir Gunnar." He reached into a pocket of his heavy long coat. "This belongs to him. Boric refused his gesture of goodwill to make amends."

Nollen recognized Gunnar's dagger with an embossed leather sheath. He hooked it onto his belt.

Carl seized Nollen's arm. "Find him quickly, and never return to Markita." He gave a partial nudge. "Go! I will keep Boric's hand from acting against you."

Nollen rushed from the chamber. He fought to keep his quickened steps from drawing attention of the guards, servants, or nobles. However, he did pause to retrieve his weapons. He endured an uncomfortable wait of five minutes before he proceeded to the stables. There, he found many waited for their mounts. Not wanting to risk further trouble, Nollen found Alydar. He ignored a protesting groom to mount and leave Sproule.

Once out the gates, he turned Alydar east. A quarter mile from Sproule, he looked back. Others left and turned in various directions. No sign of soldiers. He snapped the reins. "Run!"

Alydar heeded the command. For a half-hour, Nollen urged Alydar to continue at a blistering pace. The mighty unicorn-horse grunted several times, yet never slowed. Satisfied they reached a safe distance, Nollen eased Alydar from gallop, to a lope, and finally a walk.

Alydar snorted and tossed his head. "I hope there is an explanation," he chided between heavy breaths.

"Aye. We'll speak when under cover for the night."

After several miles, they entered the forest to head in an east/northeast direction. At a hollow deeply embedded in a ravine, Nollen dismounted. The orange glow of sunset peeked through the bare branches and stalwart pines.

Grateful, Nollen leaned his forehead against Alydar's cheek. "Thank you. I fear that hasty ride is something Gilen could not have managed."

"He would have done it for you."

Nollen removed his bedroll, saddlebags, and sack. "Find what you need for fodder and drink. We'll wait for Ajax and Callie to arrive."

While Alydar took advantage of the stream for water and bank scrub, Nollen spread out his bedroll and built a small fire. Startled, he jumped up when a small rabbit carcass fell in front of him.

Ajax landed on the ground. "I thought you could use some nourishment after that ride." He stretched his neck out toward the rabbit.

"Thanks." Nollen removed his dagger to prepare the rabbit for roasting. He just placed it over the fire when Callie arrived.

She panted heavily. "What made you flee the castle?"

In response to the question, Nollen described the events in Peitro, and his audience with Archduke Boric.

"No soldiers followed you," Ajax said.

"They couldn't at my speed," boasted Alydar.

"Even so, Lord Carl kept his word." Nollen tested the rabbit for cooking. "At least we know Gunnar is alive, though still somewhere unknown." He unhooked Gunnar's dagger from his belt. "I have something of his. Hopefully, your wolf senses will determine his presence." He held it out for Callie to sniff.

"There are multiple scents. One I recognize as you."

"Carl said Gunnar offered it to Boric in a gesture of good will."

"Will you recognize Gunnar for the others?" asked Ajax.

"Aye, once I pick up a fresh scent."

"Tomorrow, we continue on our original course to the Black Mountains," began Nollen. "More than likely Gunnar went that way, so it should narrow down the scent." He removed the rabbit from the spit. "Enough to share," he told Callie and Ajax.

"Shouldn't we resume night travel to avoid trouble?" asked Alydar.

Nollen paused in eating to reply. "Not in unfamiliar territory. I like to see where I'm going so I can recognize landmarks."

"We traveled at night until Peitro."

Nollen washed down the rabbit with water. "I know the route. It's one Gunnar and I took when we came to negotiate the treaty. Although I've been here before, my knowledge is limited past Sproule. When Boric took us to Miska to meet with King Montre, we rode in a carriage with blinds down."

"They didn't want you to learn the lay of the land," said Callie.

Nollen nodded. "Pathfinding is part instinct, and part memorization. I have enough experience to navigate any terrain, just not the particulars of Markita—yet." He flashed a cocky smile. "Since the Black Mountains are on the far eastern border of Markita, that is our general direction."

Chapter 10

IN THE COURTYARD OF SPROULE'S CASTLE, SVETA CAREFULLY circumvented the thinning crowd. At one point, she stumbled, and caught herself on a wall to keep from falling. Her pallor had grown pale, and she breathed heavily. Frantic, her eyes searched the courtyard until she saw it. Without thought of discovery, she hastened to the well. She quickly splashed her face with water then took a long drink. She tried to see her reflection in the water, but the dim light of torches made it difficult.

"Old woman, what are you doing?" A soldier accosted her.

"Quenching my parched thirst," she replied in a frail voice.

"Get inside. It's almost curfew." He waved to the servants' quarters.

She made a feeble nod yet hid a smile as she left the well. His comment told her what she needed to know. With each step, she felt stronger. When she reached the door to the servants' quarters, she darted into the shadows between the buildings. Certain the soldier was gone; she made her way to a rear door of the main house. Fortunately, it had yet to be locked for the night. She entered, and carefully closed it.

She made her way along the back corridor to the servants' staircase. That time of night most served supper or prepared rooms for Boric and others. She continued upstairs to the opulent hall of the guest quarters. Several soldiers stood guard. She paused, spoke under her breath, and flicked her fingers towards the soldiers. Droplets of water flew through the air followed by a sudden noise down the end of the hall. The sound drew the soldier's attention just enough for her to enter a room two doors from the stairwell. Servants performed their duties with lamps lit, and a fire roaring in the hearth. She sneered at the flames and crossed to the far side of the room. She blew out the lamp then opened a window just enough for a breeze. She sat on the sill welcoming the soothing coolness.

After supper, Boric retired to his chambers. Upon opening the door, he felt the coldness of the room, and slightly shivered. He stoked the fired in the hearth. Startled, he stepped back when a stream of water doused the flames. From the shadows, Sveta emerged into the lamplight.

"You!" Boric stammered in surprise. He glanced at the door. "How?"

"No one saw me." She approached him. "You disappoint me."

"What do you mean?"

"The Eldarian from earlier. You let him leave."

Boric sneered. "You don't expect me to arrest every ambassador and emissary Axel sends, do you?"

"I *expect* you to keep our agreement!" she angrily rebuffed.

Despite a brief glimmer of fear, Boric lashed back. "What of Montre? *If* I continue to adhere to our agreement, there could be war, and he won't like that."

"Convince Montre that Axel is a threat. It shouldn't be too difficult, especially with Chika aroused by the arrival of the Eldarians." She moved close to whisper in his ear. "What could they want so badly as to cross the border in secret? Are they advanced scouts for an invasion? What calamity can befall Markita if they reach the Black Mountains?"

With level brows of anger and concern, he stared at her. "I will leave for Miska in the morning." When he reached to pull a bell cord to summon a servant, she stopped him.

"Send word to the Archduke Council to meet you at Miska, and that it is urgent." When he again tried to ring the bell, her grip tightened. "No! Verbally, to give me time to leave!" She hid in a such a way as to remain unseen when he opened the door.

He instructed the guard, "Fetch Lord Carl."

The soldier immediately complied, which cleared the way for Sveta to dart from the room to the back stairwell. By the time she reached the bottom step, fatigue again threatened to overtake her. Instead of heading to either the main gate or postern, she staggered to the water grate. By the time she reached it, she collapsed to her knees. Her mortal facial features began to alter. She took a deep breath and submerged.

Underwater, her entire body transformed to reptile-like in form. She gracefully slipped through the bars. She didn't surface until she reached the river a quarter mile from the castle. The old hag became half-human, half-reptile. With a satisfied smile, she again submerged and headed down river.

Carl arrived in Boric's apartment wearing a dressing gown. At Boric's disapproving scowl, he said, "Forgive me, Your Grace, I was about to retire when told you required my immediate presence."

"We leave for Miska in the morning."

Surprised, Carl asked, "Why? Has something happened?"

Boric accosted Carl. "You can ask that after *you* allowed the Eldarian to leave?"

Although his surprise turned to concern, Carl kept his voice an even tone. "I did not believe Master Nollen came to cause trouble."

"Oh? What about Chika's reprisal to Sir Gunnar's scouting of Markita?"

Carl curiously regarded Boric at the word *scouting.* "Your Grace believes there is a more nefarious reason for their arrival?"

"What else could it be, but scouting for a possible invasion? They neglect the common courtesy to inform us of their presence."

"Your Grace, that would hardly seem wise considering the lengths they went to negotiate a trade treaty—"

"A ruse! We leave in the morning." Boric waved in dismissal.

Perplexed and disturbed, Carl returned to his chamber. Whereas, Gunnar's presence did not follow protocol, he could hardly believe it bore ill. Despite Nollen's shrewdness for trade, he seemed an engaging young man of integrity. All the same, Boric commanded, and he obeyed.

Carl unlocked a secret compartment in his desk to withdraw a book. The expensive leather cover was embossed with a lion and eagle interwoven. He opened to the first page, with the inscription:

"*To His Most Serene Majesty Montre,
and Regal Archdukes of Markita,*

*The writings of Gott of Eldar is presented this day.
May these words help enlighten your minds
and strengthen Your hearts."*

From His Most Royal Majesty, King Axel of Eldar.

The date commemorated the signing of the treaty. Carl gently turned to a place marked by the length of red silk ribbon. He read a few pages, then closed the book. He chewed on his lower lip in regard of the cover. He whispered as if talking to the book. "I believe, yet am confused by recent events. I pray for some clarity."

He replaced the book, locked the compartment, and retired.

Chapter 11

FOR TWO DAYS, NOLLEN HELD A STEADY EASTERLY COURSE. They skirted any signs of civilization. On the afternoon of the third day, he again dismounted to inspect the ground.

"What do you keep looking for?" asked Alydar.

"Plants or tracks." Nollen squatted to examine a low-growing plant. He used his dagger to cut it then stood. "It helps to learn what plants are edible, and for medicinal use." He sniffed the weed before taking a tentative taste. He scowled and spit it out. "Tastes like bitterwood. Not good for anything." He tossed it aside.

His eyes scanned the ground, as he continued to walk. He occasionally used his foot to clear debris for a better view. Alydar followed then stopped when Nollen again knelt.

With cautious curiosity, Nollen lightly brushed the ground by hand then traced an impression. Finally, he placed a hand inside it with fingers spread to determine the size. The impression dwarfed his hand. He made a low whistle. "Whatever this beast is, it's massive. The print is larger than a mountain lion, but similar in appearance to a bear."

Alydar lowered his head to sniff the print. "Nothing I recognize." He raised his head to shout, "Callie!" Shortly, the she-wolf arrived. "Do you know this scent?" He lowered his head to indicate the paw print.

Callie took her time to sniff, and lowly growled. "I sense a predator."

"That's not surprising considering the print size," said Nollen. "I think the track is about a week old."

71

Callie sniffed again. "Aye."

They heard Ajax's call a moment before the eagle landed on a branch above them. "I see movement in the trees behind and parallel to us."

Nollen vaulted into the saddle. "Callie, take the point. Ajax, fly!"

The dense trees prohibited Alydar's use of any serious speed. Nollen kept a sharp eye out for signs of trouble while Alydar weaved through the forest. He drew Alydar to a stop when they reached a vast meadow with a creek running through it. The meadow foliage went seasonally dormant. A few dead trees stood scattered about with several fallen logs near the creek.

"We'll be in the open for about two miles," said Nollen.

"Predators prefer enclosed areas for ease of the kill," Alydar said.

"Thanks for that encouragement."

At a yip, Nollen spied Callie near the creek. She yipped again and bounded across the creek. There also came an eagle's call.

"The meadow is clear," Alydar said.

"Then let's go."

This time, Alydar cantered. One hundred yards into the meadow, they heard an eagle's warning screech. Nollen pitched forward when an arrow pierced his left side. He caught himself on Alydar's neck to stay in the saddle.

"Nollen?" asked Alydar with concern. When another arrow whizzed past his head, Alydar bolted forward into a fast gallop. "Hold on!"

Nollen did his best to remain seated and ignore the searing pain in his side. It took all his strength to endure Alydar's speed. Wounded, he rocked in the saddle and finally leaned on Alydar's neck to hold on

Alydar bound into the creek, and nearly toppled Nollen. He cried out in pain when he righted himself. He tried to reach the arrow but forced to seize Alydar's mane to stay upright. The intense searing pain threatened to overtake him. When Alydar leapt over a log, Nollen fell off. Impact with the ground snapped the shaft while rolling, ripped out the arrowhead. He came to a stop face down, and unconscious.

Three men on horseback rode toward them. Two were armed with longbows. Alydar placed himself between Nollen and the approaching threat. He loudly whinnied and reared up to thrust out his legs to keep them from Nollen.

A man raised his bow at Alydar. With outstretched talons, Ajax attacked the man's face. In pain, he screamed and fell from his horse.

Callie leapt at the second armed man and dragged him from the horse. They briefly separated when they hit the ground. Despite bite wounds to his neck and shoulder, he fought her off and whipped out his dagger. Callie snapped at him, yet mindful of the weapon.

Dimitri ignored the plight of his companions to continue toward Nollen. He jerked the reins of his horse to avoid Alydar's kick. His horse bucked in protest. His attempt to dismount ended with him on the ground.

Once on his feet, Dimitri drew his sword. Alydar moved to block him. Dimitri lunged. Alydar barely avoided the blade. He angrily whinnied and reared, which forced Dimitri to retreat. When Alydar's hooves touched the ground, Dimitri advanced. Again, Alydar moved to block him.

"I'll kill you too!" Dimitri shouted. Being engaged with Alydar, he didn't hear the gallop of an approaching horse.

"Leave off!"

Dimitri turned at the shout. He had no time to defend against the sword slash that impacted his chest. The force sent him off his feet and backwards to the ground. He lay in agony, unable to move due to the large deep gash. Through gritted teeth of dying pain, he glared up at the mounted man dressed in black tunic over silver chain mail. A black cowl covered his face from the nose down.

"Don't get up."

Dimitri took several deep breaths before he closed his eyes.

The man moved his horse toward Nollen. Alydar took a defensive position. The mighty stallion pawed the ground, made angry grunts, and tossed his head.

"Easy, friend Alydar." He lowered the cowl from his face. Now, age forty-eight, more gray invaded his dark hair, though his features showed little aging over the past three years. He had a week's growth of salt and pepper whiskers.

Alydar approached. "Sir Gunnar," he whispered in greeting.

He stroked Alydar's cheek. "Noble friend. Let's tend to him." Gunnar dismounted to kneel beside Nollen.

Callie arrived. Her hackles up and ears back.

"It's Sir Gunnar," Alydar told her.

She sniffed in Gunnar's direction then assumed a contrite posture. "My lord," she greeted. Concerned, she nudged Nollen's wounded side. "Something smells wrong about his wound."

Gunnar examined Nollen. "Jagged. Probably caused by being dislodged in the fall." Further investigation. "His belt and pouch kept it from going deeper." He carefully turned Nollen over. A low groan told them Nollen was alive.

Callie moved about the area to sniff the ground. She discovered the arrowhead. She back away, sneezed, and shook her head. She returned to report. "The same scent is powerful on the arrowhead."

Alydar lowered his head to take a whiff of Nollen's wound. "Poison?"

"We'll get him to safety before I treat it." Gunnar lifted Nollen onto Alydar. He took the reins to mount his horse and left the meadow.

They made slow progress, as Gunnar kept watch of Nollen so he wouldn't slip off Alydar. Thirty minutes later, they stopped in a shallow cave. Gunnar made Nollen comfortable on his bedroll before he built a fire. He remained unconscious the whole time. Callie lay near Nollen's head to lick his face in an attempt to rouse him.

"What is your name, she-wolf?" Gunnar rummaged through his saddlebag and pulled out several items.

"I am Callie of the Halvor Wolves."

"Ajax, son of Artair," he said when Gunnar glanced at him.

"Well, friends, welcome to Markita. Though I am curious why you are here, I will tend Nollen first. Explanation can come later."

"If it is poison, how will you tend him?" asked Callie.

"Othniel gave a Ganel physician instruction for a special poultice should we encounter any evil creatures." He shrugged. "I'm not sure if it will work on poison, but it's all I have. Along with a tea blend to take internally."

Alydar, Callie, and Ajax watched Gunnar prepare then administer the poultice. He finished by wrapping the wound. Still, Nollen did not wake.

Disturbed by the lack of response, Gunnar sat back on his heels. "It must be poison to keep him unconscious this long. The wound itself should not be life-threatening."

"If I still had my magic," said Alydar with regret.

Gunnar stood and patted Alydar's cheek. "Prayer works when everything else fails."

"We shall keep watch while you seek the Almighty. Ajax, fly. Callie, the perimeter. Joslin and I at the stream." Alydar spoke in soft grunts and whinnies to Gunnar's horse. There came an affirmative reply, as told by the tossing of the head.

"Wish Joslin would listen to me like that. She's usually contrary," Gunnar comment.

Joslin snorted, and grunted.

Alydar lowly replied to Joslin then chuckled to Gunnar. "She says it's fun to frustrate you." He listened to Joslin again. "For this journey, she will serve you as faithfully as when you came to Eldar." Alydar and Joslin disappeared into the darkness.

For the remainder of the night, Gunnar went between tending Nollen's wound, and deep prayer for his recovery. It didn't take much to imagine the reason for Nollen's presence in Markita. He often traveled for trade. However, Nollen was nowhere near a main road or highway. Of course, he could ask Alydar, but he needed to keep his mind on the task at hand—Nollen's recovery. Not until nightfall did Nollen stir. He groaned in pain when he moved.

"Alydar!" Gunnar called. He gripped Nollen's shoulder to encourage him to wake up. "Nollen, lad, can you hear me?"

Nollen's brows furrowed, and his eyes blinked open. He appeared confused by the darkness, firelight, and—"Gunnar?"

"Aye, lad."

Nollen looked around then noticed Alydar's arrival. "Where am I?"

"A cave. Safe from those men, who were intent on killing you."

"The same ones who attacked us outside Peitro," added Alydar.

"Peitro? You went there?" Gunnar asked, perturbed.

Nollen blinked before he replied. "I took our former route. I learned you caused a lot trouble. So much so, that Dimitri hates all Eldarians. This wasn't our first encounter." He squirmed to get comfortable.

Gunnar retrieved a cup from near the fire. "Tea with herbs to help you heal." He lifted Nollen's head to help him drink. Nollen coughed several times while drinking the tea. When finished, Gunnar gently laid Nollen's head down. "Trouble wasn't intentional, I assure you."

"Sylvan said you were captured," Nollen spoke in a weary voice.

Gunnar paused in placing the cup aside. "Sylvan's alive?"

"If you can call it that," droned Nollen. "He reached Sener only to lose his mind. Something about a creature called Sirin."

Gunnar's features hardened. The firelight reflected in narrowed eyes. "A devilish beast. I thought we eluded it. We stopped at Peitro because Sylvan needed to rest. Unfortunately, the attack told us it followed us." When he noticed Nollen shiver, he tossed a log on the fire.

Nollen swallowed back discomfort to ask, "What exactly happened?"

Gunnar shrugged. "Chaos. When it attacked, everyone panicked. We became separated during the confusion. Next thing I knew ... Sirin had him. I tried to help but ..." he went silent with discomposure.

Sympathetic, Nollen listened. "He said he witnessed your capture."

Again, Gunnar balked. "I don't know what he *saw*, but when Sirin disappeared with Sylvan, I assumed the worst. He must have escaped somehow." With urgency, he asked, "Did he say anything else?"

"No. He babbled, which made it difficult to discern past you and Sirin. He said enough for Axel dispatched me to find you."

Gunnar's anger returned. He poked the fire. "He shouldn't have."

"His cousin lost his mind. He wasn't about to lose you too." Nollen's voice trailed off into a low moan

Gunnar's irritation softened at hearing Nollen's discomfort. "I supposed it's fitting he sent you." When Nollen squirmed to get comfortable, Gunnar pulled up the covers. "Enough talk. Rest."

After Nollen closed his eyes, Alydar grabbed Gunnar's shoulder to pull him up. The unicorn-horse led Gunnar a few yards away to speak privately. "Why do you shun Axel's concern for your welfare?"

"Not shun. More worried." Gunnar glanced back at Nollen then spoke with urgency. "You know what we face in the Black Mountains. Sirin is just the beginning." He cast another look to Nollen. "Does he know who and why?"

"No. Othniel advised Axel not to tell him."

"I'm not sure if that is better or worse for him," said Gunnar, thoughtful.

"Since traveling together, I've learned Nollen of Far Point is a brave and resourceful human. Do not underestimate him."

"Oh, I am well aware of his mettle. Like Axel, I've developed a soft spot for him." He wryly grinned. "I'm old enough to be his father."

"Then treat him like a son willing to help."

Gunnar patted Alydar and returned to the fire to keep watch.

Chapter 12

LEON SAT ALONE AT A CORNER TABLE OF THE GILROY INN. The fading colors of outside light showed the coming of twilight. He paid no attention to time or anything. His slumped posture and disheveled appearance showed he drank too much.

Concerned, Sharla approached. "Is there something I can help you with, my lord?"

Blood-shot eyes battled to focus. "Go away," he slurred.

"My lord, it's getting dark. You should go home."

"Home, bah! Empty house."

Two men entered. Their demeanor and clothes suggested foreigners. Both were dark headed with beards. The heavy embroidered outer coat closed over the inner vest by way of a sash. Each wore a round hat with a flat top.

Sharla greeted them. "Welcome."

"Food and drink," one brusquely said in heavily accented Eldarian.

"Take a seat." She motioned to a table. While they followed her instruction, she signaled Abe. The teen quickly filled tankards. Although, she eyed the strangers, she returned to Leon. "Let me bring you food to help with the ale."

Leon made a curt wave. "You don't know what it's like to be discharged! Tossed aside for worthless creatures."

He spoke too loudly for her liking. "Please, my lord, less ale and more food."

He didn't take kindly to the rebuke and banged the empty tankard on the table. "Ale! And keep it coming." When she hesitated to leave, he awkwardly tried to shove her away. He nearly fell off the chair. "Away, woman! Tend to others and leave me alone." He then thought better of it. "Bring the ale!"

Bart arrived from the stables to join Sharla and Abe at the bar. She complained to her sons, "Bad time for your father to visit Laren."

"Because of the foreigners?" Abe discreetly asked.

"No. Last time Lord Leon was this drunk, his wife died. Jonas spent days helping to sober him." Her glance of concern shifted from Leon to the strangers. "Bart, fetch your father. I will serve the strangers." She went to the kitchen.

Leon cast several curious glances at the strangers. He tried to drink, only forgot the tankard was empty. He slammed it down. Again, he looked at the strangers. The chair tipped over when he rose. He shuffled over to their table.

"You are not from here. Funny clothes."

They were reluctant to engage, but that didn't stop the inebriated Leon. He slapped his hand on the table in a clumsy attempt to lean down.

"Take my advice, leave Eldar. This place isn't worth visiting."

Sharla hurried to arrive. She put plates of food in front of the strangers. "Please, excuse him. He's not himself today. Come away, my lord." She tried to urge him from the table.

He jerked away. "Leave off. Silly women don't know their place," he chided to the strangers.

"I *know* that this is *my* inn!" Sharla stoutly rebuffed. "And you are drunk. Abe! Escort Lord Leon to the door."

Unseen by her, the foreigners perked up when she spoke Leon's name. They exchanged deliberate glances.

Leon tried to swat the teenager away, only Abe wouldn't be put off. He made certain Leon left.

"I'm sorry you experienced such ill-mannered conduct," Sharla apologized. They simply nodded and began to eat. She returned to the bar where Abe joined her. Disconcerted, she rubbed her arms. "There is something disturbing about them."

"Aside from their clothes?" Abe dryly commented.

She tightened her arms about herself. "I get a cold sense in the pit of my stomach."

To this, Abe grew serious. He cast a circumspect look to the strangers. "You want me to ask them to leave?"

She turned her back to the men. "Go help Bart find your father."

"More!" one of the strangers shouted. He lifted an empty plate.

Sharla waved an acknowledgement and went to the kitchen. It only took a few moments to bring two more plates of stew. However, upon return, she discovered them gone! A few unknown coins were left at the table. She set the plates down to examine the money.

"Sharla?" Jonas arrived with Bart and Abe.

"Have you seen these before?" She held out the coins to Jonas.

He took one to inspect it. He held it up toward the overhead lamp. "No. Who gave them to you?"

"Foreigners. They wanted more food, but while I fetched it, they left."

Jonas frowned in regard of the coins. "I need to speak to the sheriff."

"Why?" asked Sharla, anxious.

"Royal orders to be wary of foreign spies in The Doane. Laren just told me when Bart came to fetch me."

"Merciful heaven! You think they—?" she couldn't finish due to fear.

"Boys, stay with your mother," Jonas instructed the twins.

Leon staggered down the street. Now, past twilight, he encountered few people. Most made their way indoors for the night. He stumbled and fell on his rump into a building. He tried to stand but failed the first attempt. For the second attempt, he felt hands lift him to his feet. He came face-to-face with the strangers.

"Thanks." He tried to move away, only the man wouldn't let go. Again, he focused on them. "Who are you?"

"Friends to help you."

"Help! Ah!" Leon forcefully jerked away. "I have no friends here."

"Sirin is your friend."

To this, Leon straightened. His eyes narrowed to search their faces. He balked when one lifted a fist, then opened it to reveal a diamond. Leon began to smile with delight at sight of it then snarled.

"You took time getting here," he scolded.

"We camped outside."

Leon shook his head. "The gate is closed." He leaned close to them; his breath reeked. "I know a secret way out." He made a wimpy wave to follow him.

They kept a keen eye out while Leon zigzagged down streets and alleys. Several times he stopped to get his bearings. Finally, they reached a deserted, rundown part of the town wall. When Leon couldn't open the old wood and wrought iron door, the men took their turn. With effort, the door gave way. The hinges creaked, which caused a stop in progress. When no one appeared to hear, they proceeded to open it wide enough for passage.

"It's dark," chided one.

"Of course, it's a tunnel," snorted Leon.

One quietly spoke a few unknown words, which sent the second scurrying from the alley. A few moments later, he returned with a lantern.

Leon made an exaggerated expression. "Looks like the tailor's lamp."

"Go!" A man shoved Leon to the door.

The other attempted to shut the door. When it wouldn't budge, he turned to follow the others.

In the foyer of his house, Sheriff Ezer met with Jonas. Ezer held the coins. His lips pursed in consideration. "Any mention of diamonds?"

"No. Sharla found the coins on the table after they left."

"The gates are closed, so they're probably still here. Either at the boarding house or chapel. Devin is known to house an unfortunate traveler, who can't afford lodging."

"Could they be the spies?"

Ezer shrugged. "Unknown. However, a simple interview shouldn't be met with resistance—*if* they are innocent." He closed his fist on the coins. "I'll need to keep these as evidence for the interview."

"Of course. If they are spies, I wouldn't take money."

Ezer flashed a smile. "Good night, Jonas. And thank you." He escorted Jonas to the door. Certain Jonas left, he strapped on his sword. "Celena! I'm going out," he called to his wife. He didn't wait for a reply.

Being very familiar with Gilroy, Ezer made his way to the boarding house. Despite being the dinner hour, he knocked on the door. When the answer was slow in coming, he pounded harder. "Fabian! Open up, it's Sheriff Ezer."

He heard the sound of running feet and hasty words from inside. Soon, an older man of sixty appeared in the threshold.

"Sheriff."

"Fabian. I'm looking for two strangers. Foreigners. Colorfully dressed. Do you have any such boarders this evening?"

"No, Sheriff. There are no foreigners here."

"Would you mind if I ask your guests if they have seen these individuals?"

"Come, and welcome." Fabian escorted Ezer to the dining room. Four men gathered at the table to eat.

"Lois." Ezer gave a nod to the wife. He studied the men, their clothes and features. "Sorry to interrupt, but I am Sheriff Ezer. I assume you are all Eldarian."

"Aye. We're from the Freelands," answered one.

"Are you here on business or pleasure?"

"Business. We leave in the morning."

Ezer nodded. "I must ask if you know of, or recently encountered, any foreigners?"

"Does this question relate to the royal orders?" asked a second man.

"It does."

"We've kept our eyes out since leaving the Freelands but haven't run across any."

"Very well. Enjoy your meal. Lois." Ezer left the boarding house.

At the chapel, he inquired of Devin, only to receive the same negative answer. The only ones reporting an encounter were at the inn. Despite Jonas' past, he has shown himself once again to be a loyal Eldarian and citizen of Gilroy. The coins proved his story, while Sharla would not lie.

Ezer heard running feet on cobblestone, and shouting. He ran toward the commotion. He discovered four soldiers and the tailor on the derelict side of town near a partially opened door.

"Sergeant, what's going on?"

"Ah, good Sheriff," said Rogan, the tailor. "When the guards made rounds, I reported the theft of my exterior lantern."

"We found several broken pieces and followed the trail here to discover this open door," reported the sergeant.

Ezer took a torch from a guard to inspect the opening.

"Where does it lead?" asked Rogan.

Ezer shook his head. "I don't know. You, report this to Captain Castor," he told the guard he took the torch from. "Sergeant, you and others determine where this leads. I suspect some foreigners may have used this to slip out of Gilroy." He gave the torch to the sergeant. "Rogan, return home."

Chapter 13

A SHORT DISTANCE FROM GILROY, LEON JOINED THE MEN AT A makeshift camp. Two horses stood saddled and ready. A lean-to had been built for shelter.

Leon folded his arms in an attempt to get warm. "If I knew we were going camping, I would have worn my cloak," he complained.

"Sit. We'll make a fire," one said; his accent suddenly gone.

"Not too big. Don't want to attract unwanted attention," said the other in Eldarian, and without a foreign accent.

Leon nearly fell when he tried to sit.

The first one leaned to his companion. "We need to sober him up."

Leon heard whispering. "What are you saying?"

"Nothing important." He encouraged a small fire.

Leon scowled. "Which one of you is Cordel and which is Kade?"

The first became angry. "It's not wise to use names."

"If you won't tell me, I'll leave." Leon struggled to stand. His effort to leave became easily thwarted when pushed back. He fell into the lean-to.

"You're not going anywhere. Not until you tell us about Sener."

"I'm a lord, your superior. Both in rank, and this mission!" Leon coughed and hiccupped.

"Won't do good to anger him." He poked his companion. "Come warm yourself." He helped Leon to the fire. "I'm Kade. He is Cordel." The glow of fire showed his clothes contained red and blue embroidery, while Cordel's clothes gold with green threading.

"You look so much alike it's hard to tell you apart," chided Leon.

"That's the idea. Dress and act like Palleteens," said Kade.

Leon swallowed back a sickening burp. "Any food?"

Cordel snickered. From a saddlebag, he brought out a loaf of bread. He sent a private wink to Kade. "It's all we got."

Leon couldn't bite the bread, so he tore off a piece to eat.

"You should have accepted the offer of food at the inn," Kade said. He and Cordel chuckled.

"Don't act so smug. Your actions have been noticed by the King. He issued an order for your arrest," Leon rebuffed.

"So?" Cordel heaved a careless shrug. "The plan is to place blame on the Palleteens."

"Sirin won't be pleased by your ineptness." Leon spit out the bread. "You have better than this. Get it!"

Cordel snatched the bread and returned to his horse. This time, he gave Leon a fresher loaf.

"What do you know of man named Nollen?" Kade asked.

"You mean Nollen of Far Point?" Leon asked with a mouthful.

"We only know *Nollen*. He thwarted our bait and switch in Edison."

Leon huffed an ironic laugh. "That would be him. He's the Royal Commissary responsible for all trade in Eldar."

"Where can we find him? We want to get the diamonds back."

Leon shook his head. "Water." He greedily drank from the flask Kade handed him. Once done, he replied. "No chance. He's in Sener for the winter."

"Are you sure?"

"I saw him last week. Before Axel dismissed me," he groused.

"Dismissed? Why? How?" demanded Cordel

"Doesn't matter. It won't affect the plan."

"What do you mean? You were our man inside the castle."

"I will fulfill my part."

"Sirin won't like that," chided Kade.

Leon confronted Kade. "Sirin isn't here! And won't be until our plan is complete."

Suddenly, they heard distant voices then spied torch light.

Cordel bolted up ready to draw his sword. "Someone's coming!"

Leon rose to stop Cordel. "No! It may be a night patrol." When the sounds grew closer, he urged, "Hit me! And flee. I'll say you kidnapped me." He glanced toward the growing torchlight, thus unaware of the blow that knocked him to the ground semiconscious.

Cordel and Kade rode off in the opposite direction.

Dazed, Leon swayed when he pushed up to his knees. Hearing voices more clearly, he called out. "Help! Help."

Three soldiers arrived. The sergeant knelt. Dim light of the fire and torch helped him to recognized Leon. "My Lord Leon. What happened?"

"Two men … kidnapped me." He sat back on his rump.

"Why?"

Leon shrugged. "Ransom. What else?"

"Do you know who they were?"

"Foreigners. I couldn't completely understand them. Wait … I think I heard the word *Palleteen*. Aye, Palleteen. It's a bit confusing." He feinted injury.

"Sergeant! Horse tracks lead this way." A soldier pointed in the direction Kade and Cordel rode.

Annoyed, the sergeant said, "We won't catch them on foot. We'll take Lord Leon back to town, and report to Sheriff Ezer and Captain Castor."

Ezer arrived at the inn with Captain Castor, a lean, lanky man of forty. With the inn closed for the night, Ezer pounded on the door. "Jonas! Sharla."

At a delay in response, Castor added his called. "Jonas of Gilroy. This Captain Castor. Open the door."

The second shout brought the sounds of stirring from inside. A bolt was drawn, and the door partially opened. Jonas carried a lamp. "Ezer. Captain. What brings you here at this hour?"

"We have some more questions about the foreigners," replied Ezer.

"I told you what I know."

"However, you weren't here to see them. Sharla was. We want to speak with her." Castor pushed the door open to enter. Jonas stepped aside.

Abe, Bart, Sharla stood at the bottom of the stairs. All wary.

"Sharla." Ezer touched his forehead in greeting.

"Mistress, we need to ask you some questions about the foreigners," Castor began. "Was Lord Leon here at the same time?"

"Aye."

"Did anything happen?"

Sharla tried to be discrete in her reply. "Lord Leon was not himself."

"You mean drunk?"

At her anxiety to Castor's questioning, Ezer reassured her. "Everyone knows of his propensity for drinking."

With that, Sharla nodded. "Aye. Drunk, loud, and obnoxious."

"What about the foreigners?" asked Castor.

"Not drunk, if that is your question."

"Could you recognize their accent? Bertrandian? Gorland? Palleteen?"

Sharla shook her head, as she considered the answer. "Not really."

"They didn't speak much, so hard to tell their origin," said Abe.

"Where you here too?" Ezer asked the teenager.

"Aye, until Mama sent me to fetch Papa because of Lord Leon."

"I have helped sober him on a number of occasions," Jonas clarified.

"Did Leon interact with the foreigners at any time?" asked Ezer.

"Aye," began Sharla. "I went to the kitchen to get them dinner. When I returned, Lord Leon was at their table."

"Did they say anything to him?"

She shook her head. "Not that I heard. He just leaned on the table."

"Lord Leon became verbally abusive toward Mama, that's when she had me escort him out," said Abe.

"How soon after that did the foreigners leave?" asked Ezer.

"A few moments. They asked for more food. I went to fetch it, but they were gone when I came back," Sharla replied.

"Leaving these on the table." Ezer produced the coins. She nodded.

"Ezer, what is this about?" Jonas inquired in a firm tone.

Hesitant, Ezer sent Castor a conferring glance. The captain nodded, so Ezer replied. "The foreigners attempted to kidnap Lord Leon."

"Oh, how horrible!" Sharla said in distress.

"We are gathering facts about what happened," said Castor.

Sharla appeared on the verge of tears. "I don't know any more than what I've told you."

Jonas placed a comforting arm about her shoulders.

Ezer stopped Castor from speaking further. "I believe we have all the answers we need. Goodnight, Sharla. Jonas. Boys." He nudged Castor from the inn.

Once outside, Castor accosted Ezer. "I had more questions."

Ezer drew Castor from the inn. "I don't believe they can provide the answers. That door is in a most obscure place on the other side of town. By its appearance, it hadn't been used in a very long time."

"This needs to be reported."

"Aye. We leave for Sener first thing in the morning."

Chapter 14

HE RODE THROUGH SENER ON A BAY HORSE. BEING THE HEIGHT of mid-morning, traffic gnarled certain streets. Impatience marked his clean-shaven countenance at the impediments slowing his progress. Finally, he reached the castle. He drew rein to speak to the guard.

"Can you tell me where I might Nollen of Far Point, Royal Commissary?"

"He should be in his office."

"How do I get there?"

The soldier pointed. "There's a smaller door to the left, near the far wall. Ring the bell, and someone will help you."

"Much obliged." He dismounted to pull the bell rope. He waited only a few moments before a servant answered.

"May I help you?"

"I'm here to see Nollen of Far Point, Royal Commissary."

"Do you have an appointment?"

"No, I'm afraid I don't. But," he quickly added to the servant's frown. "Wyck recommended I speak with him, since I'm here on business that might interest the Commissary."

"Oh, well, in that case, come in." The servant led him through a small foyer and up two flights of stairs. They entered a spacious apartment bustling with activity. "Who shall I say is waiting?"

"Percy ... a merchant from the Freelands." He tried to mask any nervousness in reply. As he waited, his eyes surveyed the room. Men went about their business with much discussion. He overheard words that suggested produce, supplies, and other necessities. He ignored them, more interested in the surroundings.

The servant returned with another man dressed in finer clothes. He knew immediately this was not Nollen.

"Master Percy, I'm Sir Hastins, the Commissary's assistant. How may I help you?"

"It's a rather delicate matter I hoped to discuss with the Commissary. And not in front of too many ears." He flashed an awkward smile.

Hastins offered a knowing nod. "I do understand. However, the Commissary isn't here at present. I'm certain I can help you."

He took a step closer to speak privately. "I heard the Commissary recently acquired the rarest kind of gem. I trade in precious stones."

Hastins' brows leveled at the disclosure. "Indeed, this is something to discuss with the Commissary. Will you be in Sener for long, Master Percy?"

"Alas, no. I leave first thing in the morning."

Hastins forced a toothy grin. "If you can delay your departure until the afternoon, I'm sure the Commissary will be most interested to speak with you."

The servant appeared to make an objection, to which Hastins pushed past him to escort Percy to the door. "I will give him your name, so he will expect you first thing," Hastins continued in a pleasant manner. He began to close the door when the servant voiced his protest.

"But he's not in Sener—"

Percy managed to overhear yet pretended ignorance. He casually walked away. Once around the corner, he hastened down the stairs. Despite the urgency, he kept the horse at a walk until away from the castle. This time he verbally expressed his frustration with traffic.

In the King's study, Axel's brows leveled, and eyes narrowed in consideration of Ezer and Castor. Ronan, Mather, and Othniel were also present to hear the report from Gilroy.

"So, you doubt Lord Leon's version of events?" Axel said to Ezer in more a statement than question.

"It's rather convenient, Sire."

"I assume you placed him under constant surveillance," Mather said to Castor.

"Aye, General."

"If the kidnapping took place as Lord Leon claims, why take him through an abandoned door on a derelict side of town? Considering the location of his home, and the inn, they had to travel to the other side of Gilroy without being seen," said Ezer.

Axel's gaze again shifted between the sheriff and captain until finally coming to rest on Ezer. "You believe Jonas and Sharla."

"Sire, Sharla is not one to lie. As for Jonas," Ezer grew discrete. "He has been a model citizen since returning. Much like before."

Axel briefly lowered his head with a soft smile then looked up to speak. "Jonas learned much that day."

"Sire, what shall we do about Lord Leon?" asked Castor.

"Continue surveillance. Do not let him leave Gilroy without being followed."

"I already included that in my orders, Sire."

Axel gave an approving nod. "Well done, Captain. Return to Gilroy and keep me apprised of the situation."

They left just as Sir Hastins arrived. He waited to receive the King's attention. "Sire, a man came to the commodities office and requested to speak with the Commissary about ... diamonds."

Axel's posture immediately stiffened at the mention of *diamonds.* "Who?"

"He claimed his name is Percy, a trader in precious gems from the Freelands. However, that is not true. Only two men from the Freelands deal in gems, and both the Commissary and I are personally acquainted with them. Nor did he sound like a Freelander. Actually, more like a Halvor mountain dialect."

"Where is he now?"

"He left." At Axel displeasure, he hastily added, "I told him to return in the morning to speak with the Commissary."

"Won't do any good since Nollen isn't here."

"He doesn't know that, Sire. I made certain he believed the absence is temporary."

Axel scowled in displeasure. "It would have been better to have kept him in the office under some pretense."

"Sire, if he wants the diamond, there is a good likelihood he will return," Hastins said, though in a less than confident tone.

"Do you really believe that? You just said it's not possible for him to be a gem trader from the Freelands. That means this was more likely a ruse to get at Nollen," refuted Axel.

"Sire, I can order men to the Commissary office at dawn, on the chance he returns as Sir Hastins suggests," said Mather.

Axel nodded then took several deep breaths to regain his temper. "Thank you for informing me, Sir Hastins." He waved in dismissal.

Othniel spoke after Hastins departed. "Joined with the report from Gilroy, this goes beyond coincidence."

"Aye." Axel tugged on his beard, eyes shrouded, as he stared at the floor deep in thought.

"If this *Percy* returns, he will be apprehended," Mather stoutly said.

Once away from Wyckton, he kicked the pony into a gallop. A mile later, he veered off the road into the woods. He followed the smell of cooking meat until he came to a makeshift camp where Cordel waited. He still wore Palleteen clothes. Over the fire, hung a fowl to roast.

Cordel prepared to draw his weapon then relaxed. "Well?"

"He's not in Sener!" Kade swore.

"What? Are you sure?"

"Aye." Kade tested the fowl. He carefully lifted the spit off the fire to cut off a leg to eat.

"Where is he?" Cordel demanded.

Kade shrugged. "Hey!" he exclaimed when Cordel grabbed the leg from him.

"We need to know where he is to get the diamonds back."

"I know!" Kade bolted up to retrieve the leg, then sat to continue eating. "His *assistant* told me to return in the morning."

"That's not a good idea."

"What choice do we have?"

"You could sneak into the office tonight and search for them." When, Kade paused in eating to consider the suggestion, Cordel continued. "There is the old sewer. That way you can avoid being seen again."

"They would be expecting me to return. Why don't *you* go instead?"

"I'm still in disguise."

"Exactly. A Palleteen infiltrator."

"One of us needs to remain at large to help Sirin's plan."

"So, I take the risk while you wait?"

"We both are at risk since we're dead men either way. Executed as traitors or face her without the diamonds!"

"I'd rather take my chances with the King than Sirin."

Cordel stared at Kade with deadly intent. "She gave us an alternative."

Kade stopped chewing to return the stare. Without another word, Cordel went to his saddlebag, and returned with a packet.

"Eat it if captured. If you're not back by morning . . ." Cordel stopped when Kade snatched the packet.

Kade tossed aside the leg to mount his horse. Rather than enter Sener again on horseback, he abandoned his mount on the outskirts of Wyckton. He pulled up the cowl to mingle with the late afternoon crowd. Being a cool autumn day, wearing a cloak didn't appear out of place.

He casually made his way to the bridge, then joined the stream of people crossing into Sener. He made certain to keep his head down to avoid eye-contact with anyone. He reached the city square before the watch called the evening warning. Despite the peace that spread across Eldar, fortified cities still shut the main gates at night to control traffic. Pedestrians were admitted until nine o'clock, while wagons and horses forbidden after sundown. Only mounted soldiers passed through the gates at night.

Being twilight people made their way either home or to an inn for the night. Kade continued to Sener Castle. He paused to let soldiers pass. Of course, he didn't expect to be followed, but with so much at stake, he had to be certain. This might be his last task. A cold shiver caused him to stop in the shadow of an alleyway across from the castle. The consequences of failure were unthinkable. The sound of a bell from the castle chapel interrupted his dreadful pondering.

He gathered his courage to walk past the castle's main gate. Guards walked the rampart to view the street. The western wall butted up against the rowhouses of royal servants, and officers. He turned down the adjacent street. He darted into a narrow opening between buildings. The cramped alleyway ended at a stonewall. The old sewer had been walled in when the new one finished construction two years ago. Wrought iron pikes secured the top of the wall to the building on each side.

From under his cloak, he produced a rope. He made a lasso at one end and tossed it up to the iron pipes. He tugged to secure the lasso. He climbed the wall, careful to avoid the pikes when he moved to the other side. Holding on to one pike, he gathered the rope and let it down the back side to climb down. Back on the ground, he took several moments to catch his breath and shake the pain from his hands and arms.

At the old rusted sewer grate, he discovered water filled the divot. Probably from recent rains. He took a deep breath, and submerged. He swam under water through the grate and fifty yards to the other side. He broke through the surface and gasped for air. He ignored the cold water to follow the old sewer into the castle. The water depth lessened so that when he reached the other end, the culvert was dry.

Kade raced to take cover in the shadow of the far west building. He crept to the corner near the main courtyard. He ducked back when two men emerged from the door he entered earlier. They wished each other goodnight and parted company. Kade tugged on the handle to discover the door unlocked, so he quickly entered.

Being night, the hallways were dim save for an occasional torch or lamp. At the door to the office, he saw no light under the threshold. A careful jiggle of the doorknob told him it was locked. Not a problem. With no one nearby, he knelt and used locksmith tools to jiggle free the lock. After he carefully shut the door, he stood for a moment to decide where to start a search. Such valuables would be kept in a safe or vault.

Shafts of outside light filtered through the windows. Though his eyes were adjusted to the darkness, he used his hands to feel for anything that might resembled a safe or vault. He seized upon a lever and pulled it. A panel slid open with a soft scraping to reveal a gap between the exterior wall and inside door-like panel. He cast a wary eye for signs of trouble. Nothing. He felt another knob that pulled outward. Suddenly, a swooshing sound, and metal bars fell from the ceiling to block the opening behind him. Trapped!

Kade tugged on the bars. No good! He heard running feet and shouting. His heart raced at the certainty of capture.

Mather entered the private room where Axel dined with Ronan, Cormac, and Irwin. His grim features alerted them to trouble.

"Sire. He didn't wait until morning to return for the diamonds."

"Bring him here! I would question him."

"Alas, he is dead."

Axel didn't appear pleased. "Are the guards responsible?"

"No, Sire. He didn't pass through the front gate. He was found dead in the Commissary office. He triggered the safety cage. No wounds or visible signs of struggle. Although his clothes are very wet. Sir Hastins identified him as the same man from earlier today."

"Then how did he die?" asked Ronan.

"How did he get in?" Irwin added, annoyed.

"Both are unknown," said Mather with a shrug.

Axel glanced to window but saw only darkness. "Is it raining?"

"No," replied Mather.

"General, we need answers as to how this man got into the castle!"

"Sire, I ordered men to search the perimeter for any signs of entry."

Ronan leaned forward on the table. "There must be something about him to give us a clue as his real identity and purpose."

"This was found on him." Mather placed a ring with four various size metal picks on the table. "Tools of a locksmith."

"Interview every locksmith in Sener!" Axel ordered.

Mather picked up the key ring intent to leave when Axel spoke again.

"Wait! Whether he simply wanted the diamonds or intended harm to Nollen, we must assume both. I want *you* to fetch Ida and her family from Far Point and bring them here for safety. Jarred may take some convincing but tell him I insist."

"The man is dead, so how are they in danger?" asked Cormac.

"Nollen reported two men in Edison, along with what happened in Ashton to the unfortunate widow. If this man was associated with the Palleteens, the effort may not stop here. In Nollen's absence, I will protect his family."

"Aye, Sire." Mather saluted and withdrew

Agitated, Axel stood to pace. "A desperate man to take his life to avoid discovery." He turned to face the Ganels. "My lords, retired to pray for the Almighty reveals the source of this threat, and for Nollen."

Chapter 15

DESPITE THE WOUND BEING MINOR, IT TOOK A WEEK FOR Nollen to completely recover from the poison and regain strength to ride. Callie and Ajax provided meat by hunting for small game. Gunnar did short foraging treks to gather berries, wild onions, and pine nuts, but focused more on tending Nollen. Conversation between them was kept to a minimum, or rather Gunnar evasive in providing detailed answers.

On the morning of departure from the cave, Nollen knelt at the stream and splashed cold water on his face to cool the skin from a quick shave. He uncorked a small ceramic bottle and carefully poured a few drops into his palm. He placed the bottle down beside a folded razor blade. He rubbed his hands together and patted his face. He corked the bottle and returned to where Gunnar saddled the horses.

"What's that smell?" Gunnar asked.

Nollen put the bottle and razor back in his saddlebag. "Lavender and clove oil. Helps soothe the skin after shaving."

Gunnar scratched his beard. "I might have to try it. I dislike facial hair. However, traveling incognito doesn't allow much time for shaving." He pulled out a wrapped item from his bag. "When you get back to Sener, give this to Axel."

"I'm not returning without you."

"He told you to *find* me, and you have."

"Oh, no. There is more to this than you simply being lost. Something that caused Sylvan to go mad, you to be evasive, and Axel to dispatch me. Something that deals with Palleteens and diamonds."

Annoyed, Gunnar scowled. "You don't understand what is at stake."

"No! Because neither you nor Axel trust me enough to be totally honest."

"This has nothing to do with trust."

"That's always the convenient answer. Either you trust fully me, or you don't."

"Boy, we are trying to protect you!"

"I'm not a boy. As for protection, I've been shot, poisoned, threatened, and beaten. I deserve answers. So, until you tell me everything, I'm going with you."

Alydar loudly snorted and used his muzzle to shove Gunnar. "Remember what I said."

Gunnar took a moment to regain his composure. "Very well." He put the wrapped item in the saddlebag.

"*Very well* you will tell me everything or I go with you?" Nollen challenged.

"Mount up."

After they left the cave, Gunnar headed north. And hour later, he turned east. Although they kept to the woods, Ajax flew overhead while Callie took the point. The journey continued in relative silence with only occasional comments about direction or weather. At mid-day, they paused by a steam to drink, rest, and grab a quick bite to eat.

"My food supplies are running low, what about you?" Nollen asked.

"We'll make do," replied Gunnar.

"That wasn't what I asked."

"We can't risk too much contact with the locals."

Nollen huffed an ironic chuckle. "You don't have to tell me that." He rose to approach a nearly bare bush. He examined the few remaining berries. He picked one, sniffed it, then popped it in his mouth. "A little overripe but tastes like a gooseberry." He picked a handful and returned to where they sat to eat. He gave some to Gunnar. He watched Gunnar grimace when he ate. He wryly chuckled. "I told you they were overripe."

"Between foraging and hunting, we should do fine."

"With winter coming, pickings will be slim. Just like that bush."

"You can always go back." Gunnar grinned, and slapped Nollen's shoulder. He fetched Joslin.

"You won't get rid of me that easy."

They continued on an easterly course. As twilight grew nigh, Callie returned from her scouting. She held a large hare in her mouth. She dropped it to report. "There is hollow ravine with an overhanging ledge a mile south. Good for shelter. I smell rain on the wind."

Ajax navigated the trees to land on a nearby branch. "Storm clouds are rolling in," he said, unaware of Callie's report.

"Hop on," Nollen told Ajax. The eagle gently landed on the bed roll.

They managed to reach the sheltered ravine before a cold rain, mixed with sleet, began. Horses, men, Ajax, and Callie fitted comfortably under the ledge.

"Quick! Fetch what wood you can before everything becomes too wet," Gunnar told Nollen. Both hastened to gather branches. "Let's hope it's enough to cook the hare. Prepare it while I start the fire."

The cooking and consuming of the hare were done in silence. Only the crackling of the fire and sleet/rain mix broke the quiet. Unsaddled, Alydar and Joslin grazed on scrub found beneath the shelter.

The precipitation added to coolness of night. Nollen gathered his cloak about him to lay down. He used the saddle for a pillow. His crossbow and quiver stood against the earthen wall beside him.

Gunnar assumed a similar position. He turned to face Nollen. "You might consider it lack of trust, but I tell you truly, that is not the case. Aside from the trust forged between Axel and me, there is no one I trust more than you. A trust you earned years ago."

"Then why not tell me everything?"

"Let me ask you something. When Arctander, or your parents, told you to trust them in a situation you didn't completely understand, did you resent it or accept it without reservation?"

After a thoughtful, pause, Nollen replied. "Mostly, I accepted it. Knowing it was for my good. Only, I may never see him again." His voice trailed off with a muted sob.

With curious concern, Gunnar asked, "Who?"

Nollen sat up to draw his legs into his chest so his chin rested on his knees. "Grandfather."

"Why do you think that? We still may survive our mission."

Nollen shook his head and swallowed to regain his voice. "His mind is going. Axel said it started shortly after you left. Old age. Nothing can be done. He barely knew I was there, and unaware I left." A low sob escaped.

Gunnar moved to sit beside Nollen. "I'm sorry, lad. Arctander is a loyal, faithful man. I'm sure Axel will take good care of him in whatever time he has remaining."

Nollen wiped the tears from his cheek. "Axel said he would."

Gunnar gripped Nollen's shoulder. "You can *trust* Axel."

"I know." Nollen nodded in acceptance of the statement. "Still, there is something very unsettling about *this* situation."

"Aye. A danger that warrants extreme caution to protect Eldar."

"I would do nothing to endanger Eldar."

"Then ask no more questions, and be content that *if* the need arises, I will tell you." Gunnar smiled with encouragement. "Now, get some rest. You'll need all your faculties for where we're heading."

Later that night, Alydar and Joslin grew agitated. Callie rushed to stand at the ravine opening. With hackles raised and ears laid back, she growled a warning that woke Gunnar and Nollen. Suddenly, two large beasts appeared out of the darkness. They were hunched at the shoulders with mottled fur of tan, brown, and black. The snout resembled a hyena-dog with salivating fangs.

Gunnar drew his sword while Nollen grabbed his crossbow. The beasts roared. They stood on hindlegs like a bear, the massive paws with sharp claws, ready to strike. Callie leapt at one, only to be swatted aside.

Nollen fired his crossbow. The dart struck one deep in the shoulder. It let out an angry, deafening roar that made Gunnar and Nollen retreat in pain. Gunnar regained his balance. He regripped his sword and charged the closest beast.

Ajax swooped down from the trees to attack the one Nollen wounded. Sharp talons pierced the back of the beast's head. Ajax narrowly avoid a retaliatory swipe. The beast jerked when a second crossbow dart struck in the back. This wound forced it down to all fours. It raced toward Nollen. He loaded the crossbow, but the beast was too close to shoot. Callie leapt on its shoulders where her powerful jaws clamped down on the thick neck. It bucked and reared to try and dislodge her. When that didn't work, it flopped on the ground to roll. Callie jumped off to avoid being crushed. This allowed Nollen time to take careful aim. The beast gurgled when the dart pierced its throat. It jerked then went still.

On his initial charge, Gunnar landed a deep gash to the beast's abdomen. He dodged massive claws to land a second slash to the rear right leg. It fell to the ground unable to stand upright. A defensive backward swing of the paw sent Gunnar flying ten feet in the air. He landed hard on his left side. He looked up at an angry horse whinny. Joslin placed herself between him and the beast. Her buck sent a vicious kick to side of the beast's head. It staggered, dazed. Another kick from Joslin downed the beast. Gunnar quickly rose to make a lethal thrust through the beast's skull. Winded from battle and effort, he backed away.

Nollen arrived. "What are they?"

Gunnar shrugged, as he tried to regain his breath. "You hurt?"

"No. You?"

Gunnar rotated his left shoulder. "Sore. Nothing's broken."

Nollen knelt to examine the paw. "I think this is the predator whose track I discovered last week."

Callie sniffed the beast. "Smells the same."

"Have you seen it before?" Nollen asked Gunnar.

"How could I?"

"Well, you've been in Markita longer than me, and traveled through the Black Mountains. It's possible, you could have seen it before."

Gunnar wiped the blood from his blade and sheathed his sword. "No." He stroked the horse's cheek and spoke soft words of thanks.

"She acted before I could," said Alydar.

"Bring me some light," Gunnar said.

Nollen carefully took a lit branch from the fire. He held it for examination. Gunnar ran his hands along Joslin's shanks and fetlocks. When he lifted her hooves, he waved Nollen to bring the light closer.

"Looks like some bruising."

"Not surprising considering the skull size," said Nollen.

Gunnar patted Joslin's rump. "Don't worry, girl. I have salve that will help." He led her back under the shelter. "Lay down." He made several clicks with his tongue and gave a gentle tug on the reins. Joslin laid down.

Alydar used soft grunts, snorts, and whinnies to communicate. Joslin replied. When Gunnar knelt to apply the salve, she used her lips to rub the back of his head.

Gunnar laughed. "That tickles."

"She's glad you're not hurt," said Alydar.

He stroked her muzzle. "I'm glad it's nothing more serious than a couple of minor bruises." When finished dressing Joslin's wounds, he replaced the salve in the saddlebag. "Now, to make sure you stay down for the night, I'm sleeping here." He reclined against Joslin.

Chapter 16

FOR THE NEXT THREE DAYS, GUNNAR WALKED JOSLIN. NOLLEN also led Alydar. However, a few times, Nollen mounted to find a path around farms, small settlements, or towns. Each night, they made certain to find secure shelter, be it a cave or abandoned shack. By the fourth day, Joslin's bruises were healed, thus Gunnar able to ride.

At twilight, they stopped on a ridge that overlooked a large city. An impressive castle dominated a lower peak just beyond the city. Gunnar pointed at the horizon.

"Miska. And King Montre's castle," he said.

"I remember. At least from what we could see," Nollen snickered.

"Fortunately, Panko's duchy is the smallest. It starts at the eastern end of this ridge."

"I remember that too. He was the most agreeable to our treaty."

"Because he profits from the mines of metals and gems." Gunnar sternly looked along his shoulder at Nollen. "It is the most dangerous duchy being at the foothills of the Black Mountains. The three days to reach the lower pass will be hazardous."

"Sounds like Ha'tar."

"Dragons can be seen and heard. Not all creatures here are visible."

"If you're trying to scare me, it won't work."

Gunnar cocked a grin at the bravado. "No, prepare you."

Nollen chuckled. "I've learned that being around you and Axel means I need to be prepared for anything."

Callie trotted over. "I found some old ruins not far from here." They followed her along the ridge top.

Gunnar dismounted behind the ruins. "This looks like an observation tower. It hasn't been used in a long time." At the corner, he viewed Miska through the young trees and overgrowth. "Any fire can be seen."

"Only if one is looking in this direction." Nollen led Alydar inside.

Gunnar came with Joslin. "I would feel better with no fire tonight."

"Well, I saved some cooked fowl from last night."

Curious, Gunnar asked, "Then what did you eat at midday?"

"The last of the pine nuts and chokeberries." At Gunnar's scowl, he added, "You said to forage. Maybe there is something like arrowroot or burdock around to supplement the fowl."

"Hopefully, we can find them before the sun goes down." Gunnar went outside. Callie dashed in front of him to sniff the ground.

Nollen used the toe of his boot to gently clear the area in his search. By the time it was too dark to search further, they returned to the tower with four arrowroots, chokeberries, and more pine nuts. Callie and Ajax each caught a rodent for their meal while the horses grazed on scrub.

Nollen held up a root. "After weeks of this, we really need a good normal meal. Shouldn't go into the Black Mountains *unprepared.* Let me trade for supplies at the next settlement."

"Agreed," mumbled Gunnar through a mouthful of bitter berries.

Late the following afternoon, they descended the ridge to cross into Panko's duchy. On the main road, they spied a settlement. Gunnar took up a secluded position in the woods with clear visibility to the village to wait. Callie stayed with him.

Nollen rode to the village. He patted Alydar's neck. "Hopefully, we won't need to flee again." Alydar snorted and tossed his head in response. Nollen heard Ajax overhead. He learned the eagle's various calls and caws. This one reminded him of Ajax's presence.

Outside the first house, a woman held a bowl. She tossed seeds to chickens that pecked at the ground around her.

Nollen spoke in accented Markitan. "Greetings, mistress. Where can a weary traveler trade for supplies?"

She paused in her task to skeptically regard him. "That depends on what you have to offer. And who you are."

"A traveler, who means no harm."

The chickens clucked in protest of the stoppage. She dumped the rest of the seeds on the ground then placed the bowl on a bench. With hands on hips, she said, "Show me what you have to trade, and I will decide."

Nollen grinned and dismounted. From his saddlebag, he pulled out an impressive mortar and pestle. "This is made from Bertrandian stone, hard and durable. It won't crack and become faded like wood. Nor will it absorb the odors of plants or food during grinding. Easy to clean with just water."

She tried to mask her eager curiosity, as she took them for examination. "Where did you get such a thing?"

"I am a trader by profession. My travels take me to many places."

"Ya, you don't sound Markitan."

"Well, Markitan or not, I offer them in fair trade for supplies."

Her considerate gaze shifted between Nollen and the items. "These are valuable?"

"Have you seen the likes of these before?"

She slowly shook her head. "No."

He widely grinned. "*That* is what makes them valuable. They are rare. Hardly seen outside of Bertrand."

Her skepticism turned to delight. "I will trade. What do you need?"

"Eight-day supply of food." At her frown, he added, "You will be the envy of your neighbors with a mortar and pestle like this."

Her smile returned. "Done!" She spat on the palm of her hand and held it out to him.

Recognizing the sign of Markitan agreement, he mimicked her actions, and they shook hands.

Once he had the needed supplies, Nollen continued down the main road to a bend that took him out of sight of the settlement. He then entered the woods to double back and rejoin Gunnar.

"I take it you were successful."

Nollen proudly smiled. "Enough to feed us both well the next four days. Lukanka, bacon, onions, carrots, potatoes, and coarse flour meal for skillet cakes."

Impressed, Gunnar laughed. "I haven't had lukanka sausage in years. How will you prepare the skillet cakes without butter and honey?"

"Bacon grease. I have a metal tin I use for storage when traveling. I can put in a few bits of lukanka for breakfast."

"A gourmet pathfinder. We just survived on foraging after our supplies ran out. Except when we reached Eldar then others fed us."

"No wonder you enjoyed Ida's stew," Nollen said jokingly.

"She's a good cook."

"Oh, I also sharpened the razor blade while waiting, in case you decide to be rid of those heavy whiskers."

"I'll shave tonight, while *you* prepare dinner."

They rode for another hour before making camp in a hidden hollow. Without fear of being spotted, Gunnar took time to shave while Nollen cooked.

After eating, Gunnar sighed with satisfaction. "I admit, that was much better than foraging for late season berries and pine nuts."

"I take it, you don't cook," Nollen teased.

Gunnar prepared his bedroll for the night. "Only roast game, when necessary. At home, my mother and aunt did most of the cooking."

"Is that why you're returning? Because you miss your family?"

Gunnar scowled at the sour tone question. "Hardly. I told you this task is to prevent danger to Eldar, not just my family."

"How many escaped with you?"

Gunnar laid down with his head on the saddle. He gazed skyward as he replied, "There were eight of us. My parents, paternal grandfather, aunt, uncle, and my two older brothers. Only my aunt and brothers were alive when we left."

"Are your brothers married?"

"Aye."

"So, you have nieces and nephews."

"Aye. Grown. Your age or older."

Nollen smiled fondly. "Ida and Jarred had a daughter a few months ago. At least I got to see her before I left."

"Why do you insist on thinking the worst?"

"I'm just being realistic. You can't deny there is a possibility of not returning. In fact, if not for you, I would have died from the poison."

Gunnar propped himself on his elbow to face Nollen. "If you recall from our earlier venture, the Almighty can overcome any *possibility*. Even death."

For a moment, Nollen stared at Gunnar. The recollection of Axel being struck dead and brought back to life by Othniel flashed through his mind. "Grandfather told me to be strong and call upon the Almighty. That he would hear me." He heaved an embarrassed shrug. "I do, when I remember."

"I pray throughout the day. In the morning, I ask protection, and at night, give thanks for surviving the day. In between, for whatever is needed."

"I remember seeing Axel in prayer, but not you. Even here in Markita."

"Prayer isn't a posture or even verbal, rather an attitude of the heart and mind. Tell me, do you consider the Almighty at any time during the day?"

"Of course. It's hard not too when I see nature, a new birth, or even talking animals." He chuckled when he motioned to Callie and Alydar.

"That is part of prayer. Meditating on what you know of the Almighty."

The statement, spoken with simplistic assurance, became an epiphany to Nollen. "I never thought of it that way. Yet it makes sense, because when I do take time to consider, there is a peace in my spirit."

Gunnar chuckled. "You pray more often than you realize. Perhaps, by doing so, you can stop being gloomy about survival."

Nollen looked studiously at Gunnar. "Like you?"

"Aye. The peace of prayer helps me hope for the best and press on with what I'm called to do. I'm certain Axel sent you because you are meant to be here."

Nollen cocked a wry grin. "You weren't happy to see me at first."

"True. Although, more out of more concern for your welfare than questioning Axel's choice to dispatch you."

Nollen fought to stifle a yawn.

"We both need sleep." Gunnar laid back down and closed his eyes.

Despite fatigue, Nollen stared skyward. His lips moved in forming words, as he silently prayed, *Help me to employ the peace you give as Gunnar has, in service of Eldar.* Sleep came quickly, tranquil, and deep.

Chapter 17

OR TWO MORE DAYS AND NIGHTS, THEY CROSSED PANKO'S duchy. Being well supplied, they avoided the populace. At twilight of the third day, Gunnar stopped at the edge of a meadow. He motioned Nollen's attention to the peaks across the way. Foggy rain shrouded the lower part of the range.

"The Black Mountains."

Nollen felt a shiver in his core that outwardly manifested in trembling. He breathed with disconcertion at the immediate reaction.

Gunnar noticed. "It is a dark place. More hazardous than Altwald and Ha'tar combined."

"Sirin's domain," said Alydar with dread.

"Tonight, we camp at the base, then proceed to the lower pass on the morrow," said Gunnar.

"I can take the lead from here." Alydar moved in front of Gunnar.

"I know the way!" Gunnar snapped the reins for Joslin to follow.

Nollen turned in the saddle. "Axel chose Alydar as my mount because he escorted the royal family from Eldar to Kranston when they first fled. I don't believe Axel anticipated me finding you before the Black Mountains."

"Fair enough."

As darkness fell, they left the meadow and entered another forest. The terrain changed from a normal forest in late autumn to dense, gnarled trees with rocky ground. An eerie sensation caused men and beasts to become uneasy. Nollen and Gunnar nervously glanced about. Alydar and Joslin pranced on their toes as they moved through the trees. Callie's ear constantly switched from laying back on her head, to straight up to listen. She sniffed both the ground and the air. Ajax moved up and down the bedroll, cocking his head, as if listening or looking for something.

"Another cursed forest," Nollen whispered over his shoulder to Gunnar.

"I don't recall this place on our journey to Eldar," Gunnar replied in breathy anticipation. "Alydar, are sure this is the way?"

"I am. Although, it has become more foreboding than last time. Another sign of Sirin's growing strength."

Joslin grew agitated. She tossed her head and even bucked. Gunnar attempted to soothe her. Alydar spoke in grunts and snorts. Joslin physically calmed down yet chomped at the bit.

"We will not stop for night," said Alydar.

"You'll get no argument from us," said Gunnar.

"Then hold on."

Alydar began a slow lope, a speed at which Joslin could keep pace. Alydar jerked to avoid trees, and sometimes jumped obstacles. Joslin closely followed. Callie ran at top speed to stay with the horses. At first, Ajax used his talons to remain on the bedroll, but gave up and took to flight within the forest. He would land on branches to watch the direction Alydar went, then take a short flight through the trees to proceed. Nollen and Gunnar held the reins and manes to remain seated.

For two hours, they stayed the course. However, when Joslin fell behind, Alydar stopped in a ravine near a creek. Joslin breathed hard and stomped her front hooves in a form of protest. She wasn't the only one laboring to breath. Nollen and Gunnar did so from exertion of the ride.

Alydar and Joslin briefly conversed before Alydar translated. "She wants to rest for your sakes. She could feel Sir Gunnar slip a few times."

Nollen coughed to cover his amusement at the statement.

"I noticed you nearly fell off," Gunnar chided to the mirth.

Nollen fought back a smile to ask Alydar, "Is it safe to stop?"

"For a few moments. Drink from your flask and give some to Callie and us. We shouldn't drink from the stream."

Callie lifted her head before it touched the water. "Why?"

"Would you trust a dark forest to contain safe water?"

"He speaks wisdom, she-wolf," said Ajax.

"Callie!" she growled.

"You must stop insulting her," Nollen scolded Ajax. He dismounted and knelt. He carefully poured water into a cupped hand for Callie. After a second helping, he stood to offer water to Alydar. Lastly, he drank.

Gunnar did the same in giving water to Joslin before he drank. He winked at Callie before asking Ajax, "Eagle-welp?" He held up the flask.

Ajax spread his wings and cawed in angry response.

Joslin's head snapped up with ears pricked forward.

Alydar reacted in the same manner. "Quick! Time to leave." He nudged Nollen toward the saddle.

The moment they mounted; loud reptile-dragon hisses filled the air. Joslin whinnied and launched forward when a large reptile-dragon lunged from behind a boulder. Another raced toward Alydar. The unicorn-horse bucked and impacted the reptile-dragon's neck. Alydar and Joslin leapt across the stream and began a reckless gallop to escape the reptiles.

Nollen glanced back. At such speed, and dodging obstacles, he couldn't use his crossbow. When Alydar ran between two trees, a trap sprung. The force sent Nollen flying over Alydar's head when the unicorn-horse became snared in the trap. Alydar whinny-screamed in anger and began to thrash to be free of the netting.

Nollen landed hard on the ground. Briefly winded, yet aware of the need to act, he stood. He saw Alydar struggle. "Stop! You'll get hurt."

Breathing hard from anger and effort, Alydar heeded. Nollen used his dagger to begin cutting Alydar free. Gunnar arrived. His violent rein made Joslin skid to a stop. He jumped from the saddle, drew his sword, and hacked at the net. Hearing the approach of reptile-dragons briefly stopped their effort.

Flaming arrows flew from the darkness at the reptile-dragons. Immediately, Gunnar and Nollen took up position to shield Alydar. Callie stood with them. Ajax cawed and swooped down at the reptile-dragons. He barely avoided more flaming arrows shot at them.

Two arrows impacted each reptile-dragon, yet only slowed the advance. Shouting preceded a group of beings bearing torches, who rushed the dragons and waved the torches. The reptile-dragons stopped, hissed at the beings. More flaming arrows. When struck again, the reptile-dragons retreated. They turned their collective attention to the tree, where Gunnar and Nollen protected Alydar.

Gunnar and Nollen watched with wary anticipation. Excited chatter could be heard. Gunnar lowered his sword. "Uoy ot ecaep," he said.

Surprised, Nollen asked, "You speak their language? I've never heard it before."

"It's Eldarian backwards," Gunnar replied, though his focus remained on the group.

Upon approach, the torchlight revealed short beings wearing leather caps or kerchiefs. It consisted of males and females, with the older males having beards. They wore clothes made of cloth, leather, and fur. All had overly large noses and ears. The tallest reached chest high on Gunnar and Nollen. One male pushed forward. He spoke a question, to which he received a reply from Gunnar.

"Ris Rannug."

"Ah!" the being laughed. "Wonder we did when return you do, Gunnar Sir."

"Vartan." Gunnar made a salute. "My companion. Nollen of Far Point."

"You welcomed."

"Thank you," said Nollen, still a bit uncertain.

"Could you free his horse?" Gunnar asked.

Vartan barked some orders, and several males immediately complied.

"Bushlik trap for. Harm no others," explained Vartan.

"Bushlik?" asked Nollen.

"We off chase." Vartan motioned in the direction the reptiles fled.

Once free, Alydar shook himself from head to rear. Nollen examined Alydar and felt wetness on the right foreleg.

"He's injured," Nollen told Gunnar.

"How bad?"

"Hard to tell exactly, though it feels like a long, bloody gash."

"Come you. Night safe not," Vartan said.

Nollen leaned close to Gunnar. "Do you trust them?"

"If we want to survive the night, we should." Gunnar fetched Joslin to lead the horses after Vartan.

Alydar slightly limped when Nollen hastened to join Gunnar. "You speak their language, so you know these creatures?

"Domovay. Dwarves," Gunnar clarified when Nollen appeared baffled. "They guard the mountain passes."

When several Domovay poked at them to move along, Gunnar privately said, "We'll talk more later."

They entered a narrow gorge between two mounds that housed a gate of lashed wooden logs. Torches and fires lit the enclosed compound of small thatched huts. Drying on racks were meat and hides, both fur and scales, like that of the reptile-dragons. All the Domovay stared at Gunnar, Nollen, two horses, a wolf, and eagle. A few males even tried to poke spears at Callie but stopped when Vartan scolded them.

"Horses put there." Vartan pointed to what appeared to be a partially enclosed lean-to corral.

Gunnar left Joslin saddled, but Nollen removed the tack from Alydar.

"Hand me the salve," Nollen said to Gunnar. He examined Alydar's leg more closely. "I'll need some bandages too."

Speaking Domovay, Gunnar made the request. Two females complied.

"More light."

Gunnar held a torch for Nollen to see the wound clearly. Once finished with the salve and bandages, he stood and patted Alydar.

"That should help. Do you want to lay down?"

Alydar grunted with an exaggerated shake of his head to the negative.

"Sleep there will you." Vartan nodded toward a small hut beside the corral. "Rain." He held up his hand when several drops began to fall.

"I'll stay here," Nollen said.

Vartan pulled Nollen out then placed a log across the lean-to opening. "Safe horse will be. Sleep dry."

The cold rain fell harder, accompanied by a stiff breeze.

"Ajax." Nollen pointed the eagle to the corral. Ajax landed on top of the thatched roof. Callie also took up position by the opening. This made many Domovay murmur and complain.

"No like wolf here," Vartan firmly said.

"Well, she isn't going anywhere," Nollen rebuffed.

Several males loudly complained to Vartan, and an argument ensued.

Gunnar leaned close to Nollen to whisper. "They are threatening to harm her if she remains in the compound."

At Vartan's angry order, the males reluctantly grew quiet. Vartan told Nollen, "With you stay or go!" He waved between Callie, the hut for them to sleep, and the gate.

"She'll stay with us out of sight," said Gunnar. "Come, Callie."

Small shafts of light from the compound filtered through the front thatching. The floor consisted of dirt with a few straw mats for sleeping. The door shut behind them with a thud.

Gunnar tried to open it. The door flexed yet remained shut. He sneered. "They barred us in."

"I guess we shouldn't trust them, even to survive the night," chided Nollen.

Gunnar drew Nollen to sit on the pallets. He spoke a harsh whisper. "You're right, they are not to be fully trusted. However," he stressed to stop an objection. "With Alydar injured and the bushlik nearby, we *are* safer here than out there."

Callie laid down placed her head on Nollen's lap. She also spoke in a whisper. "Predators follow a scent of blood."

Nollen stroked her head. "Let's hope Alydar heals quickly."

A short trickle of rain seeped through the thatched roof.

"Ajax will alert us if there is any trouble." Gunnar laid down.

For Nollen, sleep didn't come easy. He felt Callie lay back-to-back with him. Something she had done since leaving Sener. He thought about her, Ajax, and Alydar; three unlikely companions for a dangerous mission. He grew used to talking animals from his time with Axel but had not dealt with any singularly. Alydar's assessment proved correct, Gilen could not have endured the hazardous journey. He didn't know for how long he considered the events and his companions before he fell asleep.

Suddenly, an eagle cry and horse scream pierced the night. Startled, Nollen and Gunnar sat up. Callie bounded to the door where she howled. Ajax replied followed by another horse scream.

"Alydar!" Nollen hit the door with his shoulder. It didn't yield.

"Together!" Gunnar said.

Both put all their weight into hitting the door simultaneously. The door crashed open. Gunnar stumbled forward while Nollen fell to the ground. He scrambled to his feet and raced to the corral. The log had been removed. Inside, they found Alydar down and a male Domovay on his knees beside the unicorn-horse's front leg. Callie snapped at the Domovay. He tossed something at her and made for the opening. Gunnar caught him. Nollen dropped to his knees beside Alydar. The bandage had been ripped off.

"Alydar?" Nollen anxiously asked.

The unicorn-horse murmured; his eyes had difficulty focusing.

"What did you do to him?" Nollen demanded of the male Domovay.

By now, a crowd gathered outside the corral.

Gunnar practically lifted the male off his feet. "Answer him!"

Callie directed Nollen's attention to Alydar's wound. She sniffed it then growled at the male.

"Poison?" Gunnar asked Callie. In response, the she-wolf nudged Nollen's side where he was wounded. Gunnar understood, and accused the male Domovay, "You poisoned him."

Vartan interrogated the male. From the rapid exchange, they heard the word *bushlik.* Vartan ordered others to take the male, only Gunnar was reluctant to release him.

"If Alydar dies, he must face justice!" Gunnar sternly said.

"Ya," Vartan stoutly agreed.

"Hot water! Bandages!" Gunnar shouted at the gathered Domovay. He knelt beside Nollen, where he quietly spoke. "Callie believes it the same poison that made you ill. We'll treat him the same way. Wash the wound, use the salve, try to have him drink some warm elixir. And pray."

Nollen fought back great upset, as he stroked Alydar's cheek.

When the needed items arrived, Nollen washed the wound and applied the salve. During his administrations, he softly spoke encouraging words to Alydar. The unicorn-horse made an occasional grunt or muted response, thought his breath became labored.

Gunnar mixed the elixir. He handed a cup to Nollen. "Get him to take as much as possible."

Nollen gently lifted Alydar's muzzle. "Please. Try to drink."

Alydar moved his tongue in attempts to swallow the portions carefully poured into his mouth. With the liquid gone, Nollen eased Alydar's muzzle to the ground. He placed the empty cup aside and lowered his head to touch Alydar's cheek. "Please, Gott, heal him."

Gunnar patted Nollen's shoulder. "We will keep vigil this night. No one will come near him." He motioned for Callie. They took up position at the entrance. He drew his sword, and Callie stood with hackles raised and ears back. The Domovay warily regarded them.

Careful, Vartan approached. He held a sealed crock. "Cure for poison bushlik." He offered.

Harsh in features, Gunnar shook his head. "No. We will use our medicine and prayers to the Almighty. Once more, your people have shown they cannot be trusted."

Vartan initially became insulted then showed genuine remorse. "Deal with Hobart we will."

"Like last time?"

Vartan glared upward. "No. Eldar Son not here."

"It doesn't change what happened. Then or now!"

Vartan anxiously glanced about. He waved the crowd away then motioned for Gunnar to bow his head. He spoke in a confidential voice. "Sirin on move. Her people take one littles."

Gunnar's brows grew level at the admission. "Sirin's *people?*"

"Once master of Domovay. Act make us. For littles sake."

Gunnar tried to contain his rising anger when he understood. "They took your children to force cooperation."

Vartan made a curt nod of affirmation.

Gunnar studiously regarded Vartan. "I am sorry. However, it doesn't excuse Hobart's attempt to take a life."

"Offering! Hobart's …," he used his hands to show *small,* "gone."

Gunnar straightened with dreaded consideration of the circumstance.

"Use." Vartan again held up the closed crock.

"No, thank you," Gunnar spoke in soften tone.

From behind, they heard Nollen's words of prayer and encouragement for Alydar. Vartan's sympathetic gaze went from Nollen with Alydar to Gunnar before he left.

The remainder of the night passed in heavy anticipation of Alydar's grave condition. Stalwart in his watchfulness, Gunnar added muted words of prayer to echo Nollen. Callie occasionally whimpered.

At dawn, a stirring came from inside the corral. Before Gunnar and Callie could react the Domovay cautiously approached. Vartan boldly stepped forward.

"Horse?" he asked.

"See for yourself." Gunnar smiled and stepped from opening.

Vartan loudly gasped in surprise. Alydar was on his feet with Nollen unwrapping the bandage. The wound healed! No visible scar. Vartan's reaction caught Alydar's attention. The unicorn-horse turned his head to stare at Vartan. The intensity made Vartan retreat. He seized Gunnar. "How?" He pointed at Alydar.

"The Almighty. Just like the Son of Eldar." Gunnar drew Vartan aside when Nollen led Alydar into the compound. All the Domovays mirrored the stunned reaction at sight of Alydar.

Nollen's harsh glare found Hobart, though he spoke to Vartan. "The Almighty's graciousness should not negate punishment for what he did to my horse."

"Horse live. Shave. Dishonor." Vartan spoke a commanded, and three males seized Hobart.

Hobart's cries for mercy were ignored. They forced him to sit on the ground, bound his hands, and plucked off his cap. The crowd chanted and jeered, as the men proceeded to shave off Hobart's hair and beard. He wept tears of shame. When cut loose, he ran to his hut.

Vartan grabbed the tied hair that was once Hobart's beard. "Justice." He held it out to Nollen.

When Nollen hesitated, Gunnar told him, "Take it." After Nollen accepted the gesture, Gunnar said to Vartan, "We are leaving. Do not follow or impede us in any way."

Vartan told the crowd to disperse.

In silence, they saddled Alydar then rode from the compound. Once a safe distance from the settlement, Nollen spoke.

"I heard you mention Axel and *last time*. What happened?"

Gunnar grinned. "It's simple really. The Domovay traps are so cleverly hidden they are hard to detect, even in the daytime. One unseated Axel, which resulted in a broken arm. Vartan and others came to investigate the sprung trap. Again, they took us to the compound. Axel was the first to realize they spoke Eldarian backwards and became angry when he heard them speak about demanding tribute for aid. He gave them a tongue-lashing in their language."

"He could speak their language by just hearing it?" marveled Nollen.

"As I said, it's Eldarian backward. Not too terribly difficult. Only when Vartan tried to mimic our speech, he put words in the wrong order."

"I noticed that. So, did they help set Axel's arm?"

"No. Like with Alydar, we held a prayer vigil. By morning …"

"Axel was healed," Nollen concluded with a wry smile.

"Aye. When he displayed his healed arm, Vartan recognized the royal ring. Axel had yet to take it off, which I advised him to do upon departure."

"How would the Domovay know about Axel?"

"During our stay, we learned they are descendants of those enslaved by the Palleteens to work the mines. When they managed to escape, they found refuge in the *bushlik* forest. No doubt they learned about prophecy from the Palleteens, who, as you know, worship and serve Sirin."

Alydar snorted to the contrary. "This was not a bushlik forest when I escorted the royal family to Kranston. No such creatures existed then. It wasn't until we began crossing the Black Mountain that we encountered any beasts."

"Apparently, much has changed in two hundred years," said Gunnar.

"Sirin grows bolder knowing the end is near."

"What end?" asked Nollen.

Gunnar kicked Joslin to move in front of Alydar and stop their trek. "If we succeed in our mission, Eldar will be protected from Sirin's plan, and be the end of *her.* Failure, will give her the upper hand."

"Then we won't fail," Nollen said, resolutely.

Gunnar drew Joslin back for Alydar to again take the lead.

Chapter 18

SIRIN STOOD ON A HIGHER PEAK LOOKING DOWN AT THE PASS where Gunnar and Nollen rode. Two bushliks flanked her. For this observance, Sirin discarded her old hag appearance for her normal form—a cross between a beautiful woman and reptile. Her long moss-green hair reached past her waist. Scales formed a crown that arched over her head from ear slit to ear slit. The shape and color of her eyes were that of a reptile, yellow with narrow black irises. Smooth pale green skin was covered by a short gold chiffon dress. Her feet and hands were that of a reptile, three toed and fingered with black claws.

A bushlik raised its head to look at her. It hissed in speech.

Sirin stroked its head. A wry smile appeared. "No. Let them pass. The return trip is more important." She mischievously laughed. "So, they don't grow too comfortable, perhaps bit of dense fog." She waved her hands, ending with the claws pointing down at Gunnar and Nollen.

Alydar stopped. His entire body shook, as he angrily grunted.

"What's wrong?" Nollen just finished speaking when dense, heavy fog enveloped them. He and Gunnar began to cough.

"Hard ... to ... breathe," complained Gunnar.

Alydar whinnied, to which Joslin responded. The horses picked up the pace. The fog oppressive, as well as dense. Neither Nollen nor Gunnar could see past the horses' ears.

"Too … fast!" Nollen struggled to say.

Alydar ignored the protest to continue. Callie yelped from somewhere ahead. Alydar followed the she-wolf's call. The fog thinned in time for Alydar to see the edge of the cliff. He jerked left to stay on the path. Nollen grabbed Alydar's mane to remain seated. Joslin emerged from the fog almost on top of them. Gunnar sharply drew rein. Both men took deep gasps of air to recover from the suffocating fog.

"What was that?" Nollen coughed.

"Sirin," said Alydar. "I sensed a cold evil before the fog appeared."

"Sirin can command the weather?" Nollen took another deep breath.

"Many First Ones can, at least the basics."

Gunnar surveyed the surrounding peaks, cliffs, and the narrow pass. "Let's hope that doesn't include rockslides."

"Sirin is a creature of the water. Her control is limited to those elements," Alydar continued the explanation.

"Avalanches then. Snow already covers the higher peaks."

"We are on the lower pass. We will descend several plateaus before reaching the bottom."

"You are taking a different pass than we did," insisted Gunnar.

Alydar raised his head to regard the knight. "This is the original course. We hoped Sirin would concentrate on the way you went last time and ignore this one."

Gunnar leaned on the saddle bow. " *We?* You and Axel?"

"Aye."

"I said Axel didn't expect me to find you before reaching the Black Mountains," said Nollen.

"Unfortunately, Sirin out-guessed him," groused Gunnar.

"Or someone told her," Callie emphatically said.

At the comment, Gunnar swore, "Vartan!" At Nollen's befuddlement, he explained, "He told me Sirin's servants take their children to ensure cooperation. Hobart's among them."

Nollen removed the tied hair from under the strap holding his bedroll. "You told me to take this!"

"It is their form of justice. To refuse, would have been worse."

Nollen tossed it over the cliff.

"We have lingered too long." Alydar again took the lead.

For the remainder of the day, they traveled the highest plateau of the original pass. No other anomaly occurred.

Nollen drew Alydar to rein when they reached a descent. "It's getting too dark to continue safely."

"Nor is it safe to spend the night," Alydar countered.

"If not for sleep, at least for water, food, and to stretch our legs."

"As I recall, there should be a mountain stream that runs through the next plateau. We can pause there."

Alydar carefully proceeded down the incline. He skidded when he reached the bottom and did a short leap to right his footing. Ajax landed on Nollen's bedroll. An hour later, they reached a widest part of plateau. Water ran down the rocks and filled a small pool before it continued in a shallow stream through the plateau. Stiff, Nollen dismounted. He arched his back and pulled up each leg toward his chest to stretch.

Gunnar laughed. "I'm the eldest."

Nollen smirked. "Are you telling me you're not sore?"

"No. Only that I'm older." Gunnar also did some stretches.

"You can walk two miles before the plateau narrows," said Alydar.

"Can we cook our meal, or do we eat cold sausage?" Nollen rubbed his hands and blew breath on them for warmth.

"No fire. Eat as you walk. Now, use the pool to refill your flasks. We will drink." Alydar lowered his head, so did Joslin.

Callie lapped at the water. Ajax landed at the edge of the pool to scoop up water in his beak. With flasks filled, and animals satisfied, Nollen and Gunnar took the reins to continue the trek. The plateau was wide enough to walk side-by-side.

Gunnar observed the night sky. "Clouds are forming. This cold feels likes snow." He pulled up the cloak hood.

"I sense no evil," Alydar assured them.

By the time they finished walking two miles, a mix of sleet and snow started to fall. The plateau narrowed, so Gunnar and Nollen mounted. For two hours, they traveled the undulating pass. A few times Alydar, Joslin, or Callie slipped on wet rocks during a short climb or descent. By midnight, Nollen yawned and rocked in the saddle to stay awake.

Gunnar blinked and rubbed his neck with fatigue. "We need to stop. Neither of us has slept in almost two days."

"I'll find a safe place." Callie ran on ahead.

After twenty minutes, they heard Callie yelp. Alydar shifted course to find the she-wolf in front of a shallow cave. Nollen's legs gave way when he dismounted. He caught himself on the saddle to keep from falling to the ground. Gunnar managed to stay on his feet and shuffled when he led Joslin into the cave. Both were too tired to fetch the bedroll. They stumbled and fell hard on their buttocks due to fatigue. Nollen wrapped his cloak tight and laid down. He fell asleep almost immediately. Callie took up her normal position beside him.

Nollen felt something wet on his face and tried to brush it away. More wetness. A close ear-piercing cry startled him awake. Breathing hard with fright, it took a moment to realize Callie had licked his face, and the call came from Ajax. He looked to Gunnar. The knight yawned and stretched. Nollen's focus changed to the cave opening. The grey light seemed brighter than it should be for early morning.

"I guess we slept rather deeply," said Nollen.

"Aye." Gunnar drank from the flask then fetched some provision. He handed Nollen a hunk of cured sausage and two small carrots.

"Something warm would be nice," grumbled Nollen.

"No wood up here. Maybe tonight."

Exiting the cave after eating, they discovered six inches of snow fell overnight. Light grey clouds filled the sky. In silence, they continued.

"We will reach the bottom by mid-day," said Alydar.

"Good. Hopefully, it will be warmer," said Nollen.

"Just be glad we didn't have to climb any higher," said Gunnar.

The rest of the morning passed with only minimal conversation. During the final descent, they were forced to lean far back in the saddle. This helped Joslin and Alydar maintain balance for the steep climb down.

At the bottom, Nollen stopped Alydar and dismounted. "After that incline, I want to check your legs and hooves."

Gunnar did the same with Joslin. He noticed Callie laying down and chewing at her front paws. "Here, let me see." Gently, he lifted her front paws. "A few pebbles caught between the pads." He wiggled them free.

Hearing Ajax's alert call, Nollen glanced skyward. Perplexed, he surveyed their surroundings. "I don't see anything."

Gunnar stood from helping Callie. "We're close to Kranston. His vantage point gives him a great view."

"How close?"

"With no impediments, we can be there by mid-day tomorrow." Gunnar mounted. "This time, I lead."

They crossed a meadow then navigated a wooden area before reaching a riverbank. Gunnar stopped at the water's edge and pointed north.

"Kranston."

Nollen peered in the direction indicated. The river took a sharp bend east. Beyond the far bank, rose a high peak shrouded in heavy clouds. "Where?"

"That peak. It is hidden by the clouds. From there, the view is clear, and magnificent. We head north to the narrowest part of the river to cross." Gunnar turned Joslin to head in the indicated direction. After about three miles, he stopped to dismount. "No," he said when Nollen began to get down. "Be ready to cross swiftly."

Alydar snorted in anticipation. "Burkava."

"I will draw them out," said Gunnar.

"What?"

Alydar and Gunnar ignored Nollen's question. Gunnar waded into the river until the depth reached his knees. He drew his sword and slapped at the water three times before he hastened back to shore. He kept his sword ready.

Guarded and wary, Nollen watched. He jerked in the saddle at hearing a loud echoing squeal. His action pulled on Alydar's rein, which made the unicorn-horse slightly rear.

Downstream, ripples appeared in the water when two fins cut through the surface and moved side-by-side. Trail wakes showed the creatures raced towards them. Nollen grabbed his crossbow in preparation to shoot whatever appeared.

"No! Stay still." Gunnar waved at Nollen.

The squealing increased to a continuous sound. Two serpent's heads broke the surface in front of Gunnar. Long necks rose five feet above the water. The serpents continued to move toward shore. Immediately, Gunnar placed the pommel of his sword in front of his face.

"Eldar forever!" he shouted.

In amazed trepidation, Nollen's eyes grew wide when the serpents stopped their rapid approach. As if at attention, they stared at Gunnar.

"In the name of Almighty, let us pass."

The serpents faced each other and bowed their heads until their nostrils touched the water. Between them, the water subsided to create a dry passage. Gunnar quickly mounted and snapped the reins for Joslin to cross the riverbed. With Nollen too stunned to act, Alydar proceeded. Callie brought up the rear. When they reached the opposite bank, the serpents submerged, and the river continued on its course. No ripples of fins disturbed the surface.

Nollen found enough voice to ask, "What just happened?"

"I got us across the river," Gunnar casually replied. "You can put up your crossbow now." He turned Joslin to continue up the riverbank.

Nollen did as instructed then kicked Alydar to catch up. "That wasn't a simple river crossing."

"Burkava have guarded the river to Kranston for centuries. To protect the royal family and faithful Brethren."

"They serve as a deterrent to Sirin," added Alydar.

"You said Sirin is a water creature," said Nollen, still a bit confused.

"She has no control over the burkava. The Almighty deemed it so."

"We will be safe enough on this side of the river to make a fire to cook supper." Gunnar scratched at his whisker. "And hot water to prepare for final arrival at Kranston."

Nollen grinned. "You won't need much oil this time. Unless, she's worth it."

Gunnar's brief surprise at the teasing turned to a scoff. "There is no *she.*"

Chapter 19

SHORTLY AFTER NOON THE FOLLOWING DAY, THEY TRAVELED A narrow uphill path. The trek began a gentle climb that gradually grew steeper. It wound around up the mountain until they reached the dense cloud bank that shrouded the peak. Visibility went to near zero.

Nollen could barely see Joslin's rump. What seemed longer than necessary, they continued through the clouds. Frustrated, he called ahead. "I thought you said the view up here is clear?"

Gunnar didn't reply, as they emerged from the clouds into clear blue sky and bright sunshine. Before them, lay a large plateau. He drew rein to let Nollen catch up. He smiled. "Kranston."

Unusual red rock formations rose dramatically behind an ancient castle wall and gate. Evergreens and bare deciduous trees dotted the rocks. From the red stone gatehouse, the walls ran from one side of the plateau to the other – at least one mile in either direction. The rock formations appeared split down the middle, with another castle wall and archway between them. Nollen stared in awe.

From the pouch on his belt, Gunnar pulled out a small, engraved silver whistle. "Follow closely," he told Nollen. Upon approach, Gunnar blew the whistle, with three short bursts followed by a long tweet. He waited a moment, before he repeated the whistling call.

Three men appeared on the gate tower rampart. A responding whistle came in reverse, with the long tweet followed by three short bursts.

Gunnar made a very long tweet on the whistle. Two men left the rampart while one remained. He made a sweeping wave with his arms. He widely smiled and replaced the whistle in his pouch. "We are welcomed," he informed Nollen.

The gate rose to admit them. After entering, Gunnar greeted the men who opened the gate. One was near his age, the other around thirty.

"Beno. Arnie."

"Uncle!" cheered Arnie. "We could scarcely believe it was you."

"I told you I would return."

"Uncle?" Nollen repeated.

Gunnar dismounted to warmly embraced Arnie. "Aye, son of my older brother Kean."

"What of Axel?" Arnie eagerly asked.

Gunnar proudly smiled. "He is now king."

"Praise the Almighty!"

"Our prayers are answered," said Beno.

"The first part," said Gunnar with a hint of warning. "This is Nollen of Far Point. He was instrumental in aiding Axel and me."

"Welcome, friend." Beno and Arnie balked in surprise when Callie came from behind the horses. "A white wolf!"

"Be easy. She won't harm you." Nollen dismounted. "Her name is Callie of the Halvor Wolves." Ajax landed on the bedroll. "This is Ajax of the Eagles." Alydar snorted and stomped his front leg, to which Nollen grinned. "Alydar. Brother of Teva, the Unicorn queen. They volunteered, and King Axel gratefully accepted the offer."

"I escorted the royal family to Kranston centuries ago."

Beno and Arnie gaped in amazement at hearing Alydar speak.

"There is much to explain," said Gunnar. "Is Milos still alive?"

"Aye," said Arnie, smiling. "He will be most happy to see you, as will father and Uncle Jann."

Beno called to the man on the rampart. "Rendor! We're taking Gunnar and his friend to Milos." Rendor waved an acknowledgement.

Nollen observed the surroundings as they walked from the main gate through a massive field of rolling hills. The grass lay dormant for the season. He noticed plowed places, harvested crops, and even what appeared to be a small orchard bare of leaves and fruit. Among the rocks, stood carved openings and wooden doors.

Closer view of the enormous split section showed the unusualness of the rocks. Some were curved, perhaps due to wind at such a high elevation, or boulders stacked one upon another. Trees and shrubs grew at the base of the rocks or in the crevasses. It took great skill to construct the walls, gates, and houses among such unique landscape.

Arnie paused before the interior arch. "Let Beno take the horses. It narrows too much from here for them to pass."

Nollen removed his crossbow and saddlebag before handing the reins to Beno. Gunnar also took possession of his saddlebag.

"Callie, Ajax, go with them. No need to cause any undue upset," Gunnar instructed them.

Beyond the arch, the terrain grew steeper and narrow. From the main path, other worn tracks led to carved doors embedded in the rocks or earthen mounds with metal gates. In spring and summer, deciduous trees provided shade, but for now, fallen leaves covered the dormant grass.

Arnie led them down earthen steps. At the base of the stairway stood a large opening with no door or gate. The smell of food came from within. The mound housed a great room. Red stone columns and arches stabilized the earthen ceiling. Roughhewn wooden tables and chairs filled the cavernous room. A few torches helped to light the deeper portions, but the enormous opening provided enough light for normal viewing.

To one side, a large hearth was used for warmth and cooking. A stone stack chimney ran along the wall to vent the smoke. Six women ranged in age from very old to a young teen.

The eldest woman rose from the table where she sat to peel carrots. With eager eyes, and a growing smile, she approached them. "Do my aging eyes deceive me or is it you, my dear nephew Gunnar?"

Gunnar dropped his bag on a table to warmly embraced her with a kiss on both cheeks. "You see as keenly as ever." She wept, so he gently helped her back to the table and sat beside her. "You don't look any older than when I left."

"Bah! Oh! Gunnar!" She hugged him again. When they separated, she spied Nollen. "You are not Axel."

"No, ma'am. I am Nollen of Far Point."

"A good friend to both me and Axel. Nollen, my aunt Sonya."

Sonya grabbed Nollen's hand. Her wrinkled face spread into a smile. "You are most welcome. And thank you, for helping bring my nephew back safely."

Nollen graciously replied. "It is I who owe much to Sir Gunnar and the King."

"King?" Sonya's eyes danced with delight when looking to Gunnar.

Nollen's speech also brought the other women to the table.

Gunnar widely smiled. "Aye. The Elector is defeated, and the royal line reestablished."

The women wept tears of joy, while the teens squealed with excitement.

"Where is he?" he shouted. Men and women followed him.

"Here, Milos!" Gunnar stood.

Near age seventy, a few inches taller, and brawny, Milos greeted Gunnar with a bear-hug.

Nollen smiled in observance.

"You are his friend. Welcome." Milos then barked, "Women, prepare a feast where we can hear Gunnar's report."

Two women pushed their way past Milos to reach Gunnar. Nollen reckoned one to be near his age, while the other, a few years older. The younger woman had long dark hair braided, and soft brown eyes. The older had golden hair with bright hazel eyes. Anxious excitement marked their expression.

"Is he well?" the younger one hurried to ask Gunnar.

"Aye."

She covered her mouth to contain a sob of relief.

"Praise be," the elder said to the younger. She too, misty-eyed.

Gunnar opened his saddlebag and pulled out a wrapped item. "He sends you this." He gave it to the older one.

A smile of anticipation appeared. "Is it?"

Gunnar simply smiled.

In haste, she unwrapped the item. She wept with joy upon sight of an ornate ruby necklace. She put it around her neck and hugged Gunnar.

"I told you he would not forget," the young one encouraged. She saw Nollen, and composed herself to ask Gunnar, "Who is your friend?"

"Nollen of Far Point. He risked his life to help me and Axel."

"Oh, thank you!" she cheered.

Nollen froze in surprised when she hugged him and kissed his cheek.

Gunnar laughed at the embarrassment. "Nollen, this is Lexi."

"Hello." He acknowledged with a nod.

Lexi giggled. "I know my action might seem forward, but—"

"Understandable given the circumstances," Gunnar interrupted her.

At his warning expression, she assumed a more formal attitude. "Indeed. Forgive my enthusiasm, Master Nollen."

"There is nothing to forgive. Everyone is excited by Sir Gunnar's return." Nollen kindly smiled.

Lexi flashed a bashful smile and introduced the other woman. "This is Alicia."

Nollen gave Alicia the same acknowledging nod and smile.

"I share Lexi's gratitude for helping Gunnar and Axel," said Alicia.

"It was my pleasure."

Alicia touched the necklace. "You will tell us everything."

"Naturally," said Gunnar.

"Brother!"

At the call, Alicia and Lexi quietly withdrew to help the women.

By Gunnar's happy cheer, Nollen hung back to allow the family reunion. Two older men, three women, four younger children, and two teenage boys swarmed Gunnar and Arnie. The younger children displayed some shyness, while the teenagers more enthusiastic in greeting Gunnar. When Gunnar knelt to speak to a shy six-year-old, she grinned when he tickled her. Encouraged by her mother, a younger woman, the girl flung her arms around Gunnar's neck.

Nollen judged the oldest man to be around sixty with mostly gray hair. A few specks of the original browns still visible. Nollen reckoned him to be Jann, the oldest brother Gunnar mentioned earlier. Jann carried a bit more weight and thicker neck with sagging jowls of age. His wife, Meryl, a friendly woman. The other brother, Kean, appeared closer to Gunnar's age, with salt and pepper hair. All were well proportioned, hardy men. Arnie resembled his father.

The scene reminded him of the forest compound in Heddwyn where the Brethren hid to escape the slaughter. There too was always a joyous reunion when they visited the compound to find the majority still alive.

Nollen's thoughts drifted to his family. He felt sadness regarding Arctander. He could only hope his grandfather survived until he returned. He didn't want to lose Arctander while away. He fought back a sniffle. Ida. At least she was happily married and a mother. He jumped when a hand clapped his shoulder. Gunnar.

"My friend Nollen."

"Welcome!" Jann heartily slapped Nollen on the back.

Nollen simply grinned. The rest of the conversation became a blur. He estimated triple the number of people at Kranston than Heddwyn. He couldn't keep track of all the names and relationships. He smiled, nodded, or gave a quick answer to any question, but mostly, he observed.

Kean practically shoved a tankard of cider into Nollen's hand when preparing for a toast. Nollen drank in response to Jann's salute. He coughed at the unexpected strength of the cider.

Gunnar laughed. "We brew it more potent to survive the winter. Much colder up here than many places in Eldar."

Nollen flashed an embarrassed smile. He would take more careful sips to the round of salutes and toasts offered by a number of men.

When the meal was ready, Milos shouted to get everyone's attention. "Today, has been long awaited. The Almighty worked wonders in restoring Eldar. Tonight, we celebrate. Tomorrow, we begin preparations for our return."

At the announcement of *return*, Nollen's head snapped around to Gunnar. He sat a long table with Gunnar and his family. Gunnar caught his intense regard. The knight gave a short nod of confirmation, which made Nollen sit back to consider the implications.

Milos offered up a lengthy prayer of thanksgiving, praise, and blessing for the meal. When finished, he shouted with exuberance, "Everyone, enjoy!"

Gunnar leaned close to Kean. "I noticed Lorraine still heads the cooking. Have the recipes improved?"

Kean lowly chuckled. "For Lorraine."

Gunnar laughed. "I'm sure Waldo appreciates that." He became startled when a bowl of stew was unceremonious dropped in front of him. Some of the contents spilled onto the table and splattered him. Annoyed, he looked up. A slender woman of fifty with light blue eyes sneered at him.

"Waldo died last year," she chided.

Stunned by the news, Gunnar became regretful. He snatched her arm when she moved to leave. "I'm sorry."

Jann defended Gunnar, and said to Lorraine, "He didn't know."

Lorraine jerked free and left.

Gunnar noticed everyone at the table stared at him. Nollen appeared confused, his brothers and Arnie sympathetic, but their wives cross at his blunder. The younger children, and the teenage boys, appeared perplexed.

Again, Jann repeated to the family, "Don't fault a man for something said in ignorance."

"What?" Gunnar pointedly asked.

Jann took a deep breath before he explained. "Plague killed nearly thirty last year. Waldo among them."

"Our numbers have fallen below two hundred," Kean dolefully added.

The news stuck Gunnar hard. "Thirty," he murmured in distress.

Jann placed a hand on Gunnar's shoulder. "There will be many familiar faces missing."

Milos's shout caught everyone's attention. "Let us hear from Gunnar about the wonders worked by the Almighty in Eldar."

Gunnar's disturbed glance shifted from Milos to Jann, to which Jann said, "We need to hear good news, brother."

Gunnar joined Milos. Over the next hour, he recounted the journey from leaving Kranston to Axel's coronation. Several interruptions of cheering and banging tankards on the table caused him to pause. He occasionally referred to Nollen, who offered brief statements or explanations about his involvement. However, Nollen knew Gunnar well enough to notice a disturbance behind his gestures and encouraging tone.

"Thus, I have returned as promised," Gunnar concluded.

To this, the loudest and longest banging of tankards and cheers.

Milos spoke, "At dawn, we gather on the commons to offer praise and thanksgiving to the Almighty. Now, off to your homes with warm hearts and filled bellies."

"You and Nollen will stay with us," said Jann to Gunnar.

Gunnar flashed a plaintive smile. "I'll be along after I see to my horse." He exited the great room yet left his saddlebag.

Jann looked slightly perplexed. "Master Nollen."

"Please, just call me Nollen." He picked up both saddlebags to accompany Jann, Meryl, and the rest of the family.

They walked a short distance from the great room, deeper into the interior of Kranston. Kean and his family broke off, as did Arnie, his wife, and their young family. Inside a hillside hovel, Nollen was pleasantly surprised by the cozy comfort. It contained a small hearth for family cooking and warmth, a few chairs, table, and alcoves from sleeping.

"Over there." Meryl motioned to an alcove. "Our sons slept there before they married."

"Thank you." Nollen placed a saddlebag on each of the cots. "How do I get to the stables from here? I also want to look in on my horse," he added to their unspoken curiosity.

"Turn left and take the main path over a short rise. At the bottom, take another right. You'll need this." Jann have him a lit candle.

"Be careful. Not being familiar with Kranston, the footing could be hazardous," Meryl added her warning.

Along the main path, Nollen was greeted by others. He smiled and acknowledged them. Several paths veered off from the main one. On the rise, he noticed Gunnar headed toward him. However, he turned left. Nollen followed though a bit nervous when the candlelight showed a drop off to the right. He tried not to lose sight of Gunnar as he navigated the steps down. He stopped in time to see Gunnar enter what appear to be a wooden structure. Upon arrival, the portico resembled a chapel. Two torches flanked the door. Carefully, he went inside. Soft candlelight illuminated the interior. Gunnar sat on the front pew. Not wanting to disturb him, Nollen silently sat on the back row. His presence didn't go unnoticed for long.

"Did you follow me for a reason?" Gunnar first spoke then turned.

"Out of concern."

Gunnar faced forward, so Nollen moved to the front to sit on the opposite bench. "It must have been difficult to learn of so many deaths."

Gunnar sighed with lament. "Aye."

"I know what that's like." He continued when Gunnar glanced sideways at him. "Not just my parents. Heddwyn. My grandmother was among the ten who died during the first winter – before they completed the compound. Each time Ida and I feared what we would find. Disease, starvation, or discovery." Nollen's glance surveyed the chapel. "Kranston is better fortified than Heddwyn. Well, you know. You were there."

"Those Brethren were hardy people."

"So, are the ones here. Sadly, some things can't be helped." Nollen gazed steadily at Gunnar. "Answer me truly, is your mission to bring everyone here back to Eldar?"

135

"Aye. With the throne secure, it is time for their return."

"Why was it so difficult for you and Axel to tell me this before now?"

"What you don't know, you can't tell."

Nollen scowled in annoyance. "After all we've been through, do you really believe I would betray you and Axel?"

"Keeping you ignorant until the last possible moment, was for their protection." Gunnar motioned to the door. "You did the same when taking us to the forest compound."

"Aye," Nollen admitted.

Gunnar tugged on Nollen's shoulder to draw him to his feet. "Your pathfinding skills will be tested with such a large group. Now, come. We both need a good night's sleep."

Chapter 20

IN THE MORNING, NOLLEN WOKE TO FIND GUNNAR VERY SUBDUED. He sat at the table with Jann while Meryl prepared breakfast. Jann appeared pale, and Meryl sniffled. Curious, yet quiet, Nollen joined the men at the table.

Gunnar barely whispered, "A nephew and his family were among those who died."

In a sympathetic tone, Nollen asked Jann, "One of your sons?"

Jann soberly nodded. "My oldest."

"I'm sorry," Nollen murmured.

"There is more you should know before we gather," began Jann, soberly.

Gunnar's already somber countenance grew more dreary. "Such as?"

"You know we have elderly and infirmed among us. It has been determined that some will remain to care for them since they are unable to leave."

Gunnar stared intently at Jann. "Who?"

"Meryl and I. Kean and his family will return with you. Twenty others also agreed to stay, for a total of thirty-six." When Gunnar's frown deepened, Jann took hold of his brother's arm. "You knew about the plan to care for them."

"I didn't know who would remain."

"No one did until we cast lots. Which happened after you left."

Meryl set breakfast on the table. "The truth," she chided Jann, then told Gunnar, "We volunteered when Kean was chosen by lot."

"As eldest, Sonya is my responsibility, as are Olga and Bram," insisted Jann. "It's not a life sentence," he said in an effort to alleviate the tension. "When the inevitable happens, we are free to leave." He filled all the cups. "This should be a happy time! The king is restored, and exiles are preparing to return." He lifted his cup. "To Eldar!"

They mimicked Jann's salute. "To Eldar!"

Gunnar grinned after taking the first bite of breakfast. "You still make wonderful quarkchen, Meryl."

"Is that what these are?" Nollen said of the small fried pancakes.

"Have you never had them before?" asked Meryl.

"No," Nollen replied with a mouthful. "They are very good."

Gunnar used his fork to motion to Nollen. "He's from The Doane."

"Quarkchen is a favorite breakfast in the Freelands. It's made from potatoes, eggs, and flour. I add apples, onions, and parsley," she said.

"Oma used to smother them with sour cream," Jann said with gleeful reminiscing.

"Oh, and her pickled beets and cabbage." Gunnar smacked his lips.

"Those I've eaten. When visiting Stellan, that is," Nollen said. This made the others laugh.

After breakfast, Gunnar and Nollen headed to the stables. Joslin and Alydar appeared well fed and stabled along with the three draft horses used for plowing. Callie and Ajax greeted them.

"How goes it with the remnant?" asked Alydar.

"As well as can be," Gunnar replied with a hint of sobriety.

At the cryptic answer, Alydar nudged Nollen, who explained about the plague and the choice for some to remain.

"It doesn't change the plan," said Alydar.

"Of course." Gunnar picked up a brush to groom Joslin.

"How long until we leave?" asked Callie.

"Uncertain," began Gunnar. "There is a meeting on the commons shortly. We'll learn more then."

"He needed some time to digest the news," Nollen quietly told them.

Gunnar paused in brushing Joslin yet made no comment.

Lexi arrived. She wore a large, friendly smile. "I went to the house, but Meryl said you came here."

Gunnar put down the brush. "Is there something you need?"

"No. Just excited! As is Alicia." She sounded giddy.

Gunnar briefly chuckled at the enthusiasm, only to have it fade. "Excitement will be tempered by reality of the journey, I'm afraid."

Lexi squared her shoulders, and proudly lifted her chin. Her eagerness dramatically shifted to staunch determination. "I'm not afraid. I am *the* shield maiden."

Nollen regarded her swift transformation with fascination. The way she stood and stared at Gunnar somehow struck him as familiar. Not to mention, he never heard the term *shield maiden.*

Gunnar made a partial bow. "I didn't mean that as an insult."

Lexi relaxed. "I didn't mean to lose my temper." She held his arm. "Oh, Gunnar." Her eyes grew slightly misty.

Gunnar noticed Nollen's interest. "Should be time for the gathering."

"Aye, that's why I came to find you," she said.

Despite curiosity at Lexi's sudden shift in attitude and claim, Nollen didn't have the opportunity to inquire. The majority already gathered by the time they arrived on the commons. Milos waved for Gunnar and Nollen to join him in front of the crowd. Lexi found Alicia, who waited with Kean and his family. Milos called for quiet, and the crowd complied.

"The long-awaited day promised by the Almighty has arrived. Those scattered shall now be brought home. Many of you have never seen Eldar, yet your burns for our homeland. The plans our ancestors made will now come to completion. Final preparations begin today!"

The crowd cheered and shouted praises to the Almighty.

Milos smiled, yet waved for silence. "Sir Gunnar, and Master Nollen, will guide us on the journey. To those who remain, think not of this as an ending, rather a beginning! A new era in Eldar! Let us rejoice with a service of thanksgiving and prayer."

As priest, Milos conducted a brief service by reciting Eldarian praise and prayers of thanksgiving. The crowd added their voices in one accord at the appropriate time. They ended with a song of joy.

"Go! And to your tasks be true," Milos dismissed them. "Gunnar, Nollen, join me."

They left the common area and passed through the inner compound to reach the western extent of Kranston. An almost endless view stretched before them. Below, the river they crossed, appeared as a sliver of shimmering white. The Black Mountains lay just beyond the river. The peak upon which Kranston stood, appeared on par with the Black Mountains in height. A large body of water lay to the north.

"A trek through the Black Mountains with one hundred and forty-three people will be hazardous," said Milos.

"That's an understatement," Nollen muttered.

"What?" asked Milos.

Gunnar clapped Nollen's shoulder. "Axel trusts Nollen as a consummate pathfinder."

When Nollen went to object, Gunnar's grip increased, so he focused on the horizon. "What body of water of is that?"

"Andros Sea. Although, it is really an enormous lake, not a sea in the true sense," Milos replied.

"Maybe we can find a path between the mountains and Andros."

"I don't know if anyone has tried to pass through Diabelek."

"Diabelek?" repeated Nollen, with curiosity.

"The Devil's Gorge, in Markitan."

With consideration, Nollen stared at the area Milos called "Diabelek". "If the gorge is anything like Ha'tar, it might be safer than a trek through the mountains."

"You can take us through there?" asked Milos, hopeful.

Nollen cocked his head. "The only way to know for sure is for me to travel it solo—"

"No! No time," snapped Milos. "We must all go else risk discovery by Panko, or worse—Sirin!"

"Easy, Milos. Nollen is being cautious, not refusing," said Gunnar.

"No, of course not," Nollen agreed.

Milos took a breath to calm down. "Forgive me. Emotions are high."

Gunnar nudged Milos. "See to the preparations. Nollen and I will plan the route."

Nollen waited for Milos to be out of ear shot. His voice a bit nervous. "I've never led this many people before. Mostly it's been me and Ida, or a handful at one time."

"You heard me tell Milos that Axel trusts you."

"I didn't know what I was getting into!"

"Axel did."

Nollen stared at Gunnar in sudden realization. His knees felt weak, so he sat on a boulder. His stunned gaze stared at the horizon.

Gunnar also sat on the bolder. "The *trust* you once questioned, goes deeper than you anticipated."

Nollen slowly nodded, his voice barely above a whisper, "Aye."

"What do you see when you look out there?" Gunnar gestured to the horizon. "Valleys? Mountains? Rivers? Or a trek home?"

"All of those."

"Let me put it another way. Do you admire nature or does your mind plot how you would travel the land?"

Nollen chuckled. "I determine how to get from one place to another. It's what I've done my entire life."

"All your ventures up till now, have been in preparation. Use those honed skills and *trust* the Almighty in the same way you are being trusted: complete, and without doubt."

Nollen stared intently at the Devil's Gorge. Soon, his focus shifted between the Black Mountains and the Devil's Gorge. He rose to walk along the plateau to study the horizon. Finally, he spoke.

"I can't see clearly what lies beyond the gorge, though it is the logical choice. Even the lower mountain pass we traveled, would be too narrow for such a large group. What I can do, is take short treks ahead with Callie once we enter the gorge."

"Then that is the plan."

"What about the river? Will those creatures let us cross like before?"

Gunnar shrugged. "I don't know." He rose from the boulder. "We'll make that determination once there. We should return to help." He began to head back to the center of Kranston.

Nollen hastened to catch up. "I have a question."

"Just one?" he chuckled.

"What did Lexi mean when she said she is a shield maiden? I've never heard that term before."

"Not surprising. Many things have been lost to antiquity. Or more rightly, the Electors sought to wipe out all knowledge of Eldar's past and heritage. The royal family, and their group, brought with them all the old practices, and passed them down from generation to generation. My family harkens back to the First Knights, personal bodyguards to the King. Shield Maidens are an ancient order of female warriors dedicated to the protection of the royal family."

"She spoke in singular with *the.*"

"There is a leader."

Impressed, Nollen said, "I don't know any female warrior. Oh, Ida and others are taught self-defense, not warriors."

"Everyone in Kranston learns how to fight. As soon as a child is old enough to hold a bow or wield a sword, training begins. Our lives depend upon it." Gunnar paused in their trek. "Fear not for what this group might face out there. Except for the very young, everyone is capable of defense should the need arise."

"That does make things easier."

Chapter 21

IN THE REVEREND'S PRIVATE CHAMBER AT SENER, IDA BUSILY rearranged the room. She instructed men to move the heavy pieces of furniture. Peace and motherhood transformed her from a wiry female, to one of vitality and certainty. Being ten years older, she always tended toward the motherly role in helping to raise Nollen. Yet in their covert activities, she yielded to his more assertive nature. Since marriage and birthing two children, she grew in her own self-confidence. At least in her mind, others thought something else.

"Mistress, that's not the way the Reverend prefers things." Mendel followed Ida to place small pieces as they were before her arrival.

"I know my Grandfather better than you. His bed would be against an interior wall, not right beside the window. He often sat in bed reading and praying while gazing out the window."

"The royal physician believes the night air is good for his ailments."

"He can get just as much fresh air opposite the window."

"Mistress—"

Ida stomped her foot in frustration. "Enough!" She spied Jarred in the threshold. She attempted to calm down. "Master Mendel, I realize you are trying to act in my Grandfather's best interest. However, love and lifelong knowledge guide my actions on his behalf. Please, let us stop quarreling."

Mendel too saw Jarred, and the warning glare directed at him. Despite reluctance, he agreed. "Aye, mistress." He past Jarred to leave.

"Is this the right location, mistress?" asked a man regarding the bed.

"Aye, thank you. I will take care of the rest." Once alone, she noticed Jarred stared curiously at her. "What?"

"You and Mendel really need to stop being so combative."

"Oh, is that it," she huffed. She began to make the bed with clean sheets and blankets.

Jarred joined to help. "You said it. You need to stop quarreling."

She glared across the bed. "You *too* know something is wrong."

"Not with Mendel."

She threw a pillow at him, which he caught. "Don't be contrary!"

Jarred went to the other side and took her arm to sit on the bed. "Being rough with Mendel won't gain any answers."

"Being nice hasn't work either," she refuted.

"Aye. Yet, I don't believe he knows."

"No one does! And that frustrates me." Her voice cracked.

Jarred held her hands so she faced him. "Dearest love, it may well be as the King and others have said, old age."

"No," she stubbornly insisted. "How can he have gone from being sharp-minded and strong to this confused man in a few short months?" She bit her lip to contain a sob of frustration.

"That is a question which puzzles me also." Axel arrived unnoticed.

"Sire." Jarred rose from the bed. "It is natural for Ida to struggle with doubt concerning Arctander's condition."

"Not doubt." She approached Axel. "Although I do not want to openly dispute you or Lord Ronan, in my heart, I feel this isn't old age."

"Nollen said the same before he left."

"Because we know him best." For a long moment, she and Axel regarded each other. Her expression confident, while his considerate.

"How would you proceed to find the answers?" Axel asked at length.

"Allow me sole charge of him. No Mendel, no Greta, no interference. Leave him wholly in my charge."

"You believe that will help?"

"Each time I feel on the verge of a breakthrough, when he is lucid in conversation, an interruption occurs."

"Mendel will be easy, but Greta brings his meals."

"Instruct her to leave the tray outside the door at specified times. I will fetch the food."

Again, Axel regarded Ida. She didn't flinch or retreat from his scrutiny. "You are that certain?"

"I am."

"What about Dinah?" asked Jarred. "A newborn needs her mother."

Ida smiled. "She will remain with me. Corey, is too rambunctious."

Jarred smiled. "I can keep him occupied."

Axel's observation shifted between them to finally rest on Ida. "Very well. I shall issue the instructions, along with ordering a prayer vigil to bolster your efforts."

"Thank you, Sire," she said with unction.

Axel held her hands. "May the Almighty grant you wisdom, whatever the outcome." He kissed her forehead then left.

Together, Ida and Jarred fetched Arctander.

"Oh? Are we in the right room?" Arctander asked, his gaze confused.

"We are. I rearranged it like your room at Far Point, and in Heddwyn," said Ida with reassurance.

Arctander wandered the room. He touched the bed and other furnishings. He smiled. "It does feels familiar." He stood at the end of the bed to face the opposite wall. "I like looking out the window."

"The fire is also to your liking. With a touch of pinecone in remembrance of the compound," said Jarred.

Arctander moved to the hearth and took a deep sniff. He exhaled a contented sigh.

"Sit." Ida gently helped him to the chair beside the hearth.

With smile upon his lips, he closed his eyes. "Roast venison."

"How did you guess?" Ida lightly laughed.

Arctander's eyes opened. "Have we some?"

"I ordered it for dinner. With roasted potatoes and mushroom gravy. Your favorite."

"And a small loaf of Ida's honey bread," Jarred added.

Again, Arctander smiled, and closed his eyes.

"Rest. It will be here shortly." She drew Jarred from Arctander.

"It is the most relaxed I've seen him since we arrived," said Jarred.

"I told you."

He kissed her cheek. "A wise woman. I need to get back to Corey. Should I stop by in the morning?"

"No. I will send for you, if I have need."

As Jarred went to leave, Greta arrived with a large tray with food. Another servant carried a second tray with bread and a pitcher. Jarred made a motion for Ida and helped her put the trays on a sideboard before he departed.

Arctander sat forward. "I smell the venison."

Ida escorted him to the room's small dining table. She fetched the food and sat opposite him.

"Shall I say the blessing?"

"Who is the priest?" he lightly refuted. He offered thanks. He paused in eating at hearing a soft cry. "What is that?"

"Dinah. She too needs to eat." Ida crossed to the bassinet and brought Dinah to the table. "Your great-granddaughter looks like my mother."

Arctander tenderly stroked the infant's cheek. "She looks more like you." He suddenly flinched in pain.

"Grandfather?" When he moaned, Ida put Dinah back in the bassinet. "What's wrong?"

"My head. Dizzy. Pain."

"I'll fetch your medicine." She acted quickly. Arctander grimaced when he drank the concoction. She removed his robes, and shoes in preparation for bed.

He slapped her hand away. "Enough! I'll sleep in my clothes."

Ida recoiled at the violence. "I'm here to help. Let me do that."

Wracked in pain, he rocked forward. She swiftly sat on the bed to hold him. "Dear Lord, grant him relief!" she pleaded.

Slowly, Arctander relaxed. "The pain is passing."

She helped him lie down. When she pulled up the cover, he seized her hand. His expression vexed, and apologetic.

"I didn't mean to hurt you."

She softly smiled. "You didn't." She kissed his forehead. "Sleep. I will be here when you wake."

Ida sat in a small sofa specifically placed between the bed and bassinet so she could tend both. Cushions were arranged for her to sleep comfortably.

For several days, the pattern continued. When inspired by the familiar, Arctander responded positively. Each day, Ida pressed a bit further to inquire about his daily activities in recent months. Yet, every time, pain would strike and end the conversation. She spoke twice with Jarred, voicing her frustration at the slow progress.

On the fourth day, a violent storm erupted. The bad weather aggravated Arctander. He paced the room. A loud clap of thunder woke Dinah and she started to cry. Ida tried to comfort the infant. The crying increased Arctander's agitation.

"Will you quiet that annoying infant!" He banged his fists on the table.

His outburst made Dinah wail louder.

"This is insufferable!"

"Grandfather, please, calm down. You're scaring Dinah more than the storm."

"I need to get out of here!" Arctander headed for the door.

"No!" Ida vacillated between soothing Dinah and stopping Arctander.

He couldn't open it. "Why won't this blasted door open?"

"It's locked for your safety. Now, please come sit." Ida grew frustrated at being unsuccessful in calming Dinah to deal with Arctander.

Angry, Arctander pulled at the gloves to remove them for a better grip. Being buttoned to the sleeve added to his vexation. He slipped the door handle between his hand and the glove to rip it off. The force sent him backwards when the glove tore from his hand and the sleeve. He fell hard to the floor where he lay stunned.

"Grandfather!" Ida put Dinah in the bassinet. The infant still cried, but Ida ignored her. Arctander lay semi-conscious. She rushed to unlock the door. "Jarred! Jarred! Help!" She hastened back to her grandfather.

Running feet came down the hall. Jarred and Mendel entered.

"Good Lord, what happened?" Jarred knelt beside Arctander.

"In a fit of anger, he tried to leave and became injured," she hastily explained. "Get him to bed. I need to tend to Dinah."

They did as instructed. "Fetch the doctor," Jarred told Mendel.

Ida held Dinah to comfort the infant.

Arctander moaned, unintelligible at first, then, "Ida … Ida"

"He wants you." Jarred took Dinah so Ida could sit on the bed.

"I'm here." She lovingly stroked his head.

He fought to focus. "What happened?"

"*Shhh.* Don't speak. Rest. The doctor will be here shortly." She again stroked his head.

Arctander's labored breathing of anxiety grew calmer under her soothing touch and words. When the doctor arrived, Ida gave a quick explanation. She moved so he could tend Arctander. As she went to join Jarred and Dinah, she stepped on something. A white object lay on the floor. She picked up a piece of a stone along with the torn glove.

"What is that?" asked Jarred.

"I don't know. But it fits in here." She replaced it where the button had torn off the glove. She held it up. It sparkled when struck with light.

"That's not an ordinary pebble used to make a button," said Jarred. Dinah grew fussy, so he turned his attention to his daughter.

"He needs quiet," said the doctor. "I'll speak with you after I tend him." He made a shooing motion.

In the hall, they were met by Axel. "I was told Arctander needed the doctor," he said with concern.

"He injured himself during a fit. He became so agitated he tore off his new gloves." She showed it to him along with the stone fragment.

Immediately concerned, Axel plucked the stone from her hand. "Where did you get this?"

His sudden intensity surprised her. "It was the button." She showed the place where it had been sewn.

Axel looked from the stone to the room. "Leave the child with a nurse and come to my study." He abrupted left.

Ida and Jarred hastened to comply thus not long in reaching the King's study. Ronan and Mather arrived a moment after them.

"It appears we might have found the reason for Arctander's *unusual* illness." Axel held up the stone. "A Palleteen diamond. At least a fragment."

Ida and Jarred stood dumbfounded with confusion. Ronan and Mather became warily guarded at the announcement.

"Are you sure?" asked Ronan.

"It passed Nollen's dagger test." Axel indicated a dagger on his desk.

"How did it come to be in his glove?" asked Mather.

Axel glanced to Ida and Jarred. "Do either of you know?"

Jarred shrugged. "Mendel told us Lord Leon gave him the pair after he lost the others." He used his hands to demonstrate. "The buttons connected the gloves to the sleeve so he couldn't lose them when he took them off."

"Leon!" Mather swore.

Ronan gave Mather a warning nudge when Ida became upset.

"I don't understand," she stammered.

"I will destroy this then explain," said Axel.

He tossed the diamond into the hearth and used the bellows to increase the heat. Once satisfied of the diamond's destruction, Axel told

Ida and Jarred the history of Eldar's battle with the Palleteens, and the diamond's magical quality. He further informed them about Sylvan's diminished mental state.

Overcome, Ida sat. "Why did the General react so about Lord Leon?"

Axel tried to be discrete. "Lord Leon is no longer at Court due to personal conflict. Whether he knew about the diamond hidden in the glove, is another issue. One we need to uncover."

Her confusion deepened by the cryptic answer. "Lord Leon has been cordial toward Grandfather, why would he wish him harm? If he knew."

"Again, his involvement requires an answer." Axel sought to change the subject, thus smiled. "Despite ignorance of history, your instincts about Arctander proved correct. His condition mirrored Sylvan of being slowly driven mad by way of a hidden diamond."

With tear-filled eyes, she asked, "Will he recover now that the source is revealed or end up void of faculties like Sylvan?" Her voice cracked with a sob.

Axel knelt to take her hands. "Tell me, at any time during his fits did you see a wild abandoned look in his eyes, as if reason had fled?"

For a moment, she considered the question then shook her head. "No. Despite the rage, he always complained of pain and dizziness. Except for this last time, I managed to calm him. Things familiar, made him lucid and peaceful."

"The influence may not have been as great," suggested Ronan.

"Aye," Axel agreed. "Sylvan's madness is a result of direct contact with Sirin. Arctander by a piece of cursed stone."

"Then he will recover?" Ida asked, a bit more hopeful.

"I believe there is a possibility. However," Ronan added with warning, "he may experience some lingering effects."

"I shall instruct the priests to perform a cleansing ceremony of his room, and a prayer service for recovery," Axel said with an underlying tone of firmness to Ronan. His attitude softened into a smile at Ida. "Your love saved him from a horrible fate. Return to him with hope." He helped her stand and gave her hand to Jarred.

When the door closed, Axel ordered Mather, "Find Leon and bring him to me for questioning!" Then to Ronan, "Interview everyone connected with both Arctander and Leon. And tell Irwin to bring me the armory records for review. Whatever his secret, it will be exposed!"

Chapter 22

MATHER RODE AT THE HEAD OF A SQUAD OF TEN SOLDIERS. With urgency, they made the normal six-day ride to Gilroy in four days to arrive just before sunset. Bardolf, five White Wolves, and Alfgar joined the soldiers on the outskirts of the town. Mather sent a soldier to fetch Sherriff Ezer and Captain Castor while he and the rest went directly to Lord Leon's home.

Mather banged on the door. "Leon! This is General Mather. Open the door." Receiving no answer, he ordered his men, "Break it down!"

Two soldiers used a nearby bench as a battering ram. The lock area splintered, and finally gave way. One soldier kicked open the door. Bardolf and the wolves ran inside ahead of the soldiers.

"Search every inch!" Mather shouted.

Shortly, Ezer and Castor arrived. "General." Castor saluted.

"Where is Leon?"

"He left yesterday. Heading south. I have men following him."

"General! We found fragments of papers in the drawing room hearth." The soldier held them out to Mather. "The damage is too extensive to read."

The papers disintegrated to charred ashes in Mather's hands. "Look for a safe. Tear down the walls if you have to."

Bardolf arrived. "We have a strong scent for tracking."

"Leon went south. Perhaps Alfgar can discover something from the Nicor. Head that way, and we'll follow in the morning."

Bardolf made a short howl. All the wolves hurried from the house.

"There is a way to bypass the ferry, so the water spirits might not have encountered him," began Castor after the wolves left. At Mather's displeasure, he explained, "After the *attempted* kidnapping, I ordered a search of the area. The men discovered a hidden passage under the falls."

"Between the wolves and unicorns, we'll track him," Mather declared.

Soldiers uncovered two small safes, one hidden behind a secret panel in the study, and the other under floorboards in the bedchamber. The bedchamber safe contained an ornate box with jewelry and a miniature painting of a woman.

"His wife?" Mather asked Castor and Ezer.

"Aye," Ezer confirmed.

Mather examined the jewelry. Many were damaged. He held them up to the lamplight. "Stones appear to be missing."

"If he plans to flee Eldar, maybe he took them to pawn instead of coins," Castor suggested.

"Possible." Mather examined the jewelry again. "These are unusual pieces, though definitely for a woman. Is there a master jeweler in Gilroy?"

"Aye, though he recently became seriously ill. So much so, he closed the shop and went south to recover in a warmer climate," said Ezer.

Mather scowled at news. "Then it will have to wait until we return to Sener for examination and identification."

"There is Jonas," said Ezer.

"The innkeeper?"

"Aye, and Nollen's cousin."

Mather stared out the window. Night had fallen. "I'll speak to Jonas. A good meal will be helpful before setting out." He pocketed the jewelry. "Sergeant, gather the men and head for inn."

At the corral, Bart and Abe quickly tended to the soldiers. Ezer and Castor accompanied Mather inside. A decent-size crowd gathered for supper. Sight of them brought Jonas immediately from the back.

"General! This is indeed a surprise."

Mather simply nodded. He told his men to enjoy a meal.

"You're in for a treat, General. We have boar and venison tonight."

"I would speak with you first." Mather drew Jonas to the bar for private discussion. He turned his back to the dining area. "Sheriff Ezer said that as Nollen's cousin, you have an eye for trade goods."

"I've been known to act as liaison during a trade from time to time," Jonas modestly replied.

Mather withdrew the jewelry from his pocket and placed them on the bar. "What can you tell me about these?"

Jonas picked up the pieces individually. "Some stones are missing."

"Aside for the obvious."

Jonas took an oddly shaped brooch and placed it next to the lamp for closer examination. Intrigued, he went around the bar, reached underneath, and drew out a small magnifying glass. Again, he held the brooch near the light, and turned to the back side. "It's not Eldarian."

"What?" said Mather, with surprise. "How can you tell?"

"Eldarian master jewelers stamp the back of their work for identification and appraisal. There is no such stamp."

Mather seized the magnifying glass and brooch to look where Jonas indicated. "Then what is it?"

Jonas shrugged ignorance. "It could be Bertrandian, Gorland, Markitan—"

"Markitan?" repeated Mather, intrigued.

"They mine gold in the foothills of the Black Mountains. That's what Nollen told me after he secured the trade treaty."

Mather studied the brooch. "What about Palleteens?"

"Possible, though I've not heard of Palleteen jewelry."

"They have diamonds."

"Aye. I'm just not aware of gold mines in Palleteen."

"Is there anything else you can tell me about these?"

"No, just they aren't Eldarian."

"That's a start," Ezer said the Mather.

"Aye," grumbled the general.

After a moment of heavy pause, Jonas asked, "Supper, General?"

Mather gave a distracted nod. He pocketed the jewelry. Ezer and Castor joined him at a separate table from his men. Sharla brought tankards of ale and was quickly dismissed.

"Why would Leon buy foreign jewelry for his wife?" Mather wondered aloud.

"An elaborate gift for her birthday perhaps," replied Castor.

Conversation ceased when Jonas and Sharla returned with food.

"Leon gave Arctander a set of knitted gloves that contained a Palleteen diamond chip." Mather held up the brooch. "Where do you think he got it?"

Both Castor and Ezer paused in eating. "Are you suggesting the missing stones were Palleteen diamonds?" asked Ezer.

"I believe it is a good likelihood. Confirmation will come when we find Leon." Mather pocketed the brooch to concentrate on supper.

"Forgive me, General," began a concerned Jonas. "I could not help but overhear. You may or may not be aware that Arctander is my uncle."

Mather took a drink to swallow his food. "Actually, now that you mention it. Being Nollen's cousin would make him your uncle."

"Has something happened to him?"

"He fell ill but is recovering."

"Because of the diamonds?" asked Jonas, a bit confused.

Mather made a careful survey of the room then motioned for Jonas to sit. He lowered his voice "Let's just say those *diamonds* possess a certain mystic quality that can affect a person. Fortunately, Mistress Ida discovered it before anything worse could happen."

Jonas' face showed relief. "And you believe the jewelry—"

Mather's hard glare and harsh clearing of his throat stopped Jonas' speech. "No more discussion. Be content that Arctander will recover."

Jonas visibly fought the impulse to dispute. He rose and gave a curt nod. "As you say, General."

Ezer confronted Mather. "Was it necessary to be so hard with him? You're talking about his family."

Mather cocked a scolding brow. "Too many ears in public. You can soothe it over with him later after we leave."

"I'm not to join the search?" asked Ezer, a bit taken back.

"Someone needs to remain and keep watch should those spies return. Castor will accompany me. We'll stay at the garrison tonight and leave before dawn to take the waterfall route."

They ate the remainder of the meal in silence. When Sharla approached to inquire about seconds or more ale, Mather declined. He signaled the sergeant for departure. To Sharla's surprise, Mather paid more than required.

"For food, and information," he explained. "Mistress." He flashed a friendly smile and left with Castor.

Ezer lingered to speak with Jonas. "The General is good man. A bit curt at times. Then again, he is a Freelander." He tried to lighten the mood.

"I remember him from the few times I visited Nollen in Sener. Can you tell me any more about Arctander?"

Ezer shook his head. "Not past what Mather said. I do know that Ida and her family remain safely in Sener."

Shock registered on Jonas' face. "Why?"

Ezer looked curiously at Jonas. "You don't know?"

"No. This is first I've heard of anything that sounds like trouble."

Ezer eyed the few patrons. "Where can we talk in private?"

"Upstairs."

Once Jonas shut the door to his private chamber, he accosted Ezer. "Explain."

"This goes beyond Leon's claim of attempted kidnapping."

"So? What does that have to do with my family?"

"I'm not sure of all the details. I only know that the King ordered Ida and her family to Sener for safety since Nollen is out of the country. That is probably when she learned about the diamond and Arctander."

"Where did Nollen go? And why is Ida in Sener? They could have come here to stay with us. Who is running Far Point?"

The questions came so rapidly that Ezer grew frustrated. "I said I don't have all the details. I simply follow orders. Somehow there is a link to your family, Lord Leon, and Palleteen diamonds."

Jonas glared crossly at Ezer. "That's hardly a satisfactory explanation."

Ezer haplessly sighed. "It's the best I can do. If I learn more, I promise to tell what I can." He gave Jonas a supportive clap on the shoulder. "For now, stay alert and pray. Wherever Nollen is, and whatever he is doing, must be very important. I'll stop by when I can, and don't hesitate to send for me if there is need."

"Aye. Thank you. I'll see you out." Jonas accompanied Ezer to the front door. He joined Sharla at the bar. "I'm going to Far Point after breakfast."

"Why? Is something wrong?"

"I need to protect our family's interest."

Shortly after full sunrise, Castor led Mather and twenty soldiers through the waterfall path. The deafening roar kept conversation to a minimum. Not until they rode far enough for hearing did Mather halt.

"Where does this lead?" he asked Castor about the river.

"It continues to the Great Falls. The Gilroy ferry serves as the normal crossing for anyone traveling south to Vanora."

Alfgar arrived. He tossed his head in greeting. "General."

"Any reports from the water spirits?"

"No. They have not sensed Palleteens. Only Eldarians have crossed the river."

At that moment, a white wolf came ran to the group. "General," the she-wolf began between panting breaths. "Bardolf sent me to find you. Two tracks have been detected."

"Two?"

"Aye. Another appears to have joined Lord Leon. Both headed south then split for a while to rejoin."

"Do they come anywhere near Far Point?"

"Within three miles."

"Lead on."

By late morning, Jonas arrived at Far Point. Five buildings made up the trading post; a house, barn with a corral, store, shed, and chicken coup. He observed no activity at either the house or store. The shutters of both remained closed. Then again, learning about Nollen and Ida, he didn't expect to find anyone there. Being family, he had a key, so taking stock of Far Point's condition wouldn't be too difficult. The constant squawking of chickens made him check on the animals first.

With harpys and jackals no longer a problem, there was no need to lock the barn. A beam with a latch still secured the doors, but no locking mechanism. To his surprise, the mules were fed and watered. Curious. Perhaps Ida arranged for someone to care for them while away. At the chicken coup, the eggs had not been gathered, so he proceeded to do so. Could never have enough eggs at the inn. He released the chickens to peck around the compound then went to the house. He set the basket of eggs on a porch bench to unlock the door and enter.

Despite being daylight, the closed shutters made the interior dark. He went to open them when someone attacked him from behind. The initial blow sent him sideways. He barely regained his balance when leapt upon. The force sent them crashing to the floor. A hard left to the jaw stunned Jonas. Unable to make further defense, hands jerked him to his feet. He swayed with dizziness from the assault. He squinted to shield his eyes when light came crashing through an open shutter.

"Jonas!" a startled voice exclaimed.

Jonas tried to clear his head and focus. He too surprised. "Leon?"

The man holding Jonas sent two hard jabs to Jonas' stomach then a solid punch square in the face. Jonas fell hard to the floor with a semi-conscious moan of pain.

"I thought you said Nollen would be here?" demanded Cordel. He still wore the Palleteen disguise.

"This is the most logical place since he's not at Sener," Leon argued.

"What about him?" Cordel kicked at Jonas, who woke with a start.

"Take him as hostage."

"He recognized you! We kill him."

Hearing the threat, Jonas pushed himself to his knees. He fell backward to avoid Cordel's attempt to grab him.

Leon stopped Cordel. "He's Nollen's cousin! We can use him as leverage to retrieve the diamonds."

From outside, came howling and shouting. Leon glanced out the window while Cordel stepped to the threshold. A pack of white wolves, a unicorn, and platoon raced toward Far Point.

"Soldiers!" Cordel shouted.

"Out the back!" snapped Leon.

Cordel drew his dagger to go after Jonas. "Can't leave a witness."

Despite pain and dizziness, Jonas stood to make defense. He swayed in an awkward side-step to elude Cordel. No use. In his dazed and injured state, he could not fight. He gasped in horror at the fatal blow.

Cordel raced after Leon. Two saddled horses waited behind the house. Leon's horse neighed in loud protest at the rough mount. Cordel went to grab the reins when an ear-piercing unicorn whinny sounded. He recoiled in pain. The horses whinnied in response, reared, and bucked. Leon was thrown. Cordel fell back into the house and narrowly avoided flying hooves. The horses ran off. Before either recovered, white wolves surrounded them with ears back, bared teeth, and growls. Six soldiers arrived with swords drawn.

Inside, Mather and Castor found Jonas. Castor knelt to feel for a pulse. He sighed in lament. "Rest in Gott's peace, Jonas."

Mather somberly frowned. "What was he doing here?"

Castor stood. "He probably came out of concern for family since you told him about Arctander."

Soldiers entered from the rear with Leon and Cordel in custody.

Mather assumed a formal posture. "Lord Leon, I arrest on the charge of high treason and murder." He motioned to Jonas' body.

"I didn't kill him. Cordel did."

Anger at the betrayal, Cordel lunged at Leon. The soldiers prevented him from attacking Leon.

Mather surveyed the manner of dress. "Cordel is an Eldarian name, yet you dress as a Palleteen."

"Halvor to be exact," Cordel proudly declared.

Mather sneered at the impertinence. "Bind them for the trip to Sener!" His tone grew subdued in speaking to Castor. "You and your men take Jonas back to Gilroy. Convey my deepest condolences to the widow. I'm sure the King will take a keen interest due to his relationship to Nollen and Ida."

Chapter 23

IN A DUNGEON CELL AT SENER CASTLE, LEON AND CORDEL WERE chained to opposite walls by ankle and wrist fetters. Cordel had been stripped of his Palleteen disguise. Disheveled and defiant, he suffered the worst injuries. Leon's marred face and soiled clothes also told of harsh treatment.

The jiggling of keys and footsteps made them look to the door. They blinked when the light of torches entered the dim cell. Leon was the first to recognize Axel, the king harsh and fixed in feature. Three soldiers, a jailer, Mather, and Ronan accompanied Axel. Mather and the jailer each held a torch.

Without a word, Axel signaled the soldiers to Cordel then jerked a thumb toward the door. The soldiers complied.

"I would do it again! Long live Sirin!" Cordel shouted, as they drew him from the cell.

The jailer closed the door behind him. Ronan and Mather remained.

Alex finally spoke. "You have one opportunity to make full confession and clear your conscious before meeting a traitor's end. I suggest you take it."

"Such an end is hardly incentive to speak."

Calmly, Axel reached into the pockets of his surcoat. He raised both hands. In one hand, he held the brooch, and in the other, the miniature painting. "You would tarnish her memory?"

A sudden sob caught in Leon's throat at sight of the miniature.

Axel regarded the painting. "She was beautiful. A man must have really loved a woman to go to such extent as to obtain an exquisite piece of Markitan jewelry."

Leon tried to contain a sob. "How did you know it was Markitan?"

"I didn't until you confirmed it."

Leon screwed his eyes shut to force back a surge of grief.

Axel sighed with compassion. He indicated the miniature. "I do not delight in this, as I too have loved. Acting in such a way as to dishonor a woman is unthinkable to me."

"She was the best wife," Leon's voice faltered.

"I heard Jonas helped you after she died. Yet, you are an accomplice to his murder."

Leon adamantly shook his head. "I wanted him as a hostage, not dead!"

"What you wanted doesn't change the fact that another woman is bereaved of her husband, and sons of their father."

Leon swallowed back discomposure. "I only wanted …"

"What?" Command crept into Axel's tone.

Leon raised his head to declare, "Revenge!"

The statement brought Ronan to stand in front of Axel to confront Leon. "On the king?"

"No. Arctander!" Leon's earlier defiance returned.

Perplexed, Axel moved Ronan aside to demand, "Why?"

"He discovered my wife's secret and threatened to expose her if she didn't recant. She took her own life rather than appease him!"

"That doesn't sound like Arctander," Ronan said to Axel.

Axel's eyes narrowed with suspicion. "Lord Ronan's right. Arctander would not threaten a woman."

"His piety overshadows common sense! Gott is not the only deity."

Enraged, Axel seized Leon by the throat. "What pretended deity did your wife worship?"

The choked words spat out the name, "Sirin!"

Axel's grip tightened. Concerned, Ronan grabbed Axel's arm. "Sire!"

Axel roughly released Leon, who gasped for breath. With realization, Axel looked at the brooch then held it up. "The missing stones were Palleteen diamonds. One *you* had sewn into Arctander's glove."

Axel kept intense focus on Leon. "Where do Cordel and the other fit into this? Why pretend to be Palleteens?"

A sadistic smile appeared on Leon's face. "Sirin is coming, and you can't stop her. We are already among you." He mockingly laughed.

When Axel stirred to fierce anger, Ronan pulled him to the door. "Jailer!" he shouted. He increased his grip when Axel resisted. "Sire, no!"

The jailer quickly appeared and opened the door for them to leave.

Sneering with intense anger, Axel ordered, "General, take him for immediate execution!" In bounding steps, he left the dungeon with Ronan at his heels. By the time he reached the top of the stairs, Axel breathed hard from exertion. He drew Ronan into an alcove where he attempted to calm down. "I'm grateful for your intervention."

"I confess, I too came close to taking action. What about Arctander?"

Axel answered with sobriety. "This news, and Jonas, will be a hard blow for him. Although, I am thankful for his recovery. Fetch him, Ida, and Jarred—only slowly. I need time to compose myself before breaking the news to them."

In the King's study, Ida wept. Jarred wiped his eyes, yet more concerned for comforting Ida. Arctander sat in a cushioned chair heavily wrapped in warm robes. He too grieved.

With tender compassion, Axel watched their reactions. "There was no easy way to tell you."

Arctander spoke under his breath, "Rest in Gott's peace, dear Jonas."

Ida took hold of Arctander's hand. "I must go to Sharla."

"Of course. My need of you is not as great as it was. Sharla and the boys ..." Arctander couldn't finish for sorrow.

"I can help Abe and Bart take over running the inn, and I'm sure Sharla will dote on Corey and Dinah." Jarred flashed a plaintive smile.

"I shall order an escort, and anything else you might require." Axel crossed to his desk to retrieve an ornately carved and painted box. "Please, give this to Sharla with my profound sympathy."

Ida took the box to open it. She gaped in surprise at the sight of gold coins with a sealed parchment on top. "Sire!"

"I realize no amount of gold can replace Jonas. However, those coins, along with the deed to the inn, and exclusion from taxes for the remainder of her life, may help to lighten her burden."

"You have been a great blessing to our family, Sire," said Arctander.

Axel warmly smiled. "The feeling is very mutual, as your family has blessed me with loyalty and friendship." He gently tugged Ida's hand to help her stand. "Ask General Mather and Lord Ronan for whatever you need for the journey."

When Axel escorted them to the door, he placed a discreet hand on Arctander's shoulder in passing. A sign for the High Reverend to remain. Once the door closed upon their departure, Arctander spoke.

"There is something you wish to tell, Sire?"

"I did not want to upset Ida further, and refrained from stating where the unfortunate incident occurred." Axel looked directly at Arctander to say, "Far Point."

"What would Palleteen spies be doing at Far Point?" asked Arctander, confused.

"An elaborate ruse of revenge by the person who orchestrated it all."

At first Arctander appeared stunned, then became angry when Axel explained his interrogation of Leon. Angry tears filled his eyes. After several moments, he found his voice.

"You were wise not to tell Ida. Let her believe the spies responsible."

Axel sat on the footstool beside Arctander's chair. "I wrestled with even telling you, for fear it might hinder your complete recovery. Still, I have questions about Leon's wife. What turned her to worship Sirin? Surely, Eldarians know their history."

"She was Markitan. That was part of her secret." Arctander shrugged. "I'm uncertain how or where they met, but upon discovery she became desperate."

"Leon said she took her own life and blames you."

Arctander frowned with annoyed regret. "No, her desperation came with the possibility of displeasing Sirin."

"Was she sent as a spy? By Montre?"

"I really don't know. I only became suspicious when she recoiled during a visit to Leon. All the other times, she was absent, so this was the first time we met. She tried to mask her discomposure; however, I experienced a cold chill." He grabbed Axel's hand with urgency. "The same cold sensation as when I encountered Dolus for the first time. The chill of *evil,*" he whispered with dread.

Axel firmly held Arctander's hand, as the High Reverend continued.

"I noticed the brooch she wore. In the shape of creature. That too gave me a deep-seeded chill. Afterwards, I prayed and consulted the Ancient Writings. In my research, I found a drawing that matched the brooch. A reptile water creature associated with Sirin."

Axel withdrew the brooch from his pocket. "This one?"

Arctander's eyes grew wide in surprise. "Aye. Where did you get it?"

"Mather found it, along with a miniature of her, during the search of Leon's home. The missing stones were—"

"Diamonds," Arctander said with understanding.

"Aye. What happened with his wife?"

"Armed with knowledge, I paid her an unexpected visit when I knew Leon was not home. I didn't want to upset him without first confronting her. She became violent and cursed me in Markitan, which is how I discovered her true nationality. She held that brooch and tried to invoke Sirin. I withstood her in the name of Gott! When she recoiled in such a grotesque manner, I realized I was not dealing with a mere mortal. I quickly left, lest harm came to both of us." He grew somber. "Alas, a week later, I learned of her death. Seeing him so devastated, I didn't have heart to tell him what I learned."

"Your compassion is understandable."

Arctander regarded the brooch. "Maybe if I had spoken to him, I could have mitigated her influence."

Axel pocketed the brooch. "You bear no responsibility for his actions." He took a brief pause before speaking again. "My friend, there is more to tell about Nollen's absence, for it is connected to what happened with Leon."

Arctander cocked a sly grin. "My body may be still weak, but my faculties are fully restored. If you recall, I was here when you dispatched Gunnar and Sylvan. Nollen didn't leave for *trading* purposes." He sat forward. "Since the time has come, we have work to do."

After drawing up a plan with Arctander for confronting possible invasion, Axel remained uneasy concerning Leon and his wife. Something more lay deep beneath the surface; something that could bring understanding to the entire situation.

He made his way to the royal archives located in west wing of the chapel. When the coup toppled Oleg, the High Priest managed to secure the most important ledgers and books regarding the royal family. He hid them in a secure vault beneath the altar. Since assuming the throne, Axel appointed Lord Cormac to oversee the scholars tasked with cataloguing the books and restore any that were damaged.

"Sire," greeted the brown-haired Ganel.

"Cormac. I want to see all books and papers dealing with the Palleteens." Axel took a seat at a long table to wait while Cormac complied. He cocked a wry brow when brought five, six, seven.... ten books in total. "Are there anymore?" he wryly asked.

Cormac sarcastic chuckled. "No, Sire."

Axel grinned. "Which is the oldest and which is the most recent?"

He placed them in front of Axel. "Older. Newer."

"Thank you. I don't want to be disturbed."

"Aye, Sire." He withdrew.

Axel became engrossed in reading, especially the older and newer books. He searched the archive desk for paper and a quill to take notes. Frustrated, he scratched through the notes, read more, and started again. Crumpled pieces of paper lay on the floor, with a dozen more heavily scratched. He sat back startled at the tankard placed in front of him.

"Ronan! I left instructions not to be disturbed."

"It's two hours past dinner. I thought you might need something to eat, or at least drink." He motioned to a tray containing cold roast beef, cheese, bread, and a pitcher of ale.

Axel noticed all the lamps in the room were lit and darkness outside the windows. "I hadn't realized the time."

Ronan sat on the corner of the table. "Have you found anything?"

Axel took a long drink of ale. He shook his head. "Nothing! At least nothing that would explain why Eldarians would pretend to be Palleteens. Or why Leon's Markitan wife worshipped Sirin when they claim Chika as the supreme goddess." He reached for the newer book. "In fact, the last entry dealt with Nandor's sound defeat of Baldon. There has been no indication of threat from Palleteen since."

"Perhaps due to the Almighty's curse."

Axel again drank. "Why now? After more than three hundred years of silence?"

"Maybe because of you."

Axel looked sharply at Ronan with an expression that required further explanation.

"The Electors didn't pose much of a threat outside Eldar's borders. They had enough trouble keeping the peace internally after making a pact with the Ha'tar and Nefal to help in the overthrow. Now, that the royal line has been restored, Eldar is united and stronger."

Axel focused on the book. "There is some truth in your assessment."

"But?" Ronan probed.

Axel placed the tankard down to sit up and confront Ronan. "You know the connection between the return and Sirin's ultimate fate. I had hoped sending Gunnar covertly would not arouse her. Alas, Sylvan showed otherwise." His eyes narrowed on the pages of the book. "Yet, there is something more that lies behind what is happening with the Palleteens. I had hoped to learn *what* from the ancient books. Alas, I have found no answers, only more questions." He shoved the book aside.

"Waiting is always the hardest part."

"Worse, when those you care about are in danger, and there is no way to help them," Axel droned.

Ronan touched Axel's shoulder. "Our plan will do that. Leave these and join us in evening prayer."

Chapter 24

FOR TEN DAYS, NOLLEN AIDED IN PREPARATION FOR DEPARTURE from Kranston. Each day, people inquired about the journey and Eldar. Questions included: *What is it like? How long will it take to reach Eldar? Are there more Brethren?* They even asked about talking animals. This especially interested the children, who delighted in speaking with Ajax, Callie, and Alydar.

Men hunted venison and boar to provide cured meat for the journey, and winter provision for those remaining. They also sharpened swords, daggers, prepared traps, and constructed new bows and arrows. Women used the lesser parts of animals to make sausage. They gathered root vegetables, and herbs were for cooking and medicinal use. Only the most essential items would be packed in carts drawn by the three draft horses. Caged chickens to provide eggs, and a few goats brought for milk and making cheese.

Gunnar organized the men into companies for guard duty, hunting, erecting tents, and other skills needed for the trek. Milos provided names for Nollen to consider as scouts or lookouts to aid him; Beno and Arnie among them. With these men, Nollen met separately.

Regardless of the weather, people gathered on the commons for arms practice. Nollen observed what Gunnar reported about men, women, and even children learning the art of self-defense and warfare. Most women used long bows, staffs, or daggers. A few wielded swords, like Lexi.

Nollen sat upon a rock to watch her practice with an older man. He didn't pull his blows, as they exchanged attacks. When he stumbled, Lexi disarmed him. He grinned and raised his arms in surrender.

"Well done. Your skills have vastly improved this past year," he said. "We're done for the day."

Lexi used the tip of her sword to flip up his sword. She spotted Nollen, who smiled rather quizzically. "You find something amusing?"

"No, actually impressive."

"You're smiling because I impressed you?"

He chuckled. "I've never seen a woman fight with a sword before."

She sheathed the blade. "Do women in Eldar not defend themselves?"

"Aye. Only the ones I know use a dagger or crossbow."

"Speaking of, isn't it time for you to give crossbow instructions?" She motioned to where five women waited, including Alicia and Lorraine.

"Oh? Aye." Nollen hopped off the rock.

She walked with him. At his inquisitive glance, she said, "I'm one of your pupils."

"Sorry, I'm late," he said to the others.

Lorraine wryly smiled. "We know why." She winked at Lexi.

Nollen slightly flushed. He reached for his crossbow and began to explain the weapon when Alicia interrupted him.

"We all know how to shoot a long bow," she said.

"There is a difference." Nollen demonstrated by shooting at a target without looking directly at it.

The women grew wide-eyed when the dart struck the center ring.

"The shaft of the crossbow tends to keep the arrow straighter, thus more likely to hit the target. Many factors disrupt the aim of a longbow. The slightest breeze can change the trajectory before the arrow is launched. Wind can effect a crossbow dart, but only after launch."

"We account for the wind when aiming," said Lexi.

"True, but the arch of the bow is still subject to shifting and warping over time. The solid construction of the crossbow provides more stability." He held up his crossbow to display the cocking mechanism. "A smaller crossbow is more easily loaded and fired compared to its larger counterpart, which requires a foot stabilizer and sheer strength to cock the bow." He moved to the roughhewn table upon which sat six rudimentary crossbows. "These are older, but just as effective. Each take one and we'll begin."

After some instruction, the women fired at the target. None hit the center circle, yet close enough to show some skill.

"Good, for the first attempt. Today, we shoot standing. Over the next few days, will use other positions that might become necessary."

As with other daily weapons practice, training lasted from mid-afternoon until sundown. Under Nollen's instruction they improved in speed and accuracy.

"Excellent, Lorraine!" he cheered, when she hit the center target. "The prone position is one of the most difficult to master."

"What is the hardest position?" asked a teenage girl.

"Shooting while riding at full gallop."

"Have you done that?" the girl asked, impressed.

"Aye. And at harpys, no less."

"What is a harpy?"

"The legendary bird that the enemy used to chase the eagles away," said Lorraine.

"I wouldn't say that exactly," Ajax countered. He sat perched on the wall to watch. "True, they made us flee to the Halvor Mountains, but we have protected the Brethren for centuries."

"I didn't mean to offend you," Lorraine said in apology. "Simply repeating what my great-grandfather told me."

"Can you teach us to shoot at full gallop?" one eagerly asked Nollen.

"I'm afraid we don't have the time for that. Besides, it requires one to be an expert rider before trying to shoot. Kranston only has a few draft horses, so I don't know if any of you can ride."

"Lexi and Alicia can ride," said the teenager.

Lexi flashed a confident smile. "I shot a long bow on horseback."

"At full gallop?" he asked, keen to her attempt to equal him. If Nollen learned anything about Lexi, it is her competitive nature.

She glared at him before admitting, "No."

The teenage girls fought to contain amusement at her thwarting.

"I am *the* shield maiden!" Lexi snapped at the girls. Angry, she dropped the crossbow on the table, retrieved her sword, and left.

"You shouldn't laugh at her," Alicia scolded the girls. They assumed a mildly chastised posture. "Or you, be so crass," she said to Nollen.

He bit back a reply. He glanced to the vanishing form of Lexi. "Training is over for today." He hastened to find her. At the rise, to the center of the compound, he called, "Lexi!" He ran to catch her.

She briefly looked back, huffed, and continued to walk.

"Wait. I want to apologize."

"Apology accepted."

"That doesn't sound too convincing."

She stopped to confront him. "Just because I haven't shot a harpy from atop a galloping horse, doesn't mean I can't!"

The outburst surprised him. "I never said that. I simply asked a question."

"It's the way you asked it, with an air of superiority."

"I'd say confidence more that superiority."

She gasped in outrage. "Confidence? Men think women don't have confidence in our abilities?"

Her continuing accusations confounded him. "I never said that either. My sister is very confident in what she can do."

The last statement began to quell her anger. "You have a sister?"

"Ida. She is ten years older." He fondly smiled. "More a mother when I was younger. After our parents died."

"Oh," she said with sympathy. "I too lost my parents when I was younger."

"I'm sorry. It explains why you stay with Kean's family."

She flashed an awkward smile. "They would be happy to see this day. Our return to Eldar." Her voice slightly cracked with emotion.

"I'm sure they were proud of you."

Tears immediately appeared. Overcome, she ran off.

"Lexi?" he asked, confused.

Gunnar arrived. "What happened?"

Nollen shrugged ignorance. "I'm not sure. We spoke of parents, and the next thing I know, she gets weepy and runs off."

"What did you say about them?" Gunnar asked with irritation.

His confusion deepened at the terse inquiry. "That her parents would be proud of her."

Gunnar's attitude softened at the response. "I know someone else who gets emotional when parents are mentioned."

Nollen understood. "Aye. It does stir deep emotions. I suppose I didn't think of that with Lexi."

Gunnar clapped Nollen's shoulder. "Lad, you have a lot to learn where women are concerned."

They heard female laughter and turned to see Lorraine.

"You're one to talk," she chided Gunnar. "Which way did Lexi go?" she asked Nollen.

Gunnar's low growl to the insult made Nollen speechless with cautious uncertainty. Rather than reply, Nollen pointed Lorraine in direction Lexi went.

"It will only take a few moments for him to teach you what *he* knows about women." She chuckled as she left.

"Gott, give me patience with that woman," Gunnar murmured.

"What did you say to make her so combative?"

"Nothing. Lorraine has always been that way. Many wondered how Waldo contended with such a woman."

"Maybe he didn't provoke her."

Gunnar laughed. "Waldo didn't provoke anyone. A mild-mannered man. She ran the roost. Overbearing at time. Yet, Waldo never spoke ill of her. In fact, he never spoke a cross word about anyone."

"So? Why take issue with her if he didn't?"

Gunnar looked thoughtfully at Nollen. "No reason, I suppose," he said at length. "She's simply irritating."

"Perhaps, because she is right. Women can be just as confident in themselves as we can."

"Go to the meeting. I'll be along shortly." Gunnar headed in the direction taken by Lexi. He found the women in a small natural alcove between dwells.

Lorraine sardonically smiled. "I knew it wouldn't take long."

Gunnar simply stared at her.

"Stay strong," Lorraine said to Lexi and left.

"Are you too going to scold me like Nollen?" Lexi asked with biting sarcasm.

"Did he scold you? He said the mention of parents upset you."

Lexi drew her sword and began some practice moves. Gunnar stopped her, so she faced him.

"He doesn't know."

"That's why you prevent me from speaking," she chided.

Annoyed, he took her sword. "You know the real reason."

Lexi frowned with frustration. "How much longer?"

"Until we safely reach Sener."

She snatched back her sword. "You don't want me to tell Nollen, but there are times he's so arrogant."

Gunnar chuckled. "The arrogance you scorn, I call confidence. And *that* confidence is what will get us home." When she rolled her eyes to the contrary, he led her to boulder to sit. "In some ways, you are both similar, being young and still learning your mind in certain matters. Yet, unlike you, sheltered in Kranston, Nollen fought his whole life to survive, and helped shield the remaining faithful. *His* parents sent the signal and died as a result."

Lexi became stricken by the stunning revelation. "He spoke of losing parents though not how."

"It is as sensitive a subject to him, as it is to you. His grandfather is the last high priest and is spiritual advisor to Axel." He watched her digest the news. "Nollen's confident arrogance was forged under great adversity. Though since tempered in peace, we need his skills. I trust him. Axel trusts him. So, should you."

Lexi simply nodded.

Gunnar grinned. "This is one time I agree with Lorraine. Stay strong."

Lexi laughed. "I'll tell her you said that."

He shrugged with indifference. "She won't believe it. Now, I have business with the elders."

Gunnar joined the men gathered in Milos's cave dwelling. This included Kean and Jann. Milos's wife placed tankards and a pitcher of ale on the table before she withdrew. Nollen and Gunnar made sixteen.

"The division of camp organization have been finalized," Milos informed them. "Ten individual encampments of roughly fourteen people with all necessary positions assigned for that group."

"The wagons are packed. Provisions and weapons ready," said a man

"There is excitement, and sorrow for parting," said another.

Jann placed a hearty arm about the man's shoulder. "Those of us who remain, gladly do so."

"All we need now, is to make certain of our trek before we leave in the morning." Milos sent a piercing glance to Nollen.

The young man's jowls flexed in anger. Milos made it a habit to goad him. "Nothing has changed," Nollen firmly replied.

"You have not determined how to cross the river without arousing the burkava."

Gunnar spoke. "No one can control the burkava. It is only by Gott's grace that the serpents guard the river to keep Kranston safe. You know that well, Milos."

Milos pursed his lips at the rebuke then stoutly nodded. "I'm concerned for my people, nothing else," he said to Nollen.

"I share your concern," Nollen said with unction.

"Remember, Axel trusts Nollen. As do I. With my life," stressed Gunnar.

"That should be enough affirmation not to question him anymore," Kean said to Milos.

"Aye," agreed Jann. "Since being here, Nollen has many made friends Myself included." He smiled with encouragement to Nollen.

Milos's attitude softened. "As I said, it is concern. Not lack of trust or disparaging of his character." He picked up his tankard. "This evening, we celebrate and rejoice, for on the morrow, we leave. To Eldar! To Gott!"

"To Eldar! To Gott!" They repeated the toast and drank.

"Fetch your families." Milos dismissed them.

Nollen headed for the western extent of Kranston. Milos's constant jabs grew tiresome. He appreciated Gunnar's defense, Kean's statement, and Jann's encouragement. In the short time here, he grew fond of Gunnar's brothers. They welcomed him with open arms, treated him like a member of the family, and expressed unquestioning trust in him same as Gunnar and Axel. *Trust.* The word echoed in his mind.

He ignored the setting sun and growing coolness of the evening to stare at the horizon. Despite Milos's testing, what disturbed him most were the expectations. Beginning tomorrow, everyone depended upon him to lead the way in an unfamiliar country. Startled by a hand on his shoulder, he jumped, and ready to make defense.

"Easy, lad," said Gunnar. "Didn't meant to scared you, but you didn't hear my call."

"No, I'm sorry. I was just thinking." He glanced back at the horizon.

"Thinking or fretting?" Gunnar wryly smiled. "I can spot worry."

"I guess I failed at hiding it." Nollen's jowls flex with discomposure.

"Only to those who know you. To the majority here, you are the confident knowledgeable guide sent by the King." Gunnar's grin turned serious. "You won't be alone, so don't bear the burden alone."

"I know I can depend upon you."

"Not just me. More importantly, Gott."

Gunnar's guiding hand drew Nollen from the overlook. They passed one of the many rock clefts. Unnoticed, Lexi emerged from the shadow of the cleft to stare intently at the departing duo.

Alicia arrived, unnoticed by Lexi. She saw the backs of Gunnar and Nollen walk away. Curiously annoyed, she confronted Lexi. "Are you spying on them?"

Startled, Lexi balked. "No. Not spying."

"Then what?"

"Considering what Gunnar told me against what we've seen of him."

"What did Gunnar tell you?"

"His parents died to send the signal."

Stunned, Alicia glanced in the direction of Gunnar and Nollen walked, who were now out of sight. "No wonder Axel sought him out when they reached Eldar," she murmured. "It fits the narrative of what was told us the night they arrived. It also explains his modesty when Gunnar tried to prompt him."

"Maybe. However, with the crossbow and pathfinding knowledge, he's extremely arrogant," Lexi spoke with sobriety.

"Axel sent him with Gunnar. For that reason alone, I trust Nollen." She flashed a prompting smile.

"You always see the good in people."

"I'm going to the chapel to pray of our journey, and for Nollen. That Gott grant him wisdom. Come with me." Alicia took firm hold of Lexi's arm. The initial tug told of one unwilling to accept a negative answer. Lexi fell in stride.

With the chapel empty, they moved to the front pew. In a humble position of head bowed, hands folded, and eyes closed, Alicia prayed.

"Dear Gott, we thank you for preserving us, and allowing this day to come. Keep us strong for what we must face on this a long, uncertain journey. Grant Nollen the wisdom needed. For the purpose he is here sent by ..." her voice quivered with delight, "Axel." She felt, Lexi squeeze her hand, and saw her warm smile. "I know all will be well, now that he is crowned." She touched the necklace

Lexi smiled. "Aye. Gott was gracious in that."

They turned when the door opened. Nollen paused in the threshold, obviously surprised at sight of them.

"I'm sorry, didn't mean to disturb you. I thought everyone would be at the celebrations," he awkwardly said.

"Nollen." Alicia smiled. She rose to take his hand. "Join us."

"Are you sure? I don't want to intrude."

"Come." She patted the bench beside Lexi, only Nollen chose to sit opposite them. "I assume you also came to pray for guidance and protection. We just finished praying for you." She motioned to Lexi, who blushed when Nollen sent her a quizzical look.

"Aye," Lexi admitted.

"Thank you. It is a formidable that task lies ahead. There is always apprehension of the unknown. It is nothing to be frightened about," he amended his speech when Alicia bit her lip in fear.

"You not very good at talking to women, are you?" Lexi chided.

With some sheepishness, he admitted, "In truth, I've dealt more with commodities and negotiating trades."

"Is that where your confidence lies, trading? What of pathfinding?"

Nollen grew offended at Lexi's provoking tone. "Since my youth, I have navigated Eldar in clandestine service of the Brethren and defiance of the Elector. Sir Gunnar and King Axel can vouch for my skill."

"Softly! Both of you," Alicia scolded. "We are here to pray for tomorrow." She motioned to the altar. "There lies our true confidence. In Gott."

Pricked by the rebuke, Nollen replied, "Aye. With Gott's help, we shall reach Eldar safely." His glance shifted to Lexi. "Whatever may come on this journey, I give you my word, I will not shrink from the duty entrusted to me by the King. I honor him too much to do otherwise."

Lexi staunchly met his gaze. "As the shield maiden, I give my word to support your endeavor. I honor the King too much to do otherwise."

A retiring smile appeared, as Alicia held Lexi's arm. She asked Nollen, "How long should the journey take?"

He shrugged. "Depends upon how far we can travel in a day. The terrain, weather—" He stopped at seeing Lexi's deep frown, and quick glance to Alicia. He amended his speech. "Roughly two to three weeks."

"Seems like a far distance to travel. When hunting or foraging, we've never gone past the river," said Alicia.

"I've traveled many places. Most topography is the same: mountains, plains, forest, rivers. The only difference are plants and animals."

Alicia tugged on Lexi's arm. "Time to join the feast." When Nollen didn't rise, she asked, "Are you coming?"

"Shortly."

After the door closed, he faced forward. Indeed, he came to pray, to seek guidance, and solace. He inwardly rebuked himself for his response to Lexi. The thought stuck him of how it was no different than Gunnar's reaction to Lorraine. Although, Lexi not as cantankerous. In retrospect, neither woman did anything to stir such a reaction.

Men think women can't have confidence in our abilities. Lexi's question echoed in his mind, followed by his statement to Gunnar; *Women can be just as confident in themselves as we can.*

"Why should confidence cause friction?" he asked himself. Then answered, "Why let it?"

He regarded the altar. *Confidence* now echoed in his mind beside the word *trust.* From his memory, he heard his Grandfather's parting words, *You must be strong! They need you to be strong ... Remain faithful, and call upon Gott, and He will answer.*

Overwhelmed, he leaned forward, elbows on his knees, and head bent into his hands. "Oh, Gott, confidence, trust, faith, and strength. I need all of them if I am to lead these people." He lifted his head, his eyes filled with pleading tears. "Help me not to fail."

Nollen became unaware of time, as he prayed and pleaded, sometimes out loud, other times silent. Tears freely fell, as he battled fear and uncertainty. Not until he felt the burden replaced by assurance of being heard did he stop praying. He wiped his face on his sleeve, stood, and turned to leave. Gunnar sat on the back bench.

"How long have you been here?"

"I slipped in when Lexi and Alicia left."

Disconcerted by the answer, Nollen said, "Then you heard everything."

Gunnar embraced Nollen. "If it's any encouragement, Axel came here for the same reason on the eve of our departure."

Nollen took a deep, composing breath. "I prayed I can be as confident as him on this journey."

"You will, lad, you will. Now, come. They are waiting for us."

Chapter 25

A T SUNRISE, NOLLEN STOOD ON THE RAMPART OF THE FRONT gate to oversee the assembly on the plain of Kranston. Gunnar and Milos shouted instructions for groups to take their assigned position. From this vantage point, Nollen memorized the order. He and Gunnar would lead them, followed immediately by Milos driving the first cart. Five groups followed Milos, then came Danor with the second cart and five groups behind him. Kean drove the final cart at the rear. Men walked on the outsides to protect the women and children.

When all were in position, Gunnar rode back to the main gate. Seeing the return, Nollen left the rampart to where Alydar waited at the gate. Jann stood with those who remained. Lexi and Alicia bade farewell to everyone at the gate. Nollen took a moment to observe. His conversations with both women told him they were orphans, and nearly inseparable. Alicia quiet in nature, kindhearted, and deeply faithful. Lexi could be brash at times yet devoted to Alicia. However, several incidents and cryptic comments made him wonder what mystery lies behind their relationship. A shield maiden and woman favored by Axel with an expensive gift. True, Gunnar's family and some others warmly welcomed him, but Kranston held many secrets tied to the past. Small wonder if the past is all they knew.

Arm-in-arm, Alicia and Lexi left to take their place in the departing assembly. Nollen flashed an encouraging smile when they passed him.

Gunnar arrived and dismounted. For a moment he and Jann regarded each other. Jann warmly smiled. "Don't think of this as a final parting. Remember, we will join you in Eldar someday."

The brothers embraced and lingered for several moments. Gunnar bade farewell to Jann's family. He hadn't words for his aunt, and Sonya saw the angst in his face.

"I take heart, dear nephew, that Gott has used you mightily in his service, and for the King."

Gunnar kissed her on both cheeks. Without looking back, he rode back to the group.

"Gott is with you, Nollen of Far Point." Jann heartily embraced him.

"You and Gunnar look out for one another," said Meryl.

"We will." Nollen rode to join Gunnar, who paused at Milos's cart. "There is a wider path for descent."

Surprised, Milos asked, "How did you discover that?"

Nollen widely grinned. "I spied a depression from the north wall. A good size gap in the landscape."

"I have lived in Kranston my entire life, and not noticed anything like that," said Milos in dispute.

"I'm certain you have seen it, only not recognized it as a pathway. In the height of summer, it wouldn't be visible. Now, bare limbs show its location."

Milos skeptically looked to Gunnar. The knight's confident grin made him grumble, "Let's hope you're right."

Nollen moved to the lead. When Gunnar joined him, he raised his hand in a signal to move.

Callie emerged from the forest. She trotted alongside Alydar to give a report. "The way is clear of predators. A few steep patches, but safe enough for the carts."

Ajax descended to hover and give his observations. "No signs of trouble on the horizon."

At Gunnar's askew side-glance, Nollen slyly smiled. "Since I was prohibited from scouting, I had Callie take advantage of the night, and Ajax the sky."

Impressed by the cleverness, Gunnar laughed. "Well played."

Once in the trees, Callie took the point with Nollen close behind. Ajax flew overheard. Although no actual foot path, the way through the forest proved wide enough for the carts and people to walk three abreast. At the few steep places, those driving the carts strategically applied the brakes to keep down speed.

Milos never said anything in regard to the chosen path. Instead, he cast cautious glances at Nollen. With short pauses to gather stragglers, it took an hour to reach the bottom where Nollen ordered a complete stop.

"Why are we stopping?" asked Milos.

"To rest. That was a hard climb down for the children. Also, to check the brakes and wheels," replied Nollen.

"We risk discovery."

"If we keep going without rest, we risk injury."

"How far can we travel each day?" Gunnar's question briefly ceased the argument between Milos and Nollen.

"Depends on the terrain, weather, and anything unexpected." Nollen added at seeing Milos's displeasure, "My hope is fifteen miles."

"That's too slow," Milos objected.

Nollen motioned to the people. "The size of this group also dictates our speed." When Milos remained stubborn, he pressed his point. "How many have traveled any distance outside of Kranston?"

"You know most have never left!"

"Exactly. They are not used to any lengthy journey. Muscles will ache, blisters form, and fatigue manifest in poor judgment."

Gunnar leaned forward on the saddle bow. His staunch expression matched his voice. "Milos, remember I told you Nollen is an experienced guide. Axel and I would not have survived in Eldar without him."

Milos glanced at path they just traveled. He reluctantly spoke. "You did get us down safely on an *unknown* path." He hoped off the cart to inspect the wheels and brakes.

Nollen scowled at the begrudging admission. Gunnar motioned for them to leave.

"Milos is a stubborn mortal," Alydar commented.

"That's an understatement." Nollen guided Alydar to the center of the group. He stood in the stirrups to shout, "Water, but no food. Our next stop, is the river." He then rode to the front.

"You may yet win Milos over," said Gunnar.

Nollen rolled his eyes. He waited fifteen minutes before calling for continuation. It took another half-hour to navigate the thinning forest and reach an open meadow. Ajax's cry drew his attention skyward. Callie's growl brought his focus down the earth.

"Trouble?" he asked Callie.

"A scent on the wind. I'll run ahead."

When Nollen glanced back to Milos, Gunnar said, "No need to alarm them until we know exactly what the trouble is."

Twenty minutes later, the meadow turned into the river basin. The water's edge came into view. Just to the south, Nollen and Gunnar spied Callie. She sniffed around the burkava carcasses on land.

Nollen raised a stiff arm with a clenched fist to stop. "Wait here!" he shouted back to Milos. He and Gunnar kicked their horses into a gallop. Both jumped off before Alydar and Joslin stopped.

"What happened?" Gunnar aske Callie.

"Unknown, though I smell the same predator that attacked us. Those the Domovay ran off."

Gunnar drew his sword to investigate the area. Nollen inspected the burkava. He observed tracks and scarring on the ground.

Milos, Danor, and Kean arrived. "What killed them?" asked Milos.

"Bushlik," replied Nollen. "They drug the burkava out of the water where they had no means of defense."

"How can you tell that?" asked Kean.

"Bushlik tracks. The burkava have only fins, not legs. The fins left scarring on the ground from the water to here. Dislodged pebbles and debris showed they tried to fight. A useless struggle."

"Have you encountered bushliks?" asked Danor.

"Aye. When they attacked us, the Domovay drove them off."

"Domovay? I thought they were wiped out ages ago."

"No, some survived."

Gunnar returned. "I found bushlik tracks further south. They disappeared into the water."

"They can swim too?" Milos asked with concern.

"Bushlik are reptiles controlled by Sirin."

Milos, Danor, and Kean balked with discomposure at Gunnar's statement.

"How are we going to cross the river now?" Milos demanded.

"Well," began Nollen with consideration. "Bushlik attacked us at night, and according to the Domovay, that is when they are most active."

"The burkava protected us, and Gunnar reports the bushlik are now in the river," Milos insisted.

"I said the tracks disappeared into the water. The bushlik could have crossed to the other side, and not necessarily still *in* the river," Gunnar stoutly corrected.

"With the burkava's help, we could have crossed the river safely, now the risk is greater," Milos countered.

"The entire journey is a *risk*," Gunnar refuted.

Nollen gazed studiously at a bend to the north. "From what I recall, the river briefly narrows at the gorge before widening into a mouth at Andros Sea."

"How far do you reckon it is from here?" asked Kean.

"A few miles, so we should be able to cross before nightfall. Of course, that depends upon the depth and current if it can be done on foot or we need rafts."

"The sooner we leave, the better." Gunnar nudged Nollen to return to the horses. Milos, Danor, and Kean followed.

They fielded some questions, and comments from the group, but when Milos briefly told of the plan, the crowd agreed and headed north.

Two miles later, Nollen dismounted beside the river. He found a good size limb then climbed an overhanging boulder to get a better view. He threw the limb into the river to check the current speed.

Gunnar remained on Joslin. Milos stood beside Gunnar to watch.

"Well?" asked Milos when Nollen returned.

"A steady current, not too swift. I reckon a hundred yards across. Now, to judge the depth." He mounted Alydar and found a way down to the river's edge. "I hope you're a good swimmer," he teased Alydar.

"Hold on." Alydar hurried into the river, which surprised Nollen.

At the halfway point, the depth reached Alydar's shoulder. Unexpectedly, Alydar grew agitated. He whinnied and breathed hard.

"What's wrong?"

Alydar didn't answer. Instead, he turned and headed back to shore. Nollen jumped down when Alydar shook off the water and stomped his front hooves.

"Did something happen?" asked Gunnar.

"There is uneasiness in the water," replied Alydar.

"Can it be crossed?" inquired Milos.

"Water came to Alydar's shoulders, so it will be too deep for children on foot," said Nollen.

"They can be carried. What about the current?"

"Tolerable for adults. Alydar's concern shouldn't be ignored." Nollen stroked Alydar's neck.

"He's a horse!" scoffed Milos.

"Unicorn!" Alydar rebuffed.

"I don't see a horn. We cross now." Milos went back to the group.

Nollen's harsh glare found Gunnar. "Why is he so contrary?"

Gunnar fought a sheepish grin. "Did I forget to tell you he is Lorraine's brother?"

Nollen hoisted himself into the saddle to pursue Milos. "Wait! We need to take precautions."

"No rafts, they won't be ready before sundown," Milos said.

"Ropes. Stretched between the shores as a guide and safety line. Hopefully, we have enough to make the distance. The smaller children can ride in the carts."

To this, Milos nodded. "Fetch the ropes," he ordered some men.

They tied ropes together then anchored one end to a tree nearest the water's edge.

"I'll take the other end across. Feed me the line as I go." Nollen then whispered to the unicorn. "Despite what you sensed; we must cross."

Alydar tossed his head in the affirmative. This time, he calmly entered the water. Once again, when they neared the center, Alydar grew nervous. Nollen heard snorting and felt the unicorn's uneasiness.

"Steady, my friend," he encouraged Alydar.

Alydar thrust forward, which nearly unseated Nollen. He managed to keep hold of the rope. He focused on staying in the saddle for the crossing. Near the other shore, Alydar stumbled and fell into the water. Thrown sideways, Nollen landed in shallows. Alydar bounded for shore. Nollen stood and snatched the rope before it could float away. The depth came to below his knees.

On the opposite shore, Gunnar cupped his hands around his mouth to call out with concern. "Nollen?"

"I'm fine! Give me more rope!"

"There isn't much left!"

"A few feet, so I can reach that tree." Nollen motioned to a dead trunk three feet to his left. He sloshed out of the water. Unfortunately, he didn't have enough rope. He ignored Gunnar and Milos to consider options.

"Alydar. Can you hold this?" Nollen indicated the rope. Alydar took the end in his mouth. Nollen unfastened his belt and wrapped it around the tree. He secured the buckle then removed extra twine he carried from a pocket in the saddlebag. He tied the twine to his belt. He tugged on the line with all his might. The belt and twine held. He moved to the water's edge to shout. "Send some men across first to help secure the rope should it be needed!"

Gunnar waved in respond. Nollen heard muffled voices from the opposite bank. Four men held the rope to cross the river. When they successfully reached shore, Nollen assigned two to the line, and two to start fires for warmth.

"People will be cold from crossing the river," he explained.

With Nollen coordinating on one side, and Gunnar on the other, the crossing of one hundred and forty people and three wagons took several hours. A few incidents occurred where some lost hold of the rope to be helped by others. The littlest children cried by the time they reached the other side, scared, and wet from splashing waves.

When it came to the carts, men aided the horses, and kept the wheels from getting stuck in the riverbed. The horses reacted with the same skittishness as Alydar. Several items fell from the carts and lost to the river. Milos crossed with the last wagon while Gunnar remained on the far side. Once Milos reached land, Nollen called to Gunnar.

"Grab the rope and join us!"

Since the knot had become tight from constant pulling, Gunnar cut the rope from the tree. He mounted Joslin and tied the rope to the saddle horn before they entered the river. Alert to the problems faced by other horses, Gunnar grabbed Joslin's mane. It didn't help. Upset, she reared, slipped, and fell backward almost on top of Gunnar.

Nollen stepped into the river when Callie leapt into the water. Frightened, Joslin hurried to shore. Nollen caught her reins.

"Whoa, girl! Easy," he soothed. His focus returned to the water.

Gunnar's head broke the surface, and he gasped for air. Callie grabbed the sleeve of his tunic in her teeth. She pulled while he swam with awkward stroke to fight against the current.

"Here!" Nollen gave Joslin's reins to the nearest man. He and Kean rushed to help Callie and Gunnar. Callie released Gunnar to them and made her way to shore where she shook off the water.

Nollen and Kean practically dragged Gunnar from the river. He collapsed to his knees with gasping coughs.

Kean knelt beside Gunnar. "Are you hurt?"

Gunnar shook his head since he coughed.

"Take him to the fire to dry off and get warm," Nollen told Kean. He patted Callie's head in gratitude. "I don't think I could have reached him in time." He joined the group with Milos. "We'll make camp and rest until tomorrow." When Milos agreed, Nollen went to find Gunnar. He sat by the fire wrapped in a blanket.

Lexi and Alicia helped tend those gathered around the fire for recovery. Alicia gave Gunnar a cup of steaming drink.

"You told Kean you're not hurt, but I've seen you swim better," said Nollen with a wry smile.

Gunnar swallowed. "Briefly stunned, that's all. How is Joslin?"

"Unhurt. Shaken-up, similar to the other horses. I believe Alydar's uneasiness dealt with the bushliks and burkava."

Lexi held out a cup for tea for Nollen. "You're still wet."

He drank. He did a sudden, surprised intake of air and coughed. "This isn't tea! What is it?" he asked in a strained voice.

Lexi, Gunnar, and Alicia laughed. "It is tea with Kirsch," said Lexi.

Nollen held his throat. "It burns."

"It's the warmth of the liquor," said Gunnar. He blew on the hot tea and sipped some more.

"I gather you haven't drunk anything stronger than ale," said Lexi.

"Wine, and some whiskey. Nothing like this." Nollen sniffed the cup.

"Don't be afraid," began Lexi. "It will warm you from the inside."

"It does have that quality." Nollen took a tentative sip.

"We only drink it during extreme cold," explained Alicia. "Sit." She gently tugged on his arm. She placed a blanket over his shoulders.

Callie moved to lay between Nollen and Gunnar.

"Thank you," Gunnar petted Callie. She licked his hand.

"I've never seen a friendly wolf before," said Lexi.

"In Eldar, the First ones were created to defend the kingdom," said Callie.

Lexi sat beside Nollen to continue speaking to Callie. "I've heard stories about the First Ones. Of course, living in Kranston, it sounded so fantastic. Almost beyond belief. You, Ajax, and Alydar have made those stories come alive. I look forward to getting to know you and the others better. To going home."

Callie rose to place a paw on Lexi's lap. "As the shield maiden, we are at your command, my lady."

Gunnar coughed, this time with purpose. He glared at Lexi.

She bashfully smiled. "I must help the others."

"What was that about?" asked Nollen.

"Clearing my throat. From the kirsch." Gunnar returned to drinking.

Nollen leaned closer to speak confidentially. "There is something you both know about her that I don't."

"There are certain *facts* which are closely guarded for security reasons. Much like when we first arrived in Eldar," Gunnar stressed his point.

Nollen looked to where Lexi handed out blankets and tea. "Very well." He absent-mindedly took a big drink of tea and began to choke on the strong flavor. "I don't know if I can get used to this."

"Children drink it in tea." Gunnar widely smiled.

Chapter 26

FROM A LARGE PLATEAU, SIRIN WATCHED THE GROUP NAVIGATE the gorge. Two bushliks hissed.

"Patience, my pets. We wait until they reach the middle of the gorge." Her gaze fixed upon the tiny form of Nollen in the lead. "Then, I shall truly test his resolve. With that, I can learn the identity I seek."

Below, Nollen's keen gaze continually checked the surroundings. Aside from the stone a red color instead of gray, the Markitan gorge did hold a sense of familiarity to Ha'tar. Both places were bleak with little to offer than rocky footing and high canyon walls. Not even weeds grew in the denuded ground. Stark gray clouds hung low in the sky, threatening to add precipitation to the difficulty.

Progress proved slow for the carts on such uneven terrain. Often men pushed from behind to aid the horse in maneuvering through the gorge.

To keep pace with the group, Nollen walked Alydar. Only when called for some purpose or to investigate a problem, did he ride. Since Milos watched him closely, he always returned to the front. He occasionally sent Callie with Beno and Arnie to scout no more than mile at a time. Ajax circled over the gorge with an occasional cry to remind Nollen of his presence. For three days, the eagle gave no warning, nor Callie sniff out a predator, nor did Alydar grow uneasy. Nollen took all these as good signs.

The confinement of the gorge made nightly camping difficult. They arranged the barest of comfort for the women and children. Men slept in the open. With no wood, meals consisted of cold sausage, cheese, and days old flat bread, softened by dipping in liquid.

Mid-morning of the fourth day, Arnie ran back to Nollen. "A landslide has blocked the gorge."

"How far ahead?"

"A mile at most. We just reached our limit when Callie smelled something. That's when we discovered the landslide."

"Halt!" Nollen shouted back to the group.

Gunnar walked beside Milos's cart, and quickly joined Nollen. "Why are we stopping?"

"A landslide. I'm going ahead with Arnie to investigate and determine if there is another path. Let Milos know." Nollen grabbed his crossbow and left Alydar to proceed with Arnie.

Along the route, Nollen took stock of the gorge. He spied several passages. Two appeared large enough to accommodate the group.

"Not sure where they lead," said Arnie to the interest.

"We'll determine that after viewing the slide."

They arrived to find Beno on top of the hundred-foot-high rock-slide. Callie continued to sniff along the base.

"What do you see?" Nollen called.

"Not much!" Beno tried to carefully move to his right. He slipped. He tumbled down the rocks where he lay semi-conscious. Nollen and Arnie ran to aid him.

"Beno?" Arnie asked with concern.

Beno began to come around and groaned. "My shoulder!"

Arnie carefully helped Beno sit up. He grabbed his left shoulder in great pain. He cried out when Arnie examined it. "Either broken or dislocated," Arnie told Nollen.

"Take him back for treatment. I'll scout those passages."

Nollen watched Arnie aid Beno until they disappeared around the bend. "Do you sense a predator or anything unusual?" he asked Callie.

"Faint traces with no clear direction."

Nollen examined the rocks at the base of the slide. Most felt solidly wedged. A few gave way and created a small slide. He quickly backed away to avoid injury. He glanced up. "Wish I could see what is on the other side."

"Not good to climb it after Beno's injury."

"Aye. Maybe one of the passages can give me a better vantage point."

Back at the location where he spied the passages, Nollen's brows furrowed in surprise. He made several treks back and forth. All the while, he peered at the canyon wall.

Callie curiously watched then finally asked, "Is something wrong?"

"There were two passages here. Now I only see one."

"Are you certain this is where you saw them?"

Nollen glared incredulously at the she-wolf. "Aye!" He pointed. "One led north, and other south. Now only the south remains. It heads into the Black Mountains," he spoke the last sentence with dread. "Tell Gunnar I'll be back by sundown."

Callie cut in front to prevent him from entering the passage. "You can't go alone."

"You smelled predators. The group needs the protection of your wolf senses. I'll be fine." He armed his crossbow.

Callie did a loud yelp that received an eagle's response. "Ajax."

Nollen smiled. "Go. Tell them to save me some supper."

He entered the passage with crossbow ready. He cautiously traveled, to scout the terrain, while keeping an eye out for trouble. The path appeared wide enough for the carts. Soon, it began a gentle climb into the mountains. The width remained. High rock walls gave way to a small plateau. He stopped to gaze down and determine if he could see beyond the slide. A fog settled over the area behind the slide. He tried to locate the second passage from this vantage point, but again, fog appeared.

"Strange," he murmured.

Suddenly, fog enveloped him. He began to choke, like when the fog engulfed them on route to Kranston. He struggled to breathe. Feeling faint, his crossbow fell from his hands. He collapsed to all fours and gasped for air.

Clawed feet appeared in front of him. His eyes grew wide in frightened awe at the beautiful woman/reptile creature standing over him. Her long moss-green hair reached past her waist. Scales formed a crown that arched over her head from ear slit to ear slit. The shape and color of her eyes resembled a reptile, yellow with narrow black irises. Smooth pale green skin was covered by a short gold chiffon dress.

She smiled, wide and mocking. "Hello, Eldarian."

Nollen could barely speak for choking. "Who …?"

"Who am I? Is that your question?"

He nodded, as he tried to breathe.

"To the Markitans I'm called *Chika*. To Eldarian, I am Sirin!" she loudly declared.

At the pronouncement of her name, he fell onto his back, the breath wrenched from his lungs. He stared in terror when she bent over him.

"You won't die. Not yet. I need something from you."

He took in a large gulp of air to ask, "What do you want from me?"

"An identity."

He groaned in confusion. The lack of oxygen muddled his mind. "What?"

She knelt. "You are escorting the enemy." She seized his throat. "I want to know which one it is."

"I don't know what you mean." His words came halting and difficult.

"Do not play coy. The last Eldarian who did so, suffered for his obstinacy."

Being deprived of air, Nollen fought to remain awake. Sirin's hand moved from the tight stricture of his throat to grab his face. The seizure made his eyes snap open. Her stare, searching and penetrating.

"I sense fear. Only not of me." Her iris slits narrowed the deeper she focused on him. "Fear of failure. A common mortal weakness."

Nollen trembled. His face twisted with fear.

"What do you see, Eldarian? Destruction. Death."

194

Visions of individuals in the group sprang before eyes. Some drowned in the river. Others crushed by a landslide. "No!" he cried. He screwed his eyes shut to block out the visions.

"Your fear will end in misery! I can help prevent that. Identify the enemy, and your confidence will be restored."

"Confidence," he murmured in repeat. "No fear. Gott, help me."

"What was that? I didn't hear clearly. Is it a name?"

His eyes snapped open to call out, "Gott, help me!"

Sirin screamed and fell backwards. She hissed in reptile anger. "A name!"

When she moved to lunge at him, Nollen again spoke, this time with boldness. "Gott is my confidence."

Sirin crumpled in pain. Two bushliks arrived. Nollen grabbed his crossbow, but the beasts didn't attack him. Instead, they protected Sirin.

In angry, painful words, she declared, "You will pay for your insolence, Eldarian! All will suffer until I find the one who hold my fate." She again screamed. A bushlik moved so she could grab it. The second came, and both withdrew with Sirin clinging to them.

For an anxious moment, Nollen watched the withdrawal. During that brief time, the fog lifted, his breathing returned to normal, and his mind became clear. Overwhelmed by what happened, he lowered his head in an attempt to regain his composure. He heard his name called and looked up to see Callie before she licked his face. Ajax landed beside him. Gunnar and Kean arrived in a rush.

Worried, Gunnar knelt. "What happened to you, lad? Ajax said you disappeared from sight, and for a brief time, Callie couldn't smell you."

Grim, yet befuddled, Nollen shook his head. Words failed him.

"Can you stand?"

Nollen shrugged. He held onto Gunnar to rise. He took a deep breath of recovery.

"Take what time you need. We'll wait," said Kean.

Surprised by what he saw, Nollen moved to the edge of the plateau. "It's back." The words forced from his mouth brought Gunnar and Kean join him, their curiosity visible. He pointed. "Passage. Hidden by the fog."

"What fog?" asked Gunnar.

Rather than directly answer, Nollen pointed their attention to the landslide. "Dead end. Beno?" The effort to speak, disconcerting.

"Don't know. We came looking for you when Callie returned," replied Kean.

Gunnar stopped Nollen from leaving. Their locked eyes: Gunnar concerned, and Nollen agitated. Silently, Gunnar released Nollen. Callie followed him from the plateau.

"What's wrong with him?" Kean asked Gunnar.

Gunnar stared after Nollen. He spoke when Kean touched his arm. "An unsettling encounter." He indicated the passage. "More than likely, he will scout ahead. Let's bring up the rest to join him."

Threat from the gray clouds turned into pelting sleet. Nollen rode in the lead. He ignored the weather to stare straight ahead. He didn't speak, rather nodded when addressed or waved to indicate direction. The path led north from the gorge yet continued longer than what he viewed from the heights. Although not hemmed in by high gorge walls, the path proved narrowed and hilly.

Three times he turned in the saddle to gauge the path in relation to the place of his encounter. Each time, he caught Gunnar's concerned expression. And each time, he abruptly faced forward. He trembled. Not for fear of Gunnar, rather gripped by panic of speaking. The encounter unnerved him to the core. Where he found the words and courage to answer and rebuke Sirin, baffled him. Since leaving the heights, he fought against sheer terror to maintain his composure. The final time of catching Gunnar's eye brought the terror to near overwhelming.

"Nollen?" Alydar questioned, but no verbal response.

Instead, Nollen gripped the reins. His panicked expression told of a desperate battle to maintain control. His breathing labored, and his whole body visibly trembled.

Feeling his quaking through the saddle, Alydar spoke with more command "Nollen!" This time, at the lack of reply, he cut sideways with a gentle buck. A move to break Nollen's transfixed state. It worked. Startled, Nollen adjusted to stay in the saddle.

Gunnar drew Joslin to quick rein, and seized Alydar's bridle. "Nollen!"

Shocked, yet befuddled, Nollen stared at Gunnar, his face pale.

"What is it, lad?" asked Gunnar in a low worried voice.

Disconcerted, yet unable to speak, Nollen shook his head.

Milos brought the cart to a halt. "Is something wrong?"

Gunnar released Alydar to reply, nonchalant. "Alydar shied at something." He observed the surroundings. Twilight began. "Over by the creek is a place large enough to erect a tent for cooking. Take the group there. We'll join you after we determine our course for tomorrow." When Milos appeared unconvinced, he sternly added, "Go."

Milos left without further comment.

Gunnar waved Nollen to dismount. With a guiding hand, he steered Nollen to the creek that ran along the base of the hilly terrain. He spoke in a discreet yet firm voice. "You can't keep silent, lad. We know something happened."

Nollen stared down at the creek. His gloved hands clenched tightly into fits. He flinched when Gunnar's grip tightened. This time he trembled enough for Gunnar to notice.

Mindful of the passing crowd, Gunnar stepped closer so his arm encircled Nollen's shoulders. In an urgent whisper, he said, "Fight it, lad. Don't let what happened to Sylvan happen to you."

The statement made Nollen's head snap up to regard Gunnar.

"Remember, I witnessed his encounter with Sirin."

Nollen fought to speak, his words halting, "Help … me."

Gunnar tightened his embrace of Nollen's shoulder. He bent his head. "Gott, hear me on Nollen's behalf. Release him of whatever wiles Sirin employed. The Brethren need him for this journey. Axel depends upon him, and me," he briefly paused, his eyes misty, "you granted me the privilege of a son, if not in blood, in affection."

A sob caught in Nollen's throat at the expressed sentiment. His trembling ceased. "Thank you," he said in a stronger voice. He straightened and took a deep breath to regain his composure.

"Ready to join them?"

"Aye."

Chapter 27

LATER THAT NIGHT, NOLLEN COULDN'T SLEEP. EACH TIME HE tried the disturbing encounter played over in his mind. Those eyes! Those reptile yet human eyes! Most of the camp slept, with only the night watch awake. Under the open-air tent, the cooking fire remained lit to provide warmth for the men standing guard.

Nollen left the natural hollow he and Gunnar shared. He pulled up the hood and gathered his cloak to protect against the night chill. Fortunately, the sleet stopped. Alert to Nollen's departure, Callie accompanied him. He made no comment to the she-wolf's action.

He briefly checked on the watch before he sat by the fire. Gunnar's prayer helped the terror to subside, but his spirit remained unsettled, and his mind, puzzled. In deep thought, he stared at the flames. The question *Who?* kept repeating in his ears, as if hearing Sirin's voice. His concentration grew more intense. Beads of sweat formed on his upper lip. Callie sensed his disturbance and placed her head in his lap. The action prompted him to whisper a quivering question.

"Gott, what is this about?"

Nollen abruptly sat back when something came in front of his face. It took a moment to recognize a handheld cup. More surprising was seeing—

"Lorraine?"

"Good morning, to you too." She chuckled.

"Morning? It's still night."

"Time to start breakfast before the others wake. Although, there is always hot tea near the fire for the watch." She indicated the cup.

He flashed an abashed smile before he sniffed the tea

"No kirsch. It's just tea this time," Lorraine spoke with light chuckle.

He took a sip and watched her move to join Lexi, Alicia, and three others in food prep. Lexi went to the creek for water. Alarmed, he tossed the cup aside. "No!" He ran to snatch her away from the water's edge.

Startled, she dropped the bucket, cried out, and held onto him. "What?"

Nollen's eyes scanned the water. "Danger."

She tried to follow his gaze and spied a small lizard. "From a lizard?"

"Bushlik. Go back." He shoved her harder than intended.

Lexi regained her balance and drew her sword. For an anxious moment, she waited with Nollen.

"I smell nothing." Callie walked beside the creek, sniffing.

"You shouldn't linger near the water," Nollen scolded Lexi.

"We need it for breakfast."

"Next time, draw it in the daylight."

Perplexed, Lexi sheathed her sword and grabbed the bucket. Gunnar arrived with Kean, and both ready for defense. Lexi sent Gunnar a prompting glance in regards of Nollen. He made a nod of understanding.

"Let's plan the route and leave the women to prepare breakfast." Gunnar beckoned Nollen. The barest shake of the head signaled Kean not to follow. "You didn't sleep."

Nollen simply shrugged.

"He asked Gott what this is all about," said Callie

Nollen scowled. "Sometimes your ability to speak is annoying."

"She's simply trying to help," Gunnar rebuffed.

Nollen sighed in lament. "I know."

"Why that question?" Gunnar asked

"Things *she* said," Nollen discreetly replied.

"Sirin."

Nollen just nodded.

Gunnar firmly gripped Nollen's arm. "Don't revert to the terror. That is her greatest weapon."

Nollen hung his head and droned, "She uses it well." Feeling Gunnar's grip tighten, he said, "I still don't understand it all." Once he spoke, the confusion came spilling forth. "She mocked my fear ... of failing. Tried to destroy what little confidence I have." He swallowed back a sudden rise of emotion. "She somehow created images, visions, right before my eyes." He motioned back to the tent where people began to gather for breakfast. "Vowed they would suffer because I couldn't answer her," he whispered in painful desperation.

"Steady, lad," Gunner soothed before asking, "What did she want?"

"A name. She wanted me to identify someone—"

Gunnar's hand covered Nollen's mouth. He sent a quick warning glance to the tent. He whispered to Nollen, "Gott and ignorance is what saved you."

Nollen removed Gunnar's hand, yet kept his voice low. "How?"

Gunnar turned his back to the tent. "She instills fear to gain intelligence. If one possesses what she wants, ... let's just say Sylvan is an example."

A gleam of comprehension registered on Nollen face. "He gave her the answer."

Gunnar nodded. "Insanity is the result of yielding to evil. Sylvan bemoaned his weakness in betraying our mission. I tried to hurry and get him back to Eldar in hopes that Axel or Ronan could help him. Yet I couldn't abandon my task. Since then, I have eluded her. Searching for a way to proceed alone." He flashed a wry grin. "Axel sent you."

With compassionate understanding, Nollen said, "You and Axel kept me ignorant for protection."

"Aye, lad. While also trusting you with a most vital task—escorting the person Sirin longs to kill safely home."

Nollen kept his steady focus on Gunnar. "Protection is the same reason; you won't tell who."

"There are over one a hundred and forty souls, whose safety depends upon us. The individual would not want to endanger them."

"Nor do I." Nollen moved to view the path. "We remain on a westerly course. Once we begin, I'll send Arnie ahead with Callie." He grinned. "Arnie has a natural awareness of nature and his surroundings."

Gunnar chuckled. "As a boy, we couldn't keep him contained to Kranston."

"That tendency is very helpful at present."

They joined the group when summoned for breakfast.

An hour later, the day's trek began. Since the trail narrowed, Nollen walked Alydar. Shortly after leaving the creek, Lexi appeared next to him.

"Thank you for trying to save me," she said. Although by her expression, she fought a smile

He smirked at the feeble attempt of sincerity. "You aren't good at talking to men, are you?"

She laughed at the sarcastic retort. "Perhaps, we both need practice." She genuinely smiled. "In truth, I came to ask if you are feeling better."

Nollen cast a quick glance over this shoulder to where Gunnar walked Joslin beside the horse drawing Milos's cart.

"Gunnar didn't tell me. I noticed it when you returned from whatever happened on the mountain."

Nollen swallowed back a rise of emotion. "I'm better. Thank you."

"I'm glad. We, Alicia, and me, were greatly concerned. We thought—"

His brows grew level at her hesitation. "Thought what?"

"It would impact our journey," she quietly admitted.

He suppressed an immediate prick of insult. Such concern was natural under the circumstances. Thus, he tempered his tone. "I won't let anything interfere. At least. what is within my control."

"You mentioned navigating Eldar in service of the Brethren. I suppose you faced many dangers."

"More than I care to count." He grew sober in reflection. "In those days, it was a matter of survival to move unseen. To keep our faith secret." Speaking the word *secret*, made him look studiously at her.

His intensity made her fidget. "Why are you staring at me like that?"

He broke off his regard. "I'm sorry. I didn't mean to make you uncomfortable. Merely struck by the thought of what we're doing."

"No," she stoutly refuted. "There is something else."

He didn't want to lie yet couldn't be forthright about a sudden uncertain suspicion. "Marveling at the similar circumstances. I thought my days of clandestine activity ended when Axel became king."

"My days haven't ended," Lexi chided.

He smiled with encouragement. "They will when we reach Eldar."

A plaintive return smile crossed her lips. "That is my hope. The hope of us all." She motioned to the group. "Tell me about Eldar. Has it changed since Axel became king?"

"Very much."

"How?"

Nollen thought about his answer. "I'm not sure where to begin. The changes have been numerous. Besides, I don't know if you can comprehend them without knowledge of life under the Electors."

"The Electors drove us out of Eldar!" she huffed in refute.

"Was your family among the last of the Brethren to flee like Gunnar?"

Lexi grew awkward. "Er, no. Long before that. However, I'm not incapable of understanding." When he appeared contemplative, she added, "It would be nice to learn something good about my ancestral homeland from a native. All we heard were tales of woe, and long held myths." She motioned to Alydar.

"I'm hardly a myth."

She chuckled. "Sight of you, Callie, and Ajax, have brought to life those cherished tales." She smiled in fond remembrance. "I loved to hear my father and grandfather tell the lore of the Unicorns. I can still hear father's voice, as he acted out the battle between King Kolyn and the invaders."

"The battle where Teva lost her horn," Alydar somberly said.

"You know about it?" asked Lexi, a bit eager.

"I was there. Teva was my sister."

She blushed with embarrassment. "Is that when you lost your horn also?"

"No. It happened during the battle to reclaim the throne for the Son of Eldar."

Lexi stroked Alydar's mane. "You and Teva sacrificed so much. How can we thank you?"

"Seeing the Son of Eldar crowned, and House of Oleg restored was enough."

She laid her head against Alydar's cheek as they walked. "I should like to see the fabled horn of Kolyn."

"It shattered after sounding the call to battle," said Nollen, soberly.

"It served its purpose," said Alydar.

"I thought I failed," muttered Nollen.

"You?" asked Lexi, with surprise.

"Axel trusted me to blow the horn at the appointed time. I didn't realize when that was until …" When his voice choked, Nollen forced himself to continue. "It all ended well."

She momentarily stared at him. "Sounds like Axel trusts you almost as much as Gunnar."

Nollen cocked a wry grin. "I wouldn't go that far. Although, he has honored me with his friendship. For that reason alone, I will do what is necessary to bring this group safely home."

Lexi deeply blushed and shied. "I'm glad you're feeling better." She made a hasty departure. On her way back, she made eye contact with Gunnar. She sent a quick glance forward to Nollen, then at Gunnar before she continued on her way. She joined Alicia and Lorraine to follow Milos's wagon.

"Well?" asked Alicia.

"He feels better," Lexi quietly replied.

"Why are you blushing?" asked Lorraine.

"Some things he said about Axel."

"Like what?" asked Alicia, anxious.

Lexi gripped Alicia's hand in a gesture of reassurance. "All good. It simply made me realize how much he trusts Nollen of Far Point."

"You doubted that?"

Lexi shook her head. "Not doubt. Some uncertainty."

"Of Axel?" asked Alicia, confused.

"Of Nollen," Lorraine replied. Her eyes keen upon Lexi.

"Duty requires I be certain!" Lexi slightly blushed. "I admit, he is a complex man. Different than any at Kranston."

"Gunnar mentioned about his parents and how hardships shaped his life when speaking of their journey for Axel to become king," Lorraine said.

Alicia linked her arm with Lexi, and confidently smiled. "Be at ease. We are safe with him."

Chapter 28

BEING THE CAPITAL OF MARKITA, MISKA WAS LOCATED IN THE central part of the country known as the King's Land. The four duchies surrounded it. To the east, Archduke Panko; to the north Archduke Tomas; to the south Archduke Luken; and to the west Archduke Boric.

Miska began as a fortress-city with the King's Castle located along the northern wall. As the centuries passed, and peace reigned, Miska grew beyond the walls. Small settlements eventually came together to form a large sprawling city. Daily business of commerce relocated outside to the city commons. The fortress became refitted for the royal family, and all necessary buildings needed to serve the King's Court. The second largest structure served as the Hall of the Archdukes, along with a council chamber for the provincial satraps serving under the archdukes.

A short, wiry, steely-eyed young man of thirty, Archduke Panko sat in an office located on the floor above the Hall of the Archdukes. Being early evening, lamps and candles illuminated the room. Panko shuffled through a stack of papers. In disgust, he tossed them aside.

Another older, white-headed nobleman worked at another desk. He noticed the abrupt action. "Something wrong, Your Grace?"

"The mines are not producing as expected. If a new vein is not found …" He leaned forward on the desk. His eyes narrowed. "Albric, we must keep this from becoming known, and used by others to weaken me!"

Albric let the spectacles drop from this face yet remain attached by a thin silver chain around his neck. With an open book in hand, he approached Panko. "I might have an idea, Your Grace."

"Hopefully, a quick one. I need to present the yearly report to Montre earlier than expected.

Albric replaced the spectacles to indicate a portion of the page. "In reviewing last year's inventory, I discovered several shipments stolen. The identity of the thieves remains a mystery."

"How will that help if the mines are not producing?" asked Panko with impatience.

"By shifting a few key numbers, and claiming more theft, the King, and others, will not suspect the mines are playing out. Hence, providing time to strike a new vein."

Panko reclined to consider the suggestion. Slowly a sly smile appeared. "I know the perfect ones to bear the blame. Domovay." Albric slightly winced at the statement, which prompted Panko to inquire, "Are the efforts of persuasion no longer working?"

"Unknown. We have yet to hear from Hobart."

Panko made a dismissive wave. "That doesn't matter. The Domovay are known to have been enslaved by the Palleteens, thus the perfect foil to enact revenge by thievery. The tales of a hidden, haunted forest adds credence to the mystery of the missing gems." At Albric's visible skepticism, he challenged him. "You find fault with this?"

Albric tried to be discreet. "Not fault, Your Grace. Merely concern at the growing ruse." He sat on the corner of the desk, removed his spectacles, and continued in a voice of warning. "Hear me, as confident of your father, and I hope yours also. You must contain the *ploy* to only the direst circumstance."

"You think discovery is not dire?"

"Discovery of mines producing less is natural. No one, not even Montre, would expect gems and precious metals to continue indefinitely."

Angry, Panko stood. The chair rocked at the sudden rising. "This isn't just about the mines!" He slammed his palms on the desk to lean toward Albric. "There is the treaty. Income from Eldar alone, has enriched the duchy to the envy of all." He slapped at the book. "That is threatened by lack of production."

"Send for Nollen of Far Point to renegotiate. He is extremely reasonable."

Panko sneered. "You don't understand, do you? Weakness of any kind will be our undoing." He waved an incriminating finger at Albric. "You altered the books. Your head will fall before mine."

His noble pride wounded, Albric squared his shoulders. "I have faithfully served you, as I promised your father on his deathbed. If my head falls, know you have betrayed his desire for you to succeed."

When Albric moved to leave, Panko intercepted him. "How dare you bring my father into this!"

Albric would not be intimidated. "Kristoff knew your weakness for riches could damage the family and endanger the duchy. He charged me to see that did not happen. I have tried to honor my promise with acts that go against my conscience."

Panko's lips quivered with anger. "I could have you permanently silenced."

Albric boldly retorted, "Silence me, and you lose everything." Seeing Panko's indecision, Albric shook himself free, and left.

In a violent burst of temper, Panko hurled the book across the room.

"Your Grace," said a new voice.

Enraged by the intrusion, he confronted the newcomer. "What is it, Captain Horst?"

Horst, a man of forty with a thin beard, took quick stock of the situation. He remained at attention, while his eyes moved in observation. "There is a report of a large group traveling through the province."

The information intrigued Panko and stilled his anger. "Military?"

"No, though some men are armed. More than likely to protect the women and children traveling with them."

"What more can you tell me about them?"

"They appear to be heading east before they disappeared into the Devil's Gorge."

Panko became surprised. "Have they come out yet?"

"No. I instructed a patrol to watch for them near the Andros Pass."

"By taking the pass, they become Tomas' problem."

"Should I inform Archduke Tomas of that possibility?"

Panko laughed out loud. "No. Let him learn it for himself."

Perplexed, Horst said, "We don't know their identity or intent, Your Grace. It would be prudent to inform the archduke of possible invaders."

"Invaders? You said they weren't military."

"No, however, with nearly one hundred and forty people, that large of a group can cause problems."

Panko considered the suggestion. At length, he spoke. "Continue surveillance until they leave the province. When that happens, I will speak with Tomas." He waved for Horst to depart.

Panko retrieved the book and sat at the desk to study the pages. He reached into an interior pocket of his doublet. He carefully pulled out a reptile shape brooch studded with diamonds and emeralds. Sight of it, renewed his vigor. He replaced the brooch then picked up a bell on the corner of the desk. He vigorously rang it while he shouted a name. A servant quickly appeared.

"Send for Baron Albric!"

A few moments later, Albric returned, and with Boric. Panko couldn't hide his displeasure at the sight of his fellow archduke.

"I'm too busy for pleasantries."

"I'm not here to exchange courtesies," Boric roughly replied. "We have a serious problem. Eldarian scouts have been discovered."

Panko's brow leveled at the news. "Are you certain?"

"Axel sent that upstart, Nollen of Far Point, in search of Sir Gunnar, who apparently is missing."

Panko's keen gaze shifted to Albric then back to Boric. "How does a missing person become a scout?"

"He never presented himself to me, as is necessary when crossing the border," Boric stoutly rebuffed.

Panko sent another sly glance to Albric before speaking again to Boric. "Sir Gunnar missing is hardly cause for concern. Nor indication of Eldarian scouts."

Roused to anger, Boric lashed out. "*His* arrival brought the wrath of Chika on my duchy! A home destroyed and two people killed. Tell me again, how that is not cause for concern!"

This news stunned Panko and Albric. Albric recovered first.

"Forgive me, Your Grace, but I fail to see the connection," then added at Boric's angry frown, "Though tragic and alarming, how did you determine this is an Eldarian scouting mission, and not truly a missing person?"

Boric's demeanor changed to disconcertion. His voice low and husky. "A *Baga* visited me!"

Albric appeared uneasy while Panko skeptical.

"Montre banished all witches," Panko disputed. He carefully drew his arm close to the part of his doublet where the brooch was hidden.

Boric grew insistent. "She told me the Eldarians' intent."

Troubled, Panko crossed to the window. "You believe her?"

"Ya! The wrath of Chika is a result of the Eldarians being here!" Boric took a deep breath to regain his composure. "I will speak of this at the meeting tomorrow. We must formulate a plan against invasion."

"What about Sir Gunnar and Nollen of Far Point? Have they been found?" Panko spoke over his shoulder.

"I sent Nollen back. As for Gunnar, I don't know where he is. And I don't care!" Boric roughly replied.

Panko turned from the window. "You should be concerned. If what this Baga said is true, and he is indeed a scout, he must be located."

"I'm sure Montre will order it after he is informed."

"You haven't told him yet?"

"No, I came to you first."

Confused, Panko asked, "Why?"

"Because she mentioned the Black Mountains, and you may have information I do not."

"Not about Gunnar, nor any Eldarians."

Boric swore. "Say nothing of this until I speak with Montre."

Panko simply nodded. A long heavy moment of silence followed Boric's departure. Finally, he said, "This changes your suggestion of sending for Nollen of Far Point. It also means we no longer need to use the Domovay. Rather, the Eldarian demand for ore and gems is to finance an invasion." After a moment of further thought, added, "That group maybe a useful scapegoat."

"Group?" asked Albric, puzzled.

Panko chuckled with scheming pleasure. "An *unknown* group Horst reported traveling through the duchy. *If* they survive the Devil's Gorge, that is." He gazed out the window at the dark horizon. "Tomorrow's meeting will prove interesting." He abruptly turned, fetched the ledger, and gave it to Albric. "Do whatever is needed to prove it is the Eldarians." Panko left.

Albric sat on the corner of his desk to digest the sudden turn of events. He felt a horrible shiver wrack his body when Boric mentioned a *Baga* witch. Now, Panko wanted to draw another country into his covert plans. He stared at the book. His lips moved to form the question his agitated mind spoke: *Kristoff, why did you bind me to such a pledge?*

When he sat in the desk chair, and flipped through the pages, his conscience and sworn duty waged war. He gritted his teeth and grabbed a quill pen to begin his task. Conscience stopped him from writing. He couldn't even force his hand to move. A drop of ink fell from the quill tip onto the page. He tossed the quill aside and use a handkerchief to carefully blot up the extra ink. Frustrated, he slammed the book shut. He had to clear his mind.

Albric donned a cloak, placed the book under his arm, and left the office. He crossed the courtyard to the guest quarters on the east side of castle. He told the guard at the entrance to have supper brought to his room. Being aide to an archduke, he had modest quarters. The room consisted of a nice bed, writing desk with chair, small table for eating, and a hearth. He frowned, as the hearth had been prepared with wood, but not lit. Moonlight and exterior torchlight helped him navigate the room. First, he placed the ledger on the desk, then found the holder for a match to light the fire. Fortunately, the dry wood caught quickly. He waited several moments for the room to warm before removing his cloak. Once comfortable, he lit several candles and took a seat at the desk.

Again, he hesitated when preparing to work on the ledger. He stared out the narrow window trying to still his unsettled mind. He didn't know for long he sat there when a knock at the door roused him.

"Come." He balked when a nobleman entered. "Carl?"

Carl chuckled. "Nice to see you too, Albric." He noticed the distracted attitude. "I gather you weren't expecting me."

"No, I thought you were a servant with the food I ordered." Albric managed to curb his initial surprise. "What brings you here?"

Carl removed his cloak and took a seat. "The same that brings you. Boric's summons of the Archduke Council."

Albric chewed on his lower lip in a nervous action.

Carl noticed yet opted for a neutral question. "How is Rebah?"

"Uh? She's well. She sends her regards, and a special treat. I have it in my luggage." He rose to open the wardrobe.

Carl smiled. "It wouldn't be honey candy, would it?"

Albric returned with a small tin.

Carl eagerly opened it. He popped a piece in his mouth. "My sister always made the best honey candy." He sighed with satisfaction. He watched Albric return to the desk. The gloomy expression had not changed since his arrival. "What of you?" When Albric hesitated Carl added, "and don't say *I'm well*. I know you better."

Albric pushed aside the ledger to lean on the desk. "What can you tell me about Nollen of Far Point and Sir Gunnar?"

At first, Carl was surprised by the question, then surmised, "Boric spoke with Panko."

"Ya. His *theory* of an Eldarian invasion ... let's just say it caused Panko to reconsider some things." Albric tried to be discrete.

Carl closely regarded Albric. "Things that disturb you?"

"It doesn't make sense!" Albric kept his agitated voice low.

Carl shook his head in agreement. "No, it doesn't. I tried to reason with Boric that King Axel wouldn't consider such a thing, but—"

"The Baga."

"Ya. Even Nollen of Far Point claimed ignorance of any trouble."

"You spoke with him, too?"

"Briefly, at the end of the audience with Boric. Frankly, I believe him. I also warned him. Find Sir Gunnar and leave Markita quickly." With curious understanding, he looked to his brother-in-law. "What is it Panko wants you to do based upon this information?"

Albric sat back in the chair. His brows leveled with discomposure. "I fear even telling you."

"We are family," Carl tried to reassure him.

"That could make it worse! I'm already bound."

Carl moved his chair closer to the table. "If you are bound, then when the matter is exposed, Rebah will be in danger. No one would believe a wife ignorant of her husband's dealings. Confide in me, and I might be able to help—*if* that time comes." He took strong hold of Albric's arm. "You can trust me to the death."

Albric rose and carefully bolted the door. He moved his chair right beside Carl. "First, tell me what you know of the Palleteens and Domovay."

"Palleteens were once a strong people, who posed a threat to both Markita and Eldar. They lived beyond the Black Mountains. It is believed they served the *witch* of the Mountains and enslaved the Domovay to work the mines. The Domovay rebelled and escaped. No one knows what has become of them, while the Palleteens have been quiet for over three hundred years."

"That is partially correct. At least about the Domovay rebellion. The rest has been greatly altered."

"How so?"

Albric gripped Carl's arm. "Swear upon all you hold dear to keep what I'm about to say secret."

"I swear."

Albric spoke so low that Carl bent over to hear. "The last time the Palleteens attempted to invade Eldar, the battle ended in utter defeat and near decimation. Only one hundred men of the ten thousand survived. King Nandor sent word to King Sigurd for help in preventing the Palleteens from ever threatening both kingdoms again. Sigurd sent patrols to capture the emperor and his remaining army, but the Palleteens managed to elude them. That was until they reached Panko's duchy. Wounds, illness, and starvation from the trek across Markita, claimed twenty-six more lives. Down to a scanty seventy plus men, the exhausted emperor pleaded with Panko's ancestor, Olin, for aid and protection. Making such an agreement could mean death. However, Olin was shrewd to the opportunity, and especially with a defeated emperor." He snorted with irony. "Panko inherited Olin's shrewdness. Or more rightly, his greed."

"What did Olin do?"

"He convinced the emperor not to return to Palleteen. Without an army, he couldn't defend his kingdom from Eldarian reprisal, so it would be better for them to integrate into Markitan society and save the last of his people. Olin promised to provide them everything they needed: homes, livelihoods, new names with forged papers. He even agreed to fetch their families from across the mountains. All in exchange for *one* thing." He tapped on the ledger.

Carl's eyes grew wide with understanding. "The mines."

Albric nodded.

Carl became confused. "But I still hear tales of Palleteens today. Soothe, even Nollen of Far Point spoke of them again threating Eldar."

"A ruse to keep the stories alive," Albric said in a breathy whisper. "And to keep the mines safe from confiscation if the truth becomes known."

Carl closely regarded Albric. "You are bound to keep this secret."

Albric became distressed. "Now, it goes beyond the occasional Palleteen and the Domovay story. Panko wants to blame Eldar because of what Boric said. This could mean war!"

Thunderstruck, Carl sat back a moment to digest the revelation. He then leaned forward, urgency in his voice. "You must tell Montre."

"That means betraying my pledge to Kristoff and exposing Panko!"

"Which means more; a pledge to one man or averting war to save many lives in two countries?"

A knock on the door and Panko's voice startled them. "Albric."

"A moment, Your Grace." Albric took a moment to compose himself. He went to the door, and carefully slid back the bolt to open it.

"Ah," Panko said upon seeing Carl. "Now, I understand why you returned to your quarters."

"We became engaged in a family discussion."

Carl took the cue. He stood with tin in hand. "A gift from my sister. Honey candy. Care for a piece, Your Grace?"

Panko selected a piece. "Oh, very good."

"Rebah's specialty is making candy." Carl donned his cloak. "Your Grace. Albric. Goodnight."

After Carl left, Panko asked, "Have you made the necessary adjustments?"

"I was in the middle of working when Carl arrived."

"I want to see the ledger first thing in the morning."

Chapter 29

PANKO AND ALBRIC CROSSED THE COURTYARD FROM THE GUEST wing toward the Hall of The Archdukes. The brisk morning air nipped at their faces. Albric carried a satchel that contained the ledger. Despite the continuing stab of a guilty conscience with each stroke of the pen, he managed to make the necessary adjustments. He felt some measure of relief when Panko appeared pleased by the changes. However, the sharp prick of conscience last night paled in comparison to the apprehension of possibly displaying the alterations for the King. He could only hope that would not be necessary.

Captain Horst hurried on an intercept course. "Your Grace."

"Horst." Panko did not pause in step when Horst drew alongside.

"Your Grace." Horst's tone of urgency and touch on Panko's arm stopped the archduke. He leaned close to say, "The *dwarf* is here." At Panko's rising color of ire, he added, "I have him contained, only he insists on speaking with you."

Panko's ire found Albric. "How is it he asks for me and not you?"

Albric appeared at a loss to answer.

Horst intervened. "There is time before the others arrive."

They followed Horst to an alley behind the kitchen. Hobart's head showed signs of new hair growth, while he had a healthy three-week beard.

"Keep watch," Panko ordered Horst. He then accosted Hobart. "What could a wretched Domovay have to say to me?"

216

Hobart's sheepish glance shifted from Albric to Panko. "He know."

"I don't know what you have to say," Albric swiftly rebuffed.

"Littles," began Hobart in distress. "Help. Sirin people take."

"Come to the point!" Panko snapped with impatience.

"Two Eldars back. Black Mountains go. I try stop, got this!" He pointed to his head.

"What does your bare head have to do with it?"

"I say, try stop. Horse live. This." He sneered.

Panko grew impatient. "It still doesn't explain why this should concern me."

"Your Grace," began Albric. "I think he means he did what was asked and received punishment as a result."

Angered by the implication, Panko snapped. "You didn't mention me or Baron Albric, did you?"

Hobart recoiled at the anger. "No!"

During a brief pause of consideration, Panko regained his temper. "How do you know they were Eldarian?"

"Gunnar Sir come before. Other Point of Far Nollen."

The information intrigued Panko and Albric.

Tentative at their pleasure, Hobart asked, "Littles home come? Please."

Panko feigned compassion. "I don't know where the *littles* are."

"Archduke know all. Must help!" Hobart's distress grew.

Panko flashed a sarcastic smile. "An archduke doesn't know everything." He tried to calm Hobart. "However, Captain Horst will help you leave Miska *unseen*." He sent a pointed side glance to Horst when speaking the word *unseen*. He continued to Hobart, "*If* I learn where the littles are, I will restore them." He abruptly left with Albric.

The interior Hall of The Archdukes matched the opulence of the King's Castle. Soaring arches of white marble were held in place by columns capped with ornate gold. Jewels were interspersed in the mosaic tiled floor and sparkled when struck by sunlight through the large stained-glass windows. An intricately woven carpet flowed down the center of the floor where it ended at a raised platform. A cushioned chair overlaid in gold sat upon the platform. Four more such chairs were arranged on the floor to face the platform. On either side of the hall, two enormous hearths glowed with blazing fire.

Even with roaring fires, the brisk morning chill could be felt close to the windows and doors. Panko refused to remove his cloak when a page arrived. He went to a hearth and took off his gloves to warm his hands.

"We appear to be the first to arrive." Albric gave his cloak to the page.

"Good. The way Boric acted yesterday, I feared he would talk before the meeting started."

"Why should that matter?"

"Because of our new plan," Panko discreetly replied. "It would be better to take the others by surprise than give them time to think." He leaned closer to Albric. "Especially after what we just learned." He turned his back to the fire. He nodded to the page, who came to fetch his cloak.

Archduke Luken arrived. A fifty-five-year-old man of few words with a stoic countenance. He shrugged the cloak off his shoulders for the page to catch. He went straight to his seat.

"His Grace is in a bad mood," Albric warned Panko.

"How can you tell? He barely speaks or smiles."

"He immediately took a seat."

Panko motioned to the door. Boric arrived with Carl. He moved from the hearth. "Boric, good morning."

"Panko."

Panko motioned to a page. The man took their cloaks. He held Boric's arm to escort him to the chairs. "A little nippy out this morning, but the warmth of friends is good any time of year."

Boric scowled with suspicion. "You are in a chipper mood this morning."

Panko smiled. "Why not?"

"I heard the mines are playing out. Almost done," Luken's grave voice caught attention.

Pricked, Panko fought to maintain his temper. "Rumors, nothing more."

"Then you found a new vein," a fourth voice entered the conversation. Tomas, archduke of the north. He turned to Luken. "That would explain his good mood. More money." He rubbed his fingers together to indicate coins.

Panko flashed a non-committal smile. "You look in fine health, Tomas. Speculation of your declining health must have been exaggerated."

Tomas' irate gaze fixed on Panko. Not much older in age, Tomas was more robust in stature. "Do I look ill?"

Panko's smile turned sarcastic. "Rumors. My mines, your health. Can't believe them, can we?"

An official herald stood before the raised chair. He held a large gold staff that he pounded on the floor for attention. "His Serene Royal Majesty, Sovereign of the United Duchies of Markita, King Montre."

Despite his age of sixty, Montre bore his bulky frame with surprising grace and dignity. The ornate crown covered the balding top of his head. Pampered white hair framed his face. Keen green eyes observed the bowing archdukes and the lords who attended them.

General Tilbic, supreme commander of Markita, accompanied Montre. Striking and distinguished features marked his countenance with salt and pepper hair, and beard. Keen dark eyes made quick assessment of any situation. While his face commanded attention, his neck and body grew thick with age at sixty-two. He assumed his position to the left of the throne.

"Be seated, my noble dukes," said Montre.

Tomas remained standing while the others sat. "Sire, I confess to being puzzled by the summons. Our annual meeting is not for another month. When questioned, the courier gave no satisfactory answer for such haste."

"The reason will become clear when Boric explains."

"Then, I assume Your Majesty is also perplexed?" Tomas recoiled at Montre's harsh glare. "Forgive me, Sire, I didn't mean to imply—" Tomas stopped, bowed, and took his seat.

"Boric!" Montre snapped.

Boric moved to the foot of the platform. "Most noble peers, I have uncovered a plot of possible invasion by Eldar."

Tomas and Luken expressed shock and outrage while Panko sneered.

"Why would Axel even consider such a thing?" demanded Tomas.

"Ya! We signed a treaty not long ago," added Luken.

"A treaty from which Eldar gained much wealth!" scoffed Panko. He rose to speak. "Everyone here thinks I have prospered from the treaty. Perhaps some, but," he heavily stressed. "The demands of Eldar for ore and gems has nearly depleted the mines."

"Why have not spoken of this before?" Montre challenged.

"Sire, I have my reports."

When Panko held out his hand, Albric fought to contain a visible shiver to give him the ledger. Albric managed to send a wary glance to Carl when their eyes briefly met. Attention became drawn to Panko when he spoke again.

"Granted, it is only preliminary since this summons was unexpected. However, the numbers show the truth." Panko gave ledger to Montre.

"That still doesn't answer the question of *why?*" insisted Tomas.

Boric told how Axel sent Nollen to find Sir Gunnar. He also spoke about his meeting with Sir Gunnar after an attack on Pietro by Chika. At the name of the feared goddess, Montre stopped reading.

"How many dead?" asked the King.

"Two. A home and farm destroyed, and the town battered."

"Sire, if I may?" began Carl. He proceeded when Montre nodded permission. "Nollen of Far Point knew nothing about Pietro or Chika."

"Is this so?" Montre asked Boric.

"Ya, Sire," Boric reluctantly replied.

"You speak as if he did," said Tomas.

Panko came to Boric's defense. "Nollen of Far Point is a shrewd trader. He might look the part of a gullible youth, but his mind is sharp for a deal and quick to offer a compromise. That, gentlemen, may well be why Axel sent him—first for the treaty, and now this ruse. He is a clever combination of youth and cunning."

"If all this is true, then how was the plot discovered? He wouldn't simply confess to Boric," said Luken, unconvinced.

"Someone even more clever," began Boric with a dramatic pause for effect, "a Baga told me."

The pronouncement brought an outraged Montre to his feet. "What?"

Boric hastened to explain. "Sire, please, hear me! I know your royal decree, however, this Baga told me for the good of Markita. People in my duchy have suffered the wrath of Chika because of the Eldarians. We have no defense against her, but we do against Eldar."

"The Baga told you to make war against Eldar to appease Chika?" asked Tomas, a bit confused.

"That is correct," a female voice came from the back of the hall. She emerged from the shadow.

"Sveta!" exclaimed Boric in surprise. He then spoke to Montre. "She is—"

"What are you doing here, witch? I could have you burned at the stake," said Montre, his voice loud and full of authority.

"Burning me will not stop the Eldarians." She turned deliberate eyes to Panko. "Ask Archduke Panko about the large group that left the Black Mountains, and are at this very moment, crossing Markita to reach Eldar."

"Panko?"

"It is true, Sire. Captain Horst informed me last evening. He doesn't believe they are military since women and children are among the roughly one hundred and forty. Nollen of Far Point and Sir Gunnar may be with the group. They entered the Devil's Gorge."

"How long ago?"

"A few days. My men are watching the Andros Pass."

"That would place them in my duchy! What didn't you tell me?" Tomas hotly demanded.

"I just did. Remember, I learned of it very late last night. Doubtful they traveled the gorge in the dark. So, they haven't moved very far."

In a loud voice, Sveta interrupted. "The group is a threat!"

"Women and children?" questioned Luken.

Sveta turned narrow, penetrating eyes on Luken. "Do not be fooled by appearances. They are not as harmless as you suppose." She lowered her head. She took a deep inhale of breath and her head snapped up. "Take heed! Destroy the Eldarians. Chika is watching!" She let out a whaling, unearthly scream so deafening that all collapsed in pain. When the scream subsided, Sveta was gone.

It took several moments to recover. When they did, Montre held onto the chair to stand. "General Tilbic, find this group! Bring me Nollen of Far Point and Sir Gunnar."

Greatly displeased, Tomas accosted Panko. "You should have told me immediately!"

"I needed to confirm the information."

"You didn't believe Horst?"

"No, I wanted to make certain of the connection between the group and Eldar."

Tomas frowned, still doubtful. "Despite your earlier argument, it doesn't seem like something Axel would do."

"Whether it does or not is immaterial. The group is here, Nollen is here, and Gunnar is here."

Tomas grumbled as he departed.

Outside, Panko and Albric were again joined by Horst.

"He is gone, Your Grace," Horst discreetly reported.

"Permanently?"

"Ya."

Albric swallowed back dismay at the confirmation. Panko noticed yet spoke to Horst.

"Help Tilbic find this group." Panko nodded for Albric to continue. Once in the office, he confronted Albric. "You object to the Domovay solution?"

"I believe it unnecessary. He acted as requested."

"He failed!"

"He was a father protecting his children. The same as another," Albric boldly said.

Color of anger immediately rose to Panko's face. "Lately, you speak too my frequently of my father. Take heed!"

"I do so because you seem to forget."

Panko slapped Albric so hard, the older man staggered a few steps. Panko clenched his fists at a cut lower lip caused by his violent outburst. He grabbed Albric, more to confront than help to stand. "I seek to protect everything my family has gained. You should consider your complicity to protect your family from reprisal." He roughly released Albric. "Go!"

Albric limped across the courtyard to his quarters. He paused to watch royal soldiers muster. By the time he reached his room, he collapsed into a chair. Whereas the assault hurt, his spirit gave way under the weight of guilt. He wiped the mistiness from his eyes before he pushed himself up from the chair.

At the wardrobe, he pulled out an ornate box from his luggage. He lifted the lid to reveal an embossed leather book. He removed it and sat upon the bed to read the elegant handwriting:

"*To His Most Serene Majesty Montre, and Regal Archdukes of Markita,*

The writings of Gott of Eldar is this day presented from His Most Royal Majesty, King Axel of Eldar.

May these words help to enlighten your minds and strengthen your hearts."

Exchanging gifts was customary to commemorate such events. Albric recalled Panko's vehement reaction when they retired from the ceremony. He threw the book and box into the fire. He stormed out mumbling angry unintelligible words. Albric managed to rescue it before any serious damage. He secretly kept it, as such a royal gift should not be discarded. Almost two years later, he felt compelled to read it.

Words of faith, trust, and courage struck him. These were not common in Markita when dealing with the goddess. Reading soothed his soul, while making him resolute in mind. When finished, he put it back in his luggage. He pulled out a small journal. He vigorously wrote in it.

The morning hours passed unnoticed. When a servant brought luncheon, he grunted acknowledgement yet kept writing. The food remained uneaten. Not until his eyes grew weary and his hand cramped, did he stop. He gazed out the window to refocus from close work. He reckoned it to be mid-afternoon. Strange that Panko didn't send for him. Still, he was grateful for the uninterrupted time.

He closed the journal and wrapped it with two strips of leather that buckled to seal it. He donned a cloak and placed the journal inside an interior pocket. He went to the office used by Boric and Carl. Carl opened the door in answer to his knock.

"Is Boric here?" Albric asked in a hurried, quiet voice.

"No. Why?" Carl barely replied when Albric pushed his way inside.

"Shut the door and draw the bolt."

Although curious, Carl did as requested. He moved to the hearth when beckoned. "Has something happened? You appear injured." He motioned to Albric's cut lip.

"More than that I can say." He withdrew the wrapped journal from his cloak pocket. "You asked me which was more important, one man or the lives of many." He held out the journal. "In here, lies my answer." When Carl went to take it, Albric seized his hand. "Promise me you will find a way to get this to Axel."

Stunned, Carl asked, "Not Montre?"

Albric adamantly shook his head. "They are under threat not us. The truth of *why* is here. Now, promise me."

"I promise."

Chapter 30

NOLLEN STRETCHED AND YAWNED. HE SLEPT DEEPER THAN HE had since Eldar. The smell of breakfast woke him. In the pre-dawn light, he made his way to the cooking tent. Two men joined the women in preparing the morning meal. He noticed Gunnar near Lorraine. He didn't hear the exact words exchanged, but Gunnar huffed and moved off with a plate of food. At his approach, Lorraine scoffed.

"Your friend is in his usual surly mood." She nodded in the direction Gunnar left.

Nollen flashed an uncertain smile. "I don't think he means any harm."

Lorraine heartily laughed. She picked up a plate of food, which he hesitated to take.

"May I ask you something personal?" When she nodded, he continued. "What caused the tension between you and Gunnar? Did he wrong you in some way?"

Instead of taking offense, she grew thoughtful. "You truly don't know about women, do you?"

Nollen immediately flushed with embarrassment. "Well, I wouldn't exactly say that."

Lorraine gently smiled, took his arm, and led him to a nearby log to sit. "You are an admirable young man, Nollen. Yet, for all your knowledge and experience, there are areas lacking. There is no shame to admit ignorance. I say that with all sincerity, not mocking."

Nollen ate rather than reply. His eyes darted about, yet no one paid them any attention.

"To answer your question; he has done nothing specific. It is simply a matter of personality." Lorraine glanced in the direction Gunnar left. He now sat with Kean and his family to eat. She returned her attention to Nollen. "Strong men tend to believe they need no one, and often find fault with men who do." A fond smile crossed her lips. "Waldo was mild in manner, temperate, and kind." She sniffled back emotions.

Nollen paused in eating at her rising upset. She grinned at his sympathy.

"I know many think I ruled the roost, and Waldo placated me. That isn't true. He needed me, and I needed him." She took hold of his arm to get his undivided attention. "Never be so strong, as to not let others help you. True strength comes in unity of heart, mind, and purpose. And that, my young friend, is what a woman truly wants. To be needed." She smiled and left him to eat.

Two hours into the day's journey, Gunnar drew Joslin alongside Nollen and Alydar. Nollen didn't immediately notice him. Not until he spoke did Nollen change his intense gaze from straight ahead.

"What nonsense did she fill your head with?"

"Who?"

Gunnar leaned over to whisper, "Lorraine."

Nollen snickered. "Sound advice actually."

"That's surprising."

"Why? Because you think she so dominated Waldo that she can't speak wisdom?"

Gunnar looked suspiciously along his shoulder. "You took her advice to heart?"

"She said something I hadn't considered before." He grew reflective in speech. "Forced to be self-sufficient since childhood, learning to rely upon others isn't an easy thing to do."

"Ah, trust," said Gunnar, with seeming understanding.

"No, strength. To be so strong, as to not accept help when needed. Some men hide behind it, while others more willing to be vulnerable." Nollen again stared ahead. "Showing vulnerability in the past could get people hurt or killed."

"It can now, if we're not careful," warned Gunnar.

"Strength also comes in unity of heart, mind, and purpose. So, she said. If it wasn't that way with my parents, Ida, and grandfather, I wouldn't be what I am today. That's what I've been thinking since breakfast." He nodded toward Gunnar. "Even you told me to rely upon you for this venture. Why do you not accept the same?"

Gunnar shifted in the saddle. "I accepted your help."

"Only after we argued."

"So, the conversation was about me."

"No, men and women in general. How strong men rarely let women know they are needed. You and Waldo are just the two extremes. The more I think about it, I see how I lean more one way than the other. Yet, in reality, it needs to be a balance. Like trust," he said pointedly.

Hearing his name called, Nollen drew rein. Arnie and Beno came racing back from somewhere ahead. Arnie paused to catch his breath.

"The gorge ends a mile further at the bank of the Andros Sea," he said.

"It's open plain westward, perhaps a day's journey to the nearest wood," added Beno.

Nollen made quick observation of the landscape. "Very well. Tell Milos to stop when he reaches the end. I'll scout ahead to find a safer path since we must travel in the open." He kicked Alydar into a quicker pace. Gunnar remained with him.

"Night travel?" asked Gunnar.

"Might be safer than broad daylight with this many."

They covered the mile quickly. Nollen drew Alydar to rein. He stood in the stirrups to survey Andros, along with the plain. He rode a bit further west. Again, he drew rein to take in the horizon.

Gunnar regarded the terrain. "That is one massive lake. I can't see a shore beyond the horizon."

"South takes us back toward the gorge. West is the way we need to go." Nollen pointed. "However, there appears to be a tributary or back water between here and those far woods."

Gunnar raise up to look in the direction indicated. "How can you tell?"

Nollen cocked a grin. "Trust me. It's there." He gathered the reins. "When the group arrives, have some men catch whatever swims in these waters. Fresh fish would be a nice change from sausage. I'm going to scout tonight's path. Ajax! Callie!" He motioned the eagle to fly and wolf to run ahead.

Gunnar returned to where the gorge opened to Andros. He dismounted, and left Joslin to graze on the sparse grass. He descended the gentle slope down to the water's edge. He removed a glove, knelt, and scooped up some water to sniff then taste. Satisfied. He climbed the bank to see Milos arrive.

"Nollen went on ahead. We'll rest here until sundown."

Milos hopped down from the wagon. "Why?"

"Safer to travel at night in the open to those woods." Gunnar pointed to the horizon. "The gorge and lake will shelter us for the time being. Don't break out a full camp, but we can fish for the midday meal."

Milos called to a few men to fetch a net and some fishing lines. He then walked about the group giving instructions about rest and cooking.

By the time Nollen returned from his scouting, the aroma of fish stew greeted him. He dismounted near the cooking fire. Most had already eaten.

"That smells wonderful."

Lexi gave him a bowl of stew. "There is skillet bread on the side table."

Nollen grabbed a piece of bread. He held it in his mouth until he found sat on a rock to eat. He coughed down a spoonful of soup. "Spicy. Like everything else."

Kean laughed, and slapped Nollen on the back of the shoulders. "Spice is good to warm you on such a raw day."

"I thought that's what kirsch is for."

"Maybe I put some kirsch in the stew," teased Lexi.

Nollen ironically chuckled. "Why am I not surprised?"

Lexi widely smiled and moved back to the cooking area.

Alicia sat beside Nollen. "Do not be cross with Lexi. She has a mischievous nature, yet a good heart. She simply wants to be certain."

"Of me?"

"Well," she began discreetly. His prompting glance made her admit, "Aye. Yet understand this. You are the first outsider to find Kranston since Gunnar and his family came almost forty years ago. The vast majority have been born there. Being cautious is part of our lives."

Nollen nodded as he ate. "When did your family arrive? With Gunnar?"

"My family came with the original group."

"I don't think I've met any of them."

Alicia somberly sighed. "I am an only child. My mother died when I was young. My father, a few years later. That's when Kean and Brita took me in. The same with Lexi when her father died."

"Explains why you two are nearly inseparable."

Alicia shied and lightly chuckled.

Nollen noticed that when nervous, Alicia fiddled with the necklace Gunnar gave her as a gift from Axel. "It's a pretty necklace."

She suddenly became self-conscience of her actions. "Oh, aye."

"May I see it for a moment?" When she hesitated, he said, "I am the Royal Commissary of trade goods. By looking at the mark, I can tell you the origin of the ruby and jeweler who made it."

"Really?" she asked, fascinated. At his confident smile, she removed the necklace to give him.

Nollen turned it over. "This was made by Gerard, a silversmith in the Ganel. His mark." He showed her the small engraving on the back. "All Eldarian jewelers have a unique mark for authenticity. Ganels are experts at intricately winding threads of silver around gems like this. I suspect the ruby is from a local mine." He curiously regarded the necklace. "Strange, I don't remember this coming into the office. I suppose Axel ordered it special." He gave it back to her.

"Do all goods come through your office?" She put the necklace back on.

"Normally." He returned to eating.

"Did you become Royal Commissary as reward for helping Axel?"

Nollen paused in eating. His expression that of pleasant reminiscing. "Aye. Though, I didn't seek the position. I was content that we won, and the Electors' evil gone." He took a spoonful of stew to cover momentary discomposure.

She placed a comforting hand on his shoulder. "Since being with us, I've come to appreciate why Axel sent you." She kindly smiled.

Nollen's brief surprise at Alicia's statement became interrupted when Milos approached.

"Have you found a way across?"

"Aye. If we start just after sundown, we should make the woods by dawn or shortly thereafter."

"I'll have the men pitch the torches."

"No!" Nollen said, with a strained voice of a hard swallow. "No torches. By my calculations, it should be a clear sky tonight, and full moon."

"I hope you're right."

"He's brought us safely this far," Alicia spoke in Nollen's defense. "Would you like some more stew?" she asked him. He nodded, so she refilled his bowl.

Once he finished the second helping of stew, he returned the bowl to Alicia. "Now, for a quick nap before we get started." He found a spot near the fire and laid down with his head on the bed roll. As usual, Callie laid beside him.

A loud growl woke Nollen. Callie stood with raised hackles and stared at the water. The sun hung low on the horizon, the red hues of twilight reflecting on the rippling waves.

"What is it, Callie?" he asked.

With sword drawn, Gunnar joined Nollen. They heard a man cry out in fear, then another man, followed by a woman's scream. Three bushliks rushed from the water. One snatched the man, who battled to escape the reptile. Others rallied to help him.

Nollen grabbed his crossbow. Callie snapped at the reptiles while Ajax dove. Two more bushliks emerged from the water, making five large reptiles on the attack.

Nollen fired several shots that inflicted only minor injury to the bushliks. Gunnar dodged a swinging tail and massive claws. He couldn't get close enough to use his sword effectively. Other men used spears to poke at the beasts.

"Torches! Get torches!" Gunnar shouted. A swipe from a tail knocked him off his feet. Callie leaped on the bushlik to distract it from Gunnar.

Lexi and two others waved torches. The bushliks hissed and spat at the swaying flames. Nollen dipped the tip of an arrow into the pitch of a torch, then fired a flaming arrow. Burned, the reptile retreated.

"We need more fire!" Nollen shouted.

Ajax flew higher. His ear-piercing eagle cry stopped the bushlik advance and made people cringe. Ajax repeated the call three times before he disappeared into the brilliance of the setting sun. From out of the blinding rays of twilight, he emerged. His entire body bathed in fire. He dove at the bushliks. His unusual screech produced a stream of fire that scorched the ground between the reptiles and group. He swung for another pass. The bushliks hissed in anger, at the stream of fire. At Ajax's second pass, the bushliks scurried toward the water. Only two made it alive. Three became incinerated by Ajax's fire.

People watched in stunned amazement. Ajax again did a high flight, accompanied by an eagle's cry. The sound returned to normal, as did his appearance. When he landed, he bent his head to where his beak touched the ground.

"Ajax?" asked Nollen, wary.

"I must rest." Ajax collapsed.

Nollen quickly cradled the eagle. "What did you do?"

Alydar lowered his head to touch Ajax. "He did what needed to be done. Transformed into a phoenix."

"Will he live?" Nollen asked, anxious.

"Keep him warm and let him rest."

"I'll fetch a blanket." Lexi quickly grabbed a small child's blanket. She helped Nollen gently wrap Ajax.

"Have the people assemble to leave. Bring the wounded," Gunnar instructed Milos.

"Hold him while I mount." Nollen gave Ajax to Lexi. Once seated, he held the eagle close to secure him in the blanket. "Take the lead when they are ready," he instructed Alydar.

Occasionally, Nollen glanced to see the direction Alydar took. He mostly focused on Ajax. Only by feeling breathing could he tell that Ajax slept. He stroked Ajax's head, and spoke soft words of encouragement.

After several hours, Gunnar pulled alongside. "How is he?"

"Alive. I didn't know eagles were capable of such transformations."

"Neither did I."

"It is a special ability granted by the Almighty for limited use under extreme circumstances," explained Alydar.

"I don't recall it during the battle with Javan's forces," said Gunnar.

"Artair and Ottlia did so briefly when fighting the dragons. You must have been otherwise engaged not to notice."

"True. I was more concerned with keeping Axel alive."

Nollen looked skyward. Clouds formed beneath the high full moon. He turned his attention to the group. "Who is in the rear?"

"Arnie and Kean," replied Gunnar.

"Help them to keep stragglers from falling too far behind or getting lost. The clouds may soon obscure the moonlight." When Gunnar left, Nollen carefully craned his neck to look ahead for Callie. He did not want to disturb Ajax. He saw the she-wolf trot back. "Well?"

"The way is clear."

"Distance?"

"Another four miles."

"Good. We should reach the woods well before sunrise." Nollen looked down at feeling movement. "Ajax?"

The eagle opened his beak as if yawning. "What time is it?"

"Near midnight."

"Oh, good. I can sleep some more." Ajax nestled back into the blanket.

Nollen softly laughed.

Two hours later, the group entered the woods. Callie led them a mile further to a hidden hollow.

"Let me hold him while you dismount," Lexi offered.

The eagle squirmed at the movement then settled down at seeing Lexi. "Water and food?" asked Ajax.

Nollen placed the water flask over his shoulder before taking Ajax from Lexi. "Callie, fetch a meal for Ajax." He found a suitable place to set the eagle on the ground. He cupped his hand to hold some water for Ajax to drink. The eagle gently used his beak to scoop up the water then titled back his head to swallow. He repeated the action four times.

"Rest. Callie will be back soon." Nollen rewrapped the blanket on Ajax.

Lexi knelt beside Nollen. "You're very gentle with animals."

He sat back against a boulder. "They are in my charge. I am responsible for their safety." He smiled when he looked at Ajax. "I also consider them my friends." He felt a snort of breath on his head when Alydar's soft muzzle ruffled his hair. "That tickles." He noticed the tenderhearted way Lexi regarded him. "What?" he asked with uncertainty.

"You are a complex individual, Nollen of Far Point. An expert pathfinder, self-professed trade negotiator, trusted by the king, with an arrogance natural to those qualities. You are also a compassionate and caring man. Almost a paradox."

"Paradox? Can a man not be confident and compassionate? Or are those traits only found in women?"

Lexi flushed with anger. "I pay you a compliment and you insult me?"

"A backhanded compliment when told I'm an arrogant paradox."

"I didn't mean that!" Lexi stammered, embarrassed. "I truly meant it as a compliment. I've never known anyone like you." She swallowed back discomposure. "In truth, I've not met anyone outside Kranston before. I'm sorry."

When she stirred to rise, he grabbed her hand.

"No, I'm sorry. I should not have reacted so rudely. Stay." At her indecision, he added, "I may need help feeding Ajax." She sat, but at her continued hesitancy he added, "Alicia told me that I am the first visitor to Kranston in decades. And, how because of that, you test me to be certain."

Lexi slightly flushed. "It's true, and I'm surprised she told you that."

"She said being cautious is a way of life."

"Aye." When he smiled, she said, "You're still a paradox." She balked when Callie dropped a dead rat in front of them. "Do we skin and cook it first?" she asked Nollen.

"No, I'll tear it into pieces for him to eat," said Callie.

Lexi leaned close to Nollen. Her expression fought becoming sick. "You don't need my help."

"We'll leave Callie to feed Ajax." Nollen helped Lexi stand.

"You heard him, she-wolf." Ajax pecked at the rat.

Chapter 31

IN THE SHELTERED HOLLOW, THE GROUP STAYED FOR THREE DAYS to tend those wounded by the bushlik attack, and for Ajax to rest. During that time, Nollen, Arnie, Beno, and Callie took turns scouting the best route.

While Nollen stood in conference with Gunnar about the reconnaissance trips, Milos and Kean approached.

"When can we leave?" asked Milos.

"It depends upon the recovery of those injured," Nollen replied.

"The men are well enough to walk. Jolene can ride in a wagon."

Nollen looked up through the branches to see the sun sinking toward twilight. "It's too late today. First light."

"No night travel?" asked Kean.

Nollen shook his head. "Unnecessary under cover."

"How much longer to reach Eldar?" asked Milos.

Nollen shrugged. "Unknown. If Ajax is strong enough, I will send him ahead to search for the border. Until then, we head due west."

At Milos's displeased frown, Gunnar added, "We reckon to be in Archduke Tomas' province. Only Boric's duchy remains, nearest Eldar's border."

Milos took the information to confront Nollen. "You don't know how vast this province is?"

Nollen stiffened at the terse tone. "No, because Boric kept us blind when we traveled from his castle to Miska. We never entered Tomas' province. We know about it from discussions with the Archdukes."

Gunnar spoke with exasperation. ""Milos, we spoke of this before we left Kranston! For the final time, Axel trusts Nollen, and I trust him!"

"Milos!" Lexi called. She arrived, stern in feature. "For you to continue questioning Nollen is disruptive to our journey. He has proven himself enough to warrant no further doubt."

Milos colored with deep embarrassment. "I'm sorry, my lady." He bowed to her and quickly departed.

Curious at the exchange, Nollen regarded Lexi.

Kean's voice diverted Nollen's marked attention. "Milos is a good man. Unfortunately, concern overshadows trust. He truly doesn't mean any harm."

Nollen huffed a disagreement. "That's hard to believe when his questions seem endless."

"He won't question you again," Lexi spoke with certainty.

Once more, Nollen stared at her. "Because he obeys the Shield Maiden?"

Despite a rush of color to her cheeks, Lexi nodded. "It is not often I speak thus. In this case, I felt it necessary." She paused in departure. With a small smile, she said, "Like Axel and Gunnar, I too trust you." She left with Kean.

Callie ran to Nollen and Gunnar. "There is a human scent about two miles south."

"Old or fresh?" asked Gunnar.

"A day, no longer."

"Near our path?"

"Not yet."

Nollen scratched his chin in consideration. "As a precaution, we'll travel a half mile north before turning west."

"I know the scent, so can tell if they come any closer."

Ajax landed on a nearby branch. "I can spot them quicker."

"No, I have another task for you. Do you feel strong enough to take a longer flight?"

"How long?"

"We need to know the distance to Eldar. Can you make that determination?"

"If I can't find a border station, I will give you an estimate by what I do see."

"Good. Leave at first light." Nollen turned his attention to the group. His gaze scanned the faces until he spotted Lexi. Her demeanor now at ease, even jovial, as she conversed with Alicia in the food prep area.

Gunnar noticed the interest. "Don't press it, lad."

"Why? She made Milos back down in a way I've not seen even from you. What command does a Shield Maiden hold?"

Gunnar stepped into Nollen's line of sight. "Remember what I told about Sirin's interest."

In a pointed whisper, Nollen asked, "Lexi?"

"No names! Nor will I confirm any." When Nollen's eyes shifted back to Lexi, Gunnar gripped his arm to get the young man's undivided attention. "Ignore anything you might consider unusual behavior, simply accept it. Until we reach Eldar, it best for everyone that the person remains anonymous."

"As you say. I won't let my curiosity overshadow trust."

Gunnar chuckled at the retort. "You're learning, lad." He threw his arm around Nollen's shoulder and guided him back to the group. He spied Lorraine with the others at the cooking fire. "What concoction—I mean—meal, are you preparing tonight?" He corrected his question when Nollen jabbed him in the ribs.

Lorraine slyly grinned. "With the fish gone, we're back to sausage and skillet potatoes."

"With some sauerkraut." Alicia fought a smile when looking at Nollen to add, "No kirsch." She giggled at her own joke.

Lexi pretended to jostle Alicia's arm in friendly rebuke.

"What? It was your idea to add it to his stew at the lake."

Lexi gaped and flushed.

Nollen flashed a friendly smile at her embarrassment. "Nice to know I'm worth extra special treatment."

Alicia, Lorraine, and Gunnar laughed, which deepened Lexi's blush. To overcome her mortification, she said, "Someone needs to help you learn to eat the spicy food children do."

At Nollen's scowl, Alicia, Lorraine, and Gunnar bit back further reaction.

Nollen spoke to Lorraine about Lexi. "Does it work the same way with strong women not allowing men to express gratitude?" He marched away.

"Your influence is rubbing off," Gunnar chided Lorraine.

She grabbed his arm to prevent departure. "We need to talk." She spoke in a tone suggesting refusal was not an option.

Gunnar's gaze briefly shifted to Alicia, Lexi, and the departing Nollen. He stoutly nodded. They traveled about twenty yards from the cooking area where he motioned for her to sit on a boulder. He remained standing.

"Speak your piece."

"No need for gruffness. Can't we speak like civilized adults?"

He nodded in agreement. "Very well."

"Then sit, to speak face-to-face rather than standing over me, as if to intimidate."

He did so and attempted to relax.

"It is true, I spoke to Nollen when he asked why there is tension between us. Since then, I have been thinking about our combative relationship, and came to realize we need to talk. The problem was getting up the courage."

"Courage isn't something I thought you had a difficulty with."

She looked crossly at him. "Is that a criticism or compliment?"

He shrugged. "A simple statement. What did you tell him?"

"He asked if you had wronged me in some way." She immediately held up a hand when he went to object. "No, you have not. That is what

I told him." She sighed with futility before proceeding. "I know you, and many others, believe I bullied Waldo. I didn't," Her voice slightly cracked. She looked down instead of at him. "What made our relationship work is … he needed me." She looked at him, her eyes misty, yet face determined. "I told Nollen that strong men often don't let women or others know they need help. I further said, our combative relationship is because we are both strong, in our own way. You because of your position, and me … to face the constant criticism."

"I have contributed to that criticism," he said with regretful understanding.

She nodded. "Now, it is happening with Lexi and Nollen." She urgently grabbed his arm. "Because of us! That shouldn't be. There is too much at stake!"

He sat thunderstruck by her poignant argument. "No, it shouldn't."

"Gunnar? Can you act civil towards me?" she asked, almost pleading.

He gazed at her, as if seeing her for the first time. A soft smile appeared. "Aye."

She sniffled with relief. "I think this is the first heart-to-heart conversation I've had with any man since Waldo …" This time, her voice faltered.

He gently touched her shoulder. "I suppose I never really understood how much you truly loved him. Appearances—"

"Are deceiving," she concluded.

"Indeed." Gunnar noticed Lexi discreetly observed them while she tended to cooking duties. Alicia drew Lexi back to the task. "If we remain away too much longer, people will talk."

"They will talk when we start to act differently," she sarcastically said.

"Let them."

Gunnar escorted Lorraine back to the cooking area. He smiled at Lexi before he left in search of Nollen. He found the young man with Kean and his family. This had become common since their arrival in Kranston. For a moment, he observed Nollen's aimable interaction with his family. The young man had come to mean a great deal to him. Listening to

Lorraine deeply disturbed him, especially the realization of how their longstanding tension influenced Nollen and Lexi.

Kean spotted Gunnar. "Brother!" He raised a cup. "Kirsch before dinner." He motioned to Nollen to pour another cup.

"Whose idea was this?" Gunnar asked after receiving the cup.

Kean laughed. "Kirsch is good for a cold night."

"Nollen, uncle," Arnie said. He gave Nollen a friendly elbow jab.

"I've grown to like it. Don't tell Lexi." Nollen chuckled.

"Why?" asked Gunnar.

Nollen shrugged and wryly grinned. "I don't know. Sport. Keep her off-balance."

"Keeping a woman off-balance isn't a good thing, lad."

Nollen grew quizzical at the somber tone. Kean spoke before Nollen could. "You seem to enjoy it with Lorraine." Kean laughed, which made Brita roll her eyes in annoyance.

"Maybe that's been my problem," Gunnar admitted. He took a drink.

A man rang a triangle bell to announce supper. As usual, Milos offered the blessing before the cooking crew served the food. When Gunnar fetched his plate, he smiled and graciously thanked Lorraine.

Nollen followed Gunnar in line. He simply nodded thanks then hurried to join Gunnar at the family area. They sat around a campfire. Gunnar appeared to ignore him to eat. No one really spoke, expect the younger ones, who complained about always eating sausage or being tired. Brita handled her grandchildren with grace and patience, which helped to counter Giselle's exasperation. Arnie intervened when it came to the teenage boys.

Once finished, Gunnar went to the cleaning barrel to wash his plate and fork. Nollen mimicked the action. Returning the plate and fork, Gunnar spoke to Lorraine.

"I don't know how you manage to keep the same meal from tasting different each time, but well done."

Lorraine smiled, genuinely. "Thank you. It's all in the preparation."

Nollen wasn't the only one baffled by the courteous exchange. He caught a glimpse of Lexi and Alicia's puzzled expressions. He hurried after Gunnar. "Is there something I should know? With you and Lorraine, I mean," he added at Gunnar's skewed glance.

"Never become too old or set in your ways that you can't change." He left Nollen to consider the short answer.

Chapter 32

AJAX SOARED HIGH ABOVE THE LANDSCAPE OF MARKITA IN A DUE westerly course. During his seventy-mile flight, the terrain varied from open plains, forest, river basin, and finally to foothills. The weather remained cold, yet clear with no rain or snow. Even the wind proved favorable for flight.

Occasionally, he landed near a settlement or town to observe. Speech of the humans indicated Markita. Near twilight of the first day, he caught a small rabbit. He took his prey to a cleft in a rocky hillside to eat and rest for the night.

At dawn, Ajax began the second day journey west. He rode the wind current over a mountain range before circling down to a lower elevation. A vast plain stretched for many miles. A river ran through the plain.

Spying a settlement, he casually flew down to land on a bare oak tree. He cocked his head to observe the humans. When one spoke, he heard Markitan. After a few moments of rest, he took off again.

By late afternoon, and fifty miles since the morning, Ajax recognized an Eldarian border station. A saddled juvenile dragon lay tethered beside the station. Although not fully grown, the juvenile stood twice the size of a horse. Elaborately forged metal bridles surrounding the dragon's snort. A large saddle protected the rider from the scales and carried weapons including a longbow, three quivers of arrows, and two lances. An Ha'tar rider sat beside a fire.

Soldiers walked the rampart. An eagle's cry alerted them to Ajax's decent. The Ha'tar became wary and alert, ready to mount. One soldier raised a bow to sight the eagle.

"Do not shoot!" Ajax called.

Another soldier grabbed his archer companion. "Wait," he shouted to the Ha'tar. He then called out to Ajax, "Friend or foe?"

"Friend of Eldar," replied Ajax.

He told his companion and the Ha'tar, "Put up your bow. Stand down." He again called to Ajax. "Land safely, friend."

Ajax settled on the wall of the border station. "My thanks. Who is your commanding officer?"

"I am Lieutenant Lothair. I thought eagles preferred the Halvors. What are doing on the border?"

"A mission for the King."

Lothair stiffened with anticipation. "Sir Gunnar and Nollen of Far Point?"

Ajax titled his head, his tone suspicious. "You know of them?"

"Orders for all border stations to be on the lookout for their return."

"And the dragon?"

"To further strengthen our defenses since Palleteen spies were discovered." Lothair took a moment to scan the horizon. "Are they nearby?"

"One hundred and twenty miles east. I flew ahead as scout."

"Then they should be here with a few days."

"Aye, if the Almighty continues to grant safe passage through Markita. Send word to the King that Sir Gunnar and Nollen were successful. I must return with news of my reconnaissance." Ajax took off to head east.

A shield owl dispatched from the Nefal Station, arrived at Sener two days later. The rare bird capable of flying great distances that even surpassed eagles. Thus, they were used for important news.

Axel received word of Gunnar and Nollen's success with some relief. However, the circumstances surrounding Leon's treachery, Jonas' death, Sylvan's unsound mind, and unanswered questions plagued him. Each day he searched the Ancient writings and royal manuscripts for anything that might provide answers. He prayed throughout the day, and at night when he couldn't sleep.

Knowing and understanding his task in returning to Eldar seemed easy compared to the present situation. Back then, he was the one taking the risky action with Gunnar in support, and Nollen lending aid. Now, the roles were reversed. They took dangerous action while he waited. His brief contemplation became interrupted by Arctander's exclamation.

"Praise be!"

Ronan, Othniel, Artair, General Mather, and Arctander gathered in the study, and privy to the news.

"Indeed. It is wonderful news," Ronan agreed.

"Sire?" asked Mather.

Drawn from his introspection, Axel gave a distracted replied. "Aye, good."

At the subdued tone, Arctander asked, "Why are you not rejoicing? Gunnar is alive, while he and Nollen are bringing them back."

"I am." Axel voice his consideration. "There remain unanswered questions, and days of travel. Why only one hundred and forty when two hundred were there when we left? What happened to the others? Or why didn't they come? Ajax's message tells me they are managing to covertly cross Markita. How will Montre respond if they are discovered? Should I send word to ask for safe passage or will that incite him? Should I have contacted him at that start?"

"No, Sire, our treaty with Markita is shaky at best," said Ronan. At Arctander's contrary cough and frown, he amended his statement. "Nollen did an admirable job in the negotiations. You must admit, the treatment he received in Markita, leaves room for speculation of how seriously they take the terms. One does not blindfold a royal emissary."

"True," Arctander agreed.

Axel crossed from his desk to a table containing a map of Eldar in great detail along with one of surrounding countries with scant details. "The message is two days old, meaning they could have traveled another twenty to twenty-four miles since." He used a ruler to calculate distance on a map of Markita. "One hundred miles would place them somewhere along this latitude. Of course, it depends on whether they took the higher or lower route through the Black Mountains."

Ronan, Mather, and Arctander gathered on either side of Axel. Othniel's head rose over the table. Artair perched on Othniel's shoulders.

"Doubtful they would travel the King's Land," began Mather. He used his finger to draw along the map. "Montre would certainly have discovered them by now if they had."

"I instructed Nollen to cross at Ashford Station. Ajax arrived at the Nefal station." With the ruler, Axel tapped the map to indicated both places, with Nefal further north from Ashford.

"Whichever they chose, they must cross Boric's border province."

Axel's brows leveled with intense study of the maps. "General, place troops along the border from the Nefal Station to Ashford Station." He then said to Ronan, "Can Irwin saddle any more juveniles for dispatch to the border?"

"I don't know. Maybe. I will endeavor to learn."

"The eagles will also patrol the border skies," said Artair.

"Gentlemen, Artair, see to it!" Axel commanded.

The men left by the door while Arctander opened the window for Artair's departure.

Axel remained at the table. He placed his hands on the tabletop to lean over the map. "Gott, grant them safe passage," he quietly prayed.

"What else weighs on your mind, Sire?" asked Arctander.

The question made Axel glance up. "Sirin and the Palleteens." He straightened to fold his arms. "According to the Ancient writings, Palleteens, and some Markitans, worship a goddess called *Chika*. She is said to have cursed the mountain mines due to disloyalty, though not exactly *how* the curse is manifested."

"We know the diamonds are dangerous."

Axel focused his attention back to the map. "Legend tells that creatures of the Black Mountains are controlled by her. Yet ..." he paused with deep consideration. "I can't help but wonder if this Chika and Sirin are somehow related, if not one and the same. The parallels are striking." He looked directly at Arctander to say, "We know who Sirin is looking for."

"Gott will not allow Sirin to succeed," Arctander confidently replied.

"Do not underestimate Sirin's determination. With her fate linked to the outcome, she will stop at nothing," warned Othniel.

"Do you doubt the Almighty?" Arctander asked.

The Great White mane shook. "No. Neither will I proceed with overconfidence. Remember, the enemy managed to incapacitate me, to the near ruin of the Son of Eldar."

Axel ignored the argument, as his gaze shifted between the Ashford and Nefal stations. He reasoned under his breath. "Northern or southern route? Where I told Nollen to go or where Ajax arrived? Gott, guide my choice." At a sudden urging in his spirit, his eyes fixed on the spot. He stood to his full height to declare, "I'm going to the Nefal Station."

"Sire?" said Arctander in surprise.

"I will be there to either meet them with a hearty embrace or aid them with every weapon at Eldar's disposal."

"That is not part of the plan."

In hot rebuke, he said, "You know what is at stake! The future of Eldar, my father's house, and my own happiness. I won't be prevented. My people are coming home!"

Othniel laughed. "Finally, the Son of Eldar is roused!"

Axel grew suspicious. "What do you mean? You have been one of the voices advising caution."

"To keep you from acting prematurely. Others had to be employed first."

Not liking the answer, Axel confronted Othniel. "Placing others in danger before I act is hardly good strategy!"

"You are not the only one affected by what has happened and will happen. The Almighty works in the lives of all involved. In that, *you* must yield. Remember, Sirin rebelled against the Almighty and betrayed the First Ones."

The statement stilled Axel's ire. At a knock on the door, he said, "Come!"

Ronan arrived with Irwin. Irwin bowed and reported, "Sire, I have four juveniles I can saddle."

"Excellent. Send two to Ashford Station, and two to Nefal Station.

Mather entered. "We will ready at dawn for dispatch to the stations, Sire."

"General, you will accompany me to the Nefal Station. It's time to show Montre and Sirin, that Eldar will not tolerate any interference with our people's return."

Mather clapped his sword in acknowledgment of the order.

"I'm coming too," said Arctander.

Axel didn't immediately reply. His staunch features enough to show his initial disapproval. This did not intimidate Arctander.

"I will accept no refusal. As High Priest, my duty is clear in this matter."

Chapter 33

RONAN SAT AT THE TABLE IN HIS BEDCHAMBER WITH PAPERS scattered about. His focus shifted from various papers, and maps. Since the news from Markita regarding the returning group, he felt unsettled. War could be on the horizon. He sat back with a sigh of fatigue and rubbed his eyes. The lamp began to diminish. He tried to prime it and discovered the oil gone. At that moment, he noticed shafts of light surrounding the curtains. *Morning?* Before he could reach the window to draw back the curtains, a knock at door and voice made him change directions. Cormac arrived, and fully dressed in Ganel armor.

"You're not ready?" Cormac eyed Ronan's disheveled condition. "Or did you not sleep?"

"Time must have slipped by."

"That's an understatement." Cormac casually glanced at the disorganized papers. "Did you find what you need?"

"No." Ronan stood at the toiletry stand to wash to refresh himself.

"Why?" Cormac sat to examine the scattered pages. "I provided all the documents available. Anything more, would require my return to Mathena, and the university vaults."

Ronan used a towel to wipe his face and neck. "Not necessary. All of these keep bringing me back to the treaty. I'm not exactly sure why? However, there may be some aspect involved with recent events. Markitan jewelry, a secret Markitan wife, Palleteen diamonds, Eldarian turncoats, Sirin," he rattled off items. He crossed to the table. "While I examine these, Axel has been searching the ancient manuscripts and royal ledgers to establish a connection. So far, nothing."

"Aye. His requests are making a shamble of the records. Or so the custodian tells me." Cormac's brief chuckle was short-lived, as he picked up a copy of the Markitan trade treaty. "Masterfully written. For all his youth, Nollen knows his business."

"Indeed." Ronan gathered the papers from the treaty to place in a special leather case for such documents. "With war possible, this may come in handy." He closed the satchel.

"We're to meet Axel in courtyard, and you're not dressed."

"My saddlebags are packed." Ronan went to a chair beside the door. He placed the leather case into a compartment in one side of the saddlebag. "Help me with my armor, and we can leave."

In the courtyard, twenty-four hundred troops mustered for departure. The total garrison at the castle held three thousand. Three officers held the reins of two horses each. Mather made his way among the troops for final inspection. Irwin and Arctander waited beside the main entrance. Irwin also wore Ganel armor while Arctander's ensemble blended military elements with his priestly vestments, including light chain mail. Othniel, Alfgar, Bardolf, and Artair also waited.

Ronan and Cormac emerged first, with Ronan now fully dressed. Both carried saddlebags, which they handed to officers for placement on the horses.

Axel followed the Ganels, dressed in resplendent kingly armor. Upon sight of him, Mather signaled the trumpeters. The call to arms announced the king's arrival. Troops snapped to attention. Mather saluted by holding a fist over his left breast.

"All is ready, Sire."

Axel mounted. He gathered the reins to address the troops. "Just as my return was spoken of in prophecy, so is the return of the lost Eldarians. Today we march with the hope of greeting them at the border.

If necessary, we will fight to defend them. Neither the Palleteens nor Markitans will prevent them from coming home!"

Mather drew his sword to shout; "For Eldar! For Gott!"

Three times, the soldiers repeated the phrase in unison. When finished, Mather sheathed his sword to mount. He rode behind Axel to leave the courtyard. Ronan and Cormac came next, with Irwin and Arctander behind them. The officers and troops marched together with wagons of supplies near the rear guard.

All Sener and Wyckton turned out to hail the King and troops. With well-wishes, prayers, and wreaths, the crowds called to them. It took over an hour for the troop to cross the bridge and leave Wyckton.

"Last time we saw this was three years ago, when we left Mathena," Cormac commented.

"I pray it turns out as well now, as it did then," Ronan said.

"I pray there is no conflict," Arctander interjected.

"The prayer of us all, Reverend," Mather called back.

Several miles outside of Wyckton, they crossed a new bridge over a narrow portion of the River Leven into Nefal. Once all the troops left the bridge, Axel called for Ronan.

"Sire." Ronan brought his horse beside Axel's mount. The road wide enough to ride three abreast.

"I couldn't help but notice you appear tired. Sluggish in movement."

At first the comment surprised Ronan, then he grinned. "Your Majesty has a keen eye."

"When you are in company almost every day, one is bound to notice changes." Axel gave Ronan a friendly smile. "Why such a state?"

"In truth, I did not sleep last night. As you search for answers about the Palleteens, I have for Markita. There is something we are missing."

"Aye. Each day I review the events and consider them against what I learn in the writings and ledgers. A mystery and puzzle devoid of the final piece to put it all together." Axel looked along his shoulder at Ronan. "What have you found?"

The Ganel shrugged. "I'm not certain, yet I feel there is a strong connection to the treaty. Other precious gems, and metals are mentioned. No diamonds. Nollen's reaction to the destruction, showed he was unaware of the curse."

"Palleteen diamonds have been reduced to legends. Until recently," Arctander said.

Axel slightly drew rein for Arctander to catch up. "Nollen mentioned an Uncle Oberon had a fragment from an ancient priestly vestment. What relation is he to you?"

"My brother. Jonas' father. He died many years ago. I had no knowledge he kept a fragment." Arctander brows grew level with worry. "Until Leon, we didn't know the connection between Palleteen diamonds and Markitan jewelry, so Nollen surely wouldn't have known when negotiating the treaty. What connection could there possibly be?" he asked Ronan.

"It is a deep sense I have, not a certain answer."

"My lords, this requires more study. When we reach the Nefal Station, I will review the treaty." Axel slyly grinned at Ronan. "Which I assume you brought."

Ronan returned the impish smile. "Naturally. When one is in company almost every day, one is bound to pick up on habits."

"Sire," called Cormac. "We are near the road to part ways."

"Very well. Proceed to Ashford Station."

Cormac shouted a command. The first company of two hundred men separated from the column to follow him and Irwin on a southern road. Alfgar and Bardolf joined the departing group. Axel and the remainder continued in an easterly course. At various points along the four-day route, other companies veered off from the main column.

Chapter 34

A BLIZZARD SLOWED PROGRESS TO A CRAWL. BATTLING THE elements, the group only managed to travel ten miles in two days. Cold and exhausted, Milos called for a halt to wait out the storm. Callie discovered a small glade surrounded by majestic pines. Men erected tents in a circle to shield the center area for cooking and a communal fire from wind. The wagons provided extra protection and made it easier to access supplies. In such weather, kirsch and hot tea were the standard beverages.

At dawn of the fifth day, Nollen emerged from a tent. The snow stopped after three days, but cloudy cold weather kept threatening more. This morning, the morning sun's rays told of good day. He heard arguing come from the other side of a wagon. He found Milos with the other wagon drivers, Danor and Kean.

"Is there a problem?"

Milos's expression showed he didn't like Nollen's interruption. He reluctantly waved him closer for explanation. "Supplies are running low."

"Why? I suggested three weeks of rations, and it hasn't been that long since we left Kranston."

"There appears to have been some thievery."

"What?" Nollen exclaimed, much to Milos's chagrin. He lowered his voice. "Why didn't you tell me before now?"

"I just now learned about it from Danor and Kean."

"We tried to secure things, but, unsuccessful," Danor dolefully said.

Nollen fought to contain his ire to ask Kean, "How long has this been happening?"

Kean shrugged. "I don't know. It could have been small amounts over time, so we wouldn't notice, or all at once in desperation. It wasn't until Lorraine and Elan came for breakfast rations that I noticed a significant drop in my wagon. We did an accounting of Danor's wagon. Less is missing. Milos came upon us conversing."

Nollen glanced about until he spied the individual he wanted. "Gunnar!" When the knight arrived, he briefly explained the situation.

"What about the night watch? Have any reported suspicious activity?" Gunnar interrogated Milos.

"No," said Danor and Kean in near unison.

"How many days rations are left?" asked Nollen.

"Four, maybe five, if we're careful," Kean replied.

Nollen frowned with thought. "From Ajax's report of our distance to the border, I estimated roughly nine to ten days based upon our rate of travel. And *that* was two days ago. Now we're further behind."

"Hard to hunt in this weather," Gunnar said to Nollen.

"Then limit meals to breakfast and dinner. No eating while traveling, only drink. Even at those meals, portions will be rationed. By doing so, we may stretch the supplies long enough to reach the border. However," Nollen stressed to Milos, "that means we resume our journey *today*. No more stopping for more than a night. Time is imperative if we are to reach Eldar safely." Nollen left with Gunnar. He quickly drew Gunnar behind the family tent for a private discussion. "You know these people. Does anyone come to mind who would do such a thing?"

Gunnar pondered the question. "Difficult for me to consider the possibility." He sighed with lament. "Alas, I have been gone three years. Learning of so many deaths, I sensed an attitude change. Thievery to the point of endangering everyone? Hard to imagine."

"Difficult or not, someone is raiding the supplies."

"Aye," droned Gunnar.

"Today, circulate. Act casual. Gain what intelligence you can." Gunnar stared at him from under shrouded brows of contemplation. Seeing the obvious conflict, Nollen added, "Such conversation would be best from you than me."

"Aye. We should start by speaking to Lorraine and Elan. They need to be instructed on limiting portions."

At the cooking area, Milos and Elan engaged in a low, yet heated conversation. Lorraine appeared worried. Gunnar inconspicuously placed a comforting hand her back, as he spoke to Milos.

"I gather you told them?" he said, in more a statement than question.

"Naturally. They must ration the food."

"Perhaps a gentler approach would have served better. No need to cause unnecessary upset."

"I've learned that shielding people from the truth is more problematic than confronting reality."

"Do you confront reality by brashness or compassion?"

"You're one to talk about brashness." Milos chuckled sarcastically under his breath as he left.

"I suppose I deserved that," Gunnar chided to himself.

Lorraine heard. "No. Milos has always been too direct for his own good. You know that."

"From what I've experienced, that's an understatement," said Nollen.

"It's his way. We'll manage," Elan spoke with encouragement.

At breakfast, Lorraine, Elan, and the others distracted people with conversation, thus no one appeared to notice less food on the plates. Silently, Nollen observed the people as they ate. All acted normally. Several times he caught concerned glances from Alicia or Lexi as they served the meal. Many more will display disconcertion when rationing becomes obvious later in the day.

Once camp was dismantled, Lexi prevented Nollen from mounting. "How bad will it get? The supplies that is," she hurriedly spoke.

He tried to soothe her anxiety. "If everyone cooperates, we should make it to the border."

"What if the thief ...? We need to consider possibilities." She corrected herself to be more discreet.

He cocked a grin. "What makes you think I haven't?"

She fought a smile. "Oh, you can be arrogant."

He curbed the initial prick of ire at the word *arrogant* in favor of her bantering tone. "Remember, I gave my word to do everything I can to get the group safely home."

"Let me ride with you."

"What?" he asked, taken back by the request.

"Unless you think Alydar can't bear the weight of two," she teased.

"Two is as easy as one." Alydar nudged her toward the saddle.

"I'll have to place my bedroll on the wagon—"

He didn't finish speaking when she unloaded the bedroll to make room. Upon her return, he mounted, then gave her a hand up to sit behind the saddle. She grabbed onto him when she slipped sideways.

"Ready?"

"Aye." However, Alydar's movement forced Lexi to place her arms around Nollen's waist to remain seated.

Even though they stayed under the cover of trees, the three-day snowstorm dropped six inches on the forest floor. For horses, the snow reached to the ankle, and didn't impede them too much. The snow proved a mild inconvenience to those walking. The smallest children either sat in a wagon or were carried. Milos steered the draft horse to follow Alydar's track through the snow. The wagon wheels bumped and shifted to create new ruts. Most kept to the horse track or wheel ruts for ease of walking.

About ten minutes into the journey, Nollen asked, "Why did you want to ride with me?"

"Why not? Being on horseback saves me from walking in the snow."

He lightly retorted. "Others are walking. Including children."

Her smile was short-lived. "I wanted to talk privately."

"Oh? What about?" he said, intrigued.

"There are *things* being kept from you. Details, even Gunnar doesn't want you to know," she carefully began.

"He has his reasons, and I accept them."

"Even when it places your life in danger?"

Nollen couldn't help but let out an ironic laugh. "Danger is something I've faced all my life. Only the past three years have I known peace and freedom."

"Peace and freedom are things I have yet to experience," she droned.

"You will soon."

"You speak with such confidence. I thought you might regret coming here. To Kranston, I mean."

"Why should I regret it?"

"Because of being kept ignorant of certain … things. Especially since Axel trusts you with such an important task."

He softly smiled at her sentiment. "Thank you for your concern. Yet, keeping secrets is something I'm very familiar with. Lives depended upon it. I view this situation the same as many others."

"Really?" Her voice filled with skepticism. "There are times you haven't exactly been *accepting*."

Again, he chuckled. "There you have me. At least, before I fully understood the situation."

Her voice lowered to whisper. "I understand more than you, and this venture frightens me."

Nollen felt her grip tighten around him. "Fear is natural. Don't mistake my seeming *confident arrogance* for lack of it from time to time."

She leaned her head against his back. "Thank you."

He gripped her hands around his waist. Hearing the short eagle's cry, he jerked Alydar to a halt.

The abrupt stop made Lexi sit up yet maintain hold of him. "What is it?" she asked with breathy anticipation.

"Nollen!" Callie bounded through the snow. "The human scent is closer. Near a ravine about a half-mile ahead."

"Stop!" Nollen carefully called to Milos. Although, the order repeated down the column, he focused on Callie. "How many?"

"Many. An exact count would require me getting closer. I discovered a way around, however, it leads to the plain."

Snow flew when Gunnar drew Joslin to rein. "Trouble?"

"Callie caught a scent of humans nearby. To change course means going north to the plain," Nollen replied.

Gunnar stood in the stirrups to look around. "Better than running into trouble."

Ajax landed on a pine branch. "A number of men south, riding parallel."

Nollen sent Gunnar a glance of concern. Gunnar drew his sword.

"What?" Lexi demanded.

"Our covert attempt to reach Eldar appears to be discovered," Gunnar answered. To Nollen, he said, "Head north. I will alert the men to form a perimeter." He kicked Joslin to head back. "Follow Nollen and prepare for defense!" he ordered Milos on his way past the cart.

"Ajax! Callie! Nollen snapped. Ajax took off while Callie ran ahead. "Hold on tight." Nollen turned Alydar to head north at a gallop. "Lexi, tell me how close they are following! I need to watch out for trouble."

"Milos just turned."

The forest snow made minimal impact on Alydar's pace.

"I lost sight of Milos!" Lexi shouted.

"Alydar, slow down. We can't lose them," Nollen instructed.

Alydar slowed to a lope. "The plain is a few hundred yards ahead."

"I see Milos now. Others are behind him or running through the trees," she said.

Clear of woods, Alydar hit the deeper snow hard. Nollen and Lexi rocked in the saddle at impact. Since the depth reached his knees, Alydar leapt to force a path through the snow.

After a hundred yards, Nollen drew Alydar to a halt. He anxiously watched. Wagons and people were all spread out, as they emerged from the trees. The draft horses protested the deeper snow. The snap of reins or crack of whip urged them on. Gunnar pushed Joslin through a cloud of snow toward them.

"The wagons won't make it! We should have stayed undercover," Nollen protested.

"Too many places for an ambush. Out here, we can see them coming, and sight with bows," Gunnar countered. "Gather up!" he shouted at the group.

"Gott, help us," Nollen prayed. He looked up at Ajax's warning call. Mounted soldiers emerged from the trees. Callie growled and bared her fangs in warning. "No, Callie! Retreat to the woods!"

"I'm not leaving!"

"Go! Take Ajax. You can't help us. Please! Axel must know."

"Do as he says," Alydar hurriedly added.

Callie yelped toward the sky then bounded back to the trees.

Nollen jerked on the reins when an arrow whizzed past him. Alydar reared to avoid being struck. Lexi cried out when she fell off backwards. Nollen jumped down and armed his crossbow.

"Are you hurt?" he asked.

"No. The snow softened my fall." She stood and drew her sword.

Hundreds of mounted soldiers came at them. A few men in the group were struck down by arrows. Several fired back at the soldiers. Women screamed.

"Alicia!" Lexi ran off.

"Wait!" Nollen hurried in pursuit.

Lexi came up behind a mounted soldier who bore down on Alicia. She swung her sword and gashed his leg. Angry at the wounding, he jerked his horse around. He hacked down at her. She fell to her knees to block him. She heard her name called yet ignored it to concentrate on the soldier. She scrambled to her feet. He again swung at her. She deflected the blade yet slipped in the snow. He took advantage to land a blow to her upper right arm. The cut numbed her hand, and she dropped the sword.

"Lexi?" Alicia reached her friend for aid.

The soldier rocked back in the saddle when struck in abdomen by a crossbow dart. Wounded, he retreated.

Nollen arrived to shield them. "How bad?"

"Cut on the arm, nothing serious," Lexi answered. She retrieved her sword. She grimaced in pain at the grip.

Seeing blood, Nollen instructed Alicia, "Bandage it, if you can." He grew worried by what took place around the plain. A quick count showed the soldiers outnumbered them at least two to one.

Gunnar arrived in a slosh of snow thrown up by Joslin. "Lexi?"

"I'll live," she groused.

"We can't defend against this many!" Nollen hissed in frustration.

Gunnar made Joslin wheel in a circle to survey the soldiers. Joslin cried out and bucked when an arrow cut her rump. He couldn't maintain control and awkwardly slipped off. He balked when a sword became leveled at his face.

"Surrender, in the name of King Montre!" Horst spoke Eldarian.

Gunnar glared at Horst. The odds were not good. "Stand down!" he yelled at the group. "Stand down." He sheathed his sword. With one hand he held Joslin's bridle, the other he raised. "We yield."

"Gunnar!" hissed Lexi in dispute.

"Better everyone stays alive." Gunnar waved for Nollen to lower his bow, and Lexi her sword.

"Wisely done," said Horst.

"You realize what capturing us means?" Gunnar challenged.

"You realize the penalty for invading our country?" Horst rebuked.

"We're not invaders. We're pilgrims on our way home."

"*You* are Sir Gunnar, First Knight of Eldar. He is Nollen of Far Point, emissary of King Axel." He pointed his sword at Nollen. "You are hardly pilgrims."

"These people are!" Nollen insisted. "They are no army."

"No more talk. Yield your weapons and come with us or risk their lives in refusal."

Gunnar drew his sword to hand hilt first to Horst. He nodded to Nollen, who let a soldier to take his crossbow. The soldier then pulled the dagger from the sheath on Nollen's belt. Lexi hesitated.

"Do it, for them," Nollen said about the others.

Lexi threw her sword in the snow for the soldier to retrieve.

"How do you know who we are?" Gunnar asked.

"I am Captain Horst, of Archduke Panko's regiment. I'm surprised you don't recognize me, Sir Gunnar."

"Hardly, after being blindfolded," chided Gunnar.

"Now, give up your horses."

"Mine is wounded, and she's not kind to strangers," Gunnar refuted.

Horst moved to see the indicated wound.

"Being a mounted officer, you should understand my reluctance."

Horst stoutly nodded. "Walk. Do not ride." He reached for Alydar. The unicorn-horse angrily snorted and pulled away.

Nollen snatched the reins. "He too is injured."

"I don't see anything," scoffed Horst.

"He became lame when we hit the snow hard and fell."

On cue, Alydar pretended his right front leg was sore.

"Walk them."

"Where are you taking us?" Gunnar demanded.

"Miska. Where you will be tried before King Montre as spies."

"We're not—" Lexi began to protest when Nollen covered her mouth.

"Softly," he said in warning.

"Listen to him, woman! And keep quiet," Horst chided.

When Horst turned to issue instructions in Markitan, Nollen urgently whispered an explanation to Lexi. "Markitans don't look favorably on women speaking." He put a hand up to still her objection. "For all concerned, keep silent. Gunnar and I understand their language."

"Wait! What are you doing?" They heard Milos shout.

Soldiers unhitched the horses from the wagons. They fetched as many supplies as possible to load onto the horses.

Horst moved his horse to cuff Milos from behind. The force sent Milos face first into the snow. "Wagons slow. We take what we want."

"Let them be, Milos," Gunnar called.

Milos stood, and brushed the snow from his face and hair.

Horst yelled more commands in Markitan, then spoke Eldarian. "Move!"

Gunnar led Joslin, as the soldiers herded the group eastward. Nollen held the reins while Alydar kept up his pretense of injury. Silently, they observed the carnage. From the group, five men lay dead, six more wounded, along with three women. Half a dozen children were also injured during the melee. A few soldiers suffered wounds with one dead. The soldiers placed their deceased companion over his horse for the return to Miska.

Lexi bit her lip to contain her emotions. "What are we going to do?" she fearfully whispered to Nollen.

"Follow instructions and pray for Gott's protection."

"We failed." She covered her mouth to muffle her sob.

He took her hand with a firm reassuring grip. "Not if I can reason with Montre and remind him of our treaty."

In the shadow of trees, Callie watched the attack with hackles up and teeth bared. Ajax landed on a branch above Callie's head. When the soldiers herded the group from the plain, Callie whimpered at seeing the dead left behind.

"I heard the soldiers are taking them to Miska. I can follow them," said Ajax.

"No, I will. You can return faster to Eldar to tell of this capture."

Chapter 35

THE NEFAL STATION COULD ACCOMMODATE THE NORMAL number of troops assigned to duty, twelve. Three Ha'tar riders and juvenile dragons camped outside the station. When Axel arrived with two hundred men, a larger encampment was pitched around the station. Artair, Othniel, and Myn, the leading Ha'tar rider and trainer, also accompanied Axel. Myn dressed in Ha'tar armor made of dragon scales, fur, and leather. The domed helmet had fur flaps to cover his ears when flying. He wore a curved sword.

Nestled between the Freelands and The Doane, weather along the Nefal border tended to change swiftly depending upon the air current. In the morning, cold snow, rain, or frost from the north dominated. By midday, winds from the south melted the snow and warmed the air to a comfortable temperature.

Axel occupied the commander's quarters. Lieutenant Lothair ordered an additional cot brought to his quarters for Arctander. Lothair joined Mather and Ronan to bunk with the men in the barracks.

All gathered around the desk where Axel sat. Two maps covered the top. Othniel laid in the threshold with Artair on his back to allow the humans into the small room. A nice fire burned in the corner metal stove. Fortunately, the compact room heated quickly to help recover from the raw morning outside.

Due to the warmth, Axel shed the more cumbersome part of his armor. Mather and Ronan remained fully suited. Lothair augmented his uniform with a plain breastplate.

"Twelve encampments of two hundred are placed every ten miles from here to Ashford," Mather reported. He poked at each interval on the map. "This distance makes it easy for swift communication."

"Eagles can fly faster," Artair said.

"Dragons fly farther with less effort," added Myn, proudly.

"All good options. However, we intend to use shield owls." Mather pointed to large cage covered with a black cloth across from the stove. "Three are housed in the cage."

"What about reserves?" Ronan asked Mather.

"Six groups, an hour behind the first line of encampments."

"An hour is a long time during battle," Ronan chafed.

"When we leave, the reserves are instructed to move to the perimeter encampments to await further orders. The shield owls will also be used to send word immediately upon engagement."

"Do Irwin and Cormac have shield owls?" asked Arctander.

"Aye, but just two. Five trained owls were all the royal hatchery had."

Confused, Axel asked, "Why so few? I remember Govert telling me ten remained after dispatching them to the border stations."

"*Trained*, Sire," Mather stressed.

Artair took up the explanation. "Shield owls lay one egg every eighteen months. It takes a year for a hatchling to reach maturity for training. From the remaining twelve Lord Sylvan kept, we now have eight more, for a total of twenty. It will be many years before shield owls can be released back into the wild to repopulate."

Axel received the explanation with a nod.

"Sire, we have done all the preparations we can."

"Thank you, General." Axel wave for dismissal.

Artair hopped off Othniel's back when the lion moved from threshold so Mather, Lothair, and Ronan could leave. Arctander stayed.

"Time for my daily patrol," said Artair.

Axel crossed to a window that faced east to open it for Artair's exit. Even after closing it, he remained to stare out the window. "Judging time and distance of Ajax's report, they should be here by now. That fact they are not …" His voice trailed off in frustration.

Arctander joined Axel at the window to offer encouragement. "There could be any number of reasons for the delay. Weather, illness, injury. Such a trek with one hundred and forty people is fraught with hazards. It's doesn't mean the worst."

With thoughtful regret, Axel stroked his beard as he continued to stare outside. "Perhaps, I asked too much of Nollen."

Othniel raised his head from his resting place beside the hearth. "The Almighty told you to employ him."

"Sire!" Lothair's shout came a second before he returned in a hurry. "The rampart. Ajax is here."

Axel didn't bother to grab his cloak in haste to leave. Arctander followed as quickly as he could. The old priest huffed upon reaching the rampart. Othniel passed him to join those gathered in front of Ajax, who perched on the wall next to Artair.

"What news?" Axel demanded.

"Not good, I'm afraid, Sire," began Ajax soberly. "Two days ago, a troop of King Montre's soldiers attacked. Nollen and Sir Gunnar did what they could, but to save lives, they were forced to surrender."

Mather and Ronan arrived in a rush to hear an Axel's anxious question, "How many dead, injured, or captured?"

"Five dead, and some injured, yet still among those captured."

Axel visibly swallowed back discomposure. "Who is dead?"

"Five men. Nollen and Sir Gunnar are safe. So is the other."

Axel exhaled with some relief. He felt Arctander's supporting hand on his shoulder. Composed, he continued the inquiry. "Where are they now?"

"On the way to Miska, to be tried as spies by King Montre."

"What?" Axel thundered with outrage.

"Easy, Sire!" Arctander cautioned.

"Hardly a time to be easy!" he chided. "Anything more you can tell me?" he asked Ajax.

"Callie is following them while Alydar remains with Nollen."

"How far was the group from Miska?" Mather inquired.

"Uncertain. We kept a northerly course through what is believed to be the province of Archduke Tomas."

"Miska is in the King's Land. Can you lead us there?"

"Sire, no!" Mather began in objection. "We can't cross the border under arms. Montre will consider it an act of war."

"He captured my people! That is already an act of war!"

"The General is right, Sire," insisted Ronan. "Any hasty action could doom out people."

Arctander seized Axel's arm. His voice urgent, yet authoritative. "Do not yield to impulse. *That* is what *Sirin* wants. To throw you off balance. Keep to the plan and trust the Almighty."

Othniel nudged Axel's hand. "Ajax can return with word from you. Encouragement to help them endure until the situation can be remedied."

For a long moment, Axel remained silent. His mind, heart, and spirit warred between impulse and reason. With hasty steps, he moved away from the others. Othniel blocked Arctander from following.

Axel lowered his head. His mind raced with thoughts to sort out the situation. Even during the most dreadful times on his journey to becoming king, his mind remained clear. Now, with the threat to those dearest to him, he found his mind clouded, heart pricked, and spirit tested. Keeping such a secret didn't feel so heavy in the early days. However, once he dispatched Gunnar, his heart urged for her again. Controlling his emotions proved most difficult. Yet now, is when he needed to be in command.

His mind finally cleared enough to pray. *Gott, help me. Grant me wisdom on how to proceed. Protect them. Do not allow Sirin to endanger my love.* The breath caught in his throat as he glanced skyward. He spoke aloud, "Strengthen Gunnar's arms, and add extra insight to Nollen's shrewdness."

He lowered his head to discreetly wiped his eyes. He took a deep breath, and slowly exhaled. Standing straight he turned around. "My lords, we need to revise our plan."

"Sire. Should I return to find them?" asked Ajax.

"Wait. Once we have a new plan, I will tell you what to say. For now, come to the window. I may have some questions."

Back in the commander's quarters, Axel picked up the map of Markita. Miska lay almost dead center. He placed it back on the desk to trace with his finger a possible course from Kranston. Nothing over the Black Mountains showed them going north.

"Open the window," Axel instructed Mather. Ajax landed on the windowsill. "How did you come down from Kranston? Over the upper or lower pass through the Black Mountains?"

"Neither, Sire. Bushliks killed the burkava, which forced a turn north to cross the river near the Andros Sea. We then headed into a place called the Devil's Gorge."

Axel easily found the Andros sea, but shook his head upon further investigation. "I don't see anything called the Devil's Gorge."

"It lies on the northern path between the Black Mountains and Andros Sea."

"*Diabelek?*" Axel tried to pronounce the name.

Ronan came to stand at Axel's shoulder. "I believe *diabel* means devil in Markitan."

Axel traced a line as if traveling Diabelek. "That should have brought them into the King's Land, not Tomas' province."

"A landslide blocked the gorge and forced the group to go further north where a side canyon ended on the shores of the sea," said Ajax.

Axel made the adjustment with his finger. "Aye, that would avoid the King's land," he commented than asked, "Did you maintain a westerly course since?"

"Aye, Sire." Ajax bobbed his head in a nod.

Axel traced the course and smiled when his finger stopped at Nefal. "That answers the question of why you flew here instead of Ashford."

"A snowstorm slowed my progress this time." Ajax ruffled his feather in a shake.

"How bad was the storm?" asked Arctander.

"Bad enough to camp for nearly five days. Some children became ill."

Ronan also studied the map. "Explains why they didn't arrive as anticipated. Taking everything into consideration, it leaves the possibility they were captured … right … about … here." He tapped the map. "Miska lay southeast."

Axel glowered at the map. His arms folded across his chest. "We can't cross the border and travel that deep into Markita under arms. Nor can we allow them to be tried by Montre—as spies?" He quizzically looked at Ajax. "Why would Montre consider them spies?"

Ajax awkwardly cocked his head, as if in negative movement. "I don't know. I simply overheard a Markitan soldier say that to Nollen and Sir Gunnar."

Ronan leaned closer to Axel. "Remember what I said about the treaty? This could be why I felt so compelled."

"Fetch it!"

The others appeared quizzical when Ronan ran out of the room. Axel made no comment as they awaited his return. The Ganel lord breathed heavy from running, but not overly exhausted when he came back with the leather case. He removed the treaty to place on the table. He took a deep breath to begin an explanation.

"Nollen did a wonderful job of wording to keep trade in favor of Eldar. This is a preferential trade agreement with reduced tariffs. It is the first step to a free trade treaty, meaning, Markita must earn the right to remove all tariffs to freely import and export goods between our countries. And be included in our annual trade fairs."

"How will this help our current situation, seeing that Nollen and the others have been captured?" asked Lothair.

"We use this to negotiate with Montre for their release," Ronan said in simple reply.

"Well, if it's that easy, I'm sure Nollen will do that if he gets the chance," Mather countered.

"Naturally. However, Montre doesn't know we are poised on the border in full arms ready to act if he balks at what is written in the terms.

Once he learns, our sheer presence strengthens Nollen's bargaining position. Currently, we have the upper hand," Ronan explained.

Axel stood with his arms folded across his chest, listening.

"Let's not forget Sirin," warned Arctander.

"Indeed," added Othniel. "To Sirin, a piece of paper is worthless. She is more concerned with destroying the one who holds her fate."

Axel deliberately raised his head. His voice full throat. "She is not forgotten. Nor her threat against my people. This," he pointed at the treaty, "gives us the advantage with our human foe, while the plan includes confronting her."

Mather and Lothair were silenced by his statement. Axel turned to Ajax. "I have a task for you. One that could be extremely dangerous, if you are willing."

"Sire, I will do whatever you ask to help Eldar, and my friends. Nollen is one of the most kind and gentle humans I've ever met. He treats animals with respect and honor."

Axel grinned at the sentiment. He sat at the desk while he continued to speak. "I want you to take my letter to Montre in Miska. Hopefully, it will make him think twice about holding my people."

Chapter 36

DESPITE THE SNOW, INJURY, OR THE PRESENCE OF CHILDREN, the Markitan soldiers pushed the pace on the journey to Miska. Gunnar managed to apply salve to Joslin's wound. Alydar kept up the pretense of being injured to remain with Nollen. Among the group, only Nollen and Gunnar understood Markitan. Very few soldiers spoke Eldarian, thus any conversation among the group became quickly silenced. However, keeping tired and hurting children quiet became more difficult the further they traveled. Between adults, exchanged glances, expressions, or touch showed concern or encouragement.

Alicia, Lexi, and Lorraine kept constant company, and usually not far from either Nollen or Gunnar. Kean tended to his family, while Milos attempted to circulate among the people.

This was not the way Nollen envisioned his mission to Markita unfolding. In truth, nothing happened the way he anticipated. From the start, his companions proved most unusual, yet he grew fond of them. After his meeting with Boric, he realized the wisdom of Axel's insistence on being covert. The treaty aside, the Markitans were not entirely trustworthy. Add Sirin's intent, and the danger increased tenfold. Even if Axel had confided in him, it wouldn't change the situation rather made it worse when he encountered Sirin.

A deep, cold shiver ran through him at the recollection of her. He closed his eyes and swallowed back the rising terror. His eyes snapped open and he jerked away when someone touched his arm. His breathing slightly labored at first, then sighed in relief at seeing Gunnar. The side-glance showed Gunnar understood. Nollen's lips moved in the barest hint of a grateful smile before he faced forward. He believed he knew Gunnar well from their early days. This adventure showed him a depth of affection he didn't realize existed. Gunnar considered him like a son. New emotions rose, and as if sensing that too, Gunnar patted his shoulder. This time Nollen openly smiled.

"Halt!" Horst commanded. "Ten minutes to eat and drink."

Grateful for the pause, women and children sat on patches of damp earth cleared of snow. Infants and young children cried, while older ones either silently wept or tried to comfort the younger.

Milos boldly confronted Horst. "How much further? The children can't take much more at this pace!"

Horst's glance swept over the group. Even the men appeared tired and haggard. "We will reach Miska by nightfall. Now, you're wasting time."

Those still strong enough, tended the weak. Lorraine moved sluggishly, in the task of feeding. At one point she stumbled. Gunnar caught her.

"When was last time you ate or drank?" he asked.

"I take my portion."

"That's not what I asked."

"This morning."

He took the flask and bread from her. "I want to see bread and water pass your lips."

She took a long drink of water then accepted a hunk of the bread.

Gunnar gave the loaf and flask to Elan. "Continue. She needs to rest." He helped her sit on the ground.

"What of you?" she asked.

He grinned. "I ate a few moments ago."

"*Tiho! Tiho!*" a soldier shouted at them.

They learned that *tiho* meant *silence*. Gunnar raised a hand of acknowledgement.

Not far away, Alicia and Lexi helped others. Nollen watched over them. Several Markitan soldiers sat guard on their horses. They conversed and made a few gestures toward the group.

"These soldiers frighten me," Alicia anxiously spoke under her breath.

Lexi and Nollen heard. "I won't let them hurt you," he said.

"Their unknown speech and actions are what make me uneasy."

"They can't wait to get home." He further explained when Alicia and Lexi appeared perplexed. "They're talking about families and getting out of the cold."

"At least you can understand them," Lexi groused.

"It's good someone can," he replied with a confident grin.

Alicia gave Lexi a good-natured poke with her elbow when Lexi tried not to smile at his response.

"Time's up!" Horst shouted.

"That wasn't ten minutes," Lexi protested loud enough to be heard by the Markitans.

The soldiers angrily shouted *Tiho* at Lexi.

Nollen picked up Alydar's rein in one hand, and with the other, took Lexi by the hand. "Remember what I said before. Markitan men aren't friendly toward women speaking out of turn," he whispered in warning.

"I'm only defending my people. It is my duty as the Shield Maiden."

"*My* responsibility, as charged by the King, is to keep *you* safe along with everyone else." He squeezed her hand to add, "Please, be silent in front of them."

She saw the earnestness in his eyes. "I'll try."

"*Tiho!*"

Nollen flinched when he felt the sting of rein slap his shoulder. Lexi gasped at the assault.

"*Premaki!*" The soldiers waved them to move. Another word they came to understand while being herded.

Alicia hurried to join Lexi and Nollen. Lexi moved so Alicia walked between them. Ahead of them, Gunnar gave Joslin's rein to Lorraine so he could walk outside of her. Kean and his family fell into a position that separated them from Gunnar and Lorraine. Brita looked terribly pale. However, Giselle's appearance caused concern. Arnie aided his wife, as she tried to hold their youngest child. Finally, Arnie took the girl to relieve Giselle's burden. One of the teen boys held his mother about the waist to help her walk.

Nollen's jowls tightened. The distressing scene became all too common during the past four days. As if the difficulty of the journey wasn't enough, the callousness of their captors brought many to the brink of utter exhaustion.

Gott, be merciful in granting enough strength to reach Miska. Once there, keep those who falter alive long enough for me to act! Act - that word repeated in his mind. He boasted to Lexi about speaking with Montre and using the treaty as leverage. What if Montre didn't grant an audience?

Gott, grandfather said you would hear me when I call upon you. All these souls depended upon me. The King depends upon me. Now, I depend upon you. I beg for wisdom, courage, and faith to do what I must. Open the ears of Montre to listen. To provide a means to free us and return to Eldar.

Nollen became so lost in prayer and consideration, he didn't realize how far or long they walked until Alicia grabbed him.

"Is that Miska?" she whispered with urgent fear.

On the horizon, lay a city with a large fortress made dazzling white by snow and fading sunlight. Although, he caught only glimpses last time, he answered with certainty. "Aye."

The soldiers herded the people into a tight group. Citizens of Miska glared with suspicion, or uncertainty at the passing throng. Once inside the fortress, Horst shouted for the gate to be closed.

Now in a huddled circle, they waited anxiously in the courtyard. This time Horst ordered Joslin and Alydar taken. Neither Nollen nor Gunnar fought the soldiers who collected the horses.

Horst dismounted when approached by a nobleman. They lowly conversed.

"Do you recognize him?" Gunnar asked Nollen.

After a moment of observation, he said, "Albric."

"I just knew he looked familiar but couldn't recall the name."

A soldier shouted at them, and they fell silent.

After a few more exchanges, Horst bowed, and Albric began to depart. However, he made eye contact with Nollen before he proceeded on his way. Nollen became distracted by Horst's speech and gestures.

"What now?" Lexi whispered.

No time to answer, as they were once more driven like cattle to a far building. Minimal torchlight helped a little to navigate the steep steps to the dungeon. They divided the group between four large cells. Women wept and children cried for their parents when roughly separated. Alicia, Lexi, and Lorraine remained together in one cell, while Kean and his family were shoved into another cell. Guards held Nollen and Gunnar back.

"You two, come with me," Horst said.

Rather than being taken to another cell, Horst led them up a far set of stairs. They entered a sparsely furnished room in a back hall. Twilight faded. A small lamp illuminated the room. Movement from a darkened corner placed Gunnar and Nollen on guard for trouble. Albric.

"Leave us," he sternly ordered Horst. Albric waited for the door to close before speaking again. "This is not the way I had hoped to see you again, Nollen of Far Point. Sir Gunnar."

"Nor is this the way to treat emissary of His Majesty King Axel and First Knight, my lord baron," Nollen harshly replied.

"Are you in Markita as an emissary? Or something more?" Albric challenged.

Gunnar sternly replied. "How and why we are here is immaterial. The fact you have captured Eldarians can be considered an act of war."

Albric's eyes darted to the door before he moved closer to them. "Many consider you spies."

"You don't believe that," said Nollen.

"What I believe is of little consequence compared to others."

"Then why bring us here to speak confidentially?"

Albric stared at Nollen. "Shrewd beyond your years. That cleverness will be tested."

"It wouldn't be the first time."

"It might be the last, if you are not careful."

"What do you want?" Gunnar roughly inquired.

Albric's expression softened as his whole posture relaxed. "This may sound strange, so hear me out." He paused to look at the door again. "The words in the book, the Ancient Eldarian one given to commemorate the treaty, are they all true?"

The question caught both Gunnar and Nollen by surprise. Gunnar was the first to reply. "We believe they are. In fact, we stake our lives on it."

"Aye. Trust and reliance upon the Almighty are the foundation of our faith," said Nollen.

A small smile of relief appeared. "Thank you. I needed to be certain." At a distant sound of commotion, Albric seized Nollen's arm. "Stay strong in faith for the trial to come." He opened the door to summon Horst.

"Our women and children need food, water, and medicine," Gunnar said.

"Horst, see what can be done." Albric waited several moments before leaving the back room. He knew the risk in meeting with Gunnar and Nollen. However, the same compulsion that kept him reading the sacred Eldarian book, compelled him to take the chance.

In the short walk from the dungeon to the office above the Hall of the Archdukes, a peace he never experienced before settled his heart and mind. Although it didn't change the current situation, he determined to help them in whatever way possible.

Upon returning to the office, he found Horst conversing with Panko. A brief tremor of fear shot through him, yet quickly countered by his own words to Nollen *stay strong in faith for the trial to come.* His new resolve would not be shaken so quickly. He ignored the staring eyes to calmly cross to his desk.

Panko waved for Horst to leave. He then approached Albric. "Why did you speak to the Eldarians?"

Albric placed the glasses over the bridge of his nose to work. He managed to keep his tone neutral. "Why not? If they are to be tried, our law requires a person understand the charge."

Panko's slapping the papers on the desk got Albric's attention. "There wouldn't be anything else, would there?"

"Like what? Being friendly to our allies? They are allies, remember?" he pointedly rebuffed. He picked up the accounting ledger.

Panko pulled the book from Albric. "They are our justification!"

"Scapegoat is a better word."

Panko slammed the book. "Take care, you do not join them!"

Albric stared at Panko. He flinched when a sense of darkness chilled his spirit. "What is driving you to such diabolical extremes?" he asked in a low, anxious voice of concern.

"Look to yourself, that whatever it is, does not include you." Panko shoved the book so hard toward Albric, it nearly slid off the desk. "Make certain the evidence is so compelling the Eldarians cannot refute it." He stormed out.

When the door slammed shut, Albric waited a moment before he unlocked a large lower drawer. It appeared empty, until he tapped something inside to reveal a false bottom. Carefully lifting it up, he sighed with relief at seeing an identical book to the ledger. He replaced the false bottom and locked drawer.

Chapter 37

SINCE THE CONVERSATION WITH ALBRIC, NOLLEN'S MIND WENT between their brief exchange to the current situation. Though uncertain of the reason behind Albric's question it, he wondered if the baron would provide assistance. *Not something to hope for,* his mind argued. However, the Markitans provided food and some medicine.

Light in the cell came from outside through two small barred windows high above the floor or torches in the hallway. Milos strongly requested extra light to tend the wounded. It came in the form of a small lantern with half a candle.

During his consideration, Nollen helped those who shared the cell. Lorraine reclined against the wall when he knelt to offer her some gruel.

"Certainly not as good as your porridge, but better than bread and water," he said with some levity.

She balked when he went to feed her. "I'm not an invalid." She took the bowl to eat. It soon became obvious that in her fatigued state, even this action proved too much.

"Here, let me." Lexi knelt. She took the bowl from Lorraine. "Milos wants to speak with you," she told Nollen.

He fought annoyance. "See she eats," he said before he joined Milos in a far corner. "You wanted to see me?" Sarcasm crept into his tone.

Milos ignored the surliness. "What is your plan? How will you convince Montre we're not spies?"

"The truth. And remind him about the treaty. Beyond that," Nollen heaved an uncertain shrug, "it is in Gott's hands."

"That's not very reassuring."

"Not reassuring to a priest that Gott is in control?"

"No!" Milos snapped. He lowered his voice when his exclamation drew attention. "*Your* plan."

Nollen's face flushed with anger. "So, you advise lying? That is the fastest way to get everyone killed!"

Despite the dim light, it became obvious all eyes focused on them. Some anxious, others afraid, and a few angry.

Gunnar quickly approached. "Softly," he chided them.

Milos partly smiled at the people. "It's all right. A mild disagreement, nothing serious."

Nollen shot Gunnar an irate glance. However, the others accepted the explanation, and returned to their tasks of helping each other.

"Milos—" Gunnar began only to be silenced by a stiff hand.

Although Milos kept his tone low, his attitude had not altered. "I wasn't suggesting lying. Just questioning if there is another way."

"The treaty is our best hope. And, I sent Callie and Ajax back to Eldar with word of what happened. Axel won't stand for it," said Nollen.

"He will do what is necessary to get us home safely," Gunnar added.

"War with us would not be in the Markita's best interest," Nollen stressed his point.

For Milos, this argument was more persuasive. "They let us pray for your success in convincing Montre to let us go."

"That, I most gladly welcome," said Nollen with relief.

Once everyone ate, and wounds tended, Milos led them in a prayer. During his lengthy supplication, his fervor rose in entreaty. Voices from the other cells joined in, as a chorus of prayers resonated in the dungeon.

The Markitan guards kept shouted "*Tiho!*" and banged on the cells with pikes to make them to stop. The opposite happened, as the efforts to halt them increased the Eldarians' zeal. Some sang. The guards loudly complained among themselves, perplexed at the cacophony of singing and praising.

Horst arrived in a rush. He chastised the guards, though unable to effectively communicate due to the overwhelming Eldarian voices. He ordered a guard to open the cell. Angry, Horst shouted in Eldarian. "Quiet!" No one seemed to notice him. "I said quiet!" He seized the nearest person, Alicia. Startled, she screamed. This drew attention.

"Let her go!" Lexi stuck Horst's arm to force him to release Alicia.

Horst's backhand sent Lexi to the floor. Gunnar assaulted Horst with a hard left to face. The Markitan captain fell back against the door. Milos and Nollen prevented Gunnar from Horst further. Horst shouted in Markitan. Two guards rushed to seize Gunnar and wrest him from the Eldarians.

"Harm him, and our king will have your head!" Nollen shouted.

"You are no in a position to threaten me or anyone." Horst sneered.

"Captain!" Albric appeared in the threshold, along with Carl. "What is going on? We heard the commotion in the courtyard."

"The Eldarians were causing a riot, my lord."

Carl glanced inside and outside the door. "How? They remain in the cells, and no guard appears injured."

"We were praying and singing, nothing more," Milos boldly said.

"Who are you?"

"Milos. Priest of the Almighty, and spiritual leader of these people."

Carl's quizzical gaze found Nollen. "You seem to have a knack for being around when trouble starts."

"We didn't start any trouble. It is as Milos said, we were simply praying and singing. Captain Horst accosted one of our women." Nollen helped Lexi stand, as she remained on the floor. "Sir Gunnar merely acted to protect those weaker from an aggressor."

Displeased, Albric confronted Horst. "Captain? Is this true?"

Horst proudly squared his shoulders and pressed his lips together in a stubborn refusal to reply.

Albric didn't accept the silence. "Captain Horst! Did you accost a woman?"

"They are foreign spies! This one is too bold for her own good." He indicated Lexi. "Women need to learn their place."

"My *place*," she began, but amended her speech when Nollen carefully nudged her, "is with the Brethren to petition Gott for our deliverance."

Horst's eyes widened in outrage at the speech.

"Captain Horst!" Albric's firm warning made Horst reluctantly back down. "Release him," he ordered the guards concerned Gunnar. "Now, get out!"

After a tense moment for Horst and the guards to depart, Carl spoke. "It would be best to keep your voices down to avoid trouble."

"I told you before, I don't want trouble," said Nollen.

"You also told me; your task was simply to find Sir Gunnar. It appears, you found more than him," Carl sternly countered.

"A rather complicated explanation," Nollen ruefully admitted.

"Better hope that explanation is acceptable to King Montre." Carl moved a step closer. His voice lowered. "There is more at stake than I believe you realize. It is best to be as cooperative as possible."

"We are not spies," Nollen insisted.

"We believe that," said Albric. "However, you must be cautious and wary. There are forces at work."

"You mean *Chika*?" Nollen carefully said the name.

Carl and Albric winced. "Heed our advice," Albric urged. He and Carl withdrew.

For several moments, they listened to the sound of fading footsteps. Finally, Nollen drew Lexi to the outer wall under one of the windows. "You really must listen and not provoke them," he scolded.

"Why do they treat women so badly?"

He heaved a shrug. "I don't know. It's their way. Aye, it is wrong," he stymied her beginning protest with agreement.

Gunnar joined them. "Nollen's right. You must restrain yourself."

"The time for secrets is past," she insisted to Gunnar.

"This is about safety from Sirin. To that, you must yield, and stay true to your duty. For all concerned. Including the *King.*"

Lexi visibly wrestled with Gunnar's argument. "If Nollen can't convince Montre then I will go before him."

"No." Nollen's objection was ignored, as they continued to argue.

"We will discuss other options *if* he fails," Gunnar stressed.

"I won't fail!" Nollen succeeded to interject.

"Confident arrogance?" Lexi rebuffed.

"Trust in the Almighty to guide my words. Such as we just prayed."

His retort briefly muted her. "Indeed, you are a perplexing man."

"I'm not trying to be. I'm simply doing the best I can to discharge my responsibility. And learning more about myself in the process. A bit unnerving really." He left her to wonder his words.

Gunnar stopped Lexi from pursuing. "Enough. We all need rest."

Alicia waved Lexi to join her and Lorraine. Gunnar crossed to Nollen, who now sat opposite the window to look out to the stars. Gunnar wrapped his cloak about him and sat.

Nollen lowly spoke so only Gunnar could hear. "Tell me truly, will knowing this secret change how I deal with Montre?"

"No. Though it could cause more danger if Sirin learns."

Nollen's gaze shifted to Lexi. She nestled on one side of Lorraine with Alicia on the other. The cloaks over lapped to help keep in body heat. "Then why is she so insistent?"

"For the same reason you are—to fulfill her duty." Gunnar positioned himself in the corner to partially recline. "No more questions. Rest. You will need all your faculties."

Chapter 38

BEING A FORMAL HIGH COURT PROCEEDING, THE TRIAL WAS scheduled for ten o'clock in the Great Hall. More noblemen and legal scholars joined the Archdukes.

Montre sat in a room adjacent to the Great Hall dressed in state attire with a royal purple and silver surcoat. Three lawyers provided advice. They wore long robes of black trimmed in silver over their clothes. Slits in the sleeves allowed for ease of movement. The black square hats were worn with one point forward over the brow. Montre grew annoyed at the contrary opinions and arguments.

"Enough!" he thundered. "I asked a simple question. Does Archduke Panko's ledger provide sufficient evidence?"

Danik, a thin-faced older man with heavy white beard, replied. "It will depend upon how the Eldarian answers. Please, Sire, allow me to explain. The Archduke's ledger does support his claim in respects to the mines. However, we need to find a connection between it and the charge of spying."

"Hence, why we gather today. To put hard questions to the Eldarians," another lawyer added.

"Then why argue among yourselves?"

"Debate, Sire, not arguing," replied Danik.

"Semantics!" Montre rebuffed.

"Semantics is the issue when forming questions, Sire. That is what we debate. How exactly to word the questions to elicit a response."

A knock on the door, followed by a call. "Five minutes to ten, Sire."

"Gentlemen, take your places before I enter."

Montre rose and moved to the door. It remained open with the herald standing ready. When the castle bell tolled the hour of ten, Montre nodded. At the formal announcement, he made his way to throne. The lawyers sat in chairs at a black draped table in front of the platform. Noblemen wore various colored formal surcoats over their doublets. The archdukes wore burgundy surcoats, their counselors donned blue, while the colors of lesser noblemen were either green or brown.

"My lords, we gather this day to determine if there is a serious threat to Markita by the Eldarians. As decreed by law, we will hear both sides." Montre then spoke to Tilbic. "General, fetch Nollen of Far Point and Sir Gunnar."

Since the wee hours of the morning, Nollen stared out the window. His mind shifted between praying, recent events, and bargaining points of the treaty. Occasionally, he observed those in the cell. Most slept huddled together.

Surprisingly, he felt no anxiety, only a desire to be prepared to give answers. Of course, he couldn't account for all possibilities, just those he considered likely. In all his mental deliberation, the answer to the central question eluded him: What made the Markitans consider them spies?

When sunlight filtered into the cell, people began to wake. Gunnar yawned and stretched. He arched his back in pain. "You think I'd be used to sleeping in odd places," he groused.

"Age and cold are a troubling combination," Nollen light retorted.

"How much sleep did you get?"

"Enough."

The jingling of keys alerted them. Breakfast, or rather a meager ration of gruel, day-old bread, and water. They finished eating when another jingle of keys sounded. Tilbic entered.

"You and you. Come with me," he singled out Nollen and Gunnar.

"Trial time," Gunnar whispered to Nollen.

"Our prayers go with you," Milos said.

Nollen simply nodded. Gunnar flashed an encouraging smile to Lexi. Four guards surrounded them, as they followed Tilbic from the dungeon to the main building. Inside the Great Hall, Nollen felt his heart race.

Gott, give me peace and wisdom, he quickly prayed. The peace he felt last night, returned. With head held high, he walked beside Gunnar from the back of the Hall to the foot of the platform. All eyes watched them.

Nollen noticed Panko stood to the right of the platform with Boric, Albric, and Carl. He avoided eye-contact with Albric or Carl. Tomas, Luken, and their assistants stood on the left side of the platform. Three men dressed in black robes sat at the table.

Tilbic bowed. "Sire, Nollen of Far Point, and Sir Gunnar of Eldar."

"Correction," began Nollen in Markitan. "I am Nollen, Royal Emissary of His Majesty King Axel, and this is Sir Gunnar, Royal First Knight of King Axel."

"You are bold to speak before being addressed," scolded Tilbic.

"Since this a high trial, formal titles are required of those being brought before the court." Nollen's attention shifted to the lawyers. "Is that not so, gentlemen?"

Danik nodded. "It is so. Let the transcript reflect it."

At Montre's silent direction, Tilbic stepped aside. Montre addressed Nollen and Gunnar. "Are you aware of the charges against you?"

"Not completely," replied Gunnar.

Montre nodded to the old lawyer, who rose to speak. "I am Magistrate Danik and tasked with conducting this proceeding." He cleared his throat to begin reading. "Nollen, Royal Commissary and Emissary of His Majesty King Axel, and Sir Gunnar, Royal First Knight of King Axel, you are charged with the high crime of being spies. Of using a covert trip to Markita as an attempt to gather information to invade with the intent to overthrow King Montre. How do you plead?"

Nollen and Gunnar stiffened, as they listened to the formal charges. "Not guilty," they spoke in near unison.

"What proof do you present to refute these charges?"

"The treaty between our countries," Nollen replied. "It would hardly be in the interest of Eldar to harm a trading partner."

"Except in the attempt to gain sole control of precious resources."

"Markita is not the only country from which Eldar receives resources. Eliminating that access would not be detrimental to Eldar. However, it would inflict serious harm to Markita's economy. There, again, hardly advantageous for us to act as described."

"Why did you cross the border in secret?"

Nollen took a deep breath. This was the one answer that reflected badly on his argument.

"To find me," Gunnar answered when Nollen briefly hesitated.

Danik looked at another piece of paper. "The same question for you, Sir Gunnar. Why did you come covertly into Markita?"

"On a mission for my King that would take me to the Black Mountains."

Mention of the Black Mountains brought verbal gasps and reactions from the men gathered. Gunnar ignored them to continue.

"Not wanting to pose a danger to the citizens of Markita, it was determined to make the trek in secret. When unforeseen circumstances happened, King Axel sent Nollen to aid me. Nothing more."

"Whereas, you might consider that a noble motive, you violated the very treaty Master Nollen seeks to use in defense by not presenting yourself to Archduke Boric," Danik countered.

"This is true. I apologize for an error in judgement. However, the mistake does not change the motive of no intent to harm."

Danik challenged Nollen. "Do you also ascribe to this motive?"

Rather than answer directly, Nollen sought to turn the tables. "Sir Gunnar honestly stated his intention was not to spy or harm in any way." At Danik's smirk, he added, "You witnessed the feared reaction from all at mention of the Black Mountains. If he had revealed his true intent to Archduke Boric, would the journey have been allowed or prevented?"

"It is not your place to question this court!"

"Since when is it Markitan practice to bring unfounded charges against emissaries of an allied king?

Another lawyer handed a ledger to Danik. "So, why does Eldar increase its demands for precious metals and gems, if not to fund a war?"

Nollen's brows knitted in confusion. "We have not done so."

"Archduke Panko's accounting shows otherwise." Danik indicated the book.

"I have no knowledge of the archduke's records, so I cannot comment on the contents."

"Then the evidence is admissible since you offer no rebuttal." Danik nodded to the lawyer taking notes.

"I can, if given time to access my records in Sener."

Danik ignored Nollen.

When Nollen cast a considerate glance to Gunnar, he caught a glint of something. A nobleman moved in such a way that a burst of light reflected off his jewel ring. This prompted Nollen to boldly speak out.

"Does the accounting include Palleteen diamonds?"

The question even stunned Gunnar, who quickly corrected his reaction.

"Palleteen diamonds, did you say?" Danik repeated.

"Palleteen diamonds," Nollen said, slow and deliberate.

Danik sat to confer with his colleagues.

The room buzzed with low conversation. Nollen caught Albric's eye. The baron held the satchel tightly to his side. His entire posture showed great anxiety. Even Carl appeared apprehensive. Boric frowned. Nollen felt a cold shiver when he met Panko's narrow, suspicious regard. Danik's voice drew Nollen's attention from his observations.

"There are mention of diamonds, but not of specific origin."

"I can say with the upmost certainty, that Eldar has not placed an order for diamonds from Markita." Out of the corner of his eye, Nollen saw Panko jab Albric. Again, his attention was drawn forward by Danik.

"Then you dispute the Archduke's accounting?"

"I do!"

"How dare you?" Panko shouted and stepped forward.

"As Royal Commissary, I know what Eldar imports and exports. Diamonds are not among those," Nollen firmly said.

"You said you could not offer rebuttal without records from Sener, so how can you suddenly be so certain?" Panko interrogated.

"I need the records for accurate comparison of *all* items in *your* ledger. However!" Nollen raised his voice when those gathered agreed with Panko, "this singular item is notorious, and not needed or wanted in Eldar since it is said to be cursed by Chika!"

Mention of the high goddess brought outrage from the nobles.

"That might not have been a good idea," Gunnar chided Nollen.

Danik called for order, while boldly Panko approached. "Sire! This foreign spy speaks blasphemy!"

"I'm not a spy!"

Gunnar grabbed Nollen. "Steady, lad."

Nollen breathed hard to contain his ire, and heed Gunnar.

Finally, Montre stood and shouted, "Silence!"

The herald pounded the staff for attention. Slowly, the nobles grew quiet, though their expressions unfavorable toward the Eldarians.

Montre waved Panko back to his place. He focused harshly on Nollen and Gunnar. "Be warned about invoking the goddess in your defense."

Nollen gave a slight nod of deference to the Montre.

The King sat. "Any more questions, Magistrate?"

"One more, Sire." Danik proceeded to inquire of Nollen and Gunnar. "This group of one hundred and forty people. How do they fit into your plan of spying?"

Nollen clenched his fist. "Pilgrims we encountered. They are returning home to Eldar. Many women and children. They pose no threat to Markita."

"They can provide a good deflection for scouting on route."

Nollen went to speak but stopped when a page hurried to Montre. He whispered a few words and gave the king a paper. Montre's glowering eyes went from the paper to Nollen and Gunnar.

"Everyone out!" he bellowed. "Tilbic, take them back the dungeon. Archdukes and counselors to the antechamber!"

The soldiers roughly escorted Nollen and Gunnar to the dungeon. Not until the cell locked, and footsteps faded, did anyone speak.

"Well?" Milos anxiously asked.

Nollen shrugged. "We made a strong defense when Montre suddenly halted the trial due to some news."

"What news?"

"Don't know. He was given a paper, then dismissed everyone."

"Was the defense strong enough to convince him to release us?" asked Lexi, hopeful.

"I suppose it depends upon this unexpected news."

Gunnar smiled, as he clapped Nollen on the shoulder. "You did well, lad. All we can do now, is wait and pray."

Chapter 39

MONTRE DIDN'T WAIT FOR THE DOOR OF THE ANTECHAMBER to close before he confronted the archdukes and counselors. "This," he waved the paper, "is from Axel. He demands the release of his people immediately or will take the necessary steps to secure them if we refuse."

"How does he know already?" asked Tomas, stunned.

"Exactly! They just arrived last night! Then this today."

"He couldn't have sent a courier so swiftly from Eldar," Luken said in disbelief.

"No. It came by way of an eagle."

Panko laughed. "An eagle? Surely, Your Majesty doesn't believe a bird—"

"It bears the royal seal of Eldar!" Montre held it out for all to see. "Something an eagle can't do." He focused on Panko. "You accused *them* of spying. So, explain this?" He waved the paper in Panko's face.

With all eyes watching, Panko blurted out, "Part of Eldar's plan." He quickly continued when Montre, Tomas, and Luken scoffed. "By including capture as part of the deception, it gives Axel a legitimate reason to invade."

While the others took a moment to consider, Tomas spoke with incredulity. "Let me see if I understand this. Axel first sends Gunnar on some mission to the Black Mountains, then when that goes awry, he dispatched Nollen to find Gunnar. They gather a group of pilgrims to head back to Eldar, all for sake of getting captured so they can invade Markita?"

When Panko hesitated to reply, Tomas continued. "Does anyone or everyone fail to see the logic in that?" he asked Montre and his fellow archdukes.

"Do not underestimate the Eldarians' cunning." Sveta emerged from a back corner of the room.

"Witch, how did you get in here?" demanded Montre.

"That is unimportant. Dealing with Eldar is paramount." She sent a scolding glare to Panko. He swallowed back discomposure that no one seemed to notice. They were more concerned with Sveta, who continued. "There is one among the group who poses a great threat to Chika."

"Why would the supreme goddess fear a mortal?" asked Luken.

"Oh, you of little understanding! It was a mere mortal, who unseated Sirin from Eldar centuries ago."

"Sirin?" Carl muttered thoughtfully to himself, unheard by any.

"Some mortals are destined for greatness, some to ruin of others. A Baga can often tell the difference."

"What do you propose, witch?" Montre asked with disdain.

"I will interview each female."

"Female?" Luken scoffed. "You want us to fear a female?"

"I am female! Chika is female." Sveta's voice filled the room with such force that the men cringed in pain. She gave them a moment to recover. "Any more stupid questions?"

"A serious one," began Montre. "How will finding this female help deter Axel from invading to free his people?"

She wickedly smiled. "Once discovered, you will never fear Eldar again."

The answer pleased Panko and Boric. Tomas and Luken remained wary, as did the counselors. Montre gave it serious consideration. Albric fought to conceal his worry, while Carl broke the silence

"Sire, with the fate of two kingdoms at stake, let us discuss this before taking action," he bravely suggested.

Sveta hissed at him in reptile fashion, which made him balk.

"Stay, witch!" Montre commanded. "He speaks wisdom."

"Chika demands obedience not discussion!"

"Who will be left to obey Chika if Markita and Eldar go to war over a female?" Carl hotly countered.

"Carl! Have you forgotten, our province suffered the wrath of Chika because of the Eldarians?" objected Boric.

"No, I have not. However, Master Nollen rightly referred to our treaty. Markita is bound by certain agreed conditions. Some of which have been broken by this trial. Discussion should be warranted before proceeding further."

Sveta slightly swayed, as if losing her balance. She pretended to right herself by accidently spilling a glass of water on a table. She placed a palm in the water. "Very well. Have your discussion. However, I will return after sunset to begin the interrogation. Have this room ready with no lights, only the drapes open." She yowled an unearthly scream that made the men collapse. When they recovered, Sveta was gone.

Tomas aided Montre to stand. Montre glowered at Carl. "What do you suggest we discuss?" he demanded.

"Sire, the treaty took a year to negotiate. It established an agreement from which many Markitans have benefited in ways not possible before."

"Not my mines!" scoffed Panko. "I'm nearly bankrupt from their demands."

Uncomfortable, Albric shifted his weight to maintain composure.

"Renegotiating terms is more preferable to war," Tomas chided.

"Ya. Not to mention that what has already been done voids the King's word and signature," Carl pointedly said.

"And ours," groused Luken to his peers.

Montre strode to a chair and sat. The lines of his face deep with distress. "That thought has not been lost upon me."

"What of the witch? We can't simply ignore her," Panko said.

"Nor can we ignore the welfare of all Markitans before proceeding to violate the entire treaty!" insisted Carl.

"Lord Carl is correct, Sire," Albric said.

"Albric!" Panko sneered in scolding.

"Your Grace, we cannot dismiss the fate of our people so lightly. New mines can be dug, but people lives are not easily replaced."

Red-faced, Panko fists clenched.

"Chika is powerful! I need to protect my people from further reprisal," Boric passionately argued.

"I seek to protect all Markitans," Carl sympathetically said.

"Ya. I know." Boric said in sober agreement. He patted Carl's shoulder.

"My lords, retire and consider how best to protect Markita, serve Chika, and appease Axel," Montre said in dismissal.

Carl and Albric exchanged brief glances of concern when Panko ordered Albric to accompany him. In resigned silence, Albric followed Panko to the office above the Hall of the Archdukes.

"Your Grace, let me explain—"

"You can't explain betrayal!"

"I have not betrayed you! I dutifully performed every task given, even those I vehemently disagree with. However," Albric boldly continued over Panko's objection, "speaking for the safety of all Markitans is not betrayal. Nay, it is our duty as provincial leaders to protect our people."

"Impertinence!" Panko shouted in rage.

"Do you think Montre and the others will accept your plea of poverty when needed to contribute to the coffers to fund the army?"

With intense anger, Panko's whole body visibly trembled. He shouted in fury, as he assaulted Albric. The older man did all his could to withstand the attack. He fell into a wardrobe when stuck in the face. Defense began to waver, as punch after punch impacted Albric.

The sound of conflict brought Horst into the room. "Your Grace!"

The intervention stopped the assault. Panko breathed heavy from passionate physical exertion. He stared at a bloodied Albric lying unconscious on the floor. "Get him out of here! And leave me!"

Horst summoned two soldiers to bear Albric from the room.

In the hall, Horst and the soldiers carrying Albric encountered Carl. He rushed to catch them. "What happened?"

Horst's jowls flexed with stubbornness.

"Did Panko do this?" Carl demanded. At Horst's nod, he ordered, "Fetch a doctor! Now, captain!" He continued with the men to the Albric's room. He pulled down the covers for the men to place Albric on the bed. "Bring me the basin, pitcher, and towels. Quickly!" Once he had the items, he dismissed them.

Albric's right eye showed signs of deep bruising and swelling. His lip cut in multiple places, cheeks red with abrasions. Albric stirred in pain.

"Easy, my friend," Carl soothed.

Slowly Albric's left eye opened. His mouth barely moved. "Who ...?"

"Carl. I'm here."

Albric tried to raise his hand so Carl took hold. "If ... I die"

"You won't. The doctor will be here soon."

Albric's head sluggishly rocked side to side. "If I do. Remember, your promise. And tell Rebah ... Remember."

"I will. I promise."

Albric winced in pain. "My luggage. A book. Take it. Read it. Keep it from Panko." He fell back into unconsciousness.

Carl just found the book when the door opened. He tucked it inside his surcoat pocket. Feeling the weight, he held his arm close to his body to help conceal it. "Ah, good, doctor. Say nothing to his condition, merely tend to his wounds."

The doctor examined Albric. Stripped of his garments showed more injury to his torso. Carl fought to keep his distress under control. All the while, he held his surcoat closed.

When finished, the doctor spoke. "His condition is grave. Such severity, I suspect internal damage. The next day or two will be critical."

Carl's eyes grew misty in regard of Albric. "Do what you can. I'll return later." He went to his room. He managed to lock the door before a sob escaped. He took out the book to toss it on the bed. He paced the room to regain his composure.

Several times Albric had written him since Kristoff's death. Each time he expressed concern of how Panko changed. Everyone knew of Panko's selfish tendencies. Even before the treaty, he sought ways to increase his holdings and expand his province. In return correspondence, Carl tried to console Albric and encourage him. Until now, he didn't fully comprehend the dangerous meaning in those letters. Regret mingled with fearful concern for his brother-in-law. He thought of Rebah. How could he break such news to his beloved sister if the worst should happen?

He sat on the bed to pick up the book. To his surprise, it was a copy of Eldar's sacred book. He should have recognized it. Then again, things happened so fast, he hid it before taking notice.

Secret. Read it. Keep from Panko, Albric's words echoed in his mind.

New tears rose. "I have read it, my brother." He wiped his eyes and placed the book in his personal luggage. He looked out the window which faced the dungeon. He considered his options. Visiting the prisoners might be risky. However, an interview could be helpful in deciding upon a course of action.

He donned his state robe for departure. He made certain to lock his room. In purposeful steps, he crossed to the dungeon and ordered the jailer to bring Nollen and Sir Gunnar to an interrogation room. Kept purposely dark and damp, the atmosphere served to intimidate prisoners.

When they arrived, Carl sternly told the jailer, "Leave us. We are not to be disturbed. Is that understood?"

Carl placed a finger to his lips for silence. He carefully peeked out the small barred window of the door. No one. "Be easy, gentlemen," he spoke in Eldarian.

"A bit late for that advice," said Nollen.

"I can well understand why you feel that way. I am here to help."

"You can help by convincing Montre to release us," chided Gunnar.

"I'm speaking with you to help facilitate that very end."

"Picking a more suitable place than a torture chamber would have helped," groused Gunnar.

"This place will allay any suspicions that might otherwise arise."

"What happened to abruptly end the trial?" Nollen asked.

"Axel sent a warning letter demanding your release or he will act."

Nollen fought a smile, as he glanced to Gunnar.

Carl grew curious at the exchange. "Montre demanded to know how Axel gained intelligence so quickly since your group only arrived yesterday. My guess, is you have the answer."

"We dispatched word immediately upon our capture," Nollen said.

"An eagle? That is how the demand for release was delivered."

"Aye. In Eldar, animals are friends to humans. One joined me on this journey," explained Nollen.

Carl lowly chuckled at the answer. "Montre wondered about spies. Not you, Markitans, for Axel to learn so quickly."

"Someone betrayed our presence for capture," Gunnar rebuffed.

"Sveta."

"Who is Sveta?"

"A Baga. A witch."

Nollen visibly balked with discomposure.

Gunnar grabbed Nollen to steady him. "What's wrong, lad?"

"A sudden chill, like ... like with *her.*"

Confused, Carl asked, "Have you met Sveta before?"

Again, the young man shivered. He exhaled to relax. "You believe she betrayed us?"

"Aye. There's more. She wants to interrogate your women."

Both Nollen and Gunnar grew wary and guarded. Gunnar tried to restrain the anger in his voice when he asked, "Why?"

"She believes one of them is a threat, though didn't say how."

"Sirin," Nollen and Gunnar said in near angry unison.

Carl observed the reaction with concern. He spoke to Nollen. "In Sproule, you wondered if Chika and Sirin were the same. I now believe they are, as Sveta mentioned Sirin being driven from Eldar in connection with this female. It is one of the reasons I'm here."

"It can't be allowed to happen!" Gunnar declared.

"I agree. I managed to persuade Montre to delay it until this evening, so we could speak. However, if this Baga is Sirin, totally forbidding her could be dangerous for all. Peitro is evidence of that."

"I will face her instead. As Royal Emissary, they are my responsibility."

Carl's brows knitted at Nollen's suggestion. "I don't know if that will be an acceptable alternative. Sveta was quite adamant."

"Our women will not be mistreated! I will face her."

Carl observed the staunch determination. "This female must be very important."

Neither Eldarian replied to the statement. Instead, Nollen changed the topic. "You said this was *one of the reasons*. Is there another?"

Carl's expression turned somber. "A personal one. Although to speak of it is not appropriate at the moment, save to say, beware of Panko. His anger and ambition rules him to the point of mindless aggression."

"Albric," Nollen said with certainty. He then explained to Carl's disconcertion, "He spoke with us last night."

"About the trial?"

"No. Our faith. Something has happened to him."

Carl soberly nodded. "He may not survive the day."

"Dear Gott," Gunner prayed under his breath.

"Indeed. May Gott hear you on his behalf. Now, I must go." Carl summoned the jailer.

Nollen hurriedly whispered to Gunnar, "Say nothing to the others about females or Sirin. No need for unnecessary upset."

Once returned to the cell, they waited for the Markitans to depart.

"What happened?" Milos inquired.

"There is another interview for this evening," said Nollen.

"Brought about by an unexpected event," said Gunnar with a sly grin. "Axel knows about us and demands our immediate release."

"Praise be!" Milos cheered.

All in the cell expressed similar sentiments.

"How did Axel learn so quickly?" asked Arnie.

"Ajax. I dispatched him and Callie before our capture," said Nollen.

"So, this next interview is about us leaving," Lexi eagerly said.

"There could be some of that," Nollen discreetly replied.

Lexi noticed the subdued attitude. "You are not happy about it?"

"Oh, I'm very glad Ajax reached Axel. However, there are many issues that need to be addressed before we can leave."

"Montre would not dare refuse Axel," Lexi staunchly declared.

"I didn't say he would." Nollen chose to be cagey, though her obstinacy, prompted further speech. "You are unfamiliar with the world outside of Kranston. Under such circumstances, points of order are common between monarchs."

Pricked by the reminder, she lashed out. "I am more familiar with monarchs than you realize!" She moved to the far side of the cell.

Nollen followed. Not angry, rather curious. "Because you're The Shield Maiden? Is that what you mean?"

Gunnar quickly intervened. "Aye. That is what she means."

Lexi's fierce eyes darted between them. "Aye," she admitted.

"Then I depend upon you as The Shield Maiden to keep others calm while I negotiate the terms of release." Nollen flashed a soft smile.

Lexi's posture relaxed. "I will."

Gunnar drew Nollen aside to speak privately. "Lad …" He struggled for words. "Volunteering to stand in place of … someone you don't yet know."

Nollen wryly grinned. "So far, my ignorance has helped."

"When I am at liberty, I will gladly tell you everything. For now, know that I am proud of you."

Chapter 40

CARL WENT DIRECTLY FROM THE DUNGEON TO BORIC'S APARTMENT in the royal guest quarters of the castle. He didn't announce his presence since it sounded like Boric spoke with someone. However, he became curious at hearing a female. Through an ornately carved partition between the small foyer and private quarters, he recognized—Sveta! Startled, he ducked back.

"Archduke Panko has been more accommodating," she chided.

"I warned you in Sproule that Montre would not take kindly to the possibility of war with Eldar," Boric countered.

"And I *warned* you of inciting Chika's wrath for breaking our agreement!"

"I haven't broken it. I speak with Montre daily. I don't have a witch's wiles to force him to act. I can only present the strongest argument."

"When I discover the female and reveal her threat, Montre will agree. Until then, keep your wits."

Taking the statement as an ending to the conversation, Carl quickly, and silently, moved to the door. He knocked and called, "Your Grace!"

"A moment!" Boric shouted.

Carl waited, satisfied that his ruse worked.

"Come."

Carl found Boric was now alone. He bowed and assumed a humble attitude. "Forgive me, Your Grace. I was wrong not to consult you before speaking out of turn earlier."

Boric huffed. "Oh, that. I know your heart, Carl. Loyal. But," he grew stern. "We need to take everything into consideration. Including, Sveta's demands."

"Can her demands prevent war?"

Boric paced. His brows drawn level. "Who knows what a witch can and can't do?"

"The only way to learn is to test her."

Boric pulled to a sudden stop. "That could be dangerous!"

"More dangerous than war? She is one individual. War will cost thousands of lives."

"An individual with Chika in support."

Carl sensed a time for boldness. "What has Chika done to help Markita? Every time she makes demands, it is with pain and destruction. Never healing or aid. People act out of fear, not hope. Is that truly what Your Grace wants for Markita? To keep people bound in terror at the mention of her? Or free them to live without fear?"

Boric's eyes narrowed in attentive regard. "What else can I do?"

"The treaty," he bravely continued despite Boric's immediate ire. "It is our best hope. Despite a mistake by Sir Gunnar, trade with Eldar has enriched our people, given them purpose to work and expand beyond small villages with limited expectations. Soothe, even Miska has grown in productivity these past two years. War would devastate that progress. And for what? To appease Chika? An absent goddess—"

"Enough!" Boric snapped. "Be warned of blasphemy, Carl."

"I mean no disrespect, Your Grace. However, you can't deny reality."

Boric again paced. "Your argument has merit. However, I must weigh it against the events of today, as that *mistake* has placed us in the middle of two dangerous choices: a king's threat of war, and a goddess' demand for obedience."

"One can be reasoned with, the other cannot."

"Exactly! No one can reason with a goddess."

"Have you tried? What has she promised in exchange for obedience?"

Boric's eyes went wide with insult then turned suspicious. "Why do ask those questions?"

Carl realized his brashness went too far and reverted to a mild manner. "Simply in response to your statement."

The answer didn't abate Boric's skepticism. "You meant something by that."

"No, Your Grace." Carl knew that when Boric became angry, the best way to calm the archduke was to remain steadfast. Thus, with unflappable composure, he withstood Boric's intense stare.

As usual, Boric blinked. His sighed with resignation. "Chika isn't here to be reasoned with, so what do you suggest?"

"Do not allow Sveta to interview the Eldarian women. Axel will take that as a grave insult."

"Why should he? They are women," Boric said in rough dismissal.

"Women are treated differently in Eldar. They are given more respect."

Boric guffawed. "Respect?"

"It's true, Your Grace. I witnessed the difference when visiting Eldar during the negotiations."

Boric tried to recover from his mocking amusement. "Ya. Ya. I remember you telling me. I laughed then, too."

"You mock women, yet fear a goddess?"

Boric's humor instantly faded, only this time, Carl did not back down.

"Hear me, Your Grace. Our women love, nurture, and care for our children. They show us respect, yet for that, we think no more of them than chattel. Why?"

"They are weak and silly minded," Boric said off-handedly.

"Do find you Lady Mari to be weak and silly minded? I know, I didn't see my wife that way. I regret her not knowing that before she died."

Boric briefly glowered at the mention of his wife yet tempered his response at Carl's lament. "Eldarians consider women better than us?"

"They are considered an important part of society. Different in task and nature, but equal in life's endeavors. This is why I believe the interview of the Eldarian women is wrong because it will show total disrespect. Such action will incite Axel beyond what we have already done by violating the treaty."

Boric plopped in a chair. He chewed on his lips. His brows knitted with great deliberation. At length he asked, "What do you suggest?"

"I ask Your Grace to trust me. I have a plan for this evening. However, it is best for you to remain ignorant of the details. If it fails, the responsibility falls on me alone. If it succeeds, we may avert war."

"You ask a great deal."

"Have I not earned your trust by loyal years of service?"

Boric snorted. "You can be tiresome with asking questions you already know the answer!" He nodded. "Now, go."

Carl bowed to hide a relieved smile. In the hall, he met Panko. Meeting the archduke's gaze, a cold sensation penetrated to the core with an intensity he never felt before. He averted his eyes with a partial bow.

"Your Grace."

"Is Boric in his chamber."

"Ya—" he went to protest when Panko marched to the door, where he pounded and shouted.

Carl fought the impulse to intervene. No. He had important matters to tend. In his mind, he prayed, *Gott, the Eldarians believe you hear those who call upon you. Please, keep Boric strong against Panko's badgering. Give me favor to help your people.*

He made his way to Albric's room. The doctor sat in a chair beside the bed reading. At first Carl balked then realized the cover was that of a medical journal. He approached the bed.

"How is he?"

"By the favor of the goddess, he is still alive."

"Leave us." When the door shut, Carl sat on the bed. "Albric?" he gently spoke with a light touch on Albric's shoulder. "It's Carl. Can you hear me?" It took several more attempts before Albric stirred and opened his eyes. Carl smiled. "It is good to see you awake."

Albric grunted. "What ... is ... happening?"

"Be quiet and listen. I have read *the book* before. Remember, the tales I told you about my days in Eldar."

Albric made a feeble smile. "Stubborn I was then. Not now."

"Place your mind at ease. I am helping the *Brethren.*"

Tears fell from Albric's good left eye. He gripped Carl's arm. "Rebah?"

"I will send word for her to leave for Sproule and my protection. Panko won't harm her."

Albric sighed in relief and closed his eyes.

For an anxious moment, Carl waited. The rhythmic rising and falling of the blanket told him Albric slept. He gently kissed his brother-in-law's forehead. He summoned the doctor with instructions to send for him if anything changes.

He went to his office. There, he wrote a quick note to Rebah, and dispatched it by way of a trusted soldier from Boric's escort. In preparation for the evening interview, he would spend the afternoon reviewing the treaty and researching Markitan law.

"Enough!" Boric shouted at Panko. In agitation, he paced his chamber. "What you are proposing is not possible!"

"Not for us. Only for Chika."

"To what purpose? Why bring the devastation of war upon our people? How can it possibly serve Chika to destroy all the recent advancements?"

Panko snarled. "We are not to question the motives of the goddess! We are duty bound to obey without hesitation."

Boric became uneasy at the implication. "You would truly sacrifice all those in your province to appease Chika?"

"True obedience demands sacrifice. The more vital the task, the higher the sacrifice."

Dumbfounded, Boric stared at Panko.

At Boric's hapless expression, Panko challenged him. "Why do you vacillate? Has not the goddess favored your province?"

"She killed and destroyed those in Peitro!"

"For aiding the enemy!"

"No, they helped to enrich our country."

Irked, Panko snarled an accusation. "You chose Eldarians over Chika?"

"No! I chose to protect my people from any threat, as is my sworn duty at archduke. Same as you."

"There is an agreement. One *we* made freely. Or have you forgotten the consequences of failure?"

Boric moved to a window that overlooked the courtyard. He spoke over his shoulder. "I have not forgotten." He winced at Panko's hard clap of his shoulder.

"Then stand with Sveta in defense of Chika at the interview tonight."

Boric didn't reply rather returned his focus back to the courtyard. He stood there long after Panko departed. The fate of everything hung in the balance.

Chapter 41

NOLLEN SAT ON THE FAR SIDE OF THE CELL AWAY FROM THE OTHERS. His posture went from head bowed to looking up at the window. He needed time to prepare. The responsibility to protect had been a priority since childhood. He witnessed it in his parents, sister, and grandfather. When old enough, he followed their example. This time felt different than a sense of duty. Since Axel told him of Gunnar's capture, a deep prompting in his spirit drove him. The sensation rose to such intensity it compelled him to volunteer to face Sirin. The words from his mouth, even surprised him, especially after the unsettling gorge encounter. Once spoken, there was no turning back. He must be ready.

Occasionally, he noticed Gunnar kept others away from him; those primarily being Lexi, Alicia, Milos, and Lorraine. Part of him desired company, while the inclination to protect demanded separation. His head rose when someone sat beside him.

"Sundown." Gunnar motioned to the fading light outside the window. "Milos wants to pray again. I agree. Only less noise." He flashed a wry smile.

Nollen went with Gunnar to join the group in a circle. Lexi took hold of his right hand. Alicia held his left hand. Gunnar gripped Nollen's shoulder. They bowed their heads when Milos began to pray.

"Gott, we come to you on behalf of Nollen, asking that you grant him wisdom; faith and trust to endure ..."

Mention of *endure* made Nollen open his eyes to watch Milos. *He couldn't know. Unless Gunnar told him.* He carefully looked to see Gunnar's head remained bowed and eyes tightly closed. His lips moved, but no speech.

Milos continued, "May the words you give him, convince the Markitans to set us free that we may proceed to fulfill this appointed hour of our return. In your Almighty name, we ask. Amen."

"Amen," they repeated.

The jingle of keys alerted them to approach.

Nollen felt Lexi and Alicia squeeze his hands. He tried to withdraw, but neither would release him.

Carl entered with Tilbic. "It's time," Carl said to Nollen.

"I have to go." Nollen removed his hands from Lexi and Alicia.

Tilbic objected. "It is females to be interviewed—"

"No!" Carl snapped at the general. "Orders are changed."

"What does he mean, *females?*" Lexi anxiously asked Gunnar.

Gunnar shook his head and he placed a finger to his lips.

The motion didn't satisfy Lexi. She seized Nollen when to stop his departure.

"Don't worry. We just prayed," he assured her.

Gunnar drew Lexi back. This time with a more forceful indication for silence. After the door closed, she confronted Gunnar.

"There is something about this interview you haven't told us!"

With contrition, he replied, "I kept silent for Nollen's benefit. Let us sit, and I will disclose all."

Torches lit the courtyard. Nollen took a moment to consider his unique relationship with Lord Carl. He helped negotiate the treaty. A consummate diplomat, accustomed to concealing his true thoughts and feelings. Knowing this, made his confession of a personal reason for meeting them highly unusual. Now, he served as escort. Nollen's pondering ended upon entering the main building. The foyer and hall were surprisingly dim. Not much different inside than outside. Although curious, Nollen didn't have a chance to wonder why when they stopped in an alcove where Carl dismissed Tilbic.

Once alone, Carl spoke in Eldarian "I'm sorry it has come to this. Yet know, other *Brethren* have prayed for you."

Nollen tried to mask his surprise. The Markitan lord softly smiled, and Nollen whispered, "Thank you."

"My lord," Tilbic summoned them from the threshold.

"Courage and faith," Carl hastily whispered to Nollen.

This room was even darker than the foyer, with just the drapes opened for light. No fire warmed the room. Another peculiarity for a cold winter evening. Being accustomed to the dimness, Nollen could make out the individual archdukes. Montre sat in a chair beside a table.

"Lord Carl! Where is the first female?" demanded Montre.

"Your pardon, Majesty," began Nollen. "Do not fault Lord Carl. No Eldarian woman will be subject to questioning. I am here in their stead."

Montre snarled. "Did you tell him why?" he scolded Carl.

"Sire—"

The door slammed shut and locked with a loud click. The silhouette of a woman stood in front of it. "Where is the female?"

Nollen clenched his fist. Despite the dimness of the room, he recognized the voice. "You will not question them, creature of darkness."

"How dare you speak to me—!" Sveta stepped out of the shadows. She hissed in a reptile-like manner at sight of Nollen. "What are you doing here?"

"Seeing you do not succeed—Sirin!"

Sveta screamed so loud and long that everyone collapsed in great pain. When she stopped, she seized Nollen by his throat and jerked him into a sitting position. "You are no match for me." Her eyes glowed yellow. Her tone lowered to a threatening whisper, as she spoke in Eldarian. "Have you forgotten how they will suffer for refusing me what I want?"

The sheer effort to withstand her penetrating eyes made sweat form on Nollen's face. He clenched his teeth to stem the pain.

She grabbed his face in both her hands to intensify her stare. "Remember!"

He trembled with great effort to ignore the visions. Sweat streamed down his face from exertion. Veins protruded in his forehead. Blood trickled from his nose. His breathing grew labored.

Angered by his resistance, she demanded, "Tell me who she is!"

He forced himself to speak. "Gott, rebuke you!"

She cried out in horror and forced to back away. Released, Nollen fell to all fours. Blood freely flowed from both nostrils. He gulped for air to remain conscious. The men, who barely recovered from her first scream, again collapsed.

"Nollen?" Carl tried to inch his way to help.

With eyes of deadly intent, she grabbed Nollen again.

"In the name of Gott, begone!" he managed to speak in command.

Sveta swayed as the impact of his words drove her back again. "Kill him! Kill the Eldarians!" She let out a reptile scream that shook in the room. This time, when the sound vanished, Sveta was gone.

Panko breathed hard in angry pain. "The Eldarians have angered Chika," he spoke in halting painful words.

Carl reached Nollen, who lay on the floor semiconscious. His hair wet from sweat, pallor ashen, and blood still flowed from his nose. "Nollen?"

"Take him to the dungeon!" Montre ordered. Boric helped him to sit.

"Sire, he is seriously injured. He needs a doctor," Carl said in dispute.

"To the dungeon! Unless you want join him for disobedience!"

Still weak from the encounter, Carl had difficultly lifting Nollen. Tilbic came to help. Each placed one of Nollen's arm over a shoulder. Outside, the night air cleared their heads. Bearing Nollen became easier. He too grew more alert, though very weak. His head spun, and he tasted the blood.

"Where is she?" Nollen wearily asked.

"Gone. At least for now," Carl replied.

Tilbic summoned the jailer to open the cell.

"Wait here," Carl told Tilbic. He alone brought Nollen into the cell.

Everyone became concerned at sight of Nollen's wretched condition. Gunnar immediately took him from Carl. Carefully, he lowered Nollen to lay on the floor.

"What happened, lad?" Gunnar asked with serious concern.

Nollen licked his lips to clear the blood yet couldn't answer.

"He unmasked Sveta," Carl quietly said.

Angry, Gunnar bolted to his feet. "She did this to him?"

Carl nodded. "She ordered the death of all Eldarians because he withstood her." He quickly added, "I believe I know how to thwart her."

Worried, Lexi knelt beside Nollen. Alicia clung to Lorraine, tears streaming down her cheeks as she gazed at Nollen.

"He needs a doctor!" Lexi pleaded to Carl.

"My saddlebag. I have medicine that might help him. Get it!" Gunnar ordered Carl.

"I don't know if that's possible."

Gunnar's harsh voice matched his features. "If he dies, expect no mercy from Axel or me."

Carl took no offense at the threat. "I'll see what can be done." He left.

"Gunnar." Nollen's weak voice brought him back. "If I die …"

"Don't say it, lad. You will survive."

"Aye! Our prayers shall be heard!" Milos added his assurance.

Through tears, Lexi asked, "Why did you take our place?"

Nollen again licked his lips to clear the blood. "Years ago, I watched a man give himself for others. I can do no less than my king, who charged me with your safety."

Lexi leaned down to speak choked words. "I am the sister of that man." She kissed his cheek.

Nollen sluggishly moved his head toward Gunnar. "Glad I didn't know before." He slipped into unconsciousness.

To hopefully allay Boric's anger, Carl collected things necessary to fully explain his plan. He also stopped at the stable to find Gunnar's saddlebags, and sent it to the dungeon.

He paused at the door to Boric's quarters to braced himself for a tongue-lashing. He knocked and entered after receiving a curt order.

"Your Grace." He bowed to Boric. The archduke's eyes glared at him in such a way, Carl realized Boric's fury defied words. "Please, hear me out." He moved to the table. Boric's eyes followed. Carl continued to speak, as he withdrew two maps from a hard leather cylinder and other parchments from a leather case. "Admittedly, the first part of my plan did not go exactly as expected. However, it did serve to keep face with Axel in regard to protecting his women. The second part, will protect Markita from war while allowing us to appease Chika, and save our dignity."

"*Not going exactly as expected* is a severe understatement!" Boric voice finally exploded. He marched to the table. His sneered with fury. "What is all this?"

"Necessary items to explain part two of the plan. Please, indulge me, Your Grace, because if I can convince you, I will need your help to approach the king."

Boric leaned on the table. His face hard set. "This had better be good, or not only will I refuse to help, I will place you under arrest for aiding the enemy."

Carl swallowed back momentary discomposure. Boric never made idle threats. He bravely spoke. "Allow me to proceed."

Chapter 42

CARL NEATLY DISPLAYED THE MAPS AND PARCHMENTS ON THE table in Montre's private study. It took several hours to convince Boric. When done, the archduke petitioned Montre for an audience. Carl barely finished the arrangement, when Boric arrived with Montre. He bowed to the king.

"Sire. Thank you for agreeing to hear me."

"Boric believes your plan will work."

Carl fought a smile with a partial bow. "Then allow me to begin—"

"Wait for others," said Montre. At Carl's curiosity, he explained, "It is fitting the entire Archduke Council be present."

Feeling nervousness rise, Carl said a silent prayer for peace and clarity of thought. *In service of the Brethren,* he concluded. Though barely five minutes, he felt the time pass painfully slow. When the archdukes and their counselors arrived, Montre gave permission for Carl to proceed.

"My lords, let me first explain why I brought Master Nollen instead of a female, and how that fits into this second phase of the plan." At Panko's snarl when he mentioned Nollen, Carl felt an intense coldness in the pit of his being. Despite the sensation, he pressed on. "Master Nollen is King Axel's representative. In Markita, we view females differently than the Eldarians. As such, any action we take in respect to their women will be viewed as a great insult. With Eldar poised on our border, we cannot afford that. We already violated the treaty."

"What about insulting Chika?" demanded Panko.

"Your Grace, are you privy to how Chika will defend us from invasion?"

Panko flushed with anger. "How dare you question the goddess?"

"No, I asked Your Grace if you possess knowledge we do not."

"Panko! Let him finish," Montre scolded.

"Sire, the goddess will protect us."

"How? She is not here to help us formulate a plan. And, we need a plan."

"Sveta told us, until *he* wrongly acted." Panko accused Carl.

"His plan is sound!" Boric interjected. "It will even appease Chika."

Panko reluctantly backed down at Montre's seething glare. The king nodded for Carl to proceed.

"This map shows ancient Markita, while this one shows the current boundaries." His gestures brought all to the table.

"Boric, your province is missing in the earlier one," Luken observed.

"That is because it originally belonged to Eldar," said Carl.

"What?"

Carl used a cartograph instrument to indicate places on each map. "The river and mountains serve as a natural division between the two countries. However, a hundred years before we or Eldar had trouble with the Palleteens, Markita and Eldar fought over this territory between these two mountain ranges."

"My province," Boric said.

Carl picked up an old book. "According to royal records, both sides fought valiantly yet, neither gained significant foothold to declare the territory. To save their countries from total bankruptcy and depletion of all resources, they made an agreement." He carefully opened the book to read; "*Let it be known that this day, a tournament will be held. Trial by combat to decide the victor according to the ancient law of Markita.* The Eldarian King, Lange, agreed."

"The Eldarian champion was defeated, and my family's province became part of Markita," Boric said.

"So, you're suggesting a similar tournament, now?" asked Tomas.

"Ya. For the release of the prisoners, or their questioning by Chika."

"How will this avoid war?" asked Luken.

"It will be part of the terms."

"I'm not sure Axel will agree since you argued how they view females differently than we do," said Montre.

"The questioning can be done in his presence …"

"Chika will not be subject to human will!" Sveta appeared.

"Witch, your presence grows tiresome!" Montre chided.

"Continuing disobedience will not be tolerated," she rebuffed.

Carl once again read from the book. "*Let it be further noted, this tournament has received the blessing of our goddess, Chika, who promised to aid our champion.*"

Panko's curious eyes darted to Sveta. "Is that true? Did Chika sanction the tournament?"

Sveta's irate stare was slow to leave Carl, who bravely endured.

"Sveta!" Panko's demanding voice broke her focus.

"It is true," she reluctantly admitted. "To defeat Eldar, Chika allowed the tournament."

"Then why would she not agree now, if it will gain us the advantage?" Montre asked.

Sveta made a threatening hiss at Carl before she replied to Montre. "There is more at stake than a plot of land."

"Would war with Eldar help whatever that is?" asked Tomas, skeptical.

"Questioning of the females would have provided the answer."

"What answer?" demanded Montre, his patience exhausted. "Speak directly, witch. What answer do you seek from the females that could avert war?"

"It would not avert war, and she knows it," Carl boldly spoke.

Again, Sveta hissed at Carl. "Unbeliever!"

"I believe in the good of my people! Is that also Chika's desire?"

Sveta waved her hands. A cloud of fog enveloped Carl's head. He began to choke. He dropped to his knees in great distress.

"No! Stop, witch." Montre shouted. When she refused to heed, he called, "General!"

When Tilbic seized her, she released her concentrated hold on Carl. He fully collapsed to the floor, where he took in large gulps of air.

"Get her out of here!" Montre ordered Tilbic

They barely reached the door when she screamed. Everyone covered their ears in pain. Once more, she escaped.

Panko recovered first. "We have angered the goddess."

"No, we angered an old witch," Tomas chided.

"An annoyingly loud, old hag." Luken tried to clear his ears.

Carl struggled to stand. His voice breathy and strained voice. "Sire, she provided no answers or directions to help us."

"Why should she?" challenge Panko.

"She claims to represent Chika, yet relies solely on mortal females for answers? That does not help us to decide on how to deal with Eldar."

"He speaks truth. Sveta offered nothing helpful," Boric agreed.

Panko grew frustrated at the inability to dispute.

After a lengthy moment of silence, Montre asked Carl, "How do we proceed?"

In the dungeon, Gunnar roused Nollen to drink the same elixir as when poisoned by the arrow. Once finished, Nollen slept.

Alicia held a bowl of water, as Lexi used a wet rag to gently wipe the blood from Nollen's face. "Will he die?" asked Lexi, anxious.

"No!" Gunnar emphatically replied. He calmed his tone when she appeared stricken by the abruptness. "The blood appears to be the result of strain, not wounds. It is exhausting to come face-to-face with evil."

"You believe this worse than what happened at the gorge?"

"Different. This time, he went willingly, and prepared."

Lexi's eyes grew misty. "That is why I had to tell him the truth."

"The ignorance that saved him is now gone," he said with lament.

Lexi bit her lip to contain a sob. Alicia set the rag and bowl aside to comfort Lexi. "You think her wrong for telling him?" Alicia asked.

"No. He deserved to hear the truth. I hoped it would be after we returned home."

"You shielded him for his own safety," Alicia said, understanding.

"Aye." He motioned for the young women to join him. In a private conversation, he explained about Sylvan, the encounter with Sirin at Peitro, and the report of him going mad as a result. "I didn't want the same to happen to Nollen. There is too much risk, for him and others." His poignant gaze shifted between Alicia and Lexi.

Lexi laid her head against Gunnar's shoulder. "You have always been the best friend to Axel and me. But," she gazed up at him. "We don't want others to be sacrificed on our behalf."

"It is our duty. Nollen, in his role, me as First Knight, and even you, The Shield Maiden."

"Aye," she dolefully sighed. "I just pray this ends soon." Hearing the jingle of keys made Lexi sit up, and Gunnar to stand.

Tilbic arrived. "You! Come with me." He motioned for Gunnar.

"We'll take care of Nollen," Alicia quickly told Gunnar.

Two soldiers formed an escort. Gunnar knew better than to inquire, as doubtful Tilbic would answer any question. He squinted and shielded his eyes when they emerged into the late afternoon sunlight. The day's brightness was heightened by fresh snow. His eyes adjusted by the time they reached main building. At an interior door, Tilbic nodded, and the soldier took up guard position. Gunnar found himself in a private room with Montre, the archdukes, and counselors.

"Sir Gunnar, First Knight of Eldar." Tilbic bowed to Montre.

Gunnar offered a respectful bow to the monarch.

"Sir Gunnar, what if we told you there is plan to avert war? Would that sound agreeable to you?" inquired Montre.

"It depends upon the response of my king."

"In this case, your response will be helpful to convince Axel."

Gunnar appeared slightly confused. "I don't understand."

"Lord Carl." Montre motioned Gunnar's attention to the table where a recovered Carl stood with open book in hand.

Carl proceeded to read the account of the war with Eldar, the subsequent tournament, and outcome. When concluded, he asked Gunnar, "Are you familiar with this portion of history?"

"Vaguely," Gunnar guardedly replied. His mind raced with numerous possibilities of why this involved him.

"Not surprising," said Carl graciously. "It took a great deal of searching Markitan history to discover it. Tell me, does Eldar hold tournaments anymore?"

"No. At least, not since Axel reclaimed the throne."

"I assume that as First Knight, you are familiar with trial by combat?"

Gunnar stared at Carl in realization. "You want me to agree to trial by combat to determine the fate of war?"

"Ya," said Montre firmly.

Gunnar's entire posture stiffened with anger. "How will this benefit Eldar?"

"The terms will be these." Carl picked up a fresh piece of paper. "Should Eldar prove victorious, Markita will immediate release the prisoners without questioning the females. We will renegotiate the treaty according to terms set forth by Eldar. Should Markita prove victorious, Chika shall question the females, all remaining prisoner become servants of Markita, and Eldar immediately withdraws from the border. The trial will take place outside the town of Fraine, in the territory once disputed, and won in days of old."

Gunnar's fists tightened to contain his outrage.

"What say you? Are the terms agreeable?" Montre sternly asked.

Gunnar swallowed back his anger to reply. "Your Majesty places me in a position in which I have no authority to give answer."

"On the contrary," began Carl, "As First Knight, you are the one to take up the mantle of challenge for your king."

Gunnar frowned at his attempt to deflect the decision being thwarted. Carl spoke truth about his station and duty as First Knight.

"Well?" probed Montre, with obvious impatience.

With no alternative, Gunnar assumed a formal posture. "If those are terms, then for the good of Eldar, and in service to my king, I am compelled to accept." He clapped his empty scabbard and bowed to Montre.

"Good! All that remains, is for you to write a few words to Axel for inclusion in the official dispatch. In three days, we leave for Fraine."

"Me?" asked Gunnar, taken back by the statement.

"Your words will lend credence to this agreement."

Carl held out a quill pen to Gunnar.

Chapter 43

IN THE STILL OF NIGHT, AXEL SAT IN THE OFFICER'S QUARTERS AT Nefal Station rereading Gunnar's note. Hours ago, he and the others discussed the dispatch. None of them expected such a turn of events. It certainly complicated the situation. Everyone offered their best advice. Arctander urged a night of fasting and prayer; Ronan advised caution, while Mather boasted about the readiness of the army for battle. Othniel gave assurance of Gott's direction in the whole affair. The meeting ended in a failure to come to an agreement of accepting the terms. Axel dismissed them to continue his solitary contemplation. If he could determine Gunnar's attitude, that would help determine a course of action. That meant, he had to read between the lines since Gunnar made no mention of Nollen, Lexi, or his love.

He blinked to break the intensity of staring at the page. To refocus his eyes, he glanced to the window. The night crisp and clear. Even sitting at the desk, he saw stars. *Gott, they were so close*, his mind lamented. *What does this mean?* Once again, he reread the short letter.

To His Most Royal Sovereign, King Axel,

Under compelling circumstances, I take pen in hand to inform you of my agreement, as First Knight, to accept the challenge of Trial by Combat to defend Eldar, and your royal honor. If, by the grace of Gott, I succeed, those precious to you will be spared, as outlined in the terms set forth by King Montre of Markita.

316

If, by a twist of fate, I fail, know that my loyalty never wavered, nor my affection, as a life-long friend. Please, look favorably on this decision, done in the line of duty, and for the protection of those in my charge.

Your most humble and obedient servant,
Gunnar, First Knight of Eldar.

Letter in hand, Axel left the room. Perhaps fresh air would clear his mind. As he passed the chapel, he heard Arctander offer fervent prayers for wisdom and guidance. Othniel sat attentive beside the altar. In spirit, he wanted to join them, yet his mind kept going back to Gunnar's letter. He ignored the cold to mount the steps of the rampart. He stood by one of the large torches used to illuminate the area. Here, he could both see the letter and feel the warmth. He stared east at the dark horizon.

"So close. I could almost see your face, my love," he whispered. He regarded the letter. "What desperate measures made you act?"

"Sire."

Startled, Axel stepped aside. He huffed in relief. "Ajax."

"I hear by your voice you are troubled. I may not be able to answer fully, but I tried to observe all I could while at Miska."

"And?" asked Axel, intrigued.

"At night, I managed to softly land as near to the dungeon as possible. The first night they were singing and praising Gott. The Markitans weren't pleased, though it ended peaceably."

"How many nights were you able to get near the dungeon?"

"Three, before receiving the reply. The other two nights were spent helping Nollen recover."

Concerned, Axel anxiously asked, "From what?"

"I'm not exactly sure. I only heard prayers offered for his recovery."

With sudden consideration, Axel glanced at the letter and read, "*for the protection of those in my charge.* My friend, I understand." He then asked Ajax, "Anything concerning the welfare of others?"

"No. However, it is not just Sir Gunnar's actions. Nollen has done much to protect them. He faced Sirin and creatures in her control."

Axel brows grew leveled. "Perhaps that is how he was injured."

"If so, it would be the second time facing her. The first time, he survived with his mind intact."

Troubled, Axel glanced skyward. "Dear Gott, may Nollen not suffer as Sylvan did. Please, spare him." With new resolve, he regarded the letter. "Thank you for telling me." He left the rampart to enter the chapel. "What words of wisdom do you have from Gott to aid me?"

Arctander moved from the altar. "You already know what to do." He motioned to the letter in Axel's hand.

"I suppose I simply needed reassurance."

"As do we all when it concerns those we love."

Axel held up the letter. "Time to write orders for immediate dispatch. Rouse the others," he instructed Othniel.

Arctander accompanied Axel to the office. Once seated at the desk, Axel furiously wrote short notes on small slips of paper. Lothair appeared first, alert for orders. Ronan yawned and stretched. Blurry eyed, Mather made his way to the small hearth to encourage the fire. Myn came last.

"General. Dispatch the shield owls with orders to arrive swiftly for the march to Fraine."

Mather paused in stoking the fire to quizzically regard Axel. "You accept the terms?"

"Aye."

"That's risky, Sire."

"War is also risky. However," Axel picked up the terms. "Montre will bring our people to Fraine. At least there, we can ascertain their condition."

Mather abandoned the hearth to join them at the desk. His contrary frown prompted Axel to speak.

"If you have a better suggestion, I'm willing to listen. If not, we support Gunnar." He ironically grinned. "Fortunately, I packed his armor among the luggage. As a precaution," he added to inquiring eyes.

"A hopeful gesture," said Arctander.

"Divine prompting," said Othniel.

"That is all well and good, however that letter could have been written under duress," Mather reminded them.

"Aye, duress to protect those in his charge. Ajax informed me of some injury befell Nollen at Miska." He sent a quick glance to Arctander to gauge the Reverend's reaction. "He doesn't know the full extent, only what he overheard in prayers. Prior to that, they were singing and praising the Almighty." He then looked straight at Mather. "If they can express such faith while in the dungeon, we being free, can do the same. Our presence will bring them hope." He held out the slips of paper.

Mather immediately rolled the papers individually to place in small cylinders. "Lothair, the window." From the cage, he brought out one shield owl at a time. To each, he attached a cylinder, and spoke a command: "Fly in service of Gott and the King." When the last owl flew out, Lothair shut the window.

"Now for our plan." Axel took out a map to locate the town. "Fraine is five miles inside the border where this river flows from a lake. It is well within sighting distance of eagle and juvenile patrols. I will take the agreed five hundred troops to the appointed place of meeting. The rest, will remain poised on the border should any treachery happen."

Mather frowned in regard of the map. "I still don't like the fact Montre didn't name the man to face Gunnar."

"I believe he withheld it on purpose," said Ronan.

"Why? It doesn't make sense."

"Actually, it does." Ronan pointed to Fraine. "Are you familiar with the history of this town?"

"No, why?"

"Do you recall learning or hearing about the battle of Hilerd?"

To this name, Mather reacted with surprise. "Aye. It was a futile attempt to secure victory with Markita centuries ago."

"The crushing defeat at Hilerd, led to Eldar losing a portion of the country from here to these mountains. What is now Boric's province."

"How do you know this?" asked Axel, intrigued.

"As you sought wisdom about Chika and Sirin, I did so with treaty, and the history between our countries. I brought a couple of books with me and discovered the chronicle of Hilerd. The lengthy conflict proved exceedingly costly for both sides, with little gain. To save what he could, King Lange foolishly agreed to a proposal by the King Delmar, for a single combat to decide the final victory."

"With the province as the prize," Axel surmised.

"Aye." Ronan tapped the map. "Hilerd was the Eldarian name of Fraine."

Everyone suddenly understood the significant of the chosen field.

"Sire, this could be a trap," warned Mather.

Axel glowered at the terms, which lay beside the map. "Or a well-planned reminder of defeat to place doubt in minds."

"Indeed, Sire. This is all calculated," said Ronan.

"Proceed with caution but go we must. The future of Eldar is at stake," said Othniel.

Axel stoutly regarded the great lion. "We will march without fear." He then said to Ronan, "Fetch those books and the treaty. I want to know everything about Hilerd, and how it could possibly relate to us now."

While Axel and Ronan read and researched, Mather, Lothair, and Myn tended to the troops and riders. Arctander returned to the chapel.

Axel rubbed his eyes with fatigue. Now, the wee hours of the morning, he ignored sleep to concentrate on the situation. Still, he fought a yawn to focus on the page of the book he read.

"Ronan, what does this mean? I've read it several times and can't understand it past the name *Sir Govert.*"

Ronan read where Axel pointed. He shrugged. "I don't understand it either. The language is not Eldarian, nor Markitan – at least according to the any translation we have."

"I assume this is another name since it has a capital *S.*"

"I thought the same, but again, couldn't find any cross-reference."

Othniel lay beside the heart. "Those are old Eldarian journals, correct?"

"Aye. I found them in the archives," replied Ronan.

"Read it aloud," said the lion.

Axel complied. *"Sirrah Govert tot im schlat durcht sirentine."*

"What?" growled the lion, now on his feet.

The angry reaction surprised Axel and Ronan. "Do you understand this?" Axel warily asked.

Othniel again growled. "Sirentine is the ancient name for Sirin. Translated, the sentence is *Sir Govert was killed in battle by Sirin.*"

"By all that's holy!" exclaimed Axel. "This is a trap. One set by Sirin using our people as leverage, with Gunnar the bait to draw us to the same place for the same purpose! Only this time to kill the one who holds her fate!" He slammed the book shut, his face hard set. "By Gott, I swear, she will not succeed!"

Othniel let out a mighty roar that shook the room. In response, came the cry of eagles, howl of wolves, bray of unicorns, and the roar of dragons. Twice more, Othniel roared and received replies.

Axel and Ronan held onto fixed objects during the shaking. When Othniel finished, the room grew still. With heavy breathing of exertion to remain standing, they stared at Othniel for an explanation.

"The animals of Eldar stand united with the King to face Sirin," the lion declared.

"Oh, good," Axel said in wry relief.

Chapter 44

NOLLEN SAT UP AGAINST THE WALL. LORRAINE FINISHED FEEDING him the evening gruel. He grimaced down the last swallow. "I wish I had spices to make it taste better," she said.

He wearily grinned. "No one will ever complain about your cooking, or anyone else's cooking, for that matter."

Gunnar joined them. "You look better, lad. There is more color to your cheeks."

"I still feel weak."

"At least you're alive." Gunnar ruffled Nollen's hair.

"You had us worried. Him most of all." Lorraine nodded toward Gunnar. "Now, rest. We leave tomorrow." She left to help others.

Nollen cast a perturbed sideways glance to Gunnar.

"I had no choice," he said in response to the silent displeasure.

Nollen soberly sighed. "If I were strong enough to withstand her without collapsing, I could have found another way. Some point in the treaty—" Gunnar's grip on his arm stopped further speech.

"You nearly died a second time. Take no reproach. No one here faults you."

"He's right," said Milos. The priest knelt in front of Nollen. His voice filled with contrition. "If anyone one is to be reproached, it is me. I made things very difficult for you. I fought against Gott and the King's appointment of you. I regret that more than I say and have confessed to

Gott and others. Now, I do so to you, and offer the most sincerest apology possible."

Not only did Nollen witness Milos's remorse, everyone watched them. He offered a gracious smile. "Apology accepted."

Milos's shoulders sagged in relief. "Thank you. We shall pray for the journey, and for Gott to continue strengthening you." He flashed a timid smile and withdrew.

"Maybe I misjudged him too," Nollen quietly said to Gunnar.

"No. The fault is entirely one sided." Gunnar became concerned when Nollen huffed and closed his eyes. "Lad? Is something wrong?"

Nollen's eyes open. "No. The mention of *appointing me* brought Alydar to mind. I hope he is well. Joslin too."

"Indeed. I need her for the lists."

Face taut with anger, Panko sat before the hearth in his chamber. He stared at the flames. Since arriving in Miska, nothing had gone according to plan. At every turn he became thwarted, first by Albric, then the Eldarians, and now Carl. The most disturbing frustration came from Chika herself. He withdrew a jewel-studded reptile brooch from a pocket.

"How exactly can mortals counter a goddess? Why do you back down?" he wondered under his breath.

"Because everything is going according to *my* plan."

Panko quickly rose to face— "Sveta!"

"To them. You know who I really am." She sneered hatefully at fire. "Douse the flames!"

"No, I'll open the terrace."

"You defy me, too?" She watched him open a terrace door.

"I have done everything you asked," he haughtily rebuffed. "And what I have received in return? Nothing! Ore and gems from the mines are dwindling. My resources stretched to the limits. You promised me more wealth than I can imagine. Where is it?"

Her hiss contained a mist. His eyes widened with trepidation as the mist drew near. "No! I spoke in frustration," he fearfully confessed.

She waved her hands, and the mist disappeared inches from his face. "Let that be a lesson to mind your tongue."

"Ya," he said in a weak voice of submission.

"I expect the champion of my choosing to be ready at Fraine. Accept no other! I don't care how you convince Montre." She moved close to him. His fear returned. "As per our agreement, your life, if it is not him."

"I swear, he will be the one."

"*Wasser!*" She stretched her hands toward the hearth. Streams of water flowed from her fingers to douse the fire.

Smoke filled the room and made him choke. He ran onto the small terrace to take in fresh air. He waited for the smoke to dissipate before returning inside. The room smelled of smoldering damp wood. He opened the hall door and shouted, "Horst, find me another room!"

Carl waited on Boric, as the archduke made ready to retire. "Has Montre chosen a champion yet?"

"No," Boric chided in frustration. "The natural choice would be General Tilbic. However, he isn't a trained knight. Although a highly skilled soldier in strategy, he has little practical battle experience. In truth, there are very few knights in Markita. We haven't had war in nearly three hundred years. Since ..."

Carl's ears pricked. "Since ... Chika? Is that what you meant to say?"

Boric sluggishly nodded. "The peace has been kept by the goddess."

"Then why is she eager to engage Eldar in battle?"

Boric first grew insulted by the question then frowned to admit, "That is a question I keep asking myself. And why, I approve of your plan. There is something that doesn't make sense. A treaty with Eldar aids our country like nothing before. War will destroy everything." He earnestly regarded Carl. "My prayer to the goddess is that your plan works to appease her, and conflict can be avoided. Whichever way it is decided," he hapless spoke the last sentence.

Carl's inward battle reflected in his skeptical expression.

"You don't agree?"

"I agree about praying for the best outcome. Prayer to whom … I'm not so certain."

Boric sat on the edge of the bed. His brows level in deep contemplation. "You spent much time with the Eldarians. Tell me truly, is their god more powerful than the goddess?"

Carl lowered his voice to confidential. "I believe so. How else can one such as Nollen, stand against her and live, if not for a greater power?"

"Ah, he lives?" he asked, surprised.

"Ya."

"That is good. Despite this chaos, he is an aimable young man."

"Do not like him too much." Sveta entered from the terrace. "Why is this *unbeliever* still here?" she demanded about Carl.

"He is my loyal counselor," Boric replied.

"Loyal? No. He doubts Chika."

"I doubt why she wants war," Carl corrected.

She hissed out mist, which made Carl retreat in avoidance.

"No! Leave him be, witch!" Boric rose in defense. The action brought him into contact with the mist. He began to suffocate.

"Your Grace!" Carl took a deep breath, held it, and dragged Boric from the mist to the terrace. He exhaled to breath in night air. He slapped Boric on the back to help him recover. "Guards!" he shouted to the soldiers in the private courtyard. "The witch tried to assassinate the archduke!"

From behind, came a hiss of anger followed by an ear-piercing scream. Carl and Boric fell to their knees against the terrace rail. The chamber door burst open with shouts. Carl pulled himself up to see the guards arrived.

"Is she out there?" a soldier asked.

"No, she must have escaped. Keep a sharp eye for her. Two of you remain with the archduke. I must report this to the King." Carl aided Boric to the bed, yet briefly detained by the archduke.

"Thank you," Boric spoke in a strained voice.

Carl kindly smiled. "I'll be back shortly."

Despite the hour, Carl urgently insisted on speaking with Montre. After finally convincing the chamberlain, he entered the antechamber to wait. A few moments later, a newly awaken Montre arrived.

"What is so urgent?"

"The witch attempted to assassinate Archduke Boric. Fortunately, I was there to stop her. Unfortunately, she vanished again."

Montre's sleepiness vanished at the report. "Find the witch!"

"I already alerted the guards to do so. I also left soldiers with him while I came to inform you."

"How badly is he injured?"

"She tried to choke him with that fog, so no serious injury."

"Thank the goddess. Or, I think so," muttered Montre. Frustrated, he waved a finger at Carl. "Now, you know why I banished witches! Interfering, troublesome lot." His attitude softened to gratitude. "Thank you for telling me. More importantly, for saving Boric. Go, rest. We have a long journey ahead of us."

Carl returned to find Boric asleep. He had the soldiers pulled the settee near the bed then quietly issued instructions. "One of you stand guard by the terrace door, the other in the hall. I will remain here."

He made himself comfortable with blankets and pillows from the linen wardrobe. *Thank you, Gott, for allowing me to be here to stop Sirin. He may not believe in you now, but perhaps in the future.*

Chapter 45

IN THE LIGHT OF EARLY MORNING, ROYAL TROOPS HOUSED IN the castle barracks assembled in the grand courtyard of Miska. Servants hurried to place final items on the wagons. Horses in full harness were hitched in teams. More soldiers mustered on the town common. The total included three thousand men and mounted cavalry, along with all the equipment needed for the journey.

Under heavy guard, the Eldarians were brought from the dungeon to an appointed place in the courtyard. Although in separate cells, the proximity made it, so everyone knew the current situation. Men walked on the outside to shield the women. Lexi made her way beside Nollen, though he refused help up the dungeon stairs. Once outside, he breathed hard from exertion. Even in the courtyard, the men formed a perimeter around the women and children.

"You, guard!" called Gunnar in Markitan. "What about our horses?"

"I don't' know. And I don't care."

Gunnar grabbed him. "We need our horses!"

The soldier went to clout Gunnar when the knight blocked him.

"Enough!" commanded General Tilbic. "What is this about?"

The Markitan soldier shoved Gunnar, who barely moved a step.

"I asked about our horses," Gunnar replied.

"You'll walk like the rest."

"Unacceptable. Nollen, *the* royal emissary," he stressed the title, "is barely recovered while I need my horse for the lists." When Tilbic

327

snarled, Gunnar challenged, "Unless you would violate your king's terms by depriving me of my horse!"

Despite his disagreeability, Tilbic ordered the guard. "Fetch their horses!" He accosted Gunnar. "If you attempt to flee, they die."

Gunnar proudly squared his shoulders. "I am a knight of the First Order. I gave my word, and it will not be broken."

Tilbic witnessed the intensity with begrudging respect. He left.

"You shouldn't antagonize him," Nollen quietly chided in Eldarian.

Gunnar snickered sarcastically. "They obviously don't have knights, otherwise he wouldn't have questioned me."

"What do you call them?" Nollen waved at a group of Markitans

Mindful of the activity around them, Gunnar gave his assessment in a low voice. "Mounted infantry. They wear only light chain mail. The swords are not heavy enough to inflict serious damage to armor. More for close combat. The horses are limber and lithe for speed, not like Joslin for strength and endurance."

"They must have someone who can challenge you."

"I may not know until entry into the list," he droned.

Nollen didn't have the opportunity to question Gunnar further when a soldier arrived with their saddled horses. "Alydar!" he happily said.

Alydar softly whinnied and placed his head against Nollen's chest in greeting.

Nollen rubbed Alydar's cheeks. "Good to see you too, my friend." He added a whisper in Alydar's ear, "Sirin is here." In response, the unicorn horse made an angry grunt and stomped his right hoof. "Easy, boy. That's right." He spoke aloud for the benefit of the guards, who noticed Alydar's action. The unicorn horse calmed down.

"Is Alydar well?" Lexi whispered to Nollen.

"Aye. Simply silent among strangers."

Joslin snorted and chopped her mouth, as if greeting Gunnar.

"Aye, girl. I'm whole." He patted her neck then his hand along her back to the flank. "I see they took care of you. Only a thin scar remains."

Joslin tossed her head, and continued to chop her mouth, as if replying. Gunnar stroked her muzzle and she grew quiet.

Montre emerged onto the portico with archdukes closed behind. All wore royal military attire complete with ceremonial breastplates, a sash around the waist, fur lined cloaks, and chaperon hats. Montre's wardrobe featured purple with gray accents. The archdukes' colors represented their province: Tomas in white and silver for the north; Panko in blue and gold for the eastern mines; Luken green and yellow for the south; and Boric red and white for the western border. All were armed with elaborately hilted swords.

Montre raised his hands for attention. He spoke in a loud voice. "Today, we ride to meet the Eldarians and halt their aggression! It is our hope," he motioned to the archdukes, "that the Eldarians will accept trial by combat to avert war. However! If war should come, we shall valiantly resist them just like our forefathers in winning a great victory at Fraine."

The troops cheered, which prompted Montre to call for silence. "These Eldarians," he indicated the group, "will serve as surety against treachery by their countrymen. As such, treat them well until their fate is determined; freedom or enslavement!" He glowered at the Eldarians.

Tomas drew his sword to raise high. "Long live Montre! Long live Markita!"

The troops repeated the salute three times before they grew quiet.

Montre led the archdukes to their awaiting horses, held by their respective counselors. All save Panko. Horst held the reins of his mount.

When Montre and the archdukes rode to the front, Nollen and Gunnar were instructed to mount. Nollen refused help from Lexi. Despite some difficulty, he pulled himself into the saddle. He heard Alydar's concern, thus leaned down in pretense of checking the stirrup. He softly spoke in Alydar's bent ear.

"A second encounter with Sirin, but better outcome."

Alydar nodded, though to the casual observer, he appeared to pull at the bridle. Nollen sat up when the call to move came.

Gunnar spoke to Lexi and Alicia before moving. "Stay between me and Nollen when you can, close behind when you can't."

"They won't be out of my sight either," Lorraine said.

"You stay close too," Gunnar added.

Nollen's askew glance passed from Gunnar to Lexi and Alicia. They tried not to giggle. Gunnar and Lorraine ignored the reaction of the young people.

Progress through the town proved slow due to throngs of people that lined the streets to encourage the troops and support the king. Many jeered at the Eldarians. A few threw rocks or dirt that were intercepted or deflected by the men. This prompted the soldiers to keep order by discouraging the crowd. No serious injuries occurred.

Wary, and anxious, the Eldarians kept watch until they reached the open road. Being out of town, brought a measure of relief. After five days in a cramped, damp dungeon, the sunshine felt refreshing. They ignored the morning chill, as the sun's rays would soon warm above freezing, and help to melt some snow.

By noon, they travelled roughly six miles north. They paused to rest and eat a light meal. Soldiers provided the group with four large sausages three feet in length, and ten loaves of bread. As usual, the cooking crew distributed the allotment food.

Gunnar's family sat in a group. Joslin and Alydar stood behind him and Nollen respectively. Brita and Giselle tore off small pieces of bread and sausage for the children.

"First meat we've had in nearly a week," said Kean.

"Definitely better than gruel," said Arnie.

"At least they fed us. Some captors aren't so *generous*," said Gunnar.

"If this is *generous* ..." Arnie began, only to hush when Gunnar kicked his foot in a warning.

Markitan soldiers drew near. "Tiho!"

Everyone understood the word for *silence*.

The afternoon sun made a good winter's day for travel. Most didn't appreciate the breathtaking snow-covered countryside, except Nollen. He kept keen memories of routes. He spoke out the side of his mouth.

"We are taking the same route as when they brought us to Miska."

"I thought so too," Gunnar replied in kind.

"Is that good or bad?" Lexi cautiously asked.

"Unknown, since I'm ignorant of Fraine's location," said Nollen.

"Doubtful it's too far inside Markita," suggested Gunnar, which drew a quizzical glance from Nollen. "Why allow an invading army too much ground?"

"I could answer that if I knew the exact terms," Nollen groused.

"They didn't tell me!" chided Gunnar, a bit louder than intended.

Walking between horses, Lorraine slapped Gunnar's leg in warning. He jerked at the assault. She followed with mild rebuke. "We can't let tension get the better of us."

"I spoke in frustrated regret, not a rebuke," Nollen said in apology.

"I know, lad. There's enough frustration for all," said Gunnar.

"Tiho! Tiho!"

In a preemptive move, Lorraine grabbed Gunnar's pant leg. He rolled his eyes at the Markitan's command.

For the remainder of the afternoon, they journeyed in silence. The glances and gestures perfected on route to Miska were once again employed when needed. Overall, the day passed without incident. The evening meal consisted of stew and bread.

"They are treating us better," Gunnar whispered.

Arnie frowned at the mouthful of stew. "If you say so," he replied in a strained voice.

Gunnar took a tentative sniff then ate. He fought against a verbal expression of disgust.

Nollen had difficulty swallowing then gapped, as if cooling off his tongue. He darted irate glance to Lexi at her giggle. He simply motioned to the bowl. With wry grin, she took the first spoonful. Almost immediately, her eyes went wide with surprise. She took a long drink of water to wash down the stew. He chuckled at her reaction.

"Even children eat such spicy food," he lowly mimicked her.

They heard snickering from the Markitans guards.

"This was done on purpose," Gunnar quietly surmised. He took a large spoonful to force himself to eat. He managed to keep a straight face. At the next spoonful, he noticed a guard's wry smile and nod. "Eat up," he told the others. "It's not bad, once you're accustomed to the taste."

Tentative at first, the rest complied.

"I hope my stomach becomes as used to it as my mouth," groused Arnie.

"Are you ill?" Nollen asked with alarm.

"No, just wondering aloud."

"Spanec! Spanec!"

They also came to recognize the word for *sleep*. Three fires lit for the group, helped thaw the ground. This also made it wet for sleeping. Only a few blankets were provided and used for the little children and some older women. Most huddled together wrapped in cloaks to conserve body heat. Kean and Arnie managed to secure a blanket for Brita, Giselle, and smaller children. The men slept on either side of their wives. The teenage boys slept at the foot or head for more protection and warmth. Milos gave a blanket to Lexi. She, Alicia, Lorraine laid on it, and used their cloaks for covers. Gunnar and Nollen lay on either side of the women with their saddles as pillows. Alydar grunted and chomped his lips. Joslin lowly replied. The horses laid beside their respected riders.

Alydar lowered his head so his mouth was near Nollen's face. "Tell me what happened with Sirin," he whispered.

"I withstood her to protect our women, and a certain identity."

"What of this campaign?"

Nollen spoke with resignation. "To meet Axel and decide our fate with trial by combat. Freedom or enslavement."

"Axel?" asked Alydar with concern.

"Gunnar. He agreed because I wasn't strong enough to negotiate the terms of conflict." Remorse filled Nollen's reply.

"So, this happened after your encounter?"

Nollen stared skyward. "Aye."

"Tiho! Spanec!" A nearby guard scolded.

"I'm praying," Nollen chided in Markitan.

The guard repeated the command more forcefully.

Lexi took hold of Nollen to stop further rebuttal. He huffed but settled back down. She moved closer to whisper so only he could hear. "You are not responsible for Gunnar's agreement. He will protect me, you, and everyone else. It is his nature. Same as it is for you to negotiate and path find. Now, try to sleep."

Despite Lexi's advice, Nollen couldn't sleep. His body might still be recovering, but his mind once again sharp. Having lost his father during the formative teen years, he stemmed the need for older male influence. Or so he thought. Yes, he looked to his grandfather for counsel. That was different. Traveling with Axel and Gunnar the first time, exposed a void left by his father's passing. This venture filled the void in an unexpected way. Learning Gunnar accepted the challenge drove to heart that he returned a son's affection for the faithful knight.

Gott, grant me wisdom so I can stop this. If not, give Gunnar strength to succeed. Free our people.

He felt Alydar soft muzzle touch his face. "Sleep. Gott even knows your thoughts," whispered the unicorn.

Chapter 46

AT THE SLOW RATE OF TWELVE MILES A DAY, IT TOOK TEN DAYS for the Markitan army to reach the outskirts of Fraine. Before leaving Miska, Montre dispatched messengers to the town mayor and aldermen with word of the impending arrival. He ordered citizens to provide all necessary supplies and construct the field for trial by combat. He also included instructions regarding the arrival of King Axel and the Eldarian contingent.

An open field lay north of Fraine near a large lake. Several canals brought water to the city. A mill at the mouth of each canal controlled the water flow and used to grind wheat grown in nearby settlements. The constant turning of the mill wheel kept the water from freezing.

Final preparations were in progress for the tournament. They cleared snow for the lists. A line of flags marked the path, while a narrow tent for each combatant placed at the end of the respective sides. A royal stand had been constructed for viewing. Five regal tents erected on the east side of the field. A lone royal tent stood opposite, on the west side nearest the border. Beside the royal stand, on the Markitan side of the field, a special holding area was created for the Eldarian prisoners.

Instead of entering town, the Markitan army encamped near the royal tents. Soldiers held Nollen and Gunnar back, while the rest secured in the pen like cattle. Told to dismount, two soldiers led them toward the tents. Moving from the area, gave them clear view across the field.

"Axel hasn't arrived yet," Nollen whispered to Gunnar.

"He won't until he knows the enemy's strength." Gunnar stumbled forward when pushed by a soldier, who also told him *tiho*.

The royal Markitan standard flew over Montre's tent. Inside, the king partook of refreshment. He eyed them over the rim of a tankard. His thirst satisfied; he spoke.

"Per the agreement, when Axel arrives, you both will be released to join him. Sir Gunnar to prepare, and you, to be our liaison. The rest, will remain as surety." Both stood rigid and stone-faced. "Have you nothing to say? You." He used the tankard to indicate Nollen. "For a master of words, are strangely silent."

"My words would only express my regret of being unable to participate in drawing up the terms."

Montre stood to confront Nollen, almost nose-to-nose. "You are a brash young man. You think others incapable of bargaining? Or brokering a deal?"

"No, Majesty," said Nollen, apologetic. "Merely the inability to aid Sir Gunnar in my capacity. I truly meant no offense."

"Take them back until needed!" Montre said in rough dismissal.

As they emerged from the tent, an eagle's cry made Nollen and Gunnar look up. Both fought a smile of recognition. Their attention became drawn by a distant trumpet. Out of the far woods, came the Eldarian contingent led by a royal standard bearer. In full armor, Axel rode behind the bearer. Othniel walked beside Axel. Ronan, Arctander. Mather, and Lothair followed.

"Grandfather," Nollen said with a catch in his voice. Immediate tears swelled to blur his vision. He wiped his eyes to look again.

A second trumpet call brought Montre from his tent. "Is that a lion?"

"Othniel, the Great White Lion of Eldar," said Gunnar, proudly.

"Are there more? Lions? Creatures?" asked Montre, a bit nervous.

"Creatures are our friends."

Montre chewed on his lips in observance. "Sergeant, under a white flag, escort them to King Axel."

"Ya, Sire." He shouted for a white piece of cloth. Upon receiving it, he drew his sword and tied the cloth to the blade. "Come!" He ordered, and they proceeded to cross the field.

At the holding area, Alicia stood near the rail to gaze across the field. The trumpet announcing Eldar's arrival caught everyone's attention. She had difficulty maintaining her emotions at sight of the standard. She recognized it from a faded flag brought by Gunnar's family when they fled to Kranston. Then she saw him, all resplendent in kingly armor. She covered her mouth to stop any audible sob. Three long years, yet still apart. "Soon," she spoke under her breath.

"Come." Lexi gently guided Alicia from the rail when supper arrived.

"I saw him. Did you?" Alicia anxiously whispered.

"Aye. I also see Gunnar and Nollen." She pointed to them crossing the field with the Markitan soldier. "They will tell Axel everything. We must be patient for a little long," she assured her with a soft smile.

The soldier, Gunnar, and Nollen reached the tent a moment before Axel and company. The soldier came to attention. He placed the sword in front of his face in salute.

Axel waved for the soldier to withdraw. He dismounted and nodded for Nollen and Gunnar to accompany him inside. The flap no sooner closed then he embraced them. "Thank Gott!"

Othniel and the others entered. Arctander warmly smiled. "My dear boy." Nollen couldn't hold back tears as he embraced his grandfather. "Hush. I am well," soothed Arctander.

"I thought I would never see you again." Nollen wiped away the tears. "How?"

"The short answer," began Axel. "Lord Leon had fragments of Palleteen diamonds sown into the button of the gloves he gave Arctander. The effects slowly rendered him senile, without anyone suspecting something else."

"Except for Ida," said Arctander. "Her tenacity led to the discovery of the diamonds, and the complete regaining of my faculties."

"What?" asked Nollen with surprised confusion.

"There is much to discuss," said Axel. "First, both of you appear to have dropped some weight. General, have cook prepare a good meal. And fetch the best ale." He looked around at the tent furnishings, all fit for a monarch. "At least the Markitans observed proper hospitality." He ushered Gunnar and Nollen to a table. He didn't need to ask, as his prompting look made Gunnar speak.

"She is well, and naturally anxious to see you again. So is Lexi."

Nollen appeared perplexed.

At the reaction, Axel ask Gunnar, "He doesn't know yet?"

"About Lexi. That's because he protected them by taking the brunt of Sirin's displeasure a second time in Miska. The encounter so severe, we feared he might die."

"Gott healed you as he did me?" asked Arctander.

"He strengthened me to endure," he replied to Arctander then said to Axel, "The objective of keeping me ignorant for my protection worked. In Miska, is when Lexi revealed herself to me."

"She felt you deserved to know the truth. I agreed," said Gunnar soberly.

Nollen wryly grinned. "Knowing it explained much about her behavior. Only, now it sounds like more than her identity was withheld."

"Remember, I told you Sirin's fate is linked to one in the group," said Gunnar.

"That person is my bride. Alicia," said Axel.

"Your bride?" repeated a stunned Nollen.

Othniel took up the explanation. "When the Almighty banished Sirin for her treachery, he foretold of her destruction by way of a marriage. When Oleg's throne was restored, those from a far would return, and among them would be the promised bride to continue the royal line."

"I sent Gunnar and Sylvan to Kranston because the time had come for their return," Axel said.

Nollen understood. "Alicia is the one Sirin wants."

"Aye. Unfortunately, Sylvan knew about Alicia. At least her name. My mistake," Axel spoke with bitter regret.

"Your trust was not misplaced," Gunnar insisted.

"No, my judgement impaired! Now Sylvan—"

"What about him?" asked Nollen, warily.

"He died the day we left Sener," Arctander somberly said.

With earnest compassion, Axel looked directly at Nollen. "That is why I didn't tell you about Alicia or Lexi. I wanted to spare you from the same fate should you encounter Sirin."

Nollen softly smiled with reassurance. "As I said, it worked. However, I do have a few questions about them."

"Just a few?" Axel chuckled.

Mather returned along with two soldiers. They brought ale, tankards, bread, and cheese for everyone. "Supper will be ready in an hour," said Mather. He poured the ale while Axel made certain Nollen and Gunnar had the first helping of bread and cheese.

"What are your questions?" Axel asked.

Nollen drank to wash down the cheese. "Lexi claimed to be The Shield Maiden, which Gunnar said is a female warrior. I never heard of it. Alicia lived with Kean's family, and so quiet in nature. How, I mean—"

Axel laughed. "Don't let Alicia's soft-spoken nature fool you. She is tenacious in her faith, generous, and loving. We've been pledged since childhood. Her parents are descendants of a royal relative of Oleg." He warmly smiled when speaking of her. "I've missed her terribly."

Nollen witnessed a side of Axel not manifested before.

Axel noticed. "It's a long-held secret, and for reasons already explained." He then looked to Gunnar. "Why was she living with Kean?"

"A plague killed over thirty. Her parents among those who died."

"Merciful heaven," Axel lamented.

"Lexi also lived with Kean," said Nollen, mindful of Axel's grief.

338

"For security reason, we joined other families after our parents died. I stayed with Jann."

"That must have been cramped in that hovel."

"On warmer nights, we," Axel motioned to Gunnar, "slept outside."

"It explains why Lexi and Alicia are close friends."

"More than friends. Sisters upon our marriage. Also, Alicia is under Lexi's protection since both came of age."

"As Shield Maiden?" Nollen asked, curious to piece things together.

"As daughter of the king, it is Lexi's duty to assume the responsibility of The Shield Maiden to protect the queen—or betrothed, in this case."

Nollen cocked a grin. "Now, everything makes sense."

For several hours, Gunnar and Nollen told all that happened in Markita. They left out no detail. Axel, with help from Ronan and the others, imparted everything that occurred in Eldar during their absence.

Struck hard by the news of Jonas, Nollen abruptly left the table. When Arctander moved to comfort him, he lashed out. "I never should have involved him with those cursed diamonds!"

"It's not your fault," Arctander said.

"He's right," began Mather. "When dispatched to find Leon in Gilroy, I asked Jonas for his opinion about the jewelry. I never mentioned where we found it, only if he could identify it. Ignorant of any trouble, he went to Far Point after learning of your absence. Sadly, he ran afoul of Leon and his accomplices."

Axel joined Arctander to speak with Nollen. "Not only did Leon seek revenge on Arctander, their larger mission was to pave the way for Sirin to invade Eldar. Everything is culminating here. Place the blame where it belongs—on the evil seeking to destroy us."

Arctander spoke to Axel. "It is late. He needs rest."

A heavy moment of silence followed their departure.

"I believe it best we all retire," said Ronan. He, Mather, and Lothair left. Othniel lay in a corner near the entrance.

Soberly, Axel regarded Gunnar. This prompted Gunnar to rise from the table. "I take it you brought my armor."

"Aye. I thought you might need it if battle came … not this."

"We can't always choose how things happen, only prepare for what may come. Even in battle, soldiers die. I am expendable."

"Not to me!"

"Especially to you."

For a moment, Axel woefully regarded Gunnar before he heartily embraced his friend. He held on tight.

Gunnar held Axel by the shoulders. "When I enter the list tomorrow, display no emotion. Let them see the strength of Eldar's King and his First Knight."

"Gott be with you."

"Come. I will tend you this night," Othniel said to Gunnar.

Despite Arctander's counseling, Nollen didn't lie down. "It's hard to believe about Jonas and you. That Leon—!"

"Men driven by revenge are often consumed by unbridled passion."

In confused anger, Nollen asked, "How can you speak so calmly?"

"Age and wisdom guide me, as Gott and justice have dealt with Leon. Do not let it preoccupy you. There is still much to face here and now."

Axel entered. He carried a cup. With compassion, he watched Arctander comfort Nollen. When they noticed him, he spoke, "I thought you might have trouble sleeping. I brought you this. Evening tea."

Nollen sniffled and wiped his face. "How can tea help?"

"Trust me." Axel gave Nollen the cup and encouraged him to drink. "Sleep. I need you tomorrow." He helped Nollen into bed.

Arctander whispered to Axel, "I hope he listens to you."

"Oh, he will. With the help of sleeping herbs." Axel grinned.

Chapter 47

THE ARCHDUKES DINED WITH MONTRE IN THE ROYAL TENT. Tension rose to fever pitch in discussing the next day's trial. Panko vigorously argued about procedures. Tomas and Luken showed great irritation with Panko. Montre sat staring at the carpet flooring as he listened to the disagreement.

"Patience," counseled Boric in response to Panko's latest outburst.

Panko pulled up short from pacing. "Patience, bah! We're here, and we have not named our champion."

"Tilbic is the natural choice," argued Tomas.

"Tilbic isn't a knight of Gunnar's renown. Horst is."

Tomas laughed with harsh sarcasm. "I have never seen him sit a horse in the lists."

"When was the last tournament?" Panko challenged.

Tomas' laughter quieted with consideration.

"Twenty years ago," Luken answered. "And Tilbic won."

"How old was he then? Forty-two?" Panko awaited the answer, which came as a nod from Luken. "Can he fit into a suit of armor at his age and girth? Fight with different weapons? Horst can do both!"

"The king will decide," Tomas interjected.

"When? We need to know tonight. We can't wait any longer!"

"Sire?" Boric urged.

Montre looked up with resignation. "Panko is right. Tilbic is older, and not a physical match for Gunnar. I have wrestled with *whom* to choose since we sent the terms."

"Not Horst," insisted Boric. "Surely there is another officer of rank Tilbic can suggest."

"Why do you object to him?" Panko demanded of Boric.

"Axel might consider it inappropriate since he does not hold a royal commission or at least a knighthood. *Sir* Gunnar is the First Knight of Eldar."

Luken scoffed at Panko. "You are the one who has been arguing procedure. Boric is making a point of order."

Panko made a dismissive wave. "A title matters little. If appointed by Montre, he becomes a *royal* representative. That *is* proper procedure."

Montre raised a hand to stop further objection from the others. "Again, Panko is correct. As king, I have the right and authority, to choose whom I will." He spoke directly to Panko in a begrudging tone. "I assume Horst is fully equipped, else why make such strong argument for his selection."

"Ya, Sire, he is prepared."

"So be it. Captain Horst is my choice to represent Markita in the lists tomorrow."

Panko curbed a triumphant smile in his bow to Montre. "Permit me to depart and inform him to make final preparations." He didn't wait for approval, and hurriedly left. He found Horst tending to the harness beside a fire at the encampment. "Montre made the right choice."

Horst rose. "Then I will have my armor and horse dispatched to the champion's tent." He snapped at several nearby soldiers.

They walked to the Markitan end of the lists. The tent contained everything necessary for the combatant: a cot and small table with a stool. Upon the table were several candles along with an emerald studded reptile figurine representing Chika. Paper, quill pen, and inkwell were also provided.

Sveta sat on the cot. She smiled with pleasure at seeing Horst. "I assume, this means our plan is proceeding."

"Ya," Panko said in terse reply.

She ignored the response to focus on Horst. "As is custom, begin with the lance. Once either is unseated, and battle continues on foot, choose the mace."

"Why?" asked Horst.

"Just listen to instructions!" she chided. "Get as close as possible to impact his shield. Ignore if the spikes become embedded. Oh, and do back away. Then strike with your sword for the kill!"

With a discreet hand gesture and slight shake of the head, Panko signaled Horst to remain quiet.

Sveta didn't see the exchange, rather remained focused on Horst. "Do you understand such simple instructions?"

"Ya. It will be as you say."

"Good. Because failure means death!" Her threatening hiss made Horst take a fearful step back.

In front of the Eldarian champion's tent, Othniel tensed, as he stared across the darkened field. Torches and fires illuminated various parts of the Markitan encampment. Othniel's growl brought Gunnar from the tent. Before he could inquire, Axel arrived in a rush.

"Are you well?" he asked Gunnar. "I sensed evil."

"Sirin is here," announced Othniel.

"We shouldn't be surprised by that," said Gunnar.

"Or dismiss it. Not after Sir Govert's fate," warned Axel.

"I dismiss nothing. This whole arrangement is for her to gain access to our women, so we should anticipate her presence. I will be on guard for anything unexpected."

Axel looked across the field. "So close," he muttered. He turned at Gunnar's hand on his shoulder.

"As with me, display no emotion upon sight of her. Do not give Sirin any indication of identity."

"Gott willing," murmured Axel.

"How is Nollen?" asked Gunnar.

Axel slowly grinned. "Asleep. Thanks to the skullcap and valerian root I slipped into his evening tea."

"Good. He needs to rest."

"Callie will make sure of that."

Gunnar huffed a chuckle. "At first I was angry you sent him. Yet, in truth, he is no longer the youth we first encountered, driven by fear of expectations."

"You doubted him?" Axel asked, curious.

"Not doubt. Similar to you, when we left Kranston."

"Ah, protective towards him," Axel said with understanding.

"He proved his mettle far beyond anything I expected. More so than with the horn." Gunnar shook his head in mild wonder. "I marvel that he survived both encounters with Sirin, especially after Sylvan."

"Gott chose Nollen for this task," Othniel said.

Gunnar regarded the great lion with consideration. "The wisdom of the Almighty is beyond human comprehension."

"Then trust that Gott has prepared *you* for the task at hand," said Othniel.

"I do." Gunnar smiled kindly at Axel. "Sleep. I am content."

Only when he saw Axel enter the royal tent, did Gunnar return inside. Othniel followed. The added company of the lion made the small tent cramped, but Gunnar didn't complain. Instead, he went to the table.

The Markitans followed custom to provide paper, ink, quill, and sealing wax for the combatant's personal dictation. Although there were candles, no figurine or representation of Eldar's god. Gunnar took quill in hand. For a moment, he stared at the blank paper before him.

Othniel observed the conflict. "You told Axel of being content."

"I am. Finding the last words to write is not so easy."

"I know. This is the fourth time you have sat and stared at the paper. Let it flow from your heart rather than search for perfect words."

Taking the advice, Gunnar dipped the quill in the inkwell and began to write. The words came quickly, and pages began to fill. Two letters, signed and sealed. He placed the pen aside and laid a hand on each of the letters. He bowed his head.

"Gott, take what I have written and use it for their good. My life is your hands."

Chapter 48

As dawn broke, Axel emerged from his tent. He wore a heavy robe over his clothes. Silhouette of the Markitan encampment was outlined by the light of morning behind them. His eyes scanned the horizon until he found the holding area. Gunnar and Nollen told him of the approximate location.

"Soon, my love, soon," he whispered. He bowed his head and took a deep breath. "Gott, you have brought us to this day. Strengthen Gunnar and save your people to fulfill the promise to my ancestor."

"Amen," said Nollen. Callie sat next to Nollen.

Axel smiled. "Indeed. I hope you slept well."

"I did, though I'm surprised I slept at all."

"Sire." Mather began. "Someone is coming." He indicated two figures crossing the field.

"Looks like Lord Carl and General Tilbic," said Nollen. Upon closer approach, the light showed him to be correct.

"I recognize Lord Carl. I have not met General Tilbic," said Axel.

"A dour man," chided Nollen.

Callie stood, her hackles raised, and she growled.

"Easy girl," Nollen soothed.

Mather met them to prevent unwanted approach. After a few short words in Eldarian, he presented them to Axel. Carl and Tilbic bowed.

"Lord Carl. What word do you bring? Are my people well?"

"They are well. King Montre ordered them to be dealt with kindly."

346

"Until the contest is decided," Tilbic added in broken Eldarian.

Axel glared at him. "Hardly a reassuring statement, General."

Tilbic made a stiff, formal bow at the rebuke.

Carl added his scolding in Markitan. Tilbic withdrew several steps. "Forgive the General, he is a blunt man."

"Then let me also be blunt. Any harm to them will not be looked upon favorably. In fact, the treatment and condition of my Royal Emissary is deeply troubling."

Carl flashed a look of concern to Nollen. "Your Majesty, please believe I did all I could to help ..." He stepped closer and lowered his voice, "the Brethren."

Axel's brows lowered in surprised concern at the statement. Rather than comment on the revelation, he demanded, "Why have you come?"

"In following protocol, I am here to inform you that Markita's chosen champion is Captain Horst of Archduke Panko's command."

"Horst?" Nollen repeated with anger. A quick hand on his arm by Axel, stopped further comment.

Carl formally continued. "His Majesty King Montre requests your presence in the royal stand two hours from now."

"You have discharged your duty, my lord."

When Carl left, Tilbic fell in step.

Axel drew Nollen into his tent. "I take it you've met Captain Horst."

"He led the troops that captured us, and ... is a callous brute." Nollen amended his speech.

Axel took note of the change. "*And* something else? Well?" He grew insistent when Nollen still hesitated.

"He briefly assaulted Lady Alicia—"

"What?" thundered Axel, his face instantly red with outrage.

"Grabbed her, actually. Lexi intervened, and ... Gunnar prevented serious harm. Horst only backed down when Lord Carl and Baron Albric arrived."

Axel's jowls flexed, as he pushed open the tent flap to glare across the field. Patches of snow now glistened in morning sun, while frost rose in a cold mist.

"They truly are well. I didn't mean to imply otherwise," Nollen spoke apologetically.

Axel let the tent flap fall back into place. "Have you been told of our plan?"

"Aye. Although, I pray it does not happen and Gunnar is successful."

"I pray for the same." Axel tossed his arm around Nollen's shoulders. "Whatever the outcome, I am pleased and proud to call you both my friends."

"Breakfast, Sire." Two servants brought food and drink.

"You eat. I need to speak with Arctander." Axel didn't wait for Nollen to answer.

His blustery entrance made Arctander and Ronan turn. The tent provided sleeping comfort for the High Priest and served as a traveling chapel. Ronan sat in a chair before the portable altar where Arctander offered prayers.

"Sire," said Arctander in friendly greeting.

Axel attempted to calm his temper. "I received word identifying the Markitan champion, and the time of meeting."

"You don't seem pleased," observed Ronan.

"No! I'm not pleased by this situation." At Arctander's rebuking regard, he added, "However, I am reconciled that it must be so. Gott, help us."

"He will," said Arctander with certainty.

A squire assisted Gunnar with the final pieces of the silver armor trimmed in gold. On the breastplate, a stamped crest of a lion and eagle interwoven. Outside, they heard noise of the gathering crowd. Axel arrived dressed in royal attire fitting the occasion. However, beneath his clothes was seen a hint of chain mail.

"Leave us," Axel instructed the squire. For a moment, he regarded Gunnar. The only part missing was the shield. That stood outside near Joslin. "I'm about to join Montre in the pavilion. I came to—"

"No further words are necessary." Gunnar kindly smiled. "I want you to have these." He picked up the sealed letters from the table. "One is for you, the other for Nollen. I don't have much. If the worst should happen, everything goes to him, as it would a son. Please, see to it."

"Of course." Axel tucked the papers inside his surcoat. "The Markitan champion is Captain Horst."

Gunnar jowls flexed in anger. "I suppose it's fitting."

Axel noticed someone missing. "Where is Othniel?"

"He left before dawn to scout the perimeter."

"Not sure if it's a good idea for him to be snooping about the Markitan camp."

"The Great Lion isn't bound by the wishes of men," Gunnar teased.

Conversation stopped at hearing the first trumpet.

"Time for me to go." Axel embraced Gunnar and kissed him on both cheeks. "Gott is with you, my dear friend."

"And with you, my king." Gunnar accompanied Axel outside. Ronan, Nollen, Mather, and Arctander waited.

"Gott strengthen you, Sir Gunnar," said Arctander in blessing.

When Axel moved toward the pavilion, Nollen said, "I'll be along in a moment." Fighting back emotion, he found words difficult.

Gunner proudly smiled. "You served Axel and Eldar well. Now, it is my turn." He heartily embraced Nollen. Hearing a muffled sob, he offered encouragement. "Don't let them see weakness."

Nollen left to join the Eldarian contingent in the pavilion. Axel sat to right of Montre, with Ronan, Arctander, and Mather gathered behind him. Axel motioned for Nollen to stand behind his chair.

"I need a translator," Axel quietly said.

Nollen observed the Archdukes and counselors near Montre. Carl carefully nodded at him, so he made a similar acknowledgement. Carl also patted the satchel he wore. Nollen found it a curious signal, yet uncertain of the meaning.

A trumpet sounded and the marshal called, "Combatants present!"

Gunnar and Horst moved to stand before the royal pavilion. The visors raised to face both kings. Horst wore an impressive black and green breastplate with diamond shaped crest. A black sash around his waist from under which came a surcoat. He wore no leg armor rather high leather boots over his thighs. He did have armored gauntlets and helmet. He sneered at Gunnar.

The marshal read the agreed terms for trial by combat in Markitan. When completed, he gave the scroll to Lord Carl, who translated into Eldarian. The marshal proceeded to give instructions, which Nollen quietly translated to Axel.

"Trial will begin in the lists until one combatant is unseated then continue on foot. The ultimate victory will be decided upon death. Combatants, to your mounts!"

Both came to attention, drew their swords, and saluted the kings. Gunnar went to give the customary salute to Horst when the Markitan turned his back and walked away.

Axel voiced his objection to Montre about the insult.

Rather than reply in bad Eldarian, Montre motioned to Nollen.

Nollen kept disagreement from his face when translating. "Apparently, Captain Horst is a soldier thus unfamiliar with the customs of the lists."

The marshal waited for Horst and Gunnar to take their mounted position. Each held a lance in their right hand, with a small jousting shield on their left arm. The marshal raised his arm then quickly dropped it. Both knights charged.

Gunnar held his lance up longer than Horst. This gave Gunnar an idea of Horst's angle of attack. He lowered his lance into the path of attack to deflect the intended strike to a simple passing blow. His lance impacted squarely on Horst's shield. Horst rocked in the saddle but managed to stay upright.

Gunnar turned Joslin to the opposite side for a second pass. Doubtful, Horst would repeat the same mistake. Gunnar lowered the lance across his body for the second charge. As predicted, Horst attempted Gunnar's tactic by lowering the lance late in the gallop. Gunnar brought his lance up to come under Horst's shield. The simultaneous impact on armor shattered the lances and sent both off their horses.

Axel's grip on the chair arms tightened until the knuckles turned white. He waited in anticipation of Gunnar rising. He heard a gasp and briefly noticed Nollen breathed hard with intense focus on the battle.

"Choose your weapons to continue. The challenger first."

"Sword and shield!" Gunnar motioned to the squire for the sword and larger shield.

When the marshal turned to Horst, he shouted, "Mace!"

Seeing Horst's weapon of choice, Gunnar removed his helmet.

"Why did take off his helmet?" asked Nollen, fearful.

"Better visibility," replied Mather. "A helmet is little protection against a mace, so better to see the angle of attack."

"Battle!" the marshal shouted.

Gunnar dodged to avoid the mace. By Horst's jerky movement, he determined the captain only marginally proficient with the weapon. Gunnar managed to use his shield to deflect a badly aimed attack. He countered with a slice from his battle sword that torn open Horst's sash and the surcoat. The cut revealed some damage to the light chain mail.

Gunnar feinted another attack. When Horst made a similar move in response, Gunnar again used the shield to push aside the mace to take a second strike at the same area. This time, the chain mail ripped away to reveal a nasty open wound across Horst's abdomen. In painful anger, Horst backed away. He tried to make quick assessment of his injury when Gunnar advanced. Horst swung the mace in a defensive move that clouted Gunnar's sword down. This threw Gunnar off balance, and he stumbled past without landing another blow.

Gunnar regained his footing in time to use his shield to stop the mace. A spike pieced the shield, and upon impact, released a cloudy mist. Gunnar choked when the cloud enveloped his head. He backed away and tried to wave the mist from his face.

"Poison fog," Nollen disconcertedly said.

Having heard, Axel demanded of Montre, "What trickery is this?"

Montre couldn't answer, also stunned by the occurrence.

Horst jerked the mace away. It remained implanted in Gunnar's shield. He tossed them aside to draw his sword.

"Gunnar!" Nollen shouted when Horst advanced with sword raised.

Gunnar looked up at the warning. He ducked and attempted to parry. The death blow averted. However, the sword tip sliced open his face from above the left eye down his cheek. He fell to one knee in pain. Blood blinded him.

"He's down! Finish him, as Chika commands!" Panko urged Horst.

"Sirin!" Nollen exclaimed at understanding Panko's shout.

Mather stopped Nollen from leaving. "You can't interfere."

"He can't survive against her!"

Axel grabbed Nollen's sleeve. "You did. Trust Gott."

Nollen's face twisted in anger at the restraint. "Gott, help him!" he prayed through clenched teeth.

Hearing a war cry from Horst, Gunnar awkwardly stood. He grabbed the hilt in both hands to brace for impact. The swords clanged together, and briefly hung suspended.

"Gott of Eldar rebuke you!" Gunnar twisted Horst' sword to disarm the Markitan. He jumped back when Horst whipped out a hidden dagger.

"Cheat! An undeclared weapon," Mather shouted.

"Right this effrontery or this trial is over!" Axel commanded Montre.

"You do not order our king," Panko rebuffed in Eldarian.

On the field, Horst stepped on Gunnar's shield and jerked out the mace. He put all his force into the blow aim at Gunnar's blinded left side.

"Down!" Nollen called out in warning.

Gunnar ducked. The momentum brought Horst and the mace to the ground with such force several spikes broke. A heavy cloud of suffocating mist engulfed Horst's head. He fell to the ground unable to breathe. His body jerked then grew still.

Panko clouted Nollen from behind. Dazed, Nollen fell from the pavilion. Mather and Ronan drew swords to defend Axel.

"Panko! Stop," Montre clamored in outrage.

Boric and Tomas seized Panko to prevent further assault of the Eldarians. Luken placed himself between Montre and Axel.

An eagle's cry came from above, followed by a mighty roar that shook the pavilion. Loud reptile hissing could be heard followed by women screaming.

"Alicia?" Axel bolted to his feet. "Any harm comes to my people—"

"I don't know what is happening!" Montre protested in broken Eldarian.

"To arms! Free our people!" Axel jumped from the pavilion to Nollen. The young man helped up by a bloodied but alive Gunnar. "To the surgeon, both of you." Axel helped them hurry toward the Eldarian encampment.

An unearthly scream pierced the sky. All mortals cringe in pain. Sirin, in her true form, rushed to the holding area. Streams of water turned the rails to ice, shattering the wood. Sirin lifted the head of the first female, who winced in pain. Her reptile eyes searched the female's eyes.

"Not you!"

Sirin reached for another, with the same result. Then a third, a fourth.

Lexi crawled to Alicia. "Quickly, go under," she hastily whispered.

After successfully crawling beneath the back rail, Lexi and Alicia ran behind a tent. Hearing a close sound, Lexi looked for anything to use as a weapon. She picked up a fallen thick branch. She raised it to strike when someone rounded the corner. Lorraine cried out first in fright then pain. She cradled her left arm.

Relieved, Lexi lowered the branch. "How badly are you hurt?"

"I think my arm is broken."

"We need to get across the field. Can you make it?"

"Oh, I'll make it."

Men began to recover and tried to stop Sirin from harming the women. She hissed her suffocating mist, sometimes with success, other times not. Kean and Arnie aided Brita and Giselle when two bushliks arrived. They ushered their wives to flee. The bushliks followed.

"I thought they only came out at night!" Arnie complained.

"Does it matter?" Kean grabbed a nearby fallen rail to swing at the reptiles. Cornered against a wagon, Kean clouted the nearest beast. The second one lunged and grabbed his cloak. Brita screamed when it dragged Kean off. Before any serious injury occurred, Sirin screamed. The bushliks left them and returned to her.

At the champion's tent, Axel withdrew a horn from under his cloak. He sounded the call. In response, came multiple eagles' caws, unicorn brays, and a lion's roar. Next to the royal tent, a servant waited beside two cages draped in black. He released two shield owls.

Gunnar whistled to summon Joslin. To Nollen's surprise, Alydar came with her. On the saddle were his crossbow and quiver. He slung the quiver over his shoulders, mounted, and armed his crossbow.

"Both of you are injured," Axel objected.

"It's just blood. I still have my eye," Gunnar retorted.

"I'm thickheaded," said Nollen.

Mounted, Mather led Axel's horse. He also carried the king's helmet.

Axel accepted the helmet then mounted. He drew his sword. "Engage if necessary, but freeing our people is first priority!" He raised his sword. "For Gott, for Eldar!"

The Eldarians raced across the field. Although surprised, and in some disarray, the Markitan army engaged them.

Outraged at her failure to find the female, Sirin's screech summoned more bushliks. Hundreds swarmed onto land from the canals. To more effectively deal with the Eldarians, she positioned herself beside the closest canal. With force, she sent water from her hands. The streams turned to ice spears and took down any approaching Eldarian. In close quarters, she hissed freezing or choking mist.

Bushliks rammed Eldarian horsemen to unseat the riders. Battling such armored beasts proved deadly for some, while inflicting serious injuries to others. Unicorns aided the mortals. They charged the bushliks using their horns as spears. Even with help, between the bushliks, and being outnumbered, the Eldarians were forced to retreat.

Soiled from battle, Axel jerked his horse to a sudden stop. "Mather, where are the reserves?"

"Only a mile away, Sire."

"Fire!" Nollen urged Alydar toward Axel. "Fire is the only way to defeat the bushliks."

"He's right," said Gunnar. "At least it worked last time." He stood in the stirrups to observe the field. "Only there weren't this many."

"General, sound the call for Myn and the Ha'tar!"

Mather made the sound used by the Ha'tar to summon the dragons. His voice cut short when struck from his horse by an arrow.

"General?" Axel questioned with concern.

Mather moaned.

"He's alive," said Gunnar.

"Take him to the surgeon. You see him too, and no objection!" Axel ordered Gunnar. Axel made the same loud Ha'tar call. When finished, he told Nollen, "Find Lexi and Alicia. Keep them safe until this is over." He rose in the stirrups to shout a command. "Regroup! Regroup!"

Nollen pushed Alydar to race toward the holding area. Dismayed at the destruction, he jumped from the saddle. "Lexi! Alicia!" he called in desperation.

"Nollen." Kean limped over.

"Have you seen Lexi and Alicia?"

"No. Our people are scattered."

"Find whoever you can and head across the field. You too, Alydar."

"I won't leave you."

"Go! Lead them to safety." Nollen readied his crossbow to begin the search. He looked behind wagons and tents while avoiding the chaos of battle. Hearing a female moan, he ventured closer. "Lorraine." She suffered numerous injuries.

"My arm. Broken. Head hurts."

At a reptile hiss, Nollen stood, and aimed. The arrow barely impacted the bushliks' scaly armor. He loaded for another shot. With an angry whinny, Alydar arrived and leapt onto the bushlik. The force of unicorn-horse diverted the beast. It limped and hissed at Alydar. Nollen fired another arrow into the bushlik's injured leg. It awkwardly retreated.

"I thought I told you to go back."

"And I said I won't leave you."

"This time you will. Lorraine needs to be taken to safety." Nollen gently helped her to mount Alydar. "Go!" He slapped Alydar's rump.

Confident, Alydar indeed left, Nollen continued the search for Alicia and Lexi. He spied them near a canal windmill. He darted between combatants to reach them. "Either of you hurt?"

"No, but Lorraine is. We became separated," Alicia fearfully replied.

"I sent her to safety with Alydar."

"Thank Gott," Alicia sobbed in relief. "What of Axel and Gunnar?"

"You probably witnessed Gunnar's wounding. He's alive. Axel too."

"Look out!" Lexi snatched up rocks to throw at advancing bushliks.

"In the mill!" Nollen ushered them inside and barred the door. He began a search that turned over items.

"What are you looking for?" asked Lexi.

"A match. Lantern. Anything that produces—" He stopped at hearing a dragon's roar. "Aye, dragons!"

"What?" said Lexi confused.

"Dragon fire will stop them. It worked at Andros when Ajax became a phoenix." Nollen peeked out the window. "No sign of it." He checked his crossbow. "Bar the door behind me."

Lexi grabbed Nollen. "What are you going to do?"

"Draw it away. Axel told me to keep you two safe. Staying in here should do that." He carefully lifted the bar. He jerked opened the door and ran out. He heard it slam behind him.

Around the corner from the door, he saw ground fires caused by dragon attacks. Markitan archers attempted to shoot down the dragons with little success. He heard hissing from behind and felt the ground shake. He ran toward one of the fires. He lit the point of a dart, turned and shot at the charging bushlik. It roared in anger when struck. The added fire helped the arrow penetrate the beast's armor. Beyond the wounded beast, more bushliks converged on the mill.

Anxious, he glanced about for something else to use. He could only fire one lighted arrow at a time. With his foot, he kicked out a burning piece of timber. He raced back to the mill where he frantically waved the flaming timber at the creatures. They hissed in anger at the deterrent.

Nollen reached the door. "Are you alright?" he shouted over his shoulder. He continued to wave the timber at the bushliks that advanced then retreated from the flames.

"Aye!" Lexi replied.

The flame began to flicker. He made the Ha'tar summoning call he heard from Axel and Mather.

Sirin appeared from around the rear of the mill. "And who are you protecting?"

Nollen didn't answer, rather remained focused on the bushliks. A stream of water doused the flame by encasing the timber in ice.

"Now, how will you protect her?" Sirin mocked.

Nollen dropped the timber to aim his crossbow at her.

"Your puny arrow will not stop them. Or me."

Thud-thump-thump. Nollen fought a smile at hearing an approaching dragon. "That will!" He briefly looked up.

A Ha'tar rider steered his dragon toward the five bushliks that pinned Nollen against the door. From a dragon's roar came a continuous stream of fire. The bushliks scrambled to avoid the flames. None escaped.

Sirin used what icy water she could muster to push Nollen away from the door. He righted himself in time to see her enter. He grabbed an arrow and thrust the tip into the burning carcass of a bushlik. When Sirin emerged with Lexi and Alicia, he shouted.

"Down!"

Immediately, Lexi and Alicia heeded.

The arrow flew between the women to strike Sirin high in the chest. The impact made her release them. Another flaming arrow struck Sirin, followed quickly by a third. She collapsed to her knees. Moisture evaporated from her due to the heat. Her face began to dry and wither. A fourth fiery arrow brought the death blow. Sirin disintegrated in to smoldering heap.

At her death, the sounds of whimpering bushliks rose from across the field. The beasts retreated into the water of nearest canal. Nollen, Lexi, and Alicia warily watched the creatures flee.

Panko roughly drew his horse to rein. His glowered eyes shifted from the ash pile of Sirin to Nollen. "Wretched interloper!" He raised his sword to charge.

Nollen reached for his quiver, only to discover he was out of darts. He shoved Lexi and Alicia aside to avoid Panko's charge. The downward blade clipped his left shoulder and sent him tumbling to the ground.

"Nollen?" Lexi went to reach for him when he batted her hand aside. Panko wheel his horse around. "It's minor. Run! I'll hold him off."

Alicia only managed to draw a reluctant Lexi a dozen yards away when Lexi turned. They fearfully watched Panko's advance.

Nollen barely got to his feet when he dove to avoid Panko's second charge. He rolled, ripped an arrow from a bushlik and aimed while on his back. Panko completed turning his horse for a third attach when *twang!* Followed by an angry whinny. The dart's impact make Panko jerk the reins so violently that the horse stumbled and fell sideways. Nollen remained on his back, staring at the aftermath. The horse rose and trotted off. Panko lay motionless.

Alicia rushed to help Nollen. Lexi snatched up Panko's fallen sword ready to make defense. His vacant eyes told her he was dead. She joined Nollen and Alicia.

Othniel arrived, which made both women balk with uncertainty. "My lady." He lowered his head in acknowledgement of Alicia. "Are you injured?"

"Nollen is wounded," she replied, tentative.

"It's not serious. This is Othniel. The Great White Lion of Eldar," said Nollen.

Alicia smiled, though still unsure. Lexi spoke to Othniel. "We've heard a great deal about you."

"Shield Maiden," Othniel formally said. He inspected the ash heap. He raised his majestic head to loudly declare, "Sirin is vanquished!"

"Alicia! Lexi!" Axel pushed his horse in gallop. He jumped from the saddle before the horse stopped. He threw off his helmet, as they both ran to embrace him. "Thank Gott." He could not hold back tears of relief and joy, as he kissed each of them repeatedly on the cheek or forehead.

"And Nollen," said Lexi.

Axel gratefully smiled at Nollen. "Indeed. Take them to my tent, while I deal with Montre."

Chapter 49

UNDER HEAVY ELDARIAN GUARD, THREE OF THE FOUR archdukes, two remaining counselors, and Montre gathered in the royal tent. Montre appeared haggard and worn beyond his years. Boric and Tomas suffered wounds, while Luken battle soiled. Carl and Luken's counselors also showed signs of battle fatigue, though Carl's satchel undamaged. The tent flap opened. Axel arrived. His expression severe. Ronan accompanied him. The Markitans backed away in fear when a white lion followed them.

Weak, yet determined, Montre pushed himself to stand. He made an awkward bow to Axel. "The day is yours. Markita yields." His Eldarian clipped, yet understandable.

Axel motioned to the chair. "Sit."

Montre's arm gave way, and he fell back into the chair.

"Were you aware of Horst's treachery?" Axel demanded of Montre.

The defeated king sluggishly shook his head. "No."

Boric spoke in broken Eldarian. "King take Panko's suggestion of Horst. Tilbic too old. No knight of Markita to face Gunnar. Sorry." He offered a humble bow.

"This was all Panko's plan?"

"Ya. He … how say …" Unable to find the words, Boric turned to Carl and asked in Markitan.

Carl translated for Axel. "Apparently, Archduke Panko was in league with Chika." He boldly took a step towards Axel, which made Ronan stop him. "Your Majesty, I bear full responsibility. I suggested the terms in an effort to avert war, and hopefully, keep Chika at bay."

Axel's touch made Ronan move aside to speak with Carl. "Were you aware of Panko's agreement with Chika?"

"No. All, we knew, was he kept insisting on pleasing Chika." Carl knelt. "I offer myself as payment to do what you will, only spare my king."

Othniel approached Carl. Though apprehensive, Carl regarded the mighty lion. For a tense moment, they stared at each other. Finally, Othniel said to Axel, "He speaks the truth."

The Markitans gaped in astonishment at hearing Othniel talk.

"Very well." Axel signaled Ronan to take custody of Carl. He continued in stern rebuke of Montre. "By Markita's actions, whether known or unknown, the treaty between our countries is now void! Nor shall there be another until Markita proves it is once again worthy of trust. Keep your men away, as we leave with *our* people."

Axel turned on his heels. Ronan followed with Carl. Othniel roared at the Markitans before he left.

Across the way, Eldarian physicians tended the wounded while soldiers and servants prepared for departure. Gunnar walked Joslin in search of Lorraine. He found her in the wagon with her head bandaged and arm in a sling. On his part, the surgeon bandaged the left side of his face. This caused his grin to appear lopsided.

"We have both looked better," he said with levity. Her stricken expression at his appearance made him add, "Just precaution. The surgeon stitched it. My eyesight will return when the bandage is removed. Though, a scar will remain."

She softly smiled. "At least you're alive."

"As are you. I think being strong helped us through this."

She lightly chuckled. "Are we too strong to accept help in recovery?"

He laughed, then admitted, "No. If anything, the return to Kranston helped me relearn the meaning of unity and collaboration." He became reflective in recollection. "When Axel and I journeyed to Eldar, secrecy and survival were paramount. Followed by reestablishing the throne. Being preoccupied, I lost sight of some things." He smiled when she held his hand.

"Now, you can help those of us who know nothing of Eldar to adjust."

"Gladly." He kissed her hand.

The call came to mount for departure.

"Are we going to Sener?" she asked.

"No. The Nefal Border Station. It's just a few miles, so the more serious can recover in the safety of Eldar."

That evening, the glow of campfires, torches, and lanterns illuminated the area in and around Nefal Station. Axel ordered Lord Carl placed in the station's single prison cell. Alicia, Lexi, and Lorraine were given the commander's private quarters for rest and recuperation. Axel joined the others in the main barracks.

After dinner, the men remained in the dining hall. During the meal, Axel read the book Carl insisted on giving him. He barely ate and only took bites of food when Arctander or Ronan insisted. Any inquiries about the content were waved aside, as he continued to read. When the servants cleared the table of dinner, Axel closed the book. He stared at the cover in the same manner those at table stared at him, curious.

"Axel?" Gunnar's query broke the silence.

Axel's head slowly rose for his glance to find Nollen. "Tell me, did Baron Albric reveal any unsavory Markitan history to you at any time?"

"No. He expressed more interested in our faith and Gott. Lord Carl spoke more of issues dealing with Sirin and Panko."

"This is why." Axel tapped the book. "Panko's family was responsible for integrating the decimated Palleteen population into Markitan society after their sound defeat by Nandor. The Emperor gave up the mines in exchange for saving what remained of his people. The Palleteen kingdom has been extinct for the past three hundred years."

All at the table sat amazed and confused.

"But the cursed diamonds? Lord Leon and his compatriots?" Mather was the first to speak.

"The diamonds were indeed cursed by Sirin, disguised at Chika, when the Palleteens failed to overthrow Eldar. However, the survival of the Palleteens became a ruse devised by Panko's family to maintain the secret. They employed it as needed. Leon confessed to being a worshipper of Sirin and charged with preparing the way for her return. Another part in a large scheme."

"Incredible," murmured Ronan in wonder.

"All this information is contained in that book?" asked Arctander.

"The part about the Palleteens. I reckoned Leon's story in association with what I read about Sirin. It's quite possible his wife was of Palleteen ancestry. Again, a speculation, though it fits the narrative." Axel sympathetically looked at the book. "This is a confession to Albric's duplicity in keeping the falsehood alive."

"Why give it to you?" asked Ronan

"I believe only Lord Carl can answer that. Mather, fetch him."

The few moments it took for Mather to follow instructions passed in silence. Carl bowed to Axel. He noticed the book on the table. Axel spoke to the interest.

"This contains very surprising information that provides answers to recent events. However, it doesn't explain why Baron Albric insisted on giving it to me."

Carl affectionately smiled. "Does Your Majesty recall the Holy Books Eldar presented the Archdukes at signing of our treaty?"

"Of course."

"Let's just say that for Albric and myself, reading them had a profound effect. So much so, we now consider ourselves part of the Brethren."

Mild murmurs came from those at the table.

Arctander rose. "You claim to have faith in the Almighty of Eldar?"

"I do. As did, Albric, my brother by marriage."

"Did?" asked Nollen.

"He died the morning we left for Fraine. His death the result of a hideous beating by Panko." Bitterness crept into Carl's tone.

"That's why you took over and aided us," Gunnar surmised.

Carl simply nodded since words failed due to renewed grief.

"Did Panko learn about the book?" Axel held it up.

Carl shook his head, still trying to recover his emotion. "Although, he felt threatened by Albric's knowledge, and … Nollen," he cast a quick glance across the table.

"Me? He beat the baron because of me?" asked Nollen, angry.

"No! I meant, he feared you. First, your boldness at the trial when you disputed his claims about the mines. Then, withstanding Sirin to prevent access to the women." He turned to Axel to continued, "That is when I devised the plan. My heart and conscience compelled me to act on behalf of the Brethren."

Thoughtful, Axel stroked his beard, as he listened and watched Carl. "Did you yield to escape Markitan justice should your new faith be discovered?"

"No. On his deathbed, I promised Albric to deliver the book to Your Majesty. Under the circumstances, I saw no other way than to offer myself as prisoner. For in truth, as originator and appointed mediator, I bear the shame of Panko's treachery. My life is yours to do with as you will."

Axel's gaze briefly shifted to Arctander, which prompted the Reverend to ask, "What if the King decides to return you to Markita?"

"Then I go."

"Even if it means your death?" asked Ronan.

"What is death to one who believes but a way to heaven?"

Axel shifted in his chair at the response. "General Mather, return Lord Carl to the cell."

"A brave man," said Gunnar. He saw Axel's wry expression in regard of the book. "You've already made a decision."

"What better way to keep an eye on Montre than with an ally?"

Nollen's brows level with befuddlement. "Sire, there is something that neither Baron Albric's book nor you have explained. If Sirin's fate was tied to Lady Alicia's return, how could I kill her?"

Axel motioned to Othniel. "That is a very good question."

"Prophecy didn't say *how* or *where* she would be destroyed, only that her fate was linked to the Son of Eldar's promised bride. Your actions protected her. The Almighty also chose *you* for this task."

Nollen sat thunderstruck by the answer. Gunnar chuckled, and slapped Nollen on back. "Well done again, lad."

The door opened, and Alicia arrived. "I don't mean to intrude."

Axel widely smiled as he rose to meet her. "No intrusion. I thought you were resting." He drew her from the door to sit at the table.

"I couldn't sleep. So many emotions."

"Come, gentlemen," Arctander spoke to the others.

"You don't have to leave on my account," Alicia kindly said.

"Oh, I think we do." Gunnar winked, and closed the door.

Axel sat beside her. "Three years. You look no different than when we left. Still beautiful" He stroked her hair.

"You look like a king!" She threw her arms around his neck.

He held her close. "We shall wed immediately upon return to Sener with a celebration that Gott has fulfilled his promises."

Nollen delayed Arctander. "Grandfather, can we talk? Outside."

"Of course, dear child."

Nollen made certain to grab their cloaks before stepping into the cold night air. Firelight and torches softly lit the area. He instantly grew tense when Arctander withdrew gloves from the pockets.

Arctander tenderly smiled. "New ones. Given me by Axel. See, leather with fur lining." He pulled on the gloves then hooked arms with Nollen to walk the encampment. "What troubles you?"

Nollen searched for the words. "Othniel said Gott chose me for this mission. Why? To stare in the face of evil? I never experienced such terror or came as close to death as I did with Sirin."

Arctander stopped to face his grandson. "Tell me, how did you feel after succeeding against Sirin?"

"Relieved."

"Was that the first or the second time?"

Nollen considered. "After the first time, I couldn't think straight or even speak. I became paralyzed and overwhelmed by fear. Gunnar had to pray for me to break her hold."

"Her hold? Or the grip of fear?"

Nollen didn't immediately answer, struck by the question. "I thought they were one in the same."

"Fear is a powerful weapon of the enemy. It is deceptive."

Nollen sat upon a short rock wall.

"Did that fear flee after Gunnar's prayer?"

"Aye."

Arctander sat beside Nollen. "Did it return the second time?"

"Aye, though not as powerful."

"Since then, have you grown stronger in resolve against such evil?" Arctander curbed a smile while asking the question.

Nollen heard female laughter. The group from Kranston enjoyed their first night of freedom, with Lexi among them. "Aye. To protect others."

"That is why Gott sent you, to hone your mettle and faith for the purpose of bringing *them* home." He motioned to the group.

"Nollen!" Kean waved. "Join us!" He lifted a cup and laughed. "We have kirsch."

"Go." Arctander nudged Nollen on his way.

Kean handed Nollen a cup then raised his cup in salute. "We owe you our lives."

"You owe me nothing. What I did was in service to Gott and the king."

"Modesty?" Lexi lightly laughed.

"Would you prefer arrogant confidence?" he retorted.

The group sang a rousing old song of Eldar. Lexi poked Nollen. He flushed, abashed for not knowing the words. He smiled in hearing words of victory, and praise. When the song concluded, him felt a soft muzzle on the back of his head.

"Alydar."

The unicorn horse whinnied and tossed his head.

"Does that mean you're glad to be home?"

Alydar chomped his lips and tossed his head again.

"Well, you can say it."

Alydar did an exaggerated shake of his head. The motion immediately concerned Nollen.

"Alydar?" he asked, wary.

Callie arrived. "He can't speak anymore."

"Why?" Nollen rose, upset.

"Before we left, Othniel told us speech was granted for our task. It is complete, and we are home."

Nollen looked for Othniel but didn't see him thus, he asked Alydar, "Is that true?" The horse nodded. Alydar then lowered his head to place against Nollen's chest. "I'm sorry." He rested his forehead against Alydar's star.

Lowly Alydar chomped and grunted.

Alfgar arrived. "He says, don't be sorry. He wouldn't trade your adventure for the ability to speak again." Alydar continued, and Alfgar translated. "It is his desire, and wants to know, if you agree, that he be your horse from now on."

The statement made Nollen momentarily mute. "I would be honored to have such a mount."

Alydar grunted and whinnied.

"There is one stipulation. That you listen to him when he tries to warn you."

Nollen laughed. "Agreed."

About the Author

Shawn Lamb is a multi-award-winning author of Christian fiction ranging from age 8 to adult. She is also an event speaker. Since 2010, Shawn has participated in homeschool conventions, book fairs, comic cons, and festivals throughout the Southeast, Midwest, and Mid-Atlantic regions.

As a former screenwriter for children's television, and author of numerous books, she brings over 30 years' experience dealing with publishing and Hollywood to her speaking engagements.

For more information about Shawn's books and possible speaking engagements, visit www.allonbooks.com.

www.ingramcontent.com/pod-product-compliance
Lightning Source LLC
Chambersburg PA
CBHW071209250626
47159CB00001B/255